"The authors have already made a name for themselves as writers of intelligent space opera, and *Echoes of Earth* is sure to further bolster that reputation. The book is chock full of marvelous events, cosmic significance, mysterious alien motivations, and the wonder of outer space."

—*Science Fiction Chronicle*

"The science in Dix and Williams's work shines, entrancing with its glitter and innovation . . . and you won't find any of their novels without fully fleshed-out characters, complex plots, vivid settings, and thoughtful exploration of issues."

—*SF Site*

"Williams and Dix bring an adventurous and expansive approach to their material."

—*Locus*

and

THE EVERGENCE TRILOGY

"A close-knit personal story told on a galaxy-sized canvas. Filled with action as well as intriguing ideas."

—Kevin J. Anderson,
New York Times bestselling author

· · · · · · · HEIRS OF EARTH

· · · · · · SEAN WILLIAMS
AND SHANE DIX

ACE BOOKS, NEW YORK

HEIRS OF EARTH

An Ace Book / published by arrangement with the authors

PRINTING HISTORY
Ace mass market edition / January 2004

Copyright © 2004 by Sean Williams and Shane Dix.
Cover art by Chris Moore.
Cover design by Judy Murello.

ISBN: 0-441-01126-8

ACE ®
Ace Books are published by The Berkley Publishing Group, a division of Penguin Group (USA) Inc., 375 Hudson Street, New York, New York 10014. ACE and the "A" design are trademarks belonging to Penguin Group (USA) Inc.

PRINTED IN THE UNITED STATES OF AMERICA

10 9 8 7 6 5 4 3 2 1

For Robin Pen, sensei

CONTENTS

ADJUSTED PLANCK UNITS: TIME

Old Seconds

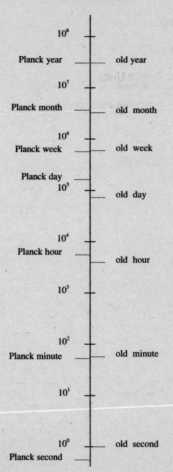

NB: For more information about Planck Units, see Appendix 1.

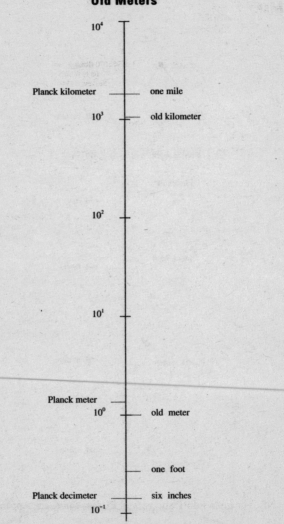

ADJUSTED PLANCK UNITS: DISTANCE

Old Meters

10^4

Planck kilometer .... one mile

10^3 ——— old kilometer

10^2

10^1

Planck meter ....
10^0 .... old meter

.... one foot

Planck decimeter .... six inches
10^{-1}

MAP

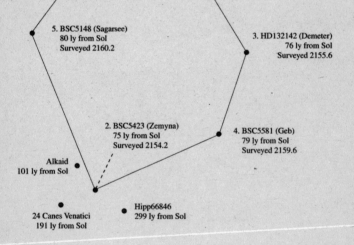

THE ALKAID SYSTEMS

1. BSC5070 (Rasmussen)
68 ly from Sol
Surveyed 2144.9

5. BSC5148 (Sagarsee)
80 ly from Sol
Surveyed 2160.2

3. HD132142 (Demeter)
76 ly from Sol
Surveyed 2155.6

2. BSC5423 (Zemyna)
75 ly from Sol
Surveyed 2154.2

4. BSC5581 (Geb)
79 ly from Sol
Surveyed 2159.6

Alkaid
101 ly from Sol

24 Canes Venatici
191 ly from Sol

Hipp66846
299 ly from Sol

SYNOPSES
ECHOES OF EARTH

2050 A.D.

The United Near-Earth Stellar Survey Program dispatches 1,000 crewed missions to nearby stars in an attempt to explore terrestrial worlds identified by Earth-based detectors. Instead of sending flesh-and-blood humans, UNESSPRO crews each mission with simulations called engrams that are intended to behave as, and function as though they in fact are, the original scientists. A core group of sixty surveyors is duplicated many times over to cover all the missions.

Twelve years after the missions are launched, all transmissions from Earth cease. Cut off from UNESSPRO, the missions continue as planned, hoping that whatever fate befell the home system will not follow them also.

2163 Standard Mission Time

Aliens come to the system of Upsilon Aquarius in the form of giant golden spindles that build ten orbital towers around the *Frank Tipler*'s target world, Adrasteia. When the towers are complete and connected by a massive orbital ring, the aliens disappear, leaving no clue as to their intentions or origins.

Peter Alander, once a highly regarded generalist but now a

flawed engram barely holding onto sanity, is sent to explore the orbital towers by the mission's Civilian Survey Manager Caryl Hatzis. Within them, Alander finds AIs that identify the towers as gifts to humanity from a powerful star-faring civilization. The Spinners are secretive and mysterious, but their gifts are to die for: a detailed map of the Milky Way, featuring details of other alien civilizations; a surgery containing exotic medical technology, such as a perfectly transparent membrane designed to keep its wearer from harm; a means of instantaneous communication with a range of 200 light-years; a faster-than-light vessel that defies known scientific laws; and so on.

Seeking assistance in studying the gifts, Petèr Alander decides to take the ftl hole ship to Sol to see what has become of Earth. What Alander finds there, however, is a civilization bearing little resemblance to the one he left. A technological Spike shortly after the launch of the UNESSPRO missions, 100 years earlier, resulted in a war between nonhuman AIs that led to, among many other things, the total destruction of Earth. A small percentage of humans have survived, in highly modified forms. The posthumans regard Alander's arrival with suspicion and disdain, since engrams are now regarded as a very poor cousin to the sort of minds that have evolved from the ashes of Earth.

A much-expanded form of Caryl Hatzis, the sole survivor of the original UNESSPRO volunteers, is pressed into service. The expanded Hatzis sends her original with Alander to Adrasteia to attest the veracity of his claims. They arrive in Adrasteia to find the colony and the gifts destroyed. Something has swept through Upsilon Aquarius and erased all trace of the *Frank Tipler*. Stunned, Alander and Hatzis retreat immediately to Sol System, only to find the same thing happening there. All the resources and technology of the posthumans can do nothing to stop the fleet of vastly superior alien vessels. Within a day, there is little left but dust.

Reeling from the double whammy, Hatzis and Alander retreat to avoid destruction at the hands of these new aliens, the Starfish. They have never been friends, in any form, and the tension between them is not helped by the revelation that Alander himself may have inadvertently brought about the destruction of humanity. By following the hails of another colony contacted by the Spinners, they determine that the Starfish home in on the omnidirectional signals broadcast by the ftl communicators provided in the gifts. Alander's attempt to call Adrasteia from Sol System drew the Starfish to the Vincula.

This pattern, they realize, will only be repeated as the Spinners sweep through Surveyed Space, dropping gifts as they go. A severely traumatized Peter Alander and the original Caryl Hatzis, very much alone without the rest of her distributed self, make it their mission to save what remains of humanity: the orphaned UNESSPRO mission engrams scattered across the stars.

ORPHANS OF EARTH

The original Caryl Hatzis (nicknamed Sol after her system of origin) sets up a headquarters on Sothis, site of an old, failed colony. From there she organizes resistance. All attempts to communicate with both the Spinners and Starfish have failed. Colonies are contacted one by one in order to warn them against using the communicators in a way that will bring the Starfish down upon them. The Starfish themselves are studied from afar to see if there is any way they can be thwarted. With the assistance of many copies of herself, Sol sets up an interstellar network that will obey her every command.

Peter Alander is her reluctant assistant in this effort. The tension between them is rising in direct proportion to the influence she has over the engrams, who regard her, the last surviving human, with something like reverence. As rumors of contact with another alien race spread through the colonies, he agrees to accompany one of her engrams, Thor, on a fact-finding mission.

Instead of aliens, they find Francis Axford (Frank the Ax), a former UNESSPRO cost-cutter and general who stowed away on a survey mission and promptly took it over, killing the remainder of the crew and copying himself many times over in the process. There are now hundreds of versions of him occupying the system of Vega, with access to the Spinners' gifts. He cautiously welcomes them and illuminates them on the nature of the new alien race, creatures he calls Roaches but which refer to themselves as the *Yuhl/Goel*. The Yuhl trail the Spinners at a distance, collecting gifts where they are able to and always staying just one step ahead of the Starfish, which, together with the Spinners, they refer to as the Ambivalence.

With the help of two captives, Alander manages to trace the source of the Yuhl migration, a vast concentration of hole ships called the *Mantissa*. There he is brought to meet yet another alien creature, the Praxis, who directs the Yuhl in their efforts at survival. Alander is literally eaten by the Praxis, who takes the information derived from his body and creates a virtual model of it, with which he converses. At the conclusion of the conversation, Alander is regurgitated in a slightly different form. He now has a real body, rather than a genetically engineered android body. It profoundly shakes him yet grounds him more firmly in the real world, making his cognition more stable.

Humanity learns ways to tease out new technology from the Gifts and from their new allies. They learn how to merge and modify hole ships, skills that may be lifesaving. As the Starfish front continues to sweep across Surveyed Space, destroying every colony it encounters, including those without gifts, the future of humanity looks increasingly in peril. Additionally, suspicions are growing that the Spinners aren't entirely what they seem, that strange holes in the Library and the Map Room may hold details humanity isn't supposed to see.

One system in Surveyed Space, pi-1 Ursa Major, has become a fatal trap for anyone who visits: of several hole ships sent to survey it, none have returned. The Hatzis engram Thor, distressed by the destruction of her home system and at odds with Peter Alander, breaks away from Sol and goes to pi-1 Ursa Major to find out what is going on.

The Yuhl cautiously accept humanity as a possible running partner, should the engrams be forced to abandon their worlds. This decision is not taken lightly, and not without resistance. Plans to confront the Starfish are quashed when it emerges that not even the technologically superior *Yuhl/Goel* will attempt it. The Starfish fleet is simply too advanced.

The decision not to fight is taken out of their hands, however, when Frank Axford betrays both humanity and the Yuhl by drawing the Starfish down on the *Mantissa* in the system of Beid and forcing a confrontation. The battle is hard and costly, but the allies do manage to cripple a cutter, one of the mighty Starfish vessels. Damage to the *Mantissa* is mitigated by the sacrifice of many human colonies in an attempt to spread the Starfish attack fleet across numerous fronts. Approximately half the *Yuhl/Goel* migration survives. Humanity loses Sothis; Frank Axford loses Vega.

Any hope the survivors can take from their slight victory over the Starfish is overshadowed by the knowledge that there are many, many more cutters where the one they crippled came from. And they are no closer to understanding why the Starfish and Spinners won't talk to them.

Meanwhile, forgotten on the edge of Surveyed Space, Thor has survived a deadly attempt on her life in pi-1 Ursa Major. Instead of attacking the mystery directly, she manages to track down a copy of Lucia Benck, Peter Alander's ex-lover and a solo scout pilot who, Thor hopes, might have seen the arrival of whatever it is in the system. Lucia is suffering from the extreme effects of engram senescence and must be uploaded into the hole ship's processors in order to function. Lucia sees her survival from that viewpoint with a mixture of wonder and dread. Her feelings are similarly mixed regarding her imminent reunion with Alander—and the fact that she might well have seen something very strange indeed in pi-1 Ursa Major.

1.1

REDUCTIO

2160.9.26 Standard Mission Time
(28 August 2163 UT)

1.1.1

Peter Alander rolled over, blinking in the dim light as he tried
to make sense of his surroundings. The room was narrow with
curved walls, and empty apart from himself, the bed he was
lying on, and the woman standing to one side with her back
facing him. Fabric slid over fabric as the woman adjusted her
clothing. The sound it made, he realized, was what had awoken
him.

"Lucia?"

The woman sighed and shook her head. "That's three times
in a row you've got it wrong, Peter." Caryl Hatzis turned with
awkward propriety to look over her shoulder at him while continuing to get dressed. "Keep this up, and I might take it personally."

Alander could only stare at her in bemusement, clutching
the small carbon disk around his neck as if this might in some
way remove his confusion. He could smell Hatzis on the mat-
tress next to him: there were sense impressions stirring strange
intimacies that seemed utterly incongruous. What on earth was
he doing in bed with *her?*

She faced him fully when her suit was sealed. If she was
aware of his confusion, she ignored it.

"Caryl . . ."

She offered a faint, disappointed smile. "You were talking in your sleep again. You really should look at laying down some new memories, you know."

"What are you doing—?" *Here*, he wanted to add, but let the question go unspoken for fear of insulting her.

"Geb called," she said. "The Spinners have arrived at Sagarsee."

His confusion persisted.

Another sigh, as though she was tired of going over the same conversation with him. "It's time, Peter. We have to act now or lose our last chance."

Finally some of it came back to him: Earth was destroyed, and the natural order of things had been destroyed with it. What little remained of humanity was caught between the Spinners and the Starfish, unsure whether to run, hide, or fight back. None of the options were particularly attractive; none offered much hope for survival.

He sat up as Hatzis made to leave the room. She stopped at the arched doorway and turned to face him. There was emotion in the stare, but nothing he would have recognized as affection. He supposed he should offer her something: a kiss or a hug maybe, but he wasn't sure what was expected of him. He wasn't even sure if they had been intimate with one another. If they had, it couldn't have been about love, surely. He felt nothing of the sort for her. The closest thing, he imagined, would be ancient hormonal imperatives operating in a tight spot.

He wondered if he even *had* hormones anymore. Or pheromones. His body consisted of an android drone into which his engram had been distilled; it had also been modified by the Praxis, the alien leader of the *Yuhl/Goel*. He didn't know what the Praxis had done to him, only that it had left him changed: the android template didn't include hair, but now he sported several days' growth across his scalp and face; the formerly regular lines of veins visible through his olive skin were flexing, shifting by minute increments; he felt stronger somehow, seeming to have more energy; and when, in strange half-memory, he touched Hatzis's skin—marveling at her own inhumanities, the advanced biomods installed in her by the posthuman regime the Starfish had destroyed in Sol—strange impulses moved through his nervous system, fleeting emotional storms that swept through parts of his cortex he didn't know he had.

"You're not going to join us?" she asked, her expression reproving. She was off to decide the course of humanity's fate. She obviously felt he should be taking an interest.

"I'll come along once the bickering is over."

"Your faith in my ability to control the rabble is as strong as ever, I see."

"Don't take it personally, Caryl. It's got nothing to do with you."

"That makes me feel a whole lot better, Peter; thanks."

"I will come by later, I promise," he assured her.

"Make your grand entrance when you're ready, then. I don't care. Just make sure you use it to good effect."

She stood in the doorway for a second longer, as though about to add something, or waiting for him to do so. He said nothing. Her words stung, but he had learned enough about her in recent weeks to know that her scorn and derision hid nervousness, uncertainty. Whatever had happened between them, he didn't want to add to that. In his present state of mind anything he said was likely to make things worse. He knew the meeting was important, in principle, but he couldn't bring himself to endure the arguments that would inevitably ensue. He could hear every one of them in advance, map out their ideological landscapes, and follow point by point the routes they'd take to utter disagreement. Maybe there was a chance that the survivors would reach consensus, but he wouldn't put money on it.

Hatzis left, fleeing his puzzled silence without a word. When she'd gone, Alander lay back on the bed with his arms folded behind his head and wondered at what he had become.

You were talking in your sleep again, Hatzis had said. That didn't surprise him. He'd been dreaming of Lucia, the lover he'd lost to the stars. Specifically, he had been dreaming of the last conversation their originals had had before the engrams left for the stars. The philosophical conundrum that had plagued opponents of the UNESSPRO missions had haunted each of the originals upon which the engrams were based at one time or another during their entrainment. How would it feel to know that hundreds of copies of yourself, echoes of the real you, were heading to places you were never likely to see? And how in turn would the echoes feel, knowing that their originals would remain behind to grow old and die at nonrelativistic rates?

Are we immortal, Lucia had once asked him, *or destined to die a thousand times?*

He still didn't have an answer for that question, despite contemplating it many times over. He—or his original, anyway, the most copied of all the mission scientists—had an innate flaw somewhere that made his engrams unstable. Of all the hundreds sent out from Earth, none had lasted more than a few weeks. All had suffered breakdowns resulting in catastrophic failure, forcing shutdown and long-term storage. He himself had survived only by virtue of being uploaded into an android body relying on its stability, its physicality, to hold himself together. It had worked, precariously, but subsequent events had shaken his confidence. He wasn't who his engram told him he was supposed to be. He was changing, evolving. Hatzis had set him free of those internal constraints, and the Praxis had given his body a semblance of natural life. But he still had no idea what he was, exactly, or where he stood in regards to his other engrams, for which he still felt a strange sort of bond.

Out of kinship? he wondered. *Or pity?*

Hatzis had a fine arrangement with her own engrams. They clicked together like pieces of a jigsaw puzzle, or so it seemed from the outside. His own copies rejected him, spurning his offer to take their memories and integrate them into a new whole. This dismayed him more than he was prepared to admit.

"There can be no greater challenge to your identity than being cast out by your own self," Hatzis had told him after the first time it happened. "It's more painful than losing a family or a home."

He found it ironic that she should be the one guiding him through this process. The one person he'd railed against since his awakening on Adrasteia, newly embodied and keenly aware of her resentment of the resources he'd been allocated. But that Caryl Hatzis had been destroyed, along with the *Frank Tipler* and all its crew, in one of the very first Starfish attacks. This was a different Hatzis altogether, the last true human alive.

"If your engram chose death over absorption, then that's his problem, not yours. Don't let his failure drag you down. You're no longer him, Peter. You're better than that. Let him go. Whatever you've become, you have an obligation to yourself to keep moving on."

But where am I moving to? he wanted to ask her.

"The only thing holding us back is ourselves, and they only win if we *let* them."

The conversation was clear in his mind. It was the first time they'd embraced, again, not out of love or lust but for comfort in the face of terrible circumstances.

"You need to have a clear idea of what it is you're clinging to," she'd said. "If your ship is sinking, then you want to at least make sure you're clinging to a life raft, and not the ship itself, right?"

"And you're my raft, Caryl?"

The memory of her laugh seemed to fill the hole ship cabin. "Cling to me, Peter, and we may well both go under."

He nodded to himself. It was true: he had to find his own center of gravity, to haul himself out of his doldrums. And to make the effort worthwhile, he had to help find a way to ensure humanity's survival. He wasn't sure that arguing en masse was the solution, but he could see that Hatzis thought it might be. That was her way, her gift. The way she had organized the resistance from Sothis had proved that she was capable of great things and that her ambition was clear. But there were times that he wondered if they might not be better off with someone more like Frank Axford. Until Axford had forced them into it, no one even considered fighting the Starfish.

With good reason, too, Alander told himself. The outcome of that skirmish had left 40 percent of the *Yuhl/Goel* scavenger fleet destroyed, along with six human colonies, Sothis and Vega included. The Starfish had lost just one of their massive cutter vessels, disk-shaped behemoths that made anything humans had ever built look paltry in comparison. That small victory might have meant something in terms of morale building had it not led to the appearance of an entirely new class of Starfish craft, one so large it made the cutters look as insignificant as motes of dust.

Despite the heavy losses, though, Alander couldn't help but

wonder if it hadn't been worthwhile. After all, they now knew more about the Starfish than they ever had before, which was undoubtedly why Frank the Ax had done what he'd done. It took a military mind to understand that to determine an enemy's capabilities, one had to make sacrifices; one had to be prepared to enter into battles that couldn't necessarily be won. When the Starfish were unknown, they were vast and terrifying. Now, though, there was a sense that maybe this faceless enemy had limitations, after all, which was something of a comfort, even if these limitations were still incomprehensibly vast.

Alander's thoughts turned increasingly to Axford, wondering what the ex-general might be up to right now. Ever since the Battle of Beid had gone so badly, there had been no sign of the man, in any of his incarnations, and his bases on Vega were in ruins, probably by Axford's own hand to cover his tracks.

"I have a message for you, Peter," the cool voice of the hole ship interjected into his thoughts. The hole ship AIs were degrees of magnitude less sophisticated than the Gifts who maintained the legacy of the Spinners, but they were still smartly sophisticated. "The transmission is coming from the hole ship you refer to as *Pearl.*"

Alander recognized the name immediately. "That's Thor's ship, isn't it?"

"I believe so, Peter."

"Well, if it's Sol she's looking for, tell her—"

"The message is addressed specifically to you," the AI cut in.

Alander frowned. The copy of Caryl Hatzis from the colony world known as Thor had been missing for days. If she was back, she should have reported to the Caryl Hatzis the engrams called Sol, not him. Maybe she was worried how Sol would react, given that she'd gone off on her own crusade without consulting anyone shortly after her colony had been destroyed. Alander could understand how she felt. He, too, had experienced the emotional trauma of seeing the world of his own mission on the *Frank Tipler* destroyed, along with all his crewmates. But he doubted that Sol would be as understanding, given the limited resources available to humanity.

"Then I guess you'd better put her through," he said, climbing to his feet.

He expected a screen to form in the wall to reveal a video image: in that fashion, the hole ships normally enabled their passengers to communicate with one another. What he got, though, was something entirely different.

The walls, floor, and ceiling retreated around him until he and the bed seemed to be hanging in a vast and giddying void. Through the darkness he sensed black shapes moving, strange limbs touching, complex senses interacting in an arcane, private dance. Then a woman stepped out of that darkness, her movements steady and assured, the smile on her face gentle and affectionate.

The shock of recognition that rushed through him was like a physical force. She was wearing a green UNESSPRO shipsuit. Her hair was highlighted in gold just the way he remembered. Her skin had a similar honeyish hue that shone in nonexistent light. Her brown eyes stared at him out of that impossible space, no less powerful for being virtual.

He climbed slowly to his feet, his jaw hanging hopelessly open as he struggled for words.

"Hello, Peter," said Lucia Benck. "It's been a long time."

1.1.2

Rasmussen was a beautiful world: green and temperate around the equator, with an even split between ocean and land-mass. Both poles were icebound and surrounded by turbulent berg-filled oceans; the air was high in oxygen, supporting a diverse ecosystem that boasted insects large enough to bite an android in two and tree trunks dozens of meters across. Its primary, BSC5070, was a G6V star slightly redder than Earth's; Rasmussen orbited close to the center of its habitable zone. *Marcus Chown,* the UNESSPRO mission sent to explore the system, had arrived fifteen years earlier and established an extensive orbital complex from which detailed biological and geological examinations had been made. Under the leadership of Rob Singh, terrestrial contamination of the environment was kept to an absolute minimum. Even during the arrival of the Gifts, the pristine ecosystem had barely been disturbed. To all intents and purposes, it was a paradise, which was what made it so hard for Caryl Hatzis to deliver her pronouncement.

"In five days," she said, "this planet and everything on it will die."

The assembly was silent.

"Three days later," she went on, "Zemyna and Demeter will follow then Geb and Sagarsee. And then—" She paused, allowing a faint echo to underline the significance of the silence with which she presaged her next words. "And then there will be no more colonies left. Everything UNESSPRO strove to achieve will be gone. All that will remain of humanity will be our ash and dust on the worlds we once visited."

Hatzis felt the pressure of eyes on her, virtual and real.

The meeting had been called at Rasmussen to coincide with the arrival of the Spinners at Sagarsee, the colony world of the BSC5148 system, the last of five loosely clustered systems known as the Alkaid Group on the opposite side of the sphere of space humanity had explored from where the Spinners had first appeared. Unless humanity's enigmatic benefactors abruptly changed their modus operandi, Sagarsee and the rest of the Alkaid Group would be the last worlds visited by the Spinners—and the last attacked by the Starfish. If humanity was to survive, then this was where Caryl Hatzis and her ragtag band of engrams would have to make their stand.

She forced herself to speak with dignity and poise when all she wanted to do was to scream out her frustration and outrage.

"We have tried communicating with the Spinners, and they haven't responded. We've tried communicating with the Starfish, and they, too, have ignored us. We've tried resisting the Starfish, and that almost got us killed. So now we have to figure out what we do next.

"If we do nothing," she said, "we die. We've seen it happen to the ostrich colonies—the ones who tried hiding in systems that had already been attacked or on worlds the Spinners hadn't visited. They thought they would be safe, that the Starfish wouldn't consider them a threat. But they were wrong, and they paid for it with their lives. To that end, should any colony represented here today choose that option, you will forfeit your gifts and your ftl communicators. This is not open to discussion; if the human race is to have any chance at all, it requires every resource it can lay its hands on."

She paused, half-expecting a reaction to this, but there was none. Everyone was fully, finally aware of the harsh reality of their situation.

"One of the options open to us is to follow the lead of the Yuhl and remain in the wake of the Spinners. We can use the gifts to fashion arks large enough to contain all our hardware, all the processors required to run the engrams and contain our memories of Earth. We can merge the hole ships, and like the Yuhl we can jump from system to system, taking what we need to keep our fleet functioning. According to the Praxis, our new friends have been doing this for two and a half thousand years, so there's no reason why we couldn't do it, too.

"This is a viable option, but for me it's not an attractive one. Many of you, I know, are still grappling with the fact that Earth was destroyed in the Spike, over a century ago. I have shown you what took its place; you've seen what the Starfish destroyed when they came to Sol." *On the heels of Peter Alander,* she added silently to herself, unable to completely suppress a twinge of resentment, even though deep down she knew it wasn't really his fault. "There's nothing left for us there, but it is *still* our birthplace. And for that reason I am loath to give up on it entirely.

"We still have some days left, and we have the resources of the gifts at our disposal. There might be something we haven't thought of yet, something that we might yet do to ensure our species' survival with dignity intact. We may yet, at the eleventh hour, find an alternative, a way in which our species could survive and somehow reclaim that which has been lost.

"We are here to decide whether to take the chance or not. We are the sole survivors of the human race; it is upon our shoulders that the future of our species rests. You must think long and hard about what you wish to do now. We must reach consensus, or we must divide.

"I ask you to consider this: to live as the Yuhl do now would mean that our future descendants, whatever they may be, will inherit nothing from us but our fear and obeisance. We will have run from our greatest challenge, and that will be our only legacy. But if today, together, we can find an alternative, then perhaps our descendants will inherit something more. If we can live through these next few days, then we could reclaim Sol System and rebuild our species, and our descendants may be heirs to a *new* Earth."

With that, as the echoes of her words filled the virtual meeting hall, she stepped back from the spotlight, glad to remove herself from the decision-making process. The sentiments she'd expressed were genuine, but in truth she didn't know for certain what was the best thing for humanity right now. Abandoning Surveyed Space for a life roaming the galaxy, caught between one alien race and another, sounded a lot like a prison sentence to her—one with no chance of parole. But was it worse than the death sentence humanity might face if they attempted to fight back?

Sol understood Alander's point all too well; she, too, was tired of endless spats, constant claims and counterclaims, petty ascendancies and power struggles. She wished her higher self, the one destroyed with the Vincula in Sol System, could magically reappear and take over. *She* would know what to do. With the resources of a post-Spike, twenty-second century humanity behind them, maybe the engrams would have had something of a chance at least.

Then again, she reminded herself, it hadn't really helped the Vincula. The Spinners had cut through its defenses like a hot knife through butter. The memory of the destruction of her home was indelibly burned into her mind, and like a recently formed scar, it itched terribly.

"We *can't* leave here," someone was insisting. "This is our home!"

"Then we must find a way to contact them—to reason with them," said another.

"The Starfish don't care about that," came the instant reply. "If we stay here, they'll destroy us as easily as they destroyed Sol."

"But who says Sol was actually destroyed?" said a third voice, entering the debate. "All we have is *her* word for that. It could be a fake designed to make us leave, to empty the colonies to allow her to take over!"

And there it was in a nutshell: all three possible responses to the situation. The engrams could refuse to accept the harsh reality and die; they could bite the bullet and leave; or they could doubt that it was even happening. The last was particularly symptomatic of newer colonies, especially those who'd been skipped by the Spinners and had yet to see any evidence of alien activity beyond the hole ships. And she could understand that. Conspiracy was so much easier to accept than the harsh reality of humanity's genocide.

Fortunately, though, survivors of Starfish attacks significantly outnumbered the newbies. Of the 1,000-odd remaining engrams attending the meeting, approximately 800 had lost homes and missions to the aliens. While they may not have seen the destruction firsthand since few had and managed to do so and survive, they were left in no doubt as to the desperate nature of humanity's plight.

Run or die, she thought to herself. *It's not a choice; it's an ultimatum.*

"I have to say, I've never been one for ultimatums."

The voice intruding upon her thoughts, *reading* her thoughts, startled her. She knew immediately to whom the voice belonged, and it was this more than anything that surprised her. She quickly sent her senses through the assembly, trying to find the source of the voice, seeking out the owner. Try as she might though, she couldn't find him.

"That's because I'm not there, Caryl," Frank the Ax said with amusement. "The others can't hear me; I'm speaking only to you, because right now yours is the only opinion that matters."

"And I'm supposed to be flattered by that, Frank?"

She heard a low chuckle. "Is that animosity I detect, Caryl?"

"I don't know. Why *should* I harbor any ill feelings toward you?" She couldn't restrain her sarcasm. "That stunt you pulled back at Beid didn't hurt us at all."

While she spoke, she ramped up her internal processing speed to its fastest setting, determined to outthink the man who'd brought so much death and destruction to humanity and its allies. But he was telling the truth: he wasn't at the meeting. There was no sign of him in the assembly nor in any of the networks attached to it. The array of hole ships docked in the upper orbits of Rasmussen was empty of his spoor, as were the gifts themselves. The only other possible place in orbit around the planet was the *Marcus Chown,* looking boxy and antiquated against the superior technology of the Spinners. It hung innocent and isolated at a lower altitude, glinting brightly in the sunlight.

"Got you," she said. His transmission was coming from the gutted survey ship, the relic of Earth that had been abandoned as soon as the Gifts arrived.

"You think I'm that stupid, Caryl?" Axford replied. "It's just a relay. I could be anywhere in the system."

"You can't be far away: your transmission lag is low."

"And what would you do if you found me, Caryl? Take me out? I'm only one of many, remember? You'd still be left with hundreds more Frank Axfords to contend with."

"That sounds like a threat, Frank."

"Listen, Caryl: either you're going to hear what I've got to say, or I'm going to leave." His voice was cool behind the amusement.

"And why should I—or anyone, for that matter—care if you stay or go? You've done nothing but hurt us in the past: stolen from the colonies, used the Starfish to cover up your thefts, sent the Yuhl almost to their deaths—"

"*And* saved your collective ass," he interjected. "You just don't know it yet."

Hatzis laughed at this. "I must have missed that part. I guess I was too busy fighting off the Starfish you set upon us."

"You seemed to do all right."

"Christ, Frank, do you even *know* how many people we lost because of you?"

"Of course I do. I was watching. The data I gleaned were exceedingly valuable."

"I'm glad the massacre gave you some amusement."

"Oh, come on, Caryl! Put your hostilities to rest and just listen to what I have to say. We're all in the same boat here. If we go down, we go down together."

"So your threat to leave was empty?"

"I need you nowhere near as much as you need me," he returned. "In a few days, we're all going to be on the run from the enemy, and from that point on, there'll be no turning back. Trust me, I'm your only shot at deflecting the Starfish."

No turning back, she echoed in her mind, tasting the notion and finding its bitterness appalling. The Yuhl had run, and were survivors as a result—but they were also scavengers, slowly devolving to the status of superstitious pirates. They practically worshiped the Spinner/Starfish migration, which they referred to in combination as the Ambivalence. Did a familiar fate now await humanity?

"Okay, Frank. I'll listen."

"But are you open to suggestions?"

She sighed to herself. "If you're going to suggest that we attack the Starfish again—"

"Fighting back is our only chance of survival, Caryl."

"You saw what happened when you forced us into doing that before."

"Look, I'm not stupid, Caryl. I know you won't stand any chance at all if you try going head-to-head with the big guns. I mean, that new ship of theirs—the Trident—that thing's so big you could use it to skewer the Moon! There's no way we'd be able to take one of those things out with anything we've got. A solar flare might do it, but there's nothing in the gifts to show how we might generate one—or how to get the Starfish to bring one of their Tridents close enough for us to even be able to use it."

"Whatever you're trying to talk me into, Frank, you're doing a shit-poor job of it. And you're not telling me anything I don't already know, either."

"If you already know it, then why bother with the big meeting? Why waste time debating over options as if you really have any choice in the matter?"

The scorn in his voice stung, like salt in an open wound.

"Because the decision can't be mine alone to make."

"But it can't be left to *them*. Christ, they're idiots, Caryl! Half of them seriously believe that, regardless of what happens, the human spirit will prevail and overcome any adversity. But you and I both know that the Starfish will storm through this region and completely remove all trace of humanity as it goes—and they won't even stop to check their heels to see what it is they've stepped in, either."

A great weariness fell over her. The fatalistic certainty of her insignificance was something that confronted her on an almost hourly basis.

"So what do you suggest we do, Frank? What's your great plan to save humanity?"

"We make them notice us, of course."

"We've tried that, remember? It didn't work."

"Then you didn't try hard enough."

"Easy to say, but do you actually have something more than just hot air and criticism to offer here?"

"I do have an idea, but I don't think you're going to like it."

"Try me anyway."

"Very well," he said. "You've already tried broadcasting messages to the Starfish. You've left satellites in vulnerable systems, radiating in all frequencies, using all known codes and media. You've sacrificed hole ships to transmit via ftl. And despite attempting to get their attention, you've never once received a reply.

"I think the reason for this is that you've been hailing the wrong people. The cutters are nothing more than drones; they're just doing a job. They're deaf to anything but their orders, and those orders are to take out any sign of intelligence in the systems they've been allocated. Maybe I'm anthropomorphizing, but that's what I see when I study their behavior. They're simply front-line soldiers, grunts, cannon fodder—they're *nothing*, Caryl.

"We need to speak to the people *giving* the orders, and I don't think we've even come remotely close to seeing them yet."

"What about the Trident?"

"It's possible, but at this stage there's no way of knowing one way or the other. All I do know is this: they probably have no idea that we even exist and no reason to suspect it. They're as blind to us as we are to the insects in the soil over which we used to walk. They're not looking for us, so they don't *see* us."

"So what's your plan, then?" She wished he would hurry up and get to the point.

"To be honest, it's not my plan," he said. "I was contacted by someone with an intriguing idea."

She wanted to ask who this person was, but she didn't have time—the engram assembly was quickly breaking down into a morass of arguments and personal insults, and she needed to get back to it—so instead she asked: "And that is?"

"It's quite simple, actually," he said. "If the Starfish won't come to us, then we'll just have to go to them."

1.1.3

In the virtual spaces of the hole ship walls, the image of Lucia Benck faced Peter Alander for the first time in 110 Adjusted Planck years. She looked exactly the same as she had during entrainment, but he had changed both overtly and subtly, from the hair to the color of his skin; from his apparent age—much younger than it had been on Earth, even taking antisenescence treatments into account—to the way he moved. There was something about him, Lucia decided, that was very different from the Peter Alander she'd known.

But it was Peter nonetheless, and that was all that mattered. She saw him through the hole ship's advanced senses, gazing at him from a thousand different angles simultaneously and in all frequencies. He was a glowing, cubist, abstract of a person, dissected and reassembled every nanosecond as her new senses swept through him. His biological functions were laid bare before her, even those specific to his android body—and others that had no analogue in human anatomy. What *they* were, she didn't know.

His Adam's apple worked. Complex glandular responses indicated anxiety that her image subconsciously imitated. He stared at her for a few seconds longer in troubled silence, finally shaking his head slowly and saying, "How did you . . . ?"

"Thor found me. She rescued me from *Chung-5* and uploaded me into her hole ship. I've been there ever since."

"You were *in* the . . . ?" He was having trouble finishing his questions. "I don't think anyone's tried that before."

She smiled. "I'm the first, actually."

He nodded in understanding. "You always were the explorer."

She didn't need to examine the tightness around his eyes to know that something other than amusement lay behind the comment. "I'm sorry I had to go, Peter. It's just that—" She struggled to recapture her rationalizations, the feelings attendant to her decision. They felt incredibly remote, and not just because they'd occurred many years earlier, even in subjective time. "Somewhere—back home, our originals—we were together, so what did it matter what *I* did? I was just one of dozens, hundreds, you know?"

"You all made the same decision," he said.

She nodded solemnly. "Thor told me. I'm sorry."

"I know you didn't do this to hurt me. You had to do what was right for you." He fell silent once more, shrugging awkwardly before moving the conversation onto a different subject. "You wouldn't have known what happened back on Earth, either—with the Spike and everything."

Another nod. "Only Caryl Hatzis survived. Which is kind of—" She tried to find the right word. *"—scary."*

He laughed at this. "I'm sure Caryl would love to hear it put that way. And I sympathize, but she's the only true human remaining. She's all we have left. She may be biomodified up to the eyeballs, and she may be a hundred and fifty years old, but she's the reason a lot of the engrams keep waking up in the morning. If humanity consisted of nothing but a bunch of dodgy programs already pushing their expiry dates, there wouldn't be any point. She's *real*; it makes a difference."

Peter shifted from foot to foot as he spoke, as though restless or nervous. His body was all smooth angles and planes, elegantly muscular yet not quite right. There was something about him that wasn't entirely human. Her image—generated by her engram but not entirely under her conscious control—folded her arms across her chest and stepped minutely away.

"You look pretty real to me," Lucia said.

Peter looked down at himself, realizing for the first time he was naked. He snatched a sheet from the bed and wrapped it around himself. She smiled at his uncharacteristic self-consciousness but didn't say anything.

"I'm a freak," he said with galling matter-of-factness. "No one would fight for me. I'm the engram with the highest failure rate in the entire program. I'm a copy of that arrogant bastard who thought the galaxy revolved around him but now can't even keep his head on right. I've been taken apart and put back together so many times I don't know *who* I am anymore."

"That's my point, Peter. You're *someone.*" Every instinct in her virtual body told her that. "If you're not the past, then maybe you're the future instead."

He exhaled explosively—something caught between a laugh and a bleat of incredulity. "No wonder the Spinners picked me to talk through, then. They obviously have a sense of humor."

For a long moment, she didn't know what to say. His readings were incomprehensible. His internal organs displayed a strange symmetry that she'd never seen before, and his brain seemed to have grown entirely new sections. There was a mysterious membrane covering his entire body. It appeared to be a film of water, shifting constantly but never evaporating.

"What's happened to you, Peter? You used to be so strong, so certain of yourself. Where did it all go?"

"In there, actually," he said, pointing at a clunky-looking solid-state data storage unit of UNESSPRO manufacture tucked into one corner of the cabin.

She frowned quizzically at him. "What do you mean?"

"You asked where the old me went," he said. "That's where Caryl puts the copies of me that don't work. She's been collecting them ever since Sothis was destroyed. She calls it the Graveyard."

Lucia grimaced in distaste; Peter smiled.

"That's what I thought, too," he said.

"But why is she doing it?"

"I have no idea. But I'm not sure that I mind it. It acts as a reminder of what I've lost—of who I'm not anymore."

"Shouldn't that be *whom?*" Out loud it sounded ridiculously irrelevant, but strangely, it was all she could think to say. The conversation wasn't going at all as she'd imagined it.

He laughed at that. "I've never really known, to tell you the truth. And neither have you, if my memory serves me correctly—and I'm sure it does. It's programmed into us, after all."

"Thor mentioned something about the programming. I'm lucky to be here, apparently. If all of the other versions of me are in as bad a shape as I was, there might not be too many operable copies of Lucia Benck out there."

"How long had you been traveling?"

"A long time," she said, injecting as much solemnity into her tone as was necessary to convey her regrets. "I went through pi-1 Ursa Major, the *Linde*'s target system, over forty years ago. My clock rate has been slow since then, but the years kept mounting." Those memories, too, seemed faint, as though they'd happened to another person. "And to think I actually had hopes of seeing another galaxy! I thought that if I kept going, there would be no stopping me. How naive I was." A glimmer of her old self found metaphorical oxygen and caught flame. "But now . . ."

Peter frowned. "But now what?"

"Thor told me all about the other aliens—the Yuhl. They travel endlessly, she said, jumping from system to system in the Starfish wake. Apparently they invited us to join them, too."

From his expression she could tell that he didn't share her excitement at the prospect.

"Well, don't you see, Peter? It means that I get to see the galaxy as I've always wanted, *and* I get to be with you at the same time! What more could I ask for?"

Thoroughly reinforced pathways in her mind glowed with the energy she poured into that thought. Her original's long-standing dilemma—to explore the stars or to opt for a life with Peter, perpetuated across all her copies—had found a solution, finally, and every fiber of her being resonated to it. She might only be an engram, and a time-weary one at that, but she had succeeded where her original had failed. She could have her cake and eat it.

"It's not that simple, Lucia," he said cautiously.

She refused to have her mood dampened. "Why not? Think of the things we could learn from the Yuhl. The things we can see!"

He sat down on the edge of the bed, looking weary. He seemed to be having trouble working out what to say. "There may be alternatives."

"Such as?"

"That's what Caryl's trying to work out now. Everyone's gathered here to discuss—"

"I know, Peter. Thor and I just missed you at iota Boötis. They said to come here, where the decision was being made. But what other decision *can* we make? It's not as if any of the alternatives are terribly attractive." Impatience was beginning to make inroads into her optimism.

He hesitated again, keeping his gaze deliberately away from her.

"What's going on, Peter? What is it you're not telling me?"

He sighed, raising his stare to meet hers. "There's a lot we need to discuss, Lucia. You've only been here a few minutes and—"

"I'm looking forward to traveling with you, Peter," she said, cutting across his cautious rambling with a knife-edge certainty.

He looked far from reassured, though. In fact, if anything, he was looking more worried than ever.

"Tell me, Lucia: How did you get in here?" he said slowly.

"I told you. Thor found me—"

"No, I mean *here,* in this hole ship. Has *Pearl* linked up with it, or have you uploaded yourself with the message Thor transmitted?"

"I uploaded myself," she said, thinking: *Why is he asking this? How is it relevant?* "I can move freely among all the hole ships except where security restrictions have been put in place. The ships let me wander, it's only the people who get in the way."

"Does Thor know you're here?"

"Does she need to know? I'm a free agent; I can do whatever I want."

"*Klotho,* shut down all internal communication with Rasmussen." he said. "Accept only incoming transmissions as legitimate, and do not reply to anything without my express permission."

It didn't register that he was talking to the hole ship until Lucia sensed the boundaries of her world contract around her.

She felt as though her head was being gripped by a vice, except she didn't have a head, and the only thing enclosing her was the hole ship's semantic space.

"What are you doing, Peter?"

"Thor has been irresponsible letting you wander freely like this," he said. "You're fixating; it's a symptom of senescence."

"So?"

"So you're not thinking properly." He sighed. "Listen, Lucia, I'm not the same Peter Alander you remember from the *Linde*. Nor am I the same as the one on Earth, either. I'm—" He hesitated uncertainly, then said: "I'm someone else altogether."

Why was he speaking to her like she was an idiot? "I *know* that, Peter!"

He shook his head. "No, you don't, Lucia. I've seen your manner before, in other engrams. You're seeing me as your memory sees me, not as I am."

She was about to protest the accusation, but he must have seen it coming and jumped in before she could say anything.

"You're probably not aware that you're doing it—no more than you could be aware of what your programming is doing to you. And I know what it's like, Lucia. Believe me, I've been there. It's like being caught in a loop, but all you're seeing is a straight line. You can only see the discontinuities from the outside."

"So what are you saying? That you don't trust me?"

He tightened the sheet around him. "It just strikes me as dangerous for you to be free to go anywhere you choose when you're not yourself, that's all. It's nothing personal."

"What do you think I am, Peter?"

"I don't know—and that's the problem. I mean, suppose you don't like something I have to tell you; how do I know that you're not going to shut off my air? Or steal another hole ship and hurt someone else? I don't even know if you *can* control the ships like that, but I'm reluctant to take the chance. I don't even know who I am, half the time." He stared, warily, at her image in the walls, which she only noticed then was flickering and distorting as though under great electromagnetic pressure. "Lucia, before we continue with this conversation, I really think you should be examined."

"I'm fine," she insisted, ignoring the stretching and strobing of her image. "Trust me."

He completely ignored her reassurances. "*Klotho*, can you confirm that I am in command of your systems?"

"That is correct, Peter," said the hole ship.

"And what status have you given the personality of Lucia Benck?"

"While you are both passengers in this vessel, she will have the same status as yourself."

"Can you lock her out of the command loop?" he asked. "I don't want her interfering with my orders or issuing any without my knowledge."

"Peter . . ." She could manage nothing else in the face of his mistrust.

"I've seen too many engrams go bad, Lucia—my own included. Until Caryl has had a chance to examine you, I can't take any chances. I'm sorry."

A wave of ugliness swept through her. She hated it, but at the same time she couldn't fight it. There was no way she would allow him to make her a prisoner in her own home. The semantic spaces of the hole ship AIs were identical from ship to ship. In the days since her awakening, they had come to seem more real to her than the solid matter they oversaw.

She felt the command pathways of *Klotho*'s AI stretching out around her. She was a dust mote wandering the transistors of a giant, antique computer, incapable as yet of seeing the whole picture but knowing how information flowed and ebbed through the greater machine. Already she could feel where to intrude if she wanted *Klotho* to take orders from her instead of Peter.

It was true what he said, too: she *could* have the ship cut off his air, if she wanted to. But hopefully it wouldn't come to that.

Ignore his command, Klotho, she instructed. *You will listen to me instead.*

You are both passengers, the hole ship replied. *I am obliged to obey you both where possible, and to follow my own judgment when orders conflict.*

Don't lock me in here! she pleaded, exerting all her will on the pressure points she sensed. All the years of confinement in

Chung-5 were fresh in her mind. She'd thought she was free, that she could travel the stars as she had always dreamed. It was a cruel joke to have that snatched away from her now—and by Peter of all people. She'd thought he understood.

"Lucia?" Peter was looking nervously around him. The fact that her image had disappeared completely, leaving the walls of his cubicle depthless and empty, had obviously unnerved him. "Lucia, are you still listening to me?"

She withdrew from *Klotho*'s complex circuitry, returning her attention to Peter. "Why should I?"

"Because I want you to understand. When I was on Adrasteia, I was desperate for you to return. In fact, at times it was only the thought of you that kept me going. You were the anchor on which I hung my sanity. But you never showed up; you never called."

"I would have if I could!" she broke in. "It was my intention to transfer data as I flew by the target system, so I could justify carrying on. I didn't want to cost the program anything or hurt anyone."

He looked up at the ceiling as if seeking her out. "You did hurt someone, Lucia. You hurt *me*. As time passed, the expectation that you would appear softened into a hope, and then it became just a dream—a dream that I never really expected to be fully realized. But it's never gone away. I've tried many times to get over you, Lucia, because I need to be free of you to find myself. But I don't know *how* to. It's not something I can switch off."

Something akin to relief washed over her at the sound of these words, but then he blinked and looked down to the floor, and in that tiny gesture she could see what was coming and a scream began to rise inside her.

"Years ago, if you had suggested we could have traveled the galaxy together, tourist and truth seeker alike, you know I would have leapt at the chance."

"But now?" she prompted her voice barely level.

"It was only when you appeared here just then, Lucia, that I realized I've already let go. It was just the taste of the dream that I was savoring, the memory of the time when we were together back on Earth. It's gone, Lucia. I can see that now; I can feel it. It switched itself off. I've moved on, I've *changed*.

And I can't just drop everything to go gallivanting across the galaxy. I have responsibilities now. I have—"

The sentence went unfinished. No words were required for her to understand what he had been about to say; it was in his expression. *I have no need for you anymore.*

The high-pitched wail that erupted from her was quite unlike anything her original mouth could have ever produced. She felt it thrill through her like a standing wave, making her entire being vibrate. The hole ship rang with it, and Peter put his hands over his ears. Wordless, agonized, the sound seemed to go on forever.

Lucia felt herself being torn apart by it, by the incomprehensible dichotomy between what was and what should have been. If it didn't stop, her mind would fly into pieces, each fragment an unfulfilled expectation—a lie propagated by the engram overseer that had kept her *her* for so long. She was a victim of programming, a continuity error—a goddamn glitch, for Christ's sake!

I can't take this, she realized, understanding and accepting not with despair, but desperation. She didn't want to die.

Klotho, you have to let me go!

What are your instructions? asked the hole ship, its voice in her mind as cool and calming as a mountain stream.

Just let me out of here! she demanded. *Let me out! Let me out!*

Whether it was her subtle nudging of the hole ship's inner workings or the force of her plea, she couldn't tell. But she felt the constrictions around her suddenly ease.

"Lucia!" Peter was trying to make himself heard over the ongoing scream. "Try to understand!"

"I don't *want* to understand!" she shouted back, and with that she felt the resistance of the hole ship crumble and the walls come down. Before it could change its mind or Peter could countermand it, she forced herself out of her prison and back out into the universe. A dizzying array of possibilities awaited her. Swept along by the power of her grief and the pain of her incomprehension, she sought somewhere quiet to hide, to lick her wounds and try to work out what was to be done. Everywhere was bright and dazzling: hole ships in complex networks dozens of nodes across, vibrating with the force of humanity's assembly; gifts shimmering with alien intentions she could only partly read; and amid it all, nestled at the center like a tiny, insignificant flaw, a tiny speck of darkness.

She headed for it, trailing her grief and confusion like a comet's tail, and dived inside.

1.1.4

The sense of something chaotic and dangerous sweeping through her made Thor glance up in alarm.

"What was *that?*" asked Axford 1041 from his half of the dual cockpit. Their hole ships had merged just far enough to allow them to talk naturally across the boundary; otherwise they were completely separate—or so she hoped, anyway.

"Lucia, I think," she said. "Expect the calls to be coming in any time now."

Barely had she finished saying this when the first transmission came through. Surprisingly, though, it was from Sol rather than Alander.

"What the *fuck* is going on, Thor?" The image of the original Caryl Hatzis appeared on *Pearl*'s curving viewscreen. "You told me at Sirius that you hadn't found anything at pi-1 Ursa Major, and now I find you've been telling Axford differently. And while we're on the subject, why are you dealing with that madman in the first place? Don't you know what he's *done?*"

A low chuckle from the other half of the cockpit cut across any answer Thor might have attempted.

"Maybe she realizes she doesn't have a choice." Axford 1041 affected a relaxed, confident pose. "If you want a solution to this problem, then you're going to *have* to talk to me."

"Any solution involving you is not a solution," Sol spat back.

"Hell of a line, Caryl. If there's anyone left after the Starfish come through here, perhaps they could engrave it on your headstone."

"And you think you can stop the Starfish?"

"I think he's worth listening to," put in Thor.

"So why doesn't he speak to the rest of the gathering?"

"They'll never reach a consensus, Sol," said Axford. "You know that."

Sol sagged at that, some of her animosity subsiding for a moment. It was clear that she *did* know that.

"If we listen to you, Frank, the Fit will rescind their invitation to become humanity-slash-Goel—again. Regardless of whatever your plan is, I know giving up *that* option will be certain suicide."

"We don't need the Fit, Caryl." The ex-general wore his best poker face: intent on the person he was talking to, with just a hint of amusement at the corners of his mouth and eyes. "And we don't need the rest of the engrams to reach a consensus, either. We just need the ones who are prepared to put their lives on the line, like I have."

Sol's expression curled into a sneer. "Remind me how you've put yourself on the line, Frank. You're just one of— how many versions of yourself, exactly?"

"It's not relevant right now, Caryl," said Axford 1041. "Let's keep to the matter at hand. We're talking survival on *our* terms, not the Ambivalence's. I'm not about to offer any shallow apologies for Beid or anything else. I've done everything I had to do to survive—and the simple fact is that we need each other if we're going to do that. So here I am. Are you interested in hearing what I have to say or not?"

Before she could respond, the *Pearl* announced another incoming transmission. The screen divided in two as Peter Alander joined the impromptu meeting.

"You're keeping a low profile," he said to Thor, glancing at Axford and Sol but, showing no surprise on his heavily stubbled face. "I don't suppose that would have anything to do with the visit I just had from Lucia Benck, would it?"

Sol looked up sharply at that. "She's *here?*"

"She was," said Alander. "I don't know where she's gone now, though. Thor set her loose, probably hoping that she'd distract us."

"That's not entirely true," Thor said. "We were hoping she'd get your attention, which she obviously did. It's not as if we forced her into anything. She *wanted* to see you, Peter. I need you to understand that she has in no way been tampered with."

"I never thought she had been," said Alander, frowning. "But why is that so important?"

"Because she's proof," said Axford. "She's given us the key to everything. Without her, we'd be as good as dead."

Alander looked confused. "I'm sorry, but would someone mind explaining to me what the hell is going on?"

"I'm here to offer you a deal," said Axford.

"Which I helped broker," Thor added, noting with satisfaction the look on Sol's face. *Yes,* she thought. *You're not the only player now, Sol.* "I found Frank and told him what Lucia told me."

Sol shook her head. "And it doesn't seem to bother you that you've been lying to me as well as making friends with a mass murderer."

Thor refused to apologize. "Judging by what you told me about Beid, he was the only one who could think big enough to use the information I had. I knew *I* couldn't, and that meant that *you* couldn't, either."

"So where *did* you find him?"

"Actually, he found me. I figured that if anyone was going to survive the destruction of Vega, it would be him, and that if he *had* survived, he'd be monitoring the system somehow. All I had to do was broadcast a request to parley, and sure enough, he appeared."

"Just like that?" said Sol skeptically. "Frank the Ax just turned himself over to you?"

"Perhaps if you hadn't been so keen to shoot him out of the skies, maybe he would have come to you, too," said Thor.

"Maybe," said Sol, nodding. "And maybe I should order an attack on him right now and blow him right the fuck out of my sight."

"Except you know it wouldn't be in your best interest to do

so," said Axford smugly. "Like I said, I hold the key to your salvation."

"I thought you said Lucia was the key?" Alander was looking increasingly lost.

"What she *knows* is the key," Axford explained.

"And what is that?" pressed Alander.

"Pi-1 Ursa Major," Sol answered for the ex-general. "That's where Thor has come from, and where she found Lucia. I'm guessing she saw something when she flew through, right? Was it the Starfish base, Frank?"

Axford smiled. "Actually, it's not a Starfish base at all. It's a *Spinner* base. Or so I reckon. Does *that* get your attention?"

Alander and Sol stared at the ex-general. Thor could practically see their minds working at superfast speed.

"You have evidence?" asked Sol.

"Enough to convince me."

"Assuming you're not bullshitting us, then, Frank, what exactly is it you're suggesting we do?"

"Simple. I suggest we force the Starfish into talking to us and, once we've done that, we offer to tell them where their enemy is hiding. I doubt there'd be a military intelligence in the universe that would ignore that kind of information."

"Or ignore the people offering it," said Thor, herself unable to suppress her smugness.

"That's the plan?" said Sol. "To run headlong into the very thing that wants to kill us?"

"Better to run to your death than run from it," said Axford.

"He's right, Sol," said Thor. "And by allying ourselves with the force destroying us, we might be able to turn the tide."

"You make it sound easy," said Alander eventually. "And I won't even go into the morality of doing it."

"Well, easy it won't be," said Axford. "Getting over that first hurdle is going to be tricky."

"Any thoughts on how we'd go about that?"

Axford's smile widened. "I wouldn't be here if I didn't."

"Wait a second," said Sol. "I'm with Peter. What about the morality of what you're suggesting? We'd be biting the hand that feeds us. Setting the Spinners up like this strikes me as being more than a little ungrateful. It could just as easily turn *them* against us, too. Then we'd end up with two enemies, not one."

"It's either this or the Starfish wipe us out once and for all," said Axford. "And it's not as if the Spinners are exactly paying us any attention or anything. They won't answer our calls. If they're not supplying any answers, then, gifts or no gifts, I say they haven't earned our gratitude."

"Just hear him out, Sol," said Thor as her original opened her mouth to protest. "What he's saying makes sense—and it could give us the edge we need to get out of this mess. Besides which, it's not as if we have unlimited time on our hands."

"We have eight days, to be precise," said Sol, intoning the deadline as though she was laying mausoleum slabs in place.

"It's all we'll need." Axford's surety was infectious. Thor could feel Sol and Alander beginning to think it over just as she had done, days earlier. Frank Axford was amoral and vicious; she knew that. And she also knew that to trust him any further than was necessary would be asking for trouble—something she had learned all too clearly when she'd heard the facts behind Beid. But if parleying with the devil was the only way to ensure hers and the rest of humanity's survival, then what choice did they really have? An opportunity like this might never present itself again.

"What makes you so keen to stay, Frank?" Sol asked.

"I'm not," he said.

Sol's eyes narrowed. "That doesn't make sense. If you're pitching us on some damfool mission designed to distract or kill us while the rest of you follow some other agenda—"

He cut her off with a laugh. "Okay, I take your point. But you're only half right. The rest of me *are* off doing something else, but nothing that's likely to conflict with your interests. You see, I'm not just banking on this plan; I'm also following the Yuhl path. I'm also migrating outward in other directions and hiding a few of myself on worlds that might be overlooked by the Starfish. I'm taking every option at once and hoping that at least some of me survive."

"Spores," said Alander, his face a picture of distaste.

Axford 1041 didn't shy from the analogy. "Exactly. Every one of me is a seed. By propagating them as widely as possible, I hope to guarantee the survival of the Axford genome."

"A plague of Axfords," Sol mused. "It doesn't bear thinking about."

His smile only widened further. "It doesn't seem so bad from my point of view, collectively speaking," he said. "And there's the rub. From *my* point of view, as an individual, this situation is a little different. The thought that one of me might survive somewhere, but not here, is only intellectually satisfying. It won't change the fact that *I'm* still dead. So I'm going to do everything I can to ensure that *this* me will survive, that *I* will pull through. And if I have to drag you along with me to do it, then I will."

"No guarantees afterward, I presume," said Sol.

Frank the Ax's smile turned predatory as he shook his head. "Once we're out the other side, then it's everyone for themselves. But it's a big galaxy. Caryl. I'm sure we can coexist peacefully enough."

Assuming anyone survives, Thor thought to herself.

"All right," said Sol, her expression guarded. "You've told me some of it. Now give me the rest. And bring Peter up to speed, too."

"What about the others?" Alander asked. "What's the point of letting them argue on if we're going to make our own plans here? Shouldn't we at least let them know there might be an alternative?"

"Perhaps when they've finished arguing, we'll consider bringing them into it," said Axford. "Once the engrams and the Yuhl have divided into their camps, then we'll know who has the guts to work with us. *They're* the people we need: the Species Dreamers determined to find a new home; the patriots willing to defend the home they already have. There's no room for fence-sitters now, people. We either stand or we fall; it's as simple as that. There is no other alternative."

Axford's words settled like a cowl over the conversation, and for a long time no one spoke. But from their expressions, Thor could tell that the ex-general's words had hit home. And when her original finally met her eyes and gave a reluctant nod of approval to the plan, Thor allowed herself a brief, self-satisfied smile.

UEH/ELLIL

There was no fanfare as the Yuhl migration divided in two. Although it took a great deal of preparation and incredible attention to detail, the occasion itself was marked only with silence by the human observers and sadness by the Yuhl. The many hundreds of hole ships comprising the *Mantissa* that had survived the Battle of Beid were split almost down the middle, with 44 percent staying behind to confront the Ambivalence and rebuild themselves a home, and 56 percent continuing onward with their great emigration. The species was well and truly divided.

Ueh/Ellil watched the separation of the *Yuhl/Goel* with resignation but no small amount of uncertainty. His species had been attending the Ambivalence for more long cycles than he'd care to count. The home worlds were legends remembered only by a handful of survivors of that time. But such memories did not belong to him. He had only ever known life in the hole ships, and sometimes it felt as though this was the only world he would *ever* know. It seemed inconceivable to him that the life he knew would ever end.

And yet for some it had already ended. Those who had voted to remain behind were no longer part of the *Yuhl/Goel*. The Species Dreamers were *Yuhl/riil* now. They were prey, the already dead—and he wasn't one of them.

He didn't know how to feel about that. Once, life had been simple. As one of a helot pair, his tasks had been simple, purely functional, and he had needed to think no more than was required to ensure those tasks were carried out effectively.

But then the bodiless humans had come along, and everything had changed. His helot pairing, *Asi/Holina*, had been taken hostage by the many-bodied human *Frank/Axford*, while he, Ueh, had accompanied *Peter/Alander* on his journey to the *Mantissa* to see the Praxis. What had become of *Asi/Holina* was unknown, but it was assumed that he had died in Axford's care. Whatever the case, without *Asi/Holina*, Ueh's position among his people had become redundant. He was effectively caught between two colliding cultures, an orphan among orphans.

He couldn't blame *Peter/Alander* for breaking up his pairing, though. The human wasn't to know the necessities of life where his culture was concerned. Alander and his kind expressed puzzlement over many things and were clearly unprepared for their first contact with an alien race. The Ambivalence had rattled them, and they were blundering now when they should have been treading lightly.

Alander had delivered *Ueh/Ellil* to the Praxis little knowing the fate that awaited either of them. Physically ingested— *eaten*—by the giant creature, they had lost everything. The Praxis had absorbed them, body and mind. For an unknown length of time neither had existed. Their regurgitation had not been guaranteed, and it came at a price. Their bodies and minds had been tinkered with, in accordance with the Praxis's inscrutable will. They had been changed to better fulfill the tasks required of them, fashioned as tools and sent back out into the universe with little knowledge of how exactly they had been altered.

The Yuhl were a species not unaccustomed to radical change. Their minds, encouraged by advanced medical science, had retained a measure of plasticity from their evolutionary past and were able to literally grow new sections to accommodate new skills. But even with such a background, *Ueh/Ellil* had been given cause to wonder. As he progressed with startling rapidity from helot to *envoy/catechist* and finally to conjugator, he had to ask where it might end.

"Who am I the same person I was before?"

Even asking that question exposed him as the freak he was. Yuhl rarely thought of themselves as individuals in isolation. Until the change, his individuality had been defined in terms of the *Yuhl/Goel* race. He was not an island; his life was not a single thread, drifting alone through space. He was a just one more strand in a much larger tapestry.

Or had been, anyway. Now that he was back among his own people, he was struck by how out of place he felt. He didn't feel like he was one of them anymore, didn't feel like he *belonged*. He was something else entirely.

"They call us the Pax Praxis," said a voice that sounded as though it could fill the universe. Ueh was standing on an observation deck, watching the *Mantissa* break in two. To the Yuhl, that meant being tightly enveloped by a glistening intestine that drooped down from the ceiling. Nanometer-thin tendrils spread through his skin to nerve endings, resulting in complex illusions of the world outside.

"The humans have much to learn," he replied.

"We all do, I suspect." Deep rumblings echoed around him, as though a meal of stones was grinding in the belly of a giant. "There's something I need you to do for me, Ueh."

"You need only to instruct me, and it will be done." He found it strange that the Praxis should word it in such a way as to make it sound like a request. Ueh's promotion to conjugator meant that he now served the Praxis exclusively, and whatever was required of him would be done without question. He was no longer bound to the Fit like others of his race.

"No, Ueh, this is different," said the Praxis. "I can't command you to do this for me. I have selected you specifically, but in this instance you are not obliged to obey me. You see, this task . . . it's not like others you would have performed."

Ueh was fascinated. He had never heard the Praxis hesitate before. "What is it you wish me to do?"

The Praxis told him then, in great detail, and he began to understand. It *was* no ordinary task, and although the thought of it was daunting, he could appreciate the symbolism of the act as well as its importance. In the history of the *Yuhl/Goel*, it would go down as a significant moment, and for that he felt profoundly honored that the Praxis had chosen him. Nevertheless, the prospect of what the Praxis was asking of him was also quite terrifying.

"But no one must know, Ueh," his new master told him. "If you decide to do this for me, you must speak to no one about it."

"But my absence—"

"Will be explained to the others," assured the Praxis. "Trust me, I will ensure that your duties are carried out. You will not be missed, Ueh. But you will be remembered, of that you can be certain."

The promise of importance piqued his pride again, and he felt strangely warmed by the Praxis's words. "And if I choose not to do this task? What then?"

"Then I shall be forced to eat my words, Ueh."

Ueh shuddered in the tight embrace of the observatory intestine. He had no doubt in his mind that "eating his words" was a metaphor for eating *him* to ensure no one else got to know about the plan.

The *Mantissa* crumbled around him like a rotten moon, then slowly recombined as two smaller orbs. A haze of hole ships attended both newly formed spheres, tidying configurations and ensuring structural soundness. Human vessels looked on in silent awe. Hole ship engineering on such a scale was at present beyond their comprehension. Joining ten ships in a viable construct was completely different than joining a thousand similar ships.

"I will do my duty," Ueh told the Praxis. The words rang hollowly in his ears. The knowledge of his certain death either way didn't make the decision any easier.

1.2

CHIEF OF MOURNERS

1.2.1

The tetrad of modified hole ships flew on thrusters with about as much grace as a dropped glass. But it didn't need grace; it just needed to be fast. And it certainly was that.

Alander stood at the rear of the command cockpit while Cleo Samson directed the modified hole ship via a slender, branched stalk protruding from the floor. The tetrad's only other passenger was Axford 1041, who sat unobtrusively to one side, his attention focused on the cockpit screens.

"The beacon has been deployed," Samson announced. "Just waiting on confirmation from Thor."

Alander forced himself not to worry. This was a test run, after all, not the real thing. Their tetrad was one of thirty arrayed across the empty zeta Dorado system. The colony there, Hammon, had been comprehensively destroyed in the wave of Starfish attacks that had accompanied the Battle of Beid. Smoke still plumed from installations on the ground where alien weaponry had eradicated all trace of human and Spinner technology. Alander had seen enough of the Starfish strikes to know that the attack would have been swift and deadly. The colonists aboard the *Steven Vogt* would have barely known what was hitting them.

Alander paced restlessly as the screens arrayed around them displayed telemetry on the mission. The other tetrads were scattered across all sectors of the system with some degree of uncertainty; it was difficult for conventional instruments to know their exact positions due to light-speed delays, and the time hadn't come to openly use ftl communications. The system contained eight planets: three gas giants and five terrestrial worlds. Hammon was one of a binary system, not quite habitable but tectonically fascinating.

With an intense look of concentration on her face, Samson tilted the tetrad into a tight turn on its nearly reactionless thrusters. The NRTs had been uncovered by Hatzis's Library research team on Juno, prior to Beid. Alander didn't understand the principles on which they operated at all; he could only take the word of the researchers, who said that they *should* work. The Yuhl employed a different drive principle again for their hole ships, and this maneuver was as much a test of technology as it was of tactics.

Seconds later, with hands tightly gripping the control stalk, Samson leveled the ship out again. She glanced over to both Alander and Axford, grinning nervously.

"Seems to work okay," she said. "Just takes a little getting used to."

"Would have been so much easier if Ueh had been here," said Axford. He looked around the cockpit as though searching the empty spaces for the alien. "Kind of quiet without the Roach, isn't it?"

Alander knew that Axford was trying to get a rise out of him by using the derogatory moniker originally attributed to the aliens. The term originated in the similarity the aliens had to insects. With their unnaturally long legs culminating in broad, triangular thighs and their thick, almost chitinous black skin, they bore a striking resemblance to grasshoppers. But they were intelligent beings, deserving of more respect than the ex-general was prepared to give them. Having spoken in some depth to Ueh, Alander had developed an understanding and appreciation for the aliens and their culture and could never bring himself to be as disrespectful toward them as Axford was, in public at least. Alander didn't doubt that Axford had a healthy respect for what the Yuhl were capable of.

"We'll just have to make do," he said, refusing to give Axford the satisfaction of rising to the bait. "He must have had his reasons for staying with the Praxis."

"I'm sure he did," said Axford, a smile tugging at the corners of his mouth. "I guess you'd understand."

"What's that supposed to mean?"

The ex-general raised his hands in mock innocence. "Hey, I'm sure the Yuhl have a lot going for them. I'm just not in any hurry to *become* one, that's all."

"No one's asking you to," said Alander.

"Not at the moment, perhaps," Axford responded. "But one must consider all eventualities, Peter. Android bodies like this one are infinitely malleable—as the Praxis proved with yours. A hybrid human-Yuhl caste might be possible somewhere down the track. I, for one, want no part of it."

"That's your decision."

"Indeed it is."

Alander bit his lip to keep his irritation contained. Of the engrams, about a quarter had expressed xenophobic concerns over the *Yuhl/Goel,* even thought their alien allies had offered significant assistance both before and after the meeting in Rasmussen. Following the failure of that meeting to reach a consensus, as he had expected, both human and Yuhl corps had split in two, leaving every human survivor with no choice but to rely on alien assistance. Approximately half of the Yuhl had remained behind to follow Thor's plan, with the endorsement of Sol, while the rest elected to continue their flight with the Praxis. A similar split divided the human camp, and tensions were running high as old alliances crumbled and new ones formed—all with the relentless ticking of the clock in the background.

"Imagine how the Yuhl must view our customs," Alander said. "I'm sure they see us as incredibly primitive. I mean, we've hardly changed since we left Africa. Even in engram form, we still cling to ancient shapes and functions. Does that make sense for a space-faring race?"

It wasn't a strong defense of tolerance, but it was the best he could do. He couldn't argue that he understood the Yuhl better just because he was more open-minded. Already a human-Yuhl hybrid, his nature counted against him in arguments with racists.

Genuinely or for effect, Axford deflected his response with a nonchalant shrug. "We get the job done."

"Maybe, but I doubt we would have thought of migrating if the Yuhl hadn't set the example."

"*I* would have."

"But you're an outlier, General. We all know that." Alander said this evenly, letting the implication—*You're a freak*—rest in the words rather than his tone.

The android laughed out loud, but before he could actually say anything in response, a vibration trilled through the tetrad. Alander and Axford both returned their attention to the screens, recognizing the distinctive sound of an incoming ftl communication.

"I guess that means go," said Samson.

Alander took a deep breath. Ftl transmissions attracted the Starfish like blood attracted sharks. The time between transmission and arrival varied; sometimes it was hours, other times they arrived after barely a few seconds, giving the unlucky broadcaster little chance of escape. Thus far, no colonies that had attracted the attention of the Starfish had survived. Alander had witnessed two attacks: one on Sol and the other on the Yuhl world-vessel *Mantissa*, and both had left him overwhelmed and stunned by the ferocity and technology of the Starfish. He had no real desire to witness such an attack a third time, but he acknowledged the necessity of it.

The tetrad rang like a bell once more: another ftl message, as expected. The first had been confirmation from Thor at the edge of the system; the second was from the beacon itself—the lure.

All thirty tetrads sounded their transmitters in synchrony, summoning the enemy with a non-Einsteinian racket that would most certainly get their attention.

The waiting was the worst part for Alander. Not knowing exactly how little time there was made evacuating dangerous and difficult. Barely 40 percent of the *Mantissa* had survived Beid, even though the Yuhl were constantly alert for an alien attack. What remained had been divided into two halves, with the slightly larger half, *Mantissa A*, accompanying the Praxis and the departing engrams on the Yuhl's ongoing migration. The rest, *Mantissa B*, remained with the Species Dreamers and the human resistance to either confront or evade the Starfish. If their gamble failed, there would be nothing left at all in less than two weeks.

Data from the distant hole ships thrilled through *Klotho* in a dissonant cacophony. The thirty tetrads were no longer hiding and therefore able to exchange telemetry at ftl rates. The instantaneous communication allowed a detailed picture of zeta Dorado to form on the screen. From the primary to the outermost gas giant, the picture was one of scarred indifference; behind the occasional puff of radioactive dust where an installation or satellite had once been, the planets and moons continued on their stately way, uncaring what happened to those who passed briefly by.

"Target acquired," said Samson, her tone sharp and touched with alarm. "Relocating!"

The screen stayed alight as the tetrad hopped across the system. Fleeting images of roiling energies and vast, disk-shaped craft peppered the screen. Alander felt his abdominal muscles tighten.

Then, abruptly, they were among the cutters, dodging the exotic weapons of the Starfish. Each had been given a nickname that in the throes of battle seemed to trivialize their potency: yellow dots, blue lances, red darts, energy whips, and more. The principles behind each were difficult to fathom. Energy whips appeared to be snaking regions of destabilized space-time, where the fundamental properties of the universe had been altered, tearing even the vacuum apart. Yellow dots blinked in and out of unspace in search of targets, materializing inside their unlucky prey and causing massive explosions as two chunks of matter tried to occupy the same space.

It was this tactic that had inspired the Yuhl to their one and only victory in the Battle of Beid. Hole ships could be divided into thirds as well as combined, and each of those thirds could be sent inside a target, equipped with weapons designed to cause maximum damage. Using this method, the Yuhl had managed to render one of the Starfish cutters totally inoperative, leading to its rescue by two of its comrades.

Alander vividly remembered the strange incident with the

rescuing craft. The two flat, giant ships were kilometers across, their edges spinning at relativistic velocities, dragging space-time around like water on the edge of a whirlpool. Spinning in opposite directions so spatial distortions made the very vacuum shimmer, the two cutters had sandwiched the damaged ship and brought it to a halt. Then, in a blaze of pulsing light, all three had disappeared.

It was at this point the Yuhl had completed their evacuation, scattering in the face of such an imposing and terrifying enemy.

The tetrad bucked violently, and Alander's attention returned to the present. Samson guided them through the thick of the battle, sophisticated algorithms in the AI combining with her increasing expertise to ride out the worst of it. A detonating red dart sent them rolling at one point, but they managed to avoid serious damage.

"How long can we keep this up?" asked Alander anxiously as he watched the thirty Yuhl/human tetrads winking in and out of unspace around the majestic Starfish craft.

"I don't know," said Axford. "But with five of those cutters slicing their way into the system, we wouldn't want to be out here too long."

The tetrad shuddered beneath them again.

"Probes away," said Samson.

She took them back into unspace as the tetrad dropped half its structure in the form of six smaller parts. Their ship instantly reduced itself in size, changing from a tetrad to a double. However, there was no appreciable change in the size of the cockpit itself or the way the ship flew. Each of the mini–hole ship probes had ftl capacities but little more than that. Their payloads consisted of sensors rather than weapons.

Klotho emerged from unspace at the far edge of the system, along with the other Yuhl pilots, safely out of the Starfish light cone. In the icy regions of zeta Dorado's Oort cloud, they viewed the five cutters from afar, relying on the instruments of the detached probes to keep a close eye on things.

There were hundreds of data streams coming in. Each of the tetrads had dropped six probes, and all of them were taking a slightly different route into and around the cutters. A quarter were destroyed within the first minute of being launched; another quarter in the next minute. Half of those were expended in collisions with the giant craft, testing the strength and nature of their exotic hulls. Every explosion was recorded by another nearby probe, the data sent to their distant observers.

Shortly after the dispersal of the tetrads, another quarter had disappeared from the screens. These hadn't been destroyed, though. They reappeared as data streams over the next fifty seconds, scattered within the cutters themselves. Having jumped inside the giant craft, they proceeded to follow a number of detailed routines designed to test their new environments. Some extruded sophisticated sensors designed to probe the nature of their surroundings. Others tested more aggressively to see what sort of reaction they would provoke. Others stayed carefully quiescent, recording their location and anything they observed with passive, patient sensors.

Alander didn't bother trying to absorb all the data coming in. That would have to wait until later, once they had jumped to safety and were well away from the Starfish. He managed to take in some of it, though, watching the scattered, bright stars of the probes wink out one by one, attacked by defensive systems within the Starfish cutters. Some activated self-destruct mechanisms; others simply fizzled out. Others clung on with admirable tenacity.

Then, suddenly, all of them were gone. Alander blinked at the empty screen in confusion. The telemetry from the probes had abruptly ceased. He couldn't see the inner system or the cutters. They were totally blind.

"What the—?"

His question was cut short when the data stream returned as abruptly as it had disappeared, only this time they were accompanied by cries of alarm and panic from the other Yuhl-human hole ship pairs. The cutters, realizing that their targets had moved, had relocated to continue the attack. Two of the pairs instantly vanished under heavy fire as the giant ships appeared directly over them, lashing out with terrifying lethality. The cutters then jumped to another location and repeated the tactic, slicing through space with an ease that belied their size.

In four of them, starlike probes still gleamed.

"We have what we came here for," said Axford 1041. He sounded surprisingly calm, given their circumstances. "I suggest we get away while we still can."

"You won't get any argument from me," said Alander. He'd seen enough.

The probes were winking out one by one, their numbers steadily eroded by conditions Alander couldn't begin to imagine.

"Just a little longer," said Samson.

"Taking evasive action," announced the hole ship a second later.

Axford called out in alarm as a cutter appeared directly over their tetrad. Vicious colors leapt out of the screen.

"I am sustaining damage." The hole ship bucked beneath them, sending Alander and Axford into the far wall. Samson remained standing, gripping the control stalk with both hands and bracing herself.

"*Klotho*, get us out of here!"

Alander's shout echoed into silence as the hole ship entered unspace. He sagged gratefully into the sudden peace, feeling his heart pounding in his throat.

"That was a little close," he said, painfully climbing to his feet.

"*Too* damned close," muttered Axford, doing likewise. Then, to Samson: "What the hell do you think you're doing?"

Samson stepped away from the controls to face Axford. "Trying to get as much data as possible," she said. "That's what we came here for, wasn't it? I only intended to stay a few seconds longer—"

"Seconds in which we could have all been killed!" Axford growled.

"Take it easy, Frank," said Alander. "She only—"

"It was a stupid and unnecessary risk," Axford cut in.

"We got out in one piece, didn't we?" said Samson.

"But we might not have," returned Axford. "What good is data if we're too dead to use it!"

"If I remember rightly, the incident at Beid was an information-gathering exercise, too. Wasn't it?" She met his glare evenly. "Funny, but I don't recall you having much concern about safety issues back then."

The ex-general glowered at her for a moment, then stormed from the cockpit, shaking his head.

Samson turned to Alander with an apologetic shrug. "He's

probably right. But we won't win this fight if we don't take chances."

He took a deep breath. "I know. Just don't cut it so fine, next time."

"Hopefully there'll only be one more 'next time.' "

Alander nodded. If the data told them what they needed to hear, there was no reason not to plough ahead with Axford's plan. He still wasn't entirely sure what he thought about that.

"Ours is not to question why . . ."

"Eh?"

"Nothing, Cleo. Just get us back home so we can see who didn't make it. We'll worry about what happens next then."

1.2.2

The total blackness was unsettling at first, but Lucia soon grew used to it. It was calm in the dark—*safe*. She had plenty of space to put herself back together, to sort out the tangle of her thoughts and examine the snarled knots in her emotions that talking to Peter had exposed. An engram was a complicated computer program designed to simulate the thoughts, emotions, memories, and actions of a human being. It wasn't perfect, but it was an excellent compromise between primitive AIs and energy-hungry humans. The UNESSPRO supervisors had anticipated problems and openly discussed the possibility of providing editing suites for the engrams, should problems arise. In the end, however, they'd opted not to allow the engrams to actively tamper with themselves, in much the same way that natural humans couldn't.

That was a shame, Lucia thought, because such an ability would have enabled Peter to fix himself without having to rely on others. He could simply shut down unreliable modules until he found the source of the instability, then modify that one to ensure that he worked properly. The idea of tinkering with one's own thoughts was discomforting, but it was better, she thought, than the notion of death and—

She forced herself to change her train of thought, to focus

more on herself. Remembering Peter only reminded her of why she was in this darkness in the first place.

What are my faulty modules? she wondered. *What conflicts are responsible for the panic I feel at losing Peter?*

She soon discovered that, as Thor had said, the problem lay in the definitional components of her engram model. They didn't affect the process of her thoughts, but they definitely influenced the initial conditions and the operating boundaries. She was constrained by certain "facts" about herself: she liked to travel, but she missed Peter; she preferred cats over dogs; she had no interest in sports; the ending of *Silent Running* still made her cry; and so on. While they existed, she was trapped by them. She couldn't change her mind, because the "her" in this case was the Lucia Benck on Earth, who had died a century before.

Engram Lucia gave up the attempt on confirming everything she'd been told, for the moment. There had to be a way to correct the problem without appealing to the others for help. She couldn't trust herself to interact coherently with them. She was beginning to assume that the only thing that had kept her alive in *Chung-5* for so long was her isolation from external input. Like a train on a roller coaster, she was perfectly safe as long as she remained on the track. The slightest nudge could send her careening to madness or even brainlock. But if she could just *switch* tracks . . .

The moment she'd fled Peter was a blur. She had no clear memory of where exactly she had fled. She suspected that she wasn't in a hole ship; in none of the alien vessels she had explored had she found anywhere like this—so dark and empty, so accommodatingly *vacant.* Here she wasn't cohabiting; she had her own space to stretch and recover. It was better even than *Chung-5*, for in the tiny probe she had been constantly aware of its constraints. Here, in the dark space, there was nothing but her.

Tentatively at first, then with greater confidence, Lucia began to explore her surroundings. Probing her dark sanctuary, she immediately became aware of three things. The first was that the dark space was permeable but defined. Beyond its boundaries, flexing and stirring like the muscles of a whale as seen from the inside, she could sense vast minds working.

There was a depth to the darkness she shied away from. Apart from that, she felt completely unthreatened.

The second thing she noticed was that her sanctuary was just a tiny fragment of the semantic world beyond. She sensed vast complexities and vistas just outside her reach. Molelike, she peered out of her burrow at a world more rich and varied than any she had expected.

The third thing she found, as she made her first cautious explorations of her new environment, was that she was being watched. Barely had the darkness begun to part around her, allowing her access to the light-filled world beyond, when she felt eyes lock on her from outside her dark sanctuary, from beyond the glowing vistas, from somewhere else entirely.

"Hello? Is anyone there?"

The voice was male and carried a hint of a familiar European accent. Close on the heels of this familiarity, though, was a sense of disorientation and confusion.

"Rob?" she said tentatively.

The owner of the voice paused slightly before answering. "Who is this? How did you get in here?"

She hesitated also, still wary of outside influences. Every instinct told her to flee, to avoid a relapse. But she knew Rob Singh; she and the good-natured pilot had entrained together in the flight simulators back on Earth. She could trust him, she was sure.

"It's Lucia."

"*Lucia?* When did you get back?"

His question gave her a sense of relief. If he wasn't aware of her return, then clearly her escape hadn't been broadcast, which meant she wasn't being actively pursued by everyone in the engram camp.

"Thor found me and brought me here," she answered. "I was in a bad way. I hid in here because it seemed safe."

Rob chuckled lightly. "I guess you could call it safe. The Dark Room is a good place to come if you're freaking out. Apparently Peter Alander used to sleep in the one on Adrasteia, back when he was unstable. Others have tried, but they say it's too empty for them. I'm not partial to it, myself."

Only a handful of his words registered. "Peter used to come here?"

"Not to this Dark Room specifically. This is Rasmussen, not Adrasteia. Adrasteia is gone; has been for weeks now. Peter has never used this particular Dark Room. I haven't actually spoken to him since he came here, but I'm told he's a lot better now than he was."

The pieces were slowly settling into place. "So that's where I am now? Rasmussen?"

"That's right."

"Inside—" Her mind grappled with difficulty at the notion. "I'm inside the *gifts?*"

"You didn't know that?" he asked, surprised. "That's why I found you. I was having a poke around on behalf of another one of me, one who died when Sothis took the bullet. He'd been finding anomalies in the Library and noting them in his PID. The records survived the attack, shipped out in a hole ship full of solid-state backups. I inherited them, if you like, and figured I'd pick up where he left off—try to see if I could add anything to his findings." A small silence encapsulated all the grief and weirdness of discussing the legacy of another version of oneself. "I've been looking into areas he ignored, hoping to find something new. But the last thing I expected to find was *you,* Lucia. To be honest, you scared the hell out of me. I thought you might be some kind of Spinner virus, come to eat me!"

The self-deprecation in his voice was a welcome relief to the strident urgencies of Alander and Hatzis, and for the first time in what felt like eons, she found herself wanting to laugh. She fought back the urge, though, nervous of any sudden, out-of-character impulses.

"Can I ask a favor of you, Rob?"

"Of course. Anything."

"Would you mind not telling anyone that I'm here right now? Everything has been kind of strange and overwhelming; I'd appreciate a little space."

"I understand. We're all a bit freaked out at the moment."

She followed his voice to its source and found a many-limbed droid gripping the edge of a doorway through which bright light streamed. Still seduced by the warm darkness, it took Lucia a moment to realize that this image was real; it wasn't virtual. It was the world outside the Dark Room in which she'd taken refuge. She was seeing the inside of one of the gifts for the first time.

"What's the Dark Room for?" she asked.

"No one's managed to work that out yet," he said. "It's a mystery. All the other spindles have a clear purpose: the Dry Dock, the Gallery, the Hub, et cetera. But not this one. It has a bunch of corridors and empty chambers, and this one room, full of darkness. Light is sucked into it, and we can't find the edges. It's very odd."

Lucia agreed. She didn't know much about the gifts—only the information that Thor had given her access to on the way back from pi-1 Ursa Major—but that was enough to capture the weirdness of the objects and the aliens that had left them behind. They were simultaneously a great boon for humanity and an irksome mystery that might never be unraveled. And they were dangerous, too, as misuse of the ftl transmitters had demonstrated. If a single word could bring down the wrath of the Starfish, eradicating all the Spinners' good works in a single stroke, what other unknown perils might lurk in the alien halls?

"By the by," Rob asked, "mind telling me how you're doing that?"

"Doing what?"

"Being . . . yourself." The telesensing robot looked like a cross between a monkey and a sea anemone, but somehow it managed a convincing shrug. "You're in engram form, you don't have a body, and yet you can obviously still see me. Do you have a processor in there or something? Or are you operating on remote, like me?"

"I'm not sure," she said. "When Thor found me, she uploaded me into her hole ship's operating memory."

"Really? I didn't know that was possible."

She wanted to shrug but lacked the physical form with which to do so. "It seems to have worked well enough."

"What brought you here?"

"I became . . . upset," she said, keen to avoid the details. "I came here to hide, to be alone."

"And here I am, interrupting you, blathering on like an idiot. Christ, Lucia, I'm sorry." Rob's voice was genuinely contrite. His robot immediately let go of the door, started to roll away like a surreal tumbleweed. "I should leave you alone."

"It's not your fault, Rob. You weren't to know." Astronaut training had reinforced in all the engrams the need for personal space, even in a virtual world. She had been alone for so long in *Chung-5*, with nothing but her thoughts to keep her amused. But Rob was a completely different person than the others she had spoken to since coming back. He seemed to have no agendas, no demands to make of her.

"Will you come back later?" she called after him.

"You can count on it." There was a smile in his voice. "I've still got work to do around here."

"Thanks, Rob," she said, meaning it. "I appreciate it."

"Sure thing. Maybe I can show you around the spindles, if you haven't seen them properly yet."

"I'd like that," she said.

"Good. Then it's a date." With that, the robot trundled off down the wide, white corridor. It tumbled around a corner and disappeared.

Lucia felt herself relax instantly. She wasn't ready for people, not without proper control over who she was. She knew that it might not be so easy to attain, but the question of *what* she was could be more easily explored. In truth, although she had agreed to let Rob show her around the spindles, she didn't know if she could leave the Dark Room. She had been interrupted in the middle of trying. As she tentatively extended herself now to test her boundaries, she found that she had an awareness of the structure that housed her—an awareness that could neither be put into words or thoughts. It was just there, a part of her, like the innate instinct a normal human had of their body's posture. With it, also, came a vague understanding of all the other spindles that girded the planet and of the transmitter they comprised.

Deciding not to wait on Rob's return, Lucia took the virtual equivalent of a deep breath and urged her pov toward the doorway.

The darkness fell smoothly behind her as she suddenly found herself—or her pov, at least—in bright light.

Embracing this newfound freedom, she began to explore.

1.2.3

A haze of stars surrounded Caryl Hatzis like a glowing mist.
She took a moment to admire it, to bathe in the light of 200
billion suns. When she breathed in, she imagined that she
wasn't breathing ordinary air but the ionized atoms and far-
flung molecules that bubbled and roiled in interstellar space.
She felt like a god, existing on star stuff, bathing in the primordial fires of creation.

She exhaled, letting the dream go with the breath she'd been
holding. It was a dream she had once cherished, of being part
of a mind that spanned the galaxy, infinite in possibility and
incomprehensible in form. Now she felt she'd be lucky to see
out the month in one piece.

"Do you know what a fovea is?"

Kingsley Oborn's voice came from behind her, followed by
the sound of footsteps. She turned to face the biotechnician as
he walked down into the pit of the Map Room.

"I'm sorry, Kingsley?"

"A *fovea*," he repeated. "Have you heard of the term?"

She nodded, still confused. "It's the part of the eye we look
at things with, isn't it? The part that takes in all the detail?"

"That's right. The rest of the cornea sees things only
vaguely, which is why we move our eyes around a lot without
knowing." Oborn came to a halt in front of her. "The eye is

constantly scanning our field of view, filling in the details. That movement is called a *saccade*. Both saccade and fovea evolved in different senses for a number of different animals, mainly in an attempt to keep the mass and complexity of the brain down. If every part of our cornea was as sensitive as the fovea, our heads would have to be fifty times larger to deal with all the information."

"I presume this is going somewhere."

He nodded significantly. "I think this is how the Starfish are sweeping the wake for anything—or anyone—we leave behind."

Hatzis frowned. "I'm not sure I follow."

Oborn seemed almost pleased with himself for having thought of something she hadn't. "There's no possible way the Starfish could sweep every cubic centimeter across such a vast front. It would take unimaginable resources to do such a thing. But they may have ways to conduct a low-level survey, looking for suspicious points, then focus in on those points with their equivalent of a fovea. This fovea confirms a suspicious sighting, then the cutters move in and get rid of it."

Her mind leapt ahead of him. "So if we want to fall behind and not be destroyed, we're going to have to find a way to evade the fovea."

He nodded again. "There's not much we can do about the low-level survey, because we have no idea how that's being conducted. But the fovea, that's a different story altogether. Look."

He held out a hand and she took it, accepting the data that flowed smoothly into her through their palms.

"We've seen enough Starfish attacks now to recognize a pattern," he continued. "There's always an anomaly shortly beforehand somewhere in the system. See here—this weird radiant point." He indicated several that had appeared in the previous weeks. "We've always assumed that these are symptomatic of the Starfish's propulsion technology. The cutters come much faster, we suspect, than the hole ship drives would allow; that they are preceded by some sort of reverse echo doesn't seem impossible. But it's always bothered me. If the Starfish are so advanced, and so aggressive, then why would they allow something like this to give their arrival away? It doesn't make sense." He shook his head. "No. I think what we're seeing are the fovea—the eyes of the Starfish watching the target as the swords approach. And if we can see them, then maybe we can learn not to be seen *by* them."

The images folded away, their job done. Oborn leaned back, looking even more self-satisfied than he had before. He had every right to be, too. Like his engram on Juno, Kingsley had been co-opted from other duties to be a leader of the research team probing the gifts for any kind of information or technology that might be of use to them in the battle against the Starfish. Although the Yuhl had been plumbing such knowledge for centuries, their access to the gifts was only secondhand, rarely stopping long enough to access the physical structures themselves and for the most part being forced to rely on recordings. An added complication was that the Gifts followed the same tactic with other species as they did with the human engrams: they chose just one member of the native population to speak with, ignoring all others. Even if the Yuhl did get their hands on one of the installations, they could only explore it, not interact with it.

"Good work, Kingsley," she said. "You've done well."

He inclined his head in acknowledgment of her praise. "Obviously we're still a long way from a working evasion technique, but we're getting there. It'd be good to have a Plan B available in case Plan A fails."

She agreed wholeheartedly, if silently, with this. "Speaking of which," she said, "I came here to look at the systems in question: Are you able to run me through them?"

The biotechnician beamed. "Of course. It'd be an honor."

Hatzis waved him forward. All the Oborns had something of a crush on her and they worked best when rewarded with personal contact. She was happy to provide it but wary of taking anything further. One of her engrams had been tempted, long before the arrival of the Spinners, but had found that the Kingsley Oborn engram became unstable if indulged. He'd been programmed with a deep-seated fear of intimacy that took precedence over any physical desires.

That didn't prevent a slight twinge of guilt, though. She had used the Oborn on Juno to head her previous research effort, and he had flown quite happily into the horror of Beid to protect her—and died in the effort. She had no room in her philosophy for noble sacrifice and was reluctant to encourage it in others.

She took the passive role as Oborn wheeled the massive star map around her. An utterly seamless and detailed three-dimensional image, the map was another of the amazing gifts from the Spinners. It showed the location and vector of every major body in the galaxy. Known objects were accurate against Earth astronomical charts: many of the previously unknown objects explained anomalous observations through dust clouds or around the galactic core. Even if it was only mostly complete—there were unexplained gaps hiding, some people thought, information the Spinners considered too sensitive for primitives—it was a boon for astronomers and astrophysicists.

"Here." The view ballooned around them, expanding and focusing on one bright white star in particular. "That's Asellus Primus. Variable F-type star; should have been visited by the *Shelley Wright* decades ago, but they didn't make it. Not that they would've found much if they had. It's a bit of a dud, really."

Hatzis knew her star maps as well as anyone. "Perhaps they kept on going to Asellus Secundus, hoping for better luck."

"If so, then they're still on their way." He smiled at her as though thanking her for an alternative and happier explanation for the *Wright*'s absence. "We're already preparing the contact point in here, orbiting the fourth planet. I think we can guarantee a fair degree of verisimilitude."

She nodded. One of the greatest concerns over the plan was that the trial run might have alerted the Starfish, put their guard up when it came to suspicious signals. Everything depended on the cutters behaving as normal in the face of an ftl transmission. If they hesitated just for a moment or failed to come at all . . .

"The map data is accurate?" she asked, shying away from the thought. It didn't serve any purpose to dwell on negative possibilities right now.

"Down to single-figure percentiles, I'm told."

"Good. And the other?"

The star map spun around her again. The second target was much more familiar to her. She instantly recognized its color and its position with respect to its nearest neighbors.

"Pi-2 Ursa Major," he said. "Five rocky worlds, six gas giants, two asteroid belts, and the usual cometary clouds. The fifth world out was the one to be colonized. You can even see the oxygen levels recorded in the map. I overheard Otto Wyra talking about this the other day. Data is actually encoded in the map image at all frequencies. The visual appearance of each image matches what we would see in the visual spectrum, but if you look outside those bounds, you can find all sorts of—" He stopped, noticing that he was drifting from the topic. "Anyway, there's nothing unusual recorded in the map. It all looks kosher."

"So do you think we're doing the right thing, Kingsley?"

He glanced at her uncertainly. "I'm not sure I know what you mean."

"The question is simple enough: Are we doing the right thing?"

He appeared suddenly flustered. "Well—I wouldn't presume to comment on something you had already—I mean. I'd only be confusing the issue, wouldn't I? And what would be the point of—?"

"Come on, Kingsley. Indulge me, won't you? I just want your opinion on this, rather than mine parroted back to me. If it makes it any easier, I'm *ordering* you to do it."

He swallowed uncomfortably before: "To be honest, Caryl, I'm absolutely terrified."

She nodded her approval and thanks. "Okay, now tell me *why.*"

"Because it's bloody dangerous, that's why. I don't know who's going to volunteer for this mission, but they'd have to be half bloody crazy to even bloody consider it."

She noted the repetition of the swear word and wondered if she might be pushing him into unstable territory, "I'll be volunteering, Kingsley."

"What? You can't be serious!"

"How can I expect my colleagues to do something that I'm not prepared to do myself?"

"But Thor's going. Surely that's enough?"

"Thor's going? How do you know that?"

"It's not a secret."

"It's a secret from me, obviously." She swallowed her confusion and the question: *What the fuck is Thor hoping to gain by broadcasting this?*

He nodded warily. "But that means you don't have to go, right?"

"I'm afraid not." She risked touching him, reassuring him with a squeeze to the shoulder. "You don't have to worry about my safety, Kingsley, and neither should anyone else. The colonies have enough concerns as it is."

"I can't help it, Sol." His eyes avoided hers. "You're all that's left. If we lose you, what's there to fight for?"

"Plenty," she said as firmly as possible. "You just keep working on Plan B and let me take care of the rest, okay?"

Starting with Thor, she added to herself as she turned and left the map—and the illusion of godhood—behind her.

*The data from the trial run flowed like honey through the high-*level simulation. Thor bathed in it, letting the raw information pour over in a slow, dense avalanche. She was assisted in the process by Marduk and Mahatala, two other Hatzis engrams who seemed happy enough to take her orders. They acted as primary filters for the data stream, weeding the information so she wouldn't be overloaded. Even at her fastest clock rate, there was too much for a single mind to absorb in one sitting.

But that didn't stop her trying. She needed to understand firsthand what she was getting into. It was all very well to take Sol's tame expert's word for what might be found in the morass of details, but she wanted to see it for herself. If she was going to leap into the fire, she wanted to know exactly how extensive the resulting burns would be.

Dozens of probes had penetrated the skins of the Starfish cutters and transmitted a wealth of data back to the waiting observers. She saw in exquisite detail everything they had experienced as they died. Explosions prompted massive and immediate defensive measures, sealing breaches and smothering fires with invisible, irresistible fingers. Lasers provoked mirror fields of perfect reflective index, sending the energy back at the probes, while chemical attacks slid off suddenly inert surfaces and were absorbed. Only the sudden annihilation of matter seemed to release enough energy to damage the cutters from within. If any serious harm was to be achieved, then it was going to require antimatter bombs and mass-superposition weapons, or the like.

At least that was the conclusion she came to from studying the up-front attacks. More subtle intrusions generated more ambiguous data. Probes that remained quiescent in their niches were for the most part ignored during the time of the test; others that had been programmed to explore their surroundings had been immediately set upon by security systems. Feeds from the dying probes reported crushing pressure, electromagnetic interference, along with anomalous readings of a dozen kinds.

Nowhere in any of the data did Thor glimpse anything that looked like it might be an alien, suggesting that perhaps the defense systems themselves might have been automatic. Although she hadn't dared hope for a glimpse of one of the mysterious Starfish, she couldn't help but feel disappointed. To be the first to sight one of the aliens would have been a great moment for her and a real slap in the face for Sol.

Ever since that moment of revelation in the ruins of Sothis, when she had understood that Sol wasn't capable of the decisions required to save humanity from the Starfish, she had felt curiously—almost alarmingly—free of any loyalty to her original. If she was going to survive, she realized now, she would have to take the steps herself. That seemed logical enough to her, although it obviously wasn't to the others.

Why me? she wondered. *What sets me apart from the other copies of me? Why am I the only one who stands up to her?*

Perhaps it was selective pressure in action. Only the strongest would survive the coming of the Starfish. While a biological species might evolve by accruing mutations in its genes, engrams could only experience copying errors through the program that ran them. Hers, she was beginning to assume, had just such an error—only her error made her stronger, more independent, than the others.

And if there was anything wrong with that, she couldn't see it.

She returned her attention to the sluggish rush of information. Of the many probes that had been sent, only twelve had remained in operation at the end of the experiment. The behavior of those probes would be examined in the finest possible detail to ascertain what, exactly, had enabled them to survive for so long in the hostile environment of a cutter while the others had failed. Was it the location they found themselves in, perhaps? Or the way they behaved? Whatever the reason, she was determined to find it. No possibility would go unexplored; every piece of information would be thoroughly investigated.

The only thing they couldn't know was how long those probes had survived *for*. When the cutters had left zeta Dorado, all ftl transmissions from the probes had ceased, meaning either they'd been taken out of range or simultaneously destroyed. Thor was keeping her fingers firmly crossed for the former. She wasn't intent on throwing herself into the lion's mouth without having at least some hope of getting out again afterward.

"Is there something you'd like to get off your chest?"

The voice—hers from another's mouth—snapped her out of the data flow. With quicksilver smoothness, her pov was back in her android body and staring at her original.

So much more beautiful and capable, came the involuntary thought. *So much more . . .* me.

Thor forced it down.

"I thought you were going to let others make the decisions," she said as she sat up. "That was the deal after Beid, right?"

"And it's still the deal," Sol replied. "Unless you'd *prefer* me to be in charge?"

Thor tore her eyes from Sol's forearms and their shockingly natural skin tones. Human flesh was available in abundance by conSense, the communal illusion inhabited by most of the engrams, but in the real world its scarcity was a source of constant despair.

"You *are* in charge, Sol," Thor said. "And well you know it, too. Worse, you encourage it. Everything's gone back to the way it was on Sothis. You let them worship you like a goddess."

Something flickered across the face of her original, then, and Thor smiled smugly for a moment, convinced she'd hit a nerve. But Sol's next words took her by surprise.

"What if it was *you* they worshiped, Thor? Would that please you more?"

She didn't have to think to answer that question, but it did take her a second to decide whether to say it aloud. Marduk and Mahatala were watching over Sol's shoulder, just as nervous and compliant as all the others were around Sol.

"Yes," Thor admitted finally. "I guess it would."

"And you think you could do a better job than me?"

It was uncertainty that made her hesitate this time. "I guess we'll never know, will we?"

Sol shrugged. "I never asked for this job, Thor, nor do I particularly want it." Her perfectly white eyes regarded Thor intently. "I was serious about leaving it up to someone else after Beid, but no one else stepped forward. You could've presented Axford's plan yourself to the Survivors' Council, but instead you went through me. And they listened to me, as you knew they would. And they're *still* listening to me, whether I want them to or not. But it's not too late. I'll happily step down any time you want me to. I'll endorse your leadership. That'll be the last order I give."

Thor studied her in return for a long moment. "You're fucking with me, aren't you?"

"No, Thor, I'm not. It would be a relief to be rid of the responsibility."

"Very well." Thor felt a slight tremor run through her. She couldn't tell if it was fear or excitement. "Then I shall relieve you of the burden."

Sol nodded once as she extended a hand. Thor took it instinctively, doubt flaring briefly in her gut as Sol's expression hardened as their palms locked together.

"*But first,*" said a voice in Thor's head, "*you're going to need this.*"

An explosion of memories and emotions blossomed in her mind. Thoughts, touches, doubts, tastes . . . The details poured through the channel Sol had opened between them, each one linking up to dozens more, catapulting her headlong into her original's experiences. The rush was inexorable and wild. It was far more intense and detailed than the high-level simulation of the test in zeta Dorado—and far more authentic than the patchwork approximation that substituted for an engram's activation memories. These were the intimate, firsthand experiences of a woman who had lived over 150 years, and they were pouring into Thor's head like a flood unleashed from a broken dam, sweeping everything away in its path.

But it wasn't like she was being invaded or being subsumed by another's mind. This came from *her*—or at least another version of her—and in a very real sense these memories already *belonged* to her. And because of this, the initial shock and fright of the experience soon wore off, and she found herself welcoming these aspects of herself.

Still, there was far too much information to assimilate. Image after image flowed through her, bringing all manner of emotional baggage with it. Seeing Sol fall to the Starfish and feeling her higher self die, piece by piece, was the culmination of a great knot of emotional scar tissue that had begun in the vicious turmoil of the Spike, during which she had witnessed the destruction of Earth and all her loved ones: her mother, her sister, her father.

Her father! She confronted a memory that had no analogue in her own mind. She remembered her father with great sadness. She had loved him, worshiped him, before his death on Io. It was that loss from which her grief sprang—or so she had always thought.

But there was so much she had never known. A tangle of memories unfolded before her now, filling spaces in her mind that until that moment she'd never realized had even been empty, each one more tragic than the last: the long and painful death of her dog, Scotty, after someone had fed him broken glass; the death of a teenage boyfriend in a car crash, and herself trapped in the wreckage with her body up against his for four hours as authorities tried to get her out; her sister on the sofa sobbing after telling her mother and father that she'd been molested by her uncle. . . .

Her uncle? Until that moment she never even knew she'd *had* an uncle. He was ruddy and short with thick hair and hazel eyes. Something of a drifter, he had come to stay at the Hatzis property to "recuperate" from some grueling job. Young Caryl remembered his hands. They were smooth-skinned and pale; his fingers were tapered and slim. They were not the hands of a hard worker; they were the hands of a pedophile.

After her sister's teary and embarrassing admission, her father had chased Uncle Ren into the orchard and shot him. Young Caryl had witnessed the murder from behind the gray trunk of an apple tree. She remembered the feel of the bark against her clutching fingers, the sickness in her gut and hot tears on her cheeks, the flash of bright red that coincided with the crack of a gunshot.

She had buried the memory as deeply as she could, keeping it from her engrams when the time came to construct their activation memories. The shame of her family was a secret she did not want spread throughout the galaxy. It was a memory too ugly to be shared with anyone else.

Until now.

Thor gradually came back to herself, realizing she was slumped forward on her knees, flailing weakly for support. Sol stood nearby, offering none.

"Too much," Thor muttered. "It's too much. . . ."

One hundred fifty years of memories had been dumped in her mind; it would probably take at least that again to sift through it all.

Sol didn't say anything at first. She just left Thor on her knees in her mental anguish. The only sounds Thor could hear were her own trembling breaths and that thin, far-off crack of a single gunshot in a long-forgotten winter.

"Do you still want it, Thor?"

As difficult as it was, she forced herself to steady her breathing and look up into Sol's penetrating gaze. Marduk and Mahatala were still watching on from nearby, and she knew that this was her first test.

She swallowed thickly in a vain attempt to moisten her throat, then nodded slowly. "I still want it."

Her original loomed over her, and for a split second she thought Sol might offer to help her up. But then Sol turned and left the room without another word, leaving Thor to wonder if she'd passed or failed the test.

"Give me a hand." She waved for Mahatala to help her up. Strong android hands gripped her arms and helped her to her feet. Thor felt the world spin around her, but she forced herself to be firm.

"Run the simulation back to where I was interrupted," she said, sitting back into her chair, grateful for its support. Every muscle in her body was trembling. "We have work to do."

Marduk and Mahatala exchanged brief and uncertain glances but then did as they were told.

1.2.4

"You did what?" Alander looked up with some alarm from the schematics he was studying. Sol sat opposite him in *Klotho*'s cockpit, casually leaning on the desk the hole ship had extruded, and repeated herself with unwavering calm.

"I gave Thor control of the engrams."

He shook his head, temporarily lost for words. "But Thor is unstable! I thought we agreed on that. She colluded with Axford; she disobeys your orders; she—" He stopped. *She was the one who told me that Lucia had rejected me*, he'd been about to say. He couldn't help but wonder if she'd done it just to hurt him.

But it was a petty concern, and one he couldn't waste time dwelling upon. Thoughts of Lucia were a distraction, as was his confusion over his relationship with Caryl. Nevertheless, he found it hard to close off his mind to both of them. Since Lucia's engram had escaped from *Klotho* no trace of her had been found anywhere, despite extensive searches of all the hole ships. The emotional part of him felt bad for what had happened, while the more rational side refused to accept grief for what he knew had needed to be done.

And as for Caryl Hatzis . . . They had shared a bed once since the meeting at Rasmussen. He had fallen into it, exhausted, and woken an hour later to feel her sliding next to him. The contact had been intimate without being sexual, but memory returned to him of it having been so, once. It had been a distraction, an experiment that hadn't worked. But the need for something more was still there, and they took what they could from each other while no other alternative existed.

"Thor can't be trusted," he finished instead. With a half-smile, he added, "But then, I suppose I would've said much the same thing about you not too long ago."

"I hope you still would say it." There was an edge to her fleeting smirk that said she wasn't entirely joking. "Thor is different from the others. Who else would you put in charge, Peter? You? Axford?" She smiled wryly. "I can't really imagine someone like Otto Wyra leading the charge, can you?"

He shook his head. "Hardly."

"Thor's the only one who's tried to take the reins of responsibility from me, and that's why I let her have it. The tweak I gave her engram is resulting in highly original behavior. Sometimes I can't tell *what* she'll do next. And I like that, because I think we need a little unpredictability right now."

Hatzis looked down at the schematics. "I thought that taking charge, making sure everything stays the way it's supposed to, is the only way to get things done. Sometimes it is, but not always. Look at Frank. He works in the background, nudging people forward against their will. Maybe I should try to be more like him."

"Spare me that much, Caryl." Alander stood to stretch his legs, finding the sudden conversational turn discomforting in the extreme. "I'm all for using him, not emulating him."

"Nevertheless, out of all of us he's the one most likely to survive."

"And you admire that?" he asked with distaste. "You think the end can justify the means?"

"Doesn't it?"

Alander offered a derisive snort as he paced the cockpit. Hatzis had turned in the chair to face him. The posture made her look startlingly vulnerable.

"Peter, I'm sick of being in charge," she said after a few more seconds of silence. "I don't intend to spend what might be my last days bickering with everyone over details that ultimately won't make a difference. But at the same time, I don't want to be completely left out, either. If I think Thor's doing a bad job or becoming unstable, then I'll pull the plug."

"And you'll take over again?"

She didn't need to think about that. "If I have to, yes."

"I presume you have a back door into Thor, then."

"Unmodified engrams are as leaky as sieves. Christ, if I *really* wanted to, I could make you dance for my entertainment." She shrugged. "But that would get boring. And besides which, I'm starting to find your company tolerable."

He wasn't sure if she was joking or throwing a backhanded compliment in his direction, like a person might toss a dog a bone. He would probably always be uncertain where he stood with her. Once part of a mind that spanned an entire solar system, what could she possibly see in him except a marginally nonandroid body able on occasion to provide a modicum of comfort?

"Besides," Sol said, "Thor found Lucia, and we have to be grateful for that. Without the information she found, we'd probably be running with the Praxis right now, just another in his pack."

He nodded, having pondered long and hard what Lucia had revealed, as relayed through Thor. Something in pi-1 Ursa Major had eliminated the *Andre Linde*, the mission she'd been due to rendezvous with in 2117. A month before Lucia's arrival, faint emissions had heralded the destruction of the *Linde* and the wholesale reorganization of the system. Days later, everything had returned to normal. Fearing that she was in danger, too, Lucia had disguised herself as an asteroid and tumbled through the system, taking snapshots as she went. Only upon awakening months later did she discover that the photos showed nothing unusual. However, upon further examination, she made another discovery: One of the photos was missing.

In Lucia's mind, the absence of that photo constituted hard evidence of foul play. Thor agreed with her findings, and so did Alander. The only problem was that the interference had taken place decades before the Spinners and the Starfish had arrived in the area. As there had been no further disturbances that Lucia had noted while continuing on her journey beyond pi-1 Ursa Major, the question was open as to what exactly was in the system, and why it was there at all.

Frank Axford reasoned that it was a Spinner base designed to coordinate the local gift-dropping exercise, or some sort of advance party. All attempts to look in the system resulted in rapid destruction and a thorough cleanup, so it was hard to tell for sure. The time lag between arrival in pi-1 Ursa Major and the deposition of the gifts was symptomatic of a galactic time-scale, he said. Forty years was nothing to beings who might cross the gulf between galaxies as if it were nothing more than a stroll across a road.

The other alternative, of course, was that Lucia was wrong—or worse, crazy—which meant the whole plan was founded upon nothing whatsoever. And in that case, Alander had nothing to be thankful to Thor for except possibly an early grave.

"We have no choice but to accept Lucia's findings," he said. "Time is ticking, and we're no closer to finding another way out of this."

Sol nodded as she turned back to the schematics. "Is there anything I should know here? And I ask only out of curiosity, you understand. Strictly as an observer."

He came back to the table but didn't sit down. "Some of the probes were attacked by forces the gifts could help us resist. It's pretty exotic stuff, and I'm not sure I follow half of it, but there are nanofacturers working on some sort of shield effect that will protect us from the worst of it. If we keep quiet and don't disturb anything, we'll probably have a chance."

She nodded as her eyes scanned the sheaves of electronic paper before her. Diagrams and explanations scrolled up and down at her touch. There was no way to tell just how much she absorbed from the casual glance, but he knew better than to underestimate her.

"This is hairy stuff," she said. "Playing around with fundamental constants is not something you do lightly or easily. I'm not sure I like the idea of being on either end of this sort of technology, especially when we only have the Gifts' word that it'll work."

"If it doesn't, I guess we won't have long to curse the fact," said Alander. "I can't imagine the Starfish taking prisoners."

"Except in a specimen jar." She sagged back into her seat, sighing. Despite advanced biomods and incredible hormonal control, she was still a victim of stress.

He came around behind her and rubbed at the muscles in her neck.

"I don't want to die, Peter."

"So take a leaf out of Axford's book. Copy yourself; leave a backup somewhere. Bury it deep enough, and it might just slip through the Starfish net."

A strange expression crossed her face. "Why should it when nothing else we've left behind has managed to survive the wake?" she asked. "If only the Gifts would fight with us. But they won't even defend themselves!"

He didn't say anything; this was ground they'd covered many times before.

"I know I shouldn't hang my hopes on someone stepping in to save us at the last minute," she said, "but I can't help it. I just can't believe that humanity could—" She shrugged, helplessly searching for the right word. Then, finally. "Could just *die!*"

"Maybe we're already dead," he said dryly. "Maybe we just haven't realized it yet."

She slipped out from under his hands and turned in her seat to face him, her expression torn between amusement and amazement.

"Of all the people I could be spending my last days with," she said, shaking her head, "why did it have to be with such a miserable bastard like you?"

"I've actually been asking myself the same thing." There was no humor in his response, just grim awareness that their situation really didn't make any sense. "Maybe it's just because our scars match."

She snorted a short laugh. "Misery loves company. Is that it?"

He turned away from her, from her facetiousness, and moved back to look at the schematics again. "How long do you think we have?" he asked after a moment's reflection.

"Until the mission, or until the end?"

"Both, I guess."

"Well, unless Thor changes the timetable, then we leave in twenty-five hours. And unless the plan works, the Starfish will be here in three days."

Her tone carried uncertainty and fear, but he had no reassurances to offer her. He had little enough for himself. All he could think of was Axford's words: *Better to run to your death than run from it.*

In the grim silence of *Klotho*'s cockpit, he found himself almost ready to believe it.

1.2.5

*There were ten orbital towers in all, each linked by a super-*strong and superconducting circuit. At first, Lucia was apprehensive about exploring them, feeling small and insignificant against the alien marvels. But the more she ventured into them, the less her trepidations bothered her.

Movement was initially slow—relatively speaking—as she followed the complex circuitry from spindle to spindle. But once she'd touched upon each of the gifts, it became easier for her to go back to them, and before long she was jumping between the spindles with instinctive ease. She just had to think of the spindle that she wanted to go to, and she immediately knew the route to take. The entire process took barely nanoseconds.

Each of the enigmatic installations had very distinct purposes: Spindle One was the Science Hall, where the Spinners provided arcane theorems in order to educate their primitive charges; Spindle Two allowed for companion experiments and materials in order to elucidate those theorems. The Library in Spindle Eight contained a vast knowledge base that would take millennia to examine thoroughly, given the chance; while the Gallery in Spindle Nine demonstrated that artistic expression was as diverse across the galaxy as it had been on Earth. There was a Surgery in Spindle Four that provided tools for medical analysis and treatments that appeared to be designed specifically for humans, although it displayed a flair for Yuhl physiognomy as well. Spindle Ten housed the Dark Room, the very depths of which she still avoided, despite her growing confidence; there was a hole ship Dry Dock in Spindle Six, and the Gifts themselves—the AIs who oversaw the entire complex—occupied Spindle Seven. Spindle Five was the Hub of the instantaneous matter transmission system, a room consisting of ten doors that offered access to each of the gifts.

Why ten? she found herself wondering. *Only nine doors would be required to access the other spindles, surely?*

Investigating this anomaly, she discovered that one of the doors looped back upon itself, back to the Hub. She remembered Rob Singh's talk of glitches in the gifts, and wondered if this was one such—evidence that the authors of these astonishing gifts were capable of error.

The Gifts themselves wouldn't talk to her as she explored, despite her attempts to ask them questions. But neither did they obstruct her, and the lesser machines in the spindles were willing to take her instructions. It was a weird feeling, seeing these alien artifacts from the inside. It felt as though she could extend herself into any of the gifts, becoming a part of them, mentally flexing here and there to examine and explore any aspect of the items contained within them. As her pov moved between the cracks in those spaces, she found that the gifts weren't as clear-cut as they appeared from an outside perspective. The Surgery, for instance, revealed to her that it could construct another I-suit to replace the demonstration model that had been appropriated by Cleo Samson, Rasmussen's mission supervisor. Furthermore, the dimensions of the I-suit could be customized to almost any setting. That raised possibilities Lucia found particularly exciting.

The more she explored the gifts, the more proficient she became at using them, effortlessly jumping between each of the spindles to further her understanding of the knowledge she found. Having examined a piece of art, for example, she could jump to the Library and find information on the species responsible for that piece of art, then cross-reference that information with star charts from the Map Room that would pinpoint the system or systems occupied by them. From there it would be just a quick trip to the Dry Dock where, had there been a hole ship available, she could have traveled to that system and witnessed the species firsthand.

That none of these species visited by the Spinners existed anymore, thanks to the Starfish, weighed heavily upon her after a while. It was depressing to think that so many lives, so many diverse cultures, had been wiped out forever. The longer she explored, the more depressed she became, until soon she felt totally exhausted and found herself needing to rest.

In no time at all, Lucia had returned to the confines of the Dark Room. With her mind expanded to the degree it was, it seemed as though an entire year had passed, when in truth it had only been a couple of hours—but she felt like an entirely different person than she had been at the start. She'd learned things, seen things, experienced things that had given her a new perspective on life. And yet she had still only touched the surface of everything within the gifts.

They were the most incredible things she'd ever seen, and she had managed to touch them. She alone had seen the awesome and beautiful mask the Gifts hid behind from *their* side. And it was a sight more wondrous than anything she could have imagined. The marvels of the Map Room rotated in her mind as she floated in the darkness, trying to absorb the information she had just accessed.

The gifts orbiting Sagarsee were the same as those deposited on all the other Earth-like worlds in Surveyed Space. It was a simple arrangement repeated on dozens of worlds. Only where physical conditions forbade it did the pattern vary. Around Hammon, where a dense cloud of orbiting rubble left over from a disintegrated moon posed a threat to geosyncronous orbits, the gifts adopted a rosette arrangement well out of danger. Sol had noted a different arrangement again in the system of Vega. There, the gifts had been built inside the core fragments of a disintegrated gas giant, where Frank Axford had built himself a sanctuary. And although these had been effectively hidden from view, the Starfish had still managed to root them out and destroy them.

That the gifts *could* be destroyed set Lucia's mind spinning. They contained such a wealth of technology and knowledge; their very nature spoke of advancements far beyond anything

Earth had ever achieved. Neither human engrams nor *Yuhl/Goel* had managed to damage one nor even get close to seeing how one worked. Yet the Starfish effortlessly reduced them to slag heaps, to clouds of energetic dust.

Humanity, she was beginning to understand, stood between the benevolence of one superpower and the destructive wrath of another. They were refugees in an incomprehensibly vast war, doing all they could just to survive.

Perhaps, then, the gifts were aid drops. She wondered if they existed to help new civilizations weather the oncoming destruction that was the Starfish migration. Maybe the Starfish weren't following the Spinners at all; maybe the Spinners were simply running ahead, doing what they could to minimize the damage to those who fell in the Starfish's path.

The thought was a disquieting one, putting as it did Thor's intended mission to contact the Spinners into serious doubt, so Lucia turned away from it. After all, it wasn't her problem. She had watched the other engrams scurry about at their highest clock speeds, frantically choosing systems, preparing for every possible contingency, expending far too much energy, she thought, in staving off the inevitable. For a brief time she considered volunteering for the mission, but that foolish notion soon passed. She'd spent what felt like an eternity locked in an electronic coffin alone; now that she was out, she wasn't about to consign herself to another more permanent tomb. She had better things to live for.

"You're back?"

Lucia had been so preoccupied that she hadn't noticed Rob's tumbling robot at the entrance to the Dark Room.

"Yes. I went exploring without you. I'm sorry."

"The gifts?"

"I visited them all, but there was too much to take in, in one scan. I spent most of my time in the Library, checking out some of the alien cultures recorded there."

His chuckle resounded in the darkness. "I wish we'd had you sooner, Lucia. It would have made our job a whole lot easier. It's a shame the hole ship isn't here, though. Now *that's* an awesome piece of technology we'd love to figure out."

"Why do you suppose there's only one of each thing per set of gifts?"

"That's one of the many mysteries we've yet to work out," he answered, his robotic limbs twitching. "There are so many things here that we just don't understand: complex machines that, for all we know, might well start a production line that could supply us with as many of each item as we need. Who knows?"

It was certainly possible, thought Lucia, especially given what she had learned about the I-suits, but it was all too alien for her to be absolutely certain of anything. She might have had the ability to explore the gifts far more effectively than anyone else, but it would still take time—time that she knew she didn't have. No one did.

She did, however, sense hidden structures behind the gifts that hinted at unseen potentials. There was enough information in the Library alone, for example, to keep a hundred researchers occupied for a century. But behind that there was an underlying purpose or function that Lucia couldn't quite fathom—and the same applied to all the other gifts, too: the Lab, the Surgery, the Science Hall, the Map Room—they all had things hidden beneath the surface.

Of all the gifts she'd investigated so far, she had no doubt that the hole ships were the linchpin of humanity's survival effort. Without them, there would be no ftl communication and no physical exchange between the colonies. Nor would there be any chance of escape, either.

And that, ultimately, was what she wanted. She had no desire to hang around like a rabbit caught in headlights as the Starfish bore down on them. Thor had brought her back against her will, and Peter had made it absolutely clear that there was nothing for her, even if she did stay. The mental pain—worse than mere anguish or grief because this was written deep down in her operating code, causing strange leaps and jumps of emotion or continuity every time she thought of him—was going to render her dysfunctional if she didn't quickly take steps to alleviate it.

"You know," Rob was saying, "sometimes I think we spend so much time wondering about the Spinners' and Starfish's motivations that we miss a very basic point."

"And that is?"

"What if their motivations are beyond our comprehension?"

he said. "Or worse: what if they have no motivations at all? I mean, we're used to empirical science having an answer—or at least promising an answer—to everything. But there might not *be* an answer in this case. The Spinners give us gifts, and we see them as being altruistic. But with so many strings attached, how can we be certain that altruism is their motivation? Why haven't they warned us about the Starfish? Why do they limit communications to just one person in each colony—and a dysfunctional person at that? Why do they give us communicators that draw attention to us? We seek answers to all of these things, when in the end it might just be that they simply don't care that much."

"Which would go against our altruistic assumptions," said Lucia, seeing his point.

"Exactly," said Rob. "We try to understand their reasoning for doing what they do, try to rationalize their activities with logic, when in truth it might just be incomprehensible to a primitive species like our own. Their reasons may be beyond our ability to understand."

She could hear the puzzlement in his voice. It was overlaid with a very real concern, for cracking this puzzle, he knew, might mean the difference between life and death for the human survivors.

"But there's another possibility that has been raised, particularly about the Starfish." He paused as if to check that she was still listening.

"Go on," she said.

"Both races exhibit extremely high technology but a relatively low sophistication when it comes to their broader actions. We assume that the Spinners were drawn here by the radio emissions of our nascent civilization, but that need not be the case. They might have stumbled across us by chance on some longer, wandering exodus. We also assume that there's some sort of method to their gift drops, but we haven't as yet been able to discern it: not all colonies get the gifts, and why some do and some don't remains a mystery. It's the same with the Starfish: we know from following the attacks that they home in on stray signals, then expand out in spheres, searching system by system. But it wouldn't take an intelligence to do this: it could just as easily be achieved by AIs."

"Machines?" The possibility was as startling as it was unsettling. "You think that's all they are?"

"It's possible. They could be autonomous systems set running thousands of years ago—maybe even *millions* of year ago. The Spinners are programmed to seek out new civilizations and give them a leg up; the Starfish could well be programmed to stamp out such attempts. And if that's the case, then surely the motivations behind the programming are irrelevant to us at the moment—and might be forever unfathomable."

He paused, and in that brief silence she heard a world of uncertainty.

"For all we know, Lucia," he muttered after a few moments, "these things could have encountered thousands of races before us. It's possible that the Praxis and the Yuhl are the only ones to have survived—and only then by barely managing to hang on. My God, Lucia, these things could be responsible for the deaths of trillions of beings! And all because a long time ago, possibly in some distant galaxy, someone set a machine or two in motion and never thought to give them a cut-off switch."

The vision of technology run rampant, of opposing impulses sweeping the galaxy clean of any sign of emerging life, troubled her greatly. And while Sol and Peter's plan to throw a spanner into that technology was a noble one, she didn't feel terribly reassured. No one had managed it in the past, so what made humanity any different? *Only its arrogance,* she told herself. *The innate belief that we are crucial to the universe and its machinations.* Despite Copernicus's discovery centuries ago that the sun and stars and planets didn't all revolve around the Earth, deep down humanity still believed itself to be the center of the universe. *But once the Starfish have finished with us,* she thought, *then that belief will be put to rest once and for all.*

"Lucia? Are you still there?"

"I'm here," she answered. "Just thinking, that's all."

"I'm sorry. I can be somewhat negative at times."

"As well you have a right to be, Rob. We all do. But I'm going to need to rest for a while now. All this information from the Library and the other spindles has left me exhausted. We'll talk again soon, okay?"

She didn't wait for him to respond; she just withdrew deeper into the spindle, with Rob's words playing in her mind. As the darkness began to seep into her, she felt a sense of terrible foreboding. Whether Rob was right or not, it didn't matter. The fact was, time was running out—and fast. If she didn't act soon, it would be too late; she'd be trampled underfoot by the mighty Starfish along with everyone else.

With most of the hole ships tied up in the resistance effort, she would have to find another way to get mobile again. Perhaps if she examined the gifts more, she would find a way to build herself another one. Or perhaps she could just steal the next one that docked there. However she was to achieve it, though, she wasn't about to stick around any longer than she had to.

1.2.6

"And so we are committed," said the leader of the *Species Dream*. *"We stand by our decision to divide the Ambivalence. We have pledged more than just our support to humanity/riil's cause. We have made their cause our own. We will live with them, or die with them. We are the Yuhl/riil."*

Sol listened, knowing that he was talking more for the benefit of the other Yuhl, not the humans participating in the decision-making process. The suffix *riil* was commonly translated into English as *prey* by the hole ships, indicating the relationship the Starfish normally had with those civilizations that chose to make a stand. She hoped that it would soon acquire a new meaning—although the fact that the section of the Fit that had remained behind were now calling themselves the Unfit suggested that their confidence was flagging.

A clamor of voices rose out of the darkness. The Yuhl didn't meet in large halls like humans did, to posture and preen before one another. They linked minds via biological helmets that plunged the senses into a virtual space that kept all distractions to a minimum. The identities of the speakers were traditionally obscured, although they did come with subtle markers designed to stop the conversation from dissolving into disconnected phrases. The voice of the Species Dream leader—a Yuhl Alander had once referred to as *Radical/Provocative*—came with the distinct smell of recently cut grass.

"Who will go?" asked one of the other Yuhl. "Who do we choose to send to their deaths?"

"Volunteers only." Thor's voice rang out clearly through the dense, heavy space. "We can only afford to send those who are committed to seeing this mission through. It is too important to risk sending anyone who might have doubts."

"And how do we choose from the many who would rather act decisively than remain behind?" said another Yuhl voice.

"I will hear recommendations," said Thor, her voice containing a clear challenge. "But the final decision will be mine. Since I am leading the team and ultimately responsible for its success, I want to know that I can trust the people that are with me."

"I wish to volunteer," said Alander.

"Me, too," said the voice belonging to Cleo Samson of Sagarsee.

That made sense, Hatzis thought. As military supervisor of the *Marcus Chown* and the colony over which the resistance effort orbited, Samson would want to be involved.

"I'll recommend Caryl Hatzis of Gou Mang and Caryl Hatzis of Inari," said Sol when it was clear that none of the Yuhl were going to volunteer. Those were the two most capable of her engrams, in her opinion, apart from Thor. She figured it couldn't hurt to load the side in her favor a little. "And I would like to put my own name forward, as well."

"*You*, Sol?" Thor asked, picking her out from the vast number of minds listening in. "I had you pegged as the one to mind the fort."

While you go in search of glory, Sol thought wryly to herself. "I'm sure the Unfit are capable of managing Sagarsee and the other colonies."

"We welcome and accept that task," said *Radical/Provocative*.

"It hasn't been offered to you yet," snapped Thor. "I'm not happy with the idea of both Sol *and* myself going. If the mission fails and both of us die—"

"Sol has abilities no one else has," put in Alander quickly. "We'd be fools *not* to include her in the mission. Besides which, if the mission does fail, then it doesn't really matter who stays behind, does it? Because if we fail, then we'll all be dead anyway."

If the mission fails . . . Alander's words echoed in Sol's thoughts. After all the death she'd seen, it still didn't seem quite real that this peaceful, prosperous colony could soon be reduced to ash—and her with it, if she stayed. The habit of life was a seductive one, and it was often too easy to pursue it in a state of denial, to sit back in the naive hope that the unimaginable might not happen.

"I'll bow to Thor's authority," she said, hearing the words as though they came from a great distance. "If she wishes me to stay, then I shall stay. But I think it would be a mistake."

"I hear you, Sol," said Thor. "But using the same argument, I would like to recommend Frank Axford for the mission also. He, too, has abilities no one else does; therefore, he, too, could contribute."

The name prompted an immediate uproar. Voices belonging to both races, Yuhl and human, protested that Axford was a traitor, a liar, a murderer, and ultimately a danger to the success of the mission. Thor didn't deny any of it, but neither did she withdraw his name from the mission roster, arguing that he had unique talents for self-preservation that could give the mission the edge it needed.

Sol wanted to laugh. Just exactly what was Axford to Thor, anyway? An anti-Sol panacea? She had to admit, though, it took a lot of guts for Thor to put his name forward, especially when the Yuhl refused to have anything to do with the mission if he was involved.

Despite the objections, the gathering reached a compromise: if Thor could locate Axford and was convinced that he would cooperate fully, she could invite him to join the mission. But under no circumstances was she to take any undue risks.

"I'm not likely to do that," said Thor. "Not when it's my life on the line, too."

And for the sake of everyone else's, Sol added to herself, *I'll make damn sure I keep my eyes on* both *of you.*

A spattering of names followed Axford's. There was room for only seven on the mission, and Sol had already created a list in her mind of those she would have had going. She didn't doubt that Thor's would be a similar list, assuming she was choosing for capability, of course, and not one-upmanship. Without the Yuhl aboard, that left easily enough room for the versions of herself she had nominated.

As the discussion wandered back to the details of the mission and what it hoped to achieve, Sol quickly lost interest. These were arguments she'd heard many times before, and it was something of a relief to know that they were Thor's problem now. She removed herself from the conference, her head coming out of the biological mask with a moist sucking sound. A tapering, six-fingered hand offered her a cloth to wipe away the contact gel. She took it gratefully, clearing her nose and mouth so she could breathe.

"*I/we* would be honored to be chosen for this mission," said a Yuhl voice from close by. "Were *I/we* allowed to go."

Sol wiped gunk from her eyes with the back of her hand. The alien loomed over her at close quarters, his hand still outstretched from proffering the towel. She wasn't as proficient at reading the facial expressions of the aliens as Alander, so she couldn't tell what he was thinking. She wondered if he had been prompted to talk to her out of rebellion against the Unfit or for other more existential reasons. For two and a half thousand years the Yuhl had been following in the Ambivalence's wake, scavenging for survival and clinging to existence by the finest thread. And now Thor planned to take a mission to actually *confront* the Starfish. If Sol had believed in God and someone had announced a mission to go have a chat with Her, then she would probably be apprehensive also.

"You know why you can't go," she said, returning the towel to the alien. "It's not my decision. It's up to Thor and the Unfit."

"It would *not be proper/be inappropriate* for *my/our* people to go on this mission," said the alien, his wing sheaths snapping, "with the traitor *Frank/Axford* involved."

She nodded. "That's a good excuse, anyway."

The alien's crazy checkerboard face adopted a series of unreadable expressions. His two oval eyes regarded her blankly.

"I'm sorry," she said. "I was just joking."

"*My/our* intentions are *genuine/noble*," he said.

"I'm sure they are."

"Should the mission succeed, *your/our* deeds will be talked about for generations to come."

Sol looked at the alien quizzically. "We're not doing this for fame, you know."

"The courage of those on the mission will be talked about regardless. Courage gives hope, and hope is a platform upon which to build a future." The Yuhl's faceplates shifted like some bizarre, organic rebus puzzle. "Those on the mission will *return/die* as heroes," the alien answered. "I am *Vrrel/Epan*. I will anticipate that moment in *my/our* thoughts."

"Thank you," she said, oddly touched by the alien's awkward words. "I hope we return, too. Keep your fingers crossed we do so in one piece and with good news."

Vrrel/Epan looked down at his hands, and she left him standing there, puzzled, while she went to get ready.

2.1.0

UEH/ELLIL

Ueh didn't wait to see Mantissa A *depart into unspace. He* was already moving on the Praxis's grisly errand.

His first objective was to get out of the places usually occupied by the Praxis's attendants. This wasn't easy to do, undetected. The spaces were cramped and crowded, and the lighting was orange-tinted and seemed dark to his human-accustomed eyes. Dozens of double-streamed voices issued from all around him, creating a dense, confused ambience. Lower gravity allowed support staff to occupy positions on walls or ceilings, giving the impression that every available cubic centimeter was thoroughly occupied.

Since when did my own people become so alien to me? he asked himself, expressing the question in the linear narrative of a human. *Since when did I cease to be one of them?*

The sight of his reflection, caught in a curving chitinous bulkhead, surprised him as it so often did these days. His legs were long, and they tended to flex more than they should with each step. His face was a mask he could read perfectly well, just as he could read those of his people around him, but at the same time it was a mask that hid the real person behind it. *What am I, exactly?* he wondered as he watched his faceplates shift.

"You are the newest," the Praxis had told him. "You have

the most potential. And I gave you that potential, Ueh, because I knew a day would come when I would have a use for it."

"Such as the use you put me to now?" Ueh had said.

"Exactly," the Praxis had answered.

"But why now?"

"I detect a strange sense of mortality creeping over me, and I am compelled to act."

Ueh followed the Praxis's instructions to the letter. As conjugator, he was not stopped or questioned by anyone. Even where his identity was unknown, chemical tags emitted by fresh new glands under his wing sheaths revealed his function to all whose duty it was to check. He moved in a cloud of purpose, assured of passage anywhere in the newly restructured *Mantissa A*. As the collection of hole ships traveled through unspace to its new destination, far outside the bubble humans called Surveyed Space, he wound his way inward, to the heart of his species' refuge. There, unseen by all and unknown except to the conjugators, lay the heart of the Praxis. As vast as the ark built around it, it beat slowly and steadily down the eons, ticking off hours with each and every pulse.

Vast, Ueh thought, *and yet so fragile* . . .

Little-used corridors took him to basement tanks storing raw mass for food makers and other devices designed specifically to support the Praxis's massive body. Unlike the Yuhl, who had grown proficient at biomodification even before the arrival of the Spinners in the home systems, the Praxis embraced his biological imperatives. He ate, he shat, and he slept; he had moods. The precise biology of the Praxis was a closely kept secret, but all knew that he was vulnerable in ways the Yuhl had abandoned many thousands of long cycles earlier. He grew tired; he was occasionally unwell; it was conceivable that he could die, one day.

The section of *Mantissa A* that Ueh entered was cramped and hot, the air uncomfortably moist. The only light came from long, sticky threads that hung in strands from the ceiling and walls. As Ueh hurried by, some of them stuck to his skin where they slowly faded and turned to gray. He didn't brush them away. They were cool and reminded him of the treatment he'd received after his wounding in the Battle of Beid. Confined to a fluid tank for more than a single cycle, he'd had numerous punctures and breaks sealed in blissful silence. The isolation had been welcome after the furies of war.

He looked back on the battle now with something approaching disbelief. Confronting the Ambivalence ran contrary to everything he'd been taught. Ever since he had emerged fully conscious from his birth cocoon, he had followed the policies of avoidance practiced by his people. They monitored the dropping of the gifts at the migration's forward edge and took those that were judged appropriate by the Praxis and the Fit. As the rear of the migration approached, death markers were prepared for the civilizations that failed to survive. The eye of the Ambivalence was avoided at all costs. To draw its attention was to invite death. Not once in all the long cycles of the *Yuhl/Goel* migration had his people ever willingly confronted the cutters, the instruments of the Ambivalence's wrath. Not until *Frank/Axford* had forced them into it.

Since the bodiless humans had come into their lives, the *Yuhl/Goel* had learned lessons in things until then unheard of. Betrayal from *Frank/Axford*, morality from *Caryl/Hatzis* . . .

Humanity has concepts such as altruism and sympathy, she had told the Fit while pleading for help for her people. They would surely die, she had said, if left to fend for themselves. *We would help you, under those circumstances.*

It would be safer to say that you would help unless it hurt you too much, Ueh had responded. *All generosity has its limits. And we know our limitations.*

Back then, he had believed what he'd said. But now he wasn't so sure. Axford had rubbed their limitations in their faces and forced them into a fight they had no chance of winning. And yet they had achieved something Ueh had never thought possible: they had *survived*. He asked himself if that wasn't apt—what the humans might call a "truth." Change was terrible at times, but then so was life. What was the purpose of survival if one was functionally dead?

He came to a pinch in the tube he was following. He squeezed through, unnerved by the fleshiness of the walls. Soon he was crawling on hands and knees, wing sheaths flinching at moisture trickling onto him from above. The surfaces around him resonated with a deep, throbbing vibration. He felt the occasional tremor roll past him, like peristalsis, and he began to worry that he might be crushed or smothered.

Soon enough, though, the passage opened up around him. He stood awkwardly in a space shaped like a tapering seed balanced on one end, long enough for two of him to stand end to end. Three puckered openings led from the chamber, one of which he'd come through. The air was fetid but breathable, and the walls were veined and shining.

Somehow without knowing, somewhere along his journey, he had crossed a boundary. He was no longer inside *Mantissa A*, he realized. He was inside the Praxis!

He waited, thinking.

"I am a complex creature," the Praxis had told him. "I have needs the *Yuhl/Goel* will never understand. Even the conjugators, to whom I grant new levels of insight into my nature, have not seen the full spectrum of my being. Before commencing my great diaspora, I was literally beyond your comprehension. But the pale shadow you see before you still has the capacity to surprise."

Ueh didn't doubt that for a second.

The air fouled around him, and his body switched automatically to internal energy reserves. The only light came from the still faintly glimmering strands clinging to his neck and shoulders, surviving briefly on the moisture that had soaked into his garments. As those last glimmers faded, he remembered a conversation he'd had with *Peter/Alander*.

The free flow of information is always desirable, he had said, *no matter where it leads us. I am here to facilitate discussion between our species. If we come away from this meeting still at war, then I will not have failed.*

In your eyes, perhaps, Alander had replied.

That response had surprised Ueh. That the human had thought it necessary to state such an obvious truth had highlighted a fundamental difference between their two species.

By what/with whose other eyes can I see?

As he pondered this in the deepening darkness of the Praxis's heart, a single, slender limb slipped out from one of the three puckered orifices, slicing him neatly open from throat to sternum and letting his life organs pour in a terrible rush from within him.

2.1

DESCENT OF ORPHEUS

2160.9.29 Standard Mission Time
(2 September 2163 UT)

2.1.1

The silence seemed to stretch forever. Observing at the high-est possible clock speed, Caryl Hatzis kept a firm grip on her autonomous nervous system. Her heart rate was down, and overactivity of her sebaceous glands was kept to a minimum. Outwardly, she would have been the epitome of calm, inwardly, however, she was screaming. This was it! There would be no turning back after this.

You'd better not be fucking us over, Axford, she thought. *Because if you are, I swear I'm going track down every last one of your goddamn engrams and—*

"I have an energy reading," said Gou Mang, her announcement dragging Thor from her thoughts.

"Where?" she asked, looking over to Gou Mang at her station in one corner of the ship's bridge.

Eight hole ships had been combined into a spiky tetrahedral octad dubbed *Eledone*. The resulting bridge was shaped like a square with sides bulging inward and corner crew stations facing toward the center. In the middle of it were seats from which screens on the concave bulges could most easily be seen. On those screens were images from the 200 hole ship pairs, tetrads, and other configurations that had gathered in Asellus Primus, lurking in whatever nooks and crannies they could find: in asteroid belts, Lagrange points, the atmosphere of gas giants, even the solar atmosphere. One view contained the mock gift installation in orbit about the system's only rocky world, a boiling hellhole too close to the primary. The decoy was radiating in the fashion typical of a gift transmitter, a lure to which the Starfish would inevitably be drawn—or so she hoped.

Gou Mang directed Sol's attention to one of the screens whose view had changed to show a burning point of energy that had appeared in the inner system, a flaring star of electromagnetism radiating at well-catalogued frequencies.

The fovea, thought Sol. *Or one of them, anyway.*

She felt like an antelope must have in the days when there were still lions and water holes, before the Spike AIs transmuted them all into raw materials for nanotech hell. They were being watched.

Spurred on by Kingsley Oborn's curiosity, sensors on half the hole ships turned to study the phenomenon while it lasted. As important as it was to scan the skies for the Starfish, every aspect of the aliens' behavior had to be observed and studied. A better understanding of the fovea might give them an idea of how to avoid the deadly wake—the *saccade*, as Oborn was insisting people call it. It might not help those about to relocate into the whale's gullet, of course, but the possibility of a Plan B would make her feel less nervous. The idea of humanity's future resting so precariously on such narrow, unreliable shoulders didn't sit comfortably with her.

If Thor was feeling the strain, she wasn't letting it show. She stood in the center of the bridge staring at the screen with her arms folded across her chest, the very picture of calm authority. Her solid android frame was clad in a formfitting black jumpsuit with numerous pockets. Over the top of that was the almost invisible shimmer of an I-suit, protecting her more thoroughly from harm than any human-made suit could ever hope to.

All seven team members were wearing identical or similar uniforms. Each had protective hoods that could be raised to cover the head, with sensory information shunted directly into the relevant nerves by induction, and each was able to recycle fluids should they be cut off from the hole ship. There was enough food to last a week should they need to, although Sol didn't need a suit to last that long; she had been biomodified almost a century ago to reduce her dependence on physical resources. She could go months without a drink and days without even breathing. Although she had rarely had to put it to the test, her survival time in hard vacuum was measured in hours, not minutes.

Thor, Gou Mang, and Inari had added colored patches—red, white, and green respectively—to distinguish them from each other. Sol's human body didn't need differentiation, and neither did Alander and Cleo Samson. Axford 1313's uniform was shot through with threads of liquid silver, as though mercury had been woven into the fabric, but he had declined to explain what they were for. Sol didn't doubt that it was something he'd retrieved from the Vega Library before it was destroyed by the Starfish—some archived technology that would increase his chances of survival in the coming mission.

They were as ready as they ever would be, given the constraints upon them. If they'd had time, she didn't doubt that they could have assembled a far more potent—and consolidated—team, but at this stage she figured anything was better than nothing.

"Contacts—three of them," Gou Mang reported as a flurry of data began to pour in.

"I keep forgetting how big they are," said Cleo Samson anxiously. "We're like mosquitoes next to them."

"That's all right," Axford muttered. "Many a human died from mosquito bites, in the past."

"Seven more contacts," said Gou Mang.

"That's more than usual," said Alander. "They're suspicious."

"Of course they are," said Inari. "They're not idiots."

Thor shushed everyone to silence. She didn't order the attack, though. She didn't need to. Everyone knew what they had to do. The human/Yuhl fleet would be ready the moment those razor-sharp edges of the cutters sliced their way out of unspace.

Eledone relocated to a superior vantage point as ftl sensors began relaying information on the disposition of the Starfish. The flurry of ftl signals prompted a splitting of the incoming formation into three: two cutters disappeared to investigate activity around the largest gas giant; four dispersed across the system, appearing and disappearing in an apparently random but actually highly synchronized pattern; those remaining swooped down on the decoy Spinner installation, strafing it with arcane weapons.

Samson took the controls, and Sol braced herself as *Eledone* relocated into position. A red marker appeared next to one of the two cutters that had jumped to the gas giant, singled out by observers in the area as the one most vulnerable.

Hatzis almost laughed aloud at the notion. Against the Starfish, *vulnerable* was a strictly relative concept. The entire hole ship fleet lying in wait for them was almost insignificant in the face of their ten cutters. The most they'd be able to do, Sol knew, was perhaps delay the inevitable. But then, a delay was all they needed.

Dozens more of the compound hole ships suddenly relocated. On the screens around her, Sol saw white spheres breaking apart and vanishing, hurling themselves into the breach. Relying on the data gained during the zeta Dorado ambush, almost a third of the hole ship fleet sacrificed itself to take the vulnerable cutter apart from the inside. Points designated weak—without even the slightest knowledge of what they were for—were targeted first, followed by major structural locations, such as the hubs at the top and bottom of the spinning vessel. *Eledone* jumped to avoid the near-instantaneous backlash—in the form of bright blue sheets that swept space clear of everything they touched—and reappeared in time to see a flicker of widely dispersed white flashes dance across the alien hull. The distorted space-time around its edge wavered, giving the starry backdrop a rippling effect. Sol imagined that she could almost hear the distress of the giant ship as the attack tore it apart from within.

The remainder of the hole ships dispersed. The tactic was simple and effective but costly, too; if the human/Yuhl fleet had millions of hole ships at their disposal, then *maybe* they might have been able to take out all ten of the cutters. But the simple fact was that there weren't enough hole ships in what remained of Surveyed Space to tackle even half of what was attacking them now.

One is all we need, Sol reminded herself. *Just one . . .*

As the rest of the fleet went to create a distraction elsewhere. *Eledone* relocated from point to point around the stricken cutter, gathering data. Between dodging Starfish attacks, Thor's team was able to glimpse what was happening to the target. Not all of the hole ship fragments had been destroyed immediately upon entering the cutter. Some lingered, broadcasting a wide range of telemetry to the waiting observers. Storms of energy poured through the craft's many chambers, with seismic waves propagating in wild and irregular surges. The relativistic velocities at the cutter's knife-sharp edge began to take their toll. Rising temperatures sent plasma coursing through chambers that had otherwise held vacuum. Clearly, the cutter was sorely damaged, perhaps dying.

Axford's eyes glittered as he watched the events unfold. Sol marveled at the man's cool assessment of the situation. He was taking everything in, not missing a single datum. She wondered what he would do if Thor made a wrong decision. Although she hadn't detected back doors other than her own in any of the engrams, there were undoubtedly other ways in. She wouldn't put it past him to try to stop her by force, if he deemed it necessary. The copy of him called 1313 had a freshness about him that indicated a newly minted body, and Sol was sure that Axford 1041 wouldn't have missed the chance to incorporate new technology into his one, best shot at survival.

"We have a locus," said Gou Mang with a mix of excitement and apprehension.

A blurry schematic of the crippled cutter appeared in one of the screens. Two-thirds in from the edge, slightly above the vertical midpoint, a green light was flashing. Gou Mang zoomed in on it. The point was on the edge of a shadowy space shaped roughly like a kidney that had been pinched at both ends and stretched to twice its normal length. The space appeared to be considerably less active than those around it, although getting a clear picture wasn't easy.

Eledone jumped again, and again, as the team examined the data. Hundreds of blue darts and red dots followed them from point to point, swarming like furiously high-tech gnats intent on destroying them. Irritated, Thor ordered Samson to take them out of the light cone of the Starfish for a moment so she could think.

Thor narrowed her eyes as Sol watched her engram consider her next move. It wasn't an easy decision. If the locus wasn't as innocent as it looked, she could be sending them to their deaths. But if she waited for another one to appear, then the Starfish might get lucky and hit the octad, effectively ending the mission before it had even begun.

"We have incoming cutters," reported Gou Mang on ftl data from the other hole ships. "The same as in Beid."

Sol examined the images. Two of the massive craft were coming to the aid of their stricken sibling. As the damaged cutter spun down, they maneuvered above and below it, preparing to dock at the poles.

"And there's the Trident!" exclaimed Axford, pointing. Everything seemed to come to a halt as the massive, incongruously slender craft slid out of the starscape and surveyed the scene.

"Okay," said Thor, breaking the moment. "No more fucking around; send the evacuation signal and take us in."

Sol's eyes were fixed to the image of the Trident and the swarms of cutters issuing from multiple openings in its side. The image was so intimidating that for a moment she considered evacuating with the others.

Who are we trying to kid? she wanted to say. *There's no way we can possibly fight this thing!*

But her mouth stayed shut as the orders went out to the hole ship fleet, now depleted to half the size it had been before. Asellus Primus was a graveyard of radiation and hole ship debris.

Slowly at first, and then with great speed, the hole ships began to wink out.

"Godspeed, Caryl," came the voice of Kingsley Oborn over the ftl communicator.

Then *Eledone* was jumping, too, and they were committed.

Alander felt a moment of déjà vu. Just under three weeks earlier, in the Mantissa, *the Praxis had sucked him into his gullet and smothered him. As* Eledone *relocated into the heart of the*

damaged cutter, there was no sense of suffocation or pressure—
or indeed of any movement at all, for the hole ships traveled
unspace with no sense of motion—but he couldn't shake the
feeling that they were diving into the belly of some vast beast
to be eaten again.

What they would find there was anyone's guess. For all the
probes and sensors dispatched in zeta Dorado and Asellus Primus, the interior of the cutter was as alien as the heart of the
sun. There could be anything inside it—anything at all. . . .

A vibration suddenly shook the cockpit, as though the hole
ship was countering resistance in unspace. Sol looked at him,
and he met her gaze helplessly. They both knew that for the
moment there was nothing they could do. The team had taken
every possible precaution. All they could do now was wait.

Eledone shuddered again.

Thor glanced over to Samson. "Is everything all right?"

"We're entering a highly turbulent region of space-time,"
she said. "Perhaps the task is too difficult for *Eledone*. The
locus is moving in a circle at many thousands of kilometers per
second."

"Eledone," Thor addressed the hole ship. "Will we be able
to occupy the coordinates you were given?"

"That is presently unknown."

"Then should we fall back and try somewhere else?"

"That is not possible," said the hole ship. "My course is set,
and it cannot be changed."

Thor frowned. "What happens if we can't make it?"

"The voyage will remain open-ended."

"Which means what?"

"It means," said Axford, "that we'll never arrive at our destination."

Alander watched Thor's eyes widen at this, and sympathized. The possibility that a hole ship might fail in a jump had
simply never arisen before.

"We'll be trapped in unspace?" she asked.

"That is correct," said *Eledone*.

"Someone should've thought of this before we left."

"Agreed," said Cleo Samson. "I didn't even bring a good
book to read."

Thor ignored her. "Then just make sure you do get us there, *Eledone*. Otherwise—"

The hole ship jolted violently to one side, causing Alander to stumble. Sol caught him by the arm to steady him, but she had to let go a second later to balance herself when another jolt shook the ship. An instant later a third one struck, making him feel as though he'd been rotated clockwise half a turn.

All eyes fell upon the pilot for an explanation.

"I think we've arrived," she obliged.

"Okay, power down. Right down." Thor's expression as she faced the flickering screens was one of intense concentration. "Passive sensors only. Keep all transmissions to a minimum. *Eledone*, I want the smallest possible profile."

"Understood, Caryl." The voice of the hole ship was smooth and unruffled. All the hole ships were able to reduce their intrusion on real space to a startling degree, with a barely basketball-sized shape performing many of the sensory functions of their usual meters-wide design.

"What's outside, *Eledone*?" asked Axford. "Are you sustaining damage at all?"

"My present environment is not optimal, but I am not in any immediate danger."

"Then let's take a look," said Sol, turning to face the screens.

A low-power and zero-emission regime left the hole ship blind except in incident frequencies. There would be no spotlights, no lasers, no radar—no broadcasts of any kind until they were absolutely certain of their safety. The few instruments Thor would allow were of ultimate simplicity. Infrared detectors painted pictures out of the heat bathing the hole ship's much-reduced profile. Visible light showed nothing but darkness irregularly punctuated by flashes of purple, while image-enhancement algorithms weren't having much luck teasing details from the murk. Ultraviolet was ambiguous at best, as were other frequencies.

"I'm picking up some weird gravitational effects," said Inari from her station. "They could be the result of the rotational slowdown."

Axford was peering at the screens from another station,

leaning forward as though shortsighted. "The navigation beacons put us right on target."

A dwindling number of unoccupied hole ship fragments were broadcasting ftl signals in and around the dying cutter to help *Eledone* pin down its position.

"No sign of countermeasures?" asked Thor.

Cleo Samson had adopted a more relaxed stance, but Alander could tell from her tight expression and the way her hands gripped the control stalk that she was as anxious as everyone else in the cockpit. Data flowed through the nerves of her hands, keeping her constantly updated on the hole ship's disposition.

"None yet," she said.

Thor let out a long sigh, as if she'd been holding her breath for a hundred years. "Then I guess it's safe to assume we've successfully completed the first leg."

"What about the shepherds?" asked Sol. Her tone suggested that she wasn't about to celebrate just yet. "Where are they?"

"Telemetry puts them almost in position," Axford replied. "One above and one below, exactly as in Beid." He looked up with a satisfied smile. "Fasten your seat belts, everybody. It looks like we're going for a ride."

Alander's skin puckered into gooseflesh at the thought. As far as he was concerned, this journey they were about to take was far more terrifying than any open-ended jump through unspace.

They had no clear view of the outside of the cutter. The hole ship fleet had long since departed, leaving only faint impressions from surviving probes and extrapolations based on previous experience.

Experience told them that that the damaged cutter was about to be taken elsewhere. Where that elsewhere was, Alander didn't know. No one did. He only hoped it wasn't an alien wrecking yard, because if it was, leg two of their mission might prove to be something of a disappointment.

The hole ship jolted again, then began to shake with a teeth-rattling, sight-blurring vibration. Alander instinctively gripped Sol's arm. Her eyes were closed, and he imagined she had opted to view the interior of the cockpit via conSense. Even now, in his new body and with the confidence of a changing personality behind it, he still found himself shying away from the virtual realm. He preferred reality over illusion any day, even when reality was as terrifying as it was now.

"How long is this going to last?" asked Thor in a raised voice.

"The ship is decelerating now," said Axford. "But there's an awful lot of angular momentum to shed. We should be thankful this is all it's doing."

The vibrations continued for another fifteen seconds, then slowly settled.

"We've stopped," said Samson, examining the instruments before her with unblinking concentration. "I think it's over."

"I think it's just beginning," muttered Gou Mang.

Alander caught a twinkle out of the corner of his eye. Looking around, he realized that the very air itself in the cockpit seemed to be sparkling!

Thor was looking warily about her, too. "What's going on?"

"It's happening," said Sol. "I think we're going!"

Alander tensed as the glow grew brighter. Sparkling motes gathered in clumps, then joined up to form intense hanging sheets that shifted in motions that suggested they were being blown in a breeze. They swirled and gleamed and continued to grow steadily brighter, until he was hard-pressed to see any of the other cockpit occupants around him. He squinted at the intensifying light, finding it almost impossible to keep his eyes open. Even Sol standing beside him appeared as a faint, shadowy blur through the burning white radiance. He closed his eyes, but that didn't keep out the light. The glow shone through the skin of his eyelids, and white sparks seemed to dance inside his brain. Light blossomed in his eyeballs, his retinas, his optic nerves. He had time to wonder briefly whether such a light might be dangerous, and then, suddenly, as though his legs had been kicked out from under him, the floor was gone and he was falling.

2.1.2

Thor dreamed. Somewhere in the distance she sensed great pain, physical and emotional, but for the time being she could hide from it, pretend it didn't exist. It was just her and the darkness. Her and her *own* memories.

She dreamed of a conversation she had had with Ueh before the alien had departed with *Mantissa A*. The recollection was perfectly clear. The alien had smelled faintly of olives basted in a chemical broth, but not offensively. Ueh's head was cylindrical and domed, with expressions delineated in sheets of black and white that slid in and out of view in constantly changing, perfectly symmetrical patterns. When he spoke, he did so through two windpipes, conveying as much meaning through the beating of two different pitches as he did by timbre alone.

"How old are you, Ueh? If you don't mind me asking."

His head tilted to face her. "*My age/why do you ask?*"

"I'm just curious," she said, remembering the first member of the *Yuhl/Goel* she had ever seen. Nicknamed Charlie, he had died while in Axford's custody. A post mortem had revealed extensive plaques and neural scarring that would have indicated great age in a human. *Possibly centuries,* Axford had said. There was also an abundance of foreign genetic material in his tissues, suggestive of highly advanced biotech including antisenescence treatments.

"*Yuhl/Goel* lifetimes differ from *humanity/riil*. I fear that you would not understand."

"What's not to understand? You're born; you live for a while; you die. How hard is it to tell me how long it's been since you were born?"

"It is hard because the concept of *birth/identity* differs between our species. I *am not a discrete individual as you imagine yourself to be/have changed*."

"We change, too," she said. "Isn't that the way of life?"

"Yet you still regard yourself as a continuous being from *birth/body* to *death/body*. Parts of *me/us* are older than others. *I am/Ueh is* different to the *birth/body* that was. How can *I/we* then reason *our/my* aggregate age?"

"I don't know," she said, beginning to wish she'd never asked the question. "Like I said, I was just curious."

The alien had thought for a moment, then, considering her with an almost sympathetic expression. Then: "In *Caryl/Hatzis* units, I was born *four hundred/eighty-six* years ago."

Thor thought she'd been ready for something like that, but the answer still startled her on a very deep level. She was talking to someone who had been alive ten times longer than she had, who was older than the entire human space program, than most countries, than the modern English language itself.

"Do you remember that far back?"

"*I have* memories from that time *are not mine*," he'd answered, obviously having difficulty trying to convey the meaning of what he was trying to say. "I was *not me then/someone else*. Those *incidents/memories* occurred to someone else. They do not interest *me/us* except as a source of *wisdom/accrued experience*."

"You mean you have no emotional attachment to those memories?"

"*This is not what* I mean *the memories do record emotions*."

"So how can you be so disconnected from them? Don't you feel sad when you remember something sad? Or happy when you remember something happy?"

"Do you feel the same sadness as someone else when they tell you one of their sad memories?"

"The *same* sadness? No, but—"

"Because the sadness is *for the person/not for the incident*. You are *removed/disconnected*. So it is with us. We do not connect. Our past selves are *gone/passed*."

Thor nodded, although she was still struggling to grasp the ramifications of what he was saying. "But if you think like that, how do you go from day to day? What's to say you won't wake up feeling like a new person, and the old one has gone? What if the old one didn't want to go?"

"Why would I resist changing? Do you fight the constant recycling of skin cells throughout your body? Do you object to the falling out of your hair?"

Remembering this, Thor smiled to herself in the darkness. It had been difficult trying to explain to Ueh that although humans changed on a cellular and psychological level, they still *saw* themselves as the same person.

"We think we're the same," she said, "despite the evidence that we change on a cellular and psychological level. You distinguish different versions of yourself despite the fact that you're inhabiting the same body and using the same name." She peered at him through the blackness. "You *do* use the same name, don't you?"

"That is an incorrect assumption, *Thor/Hatzis*. My present name is *Ueh/Ellil*. Before that, it was *Ashir/Ueh*. And before that it was *Baah/Ashir*. One day it will change again."

This was a detail Thor could follow. "To Ellil-slash-something. Right. That does make sense. I'm sorry for assuming otherwise."

"There is no need to apologize, *Thor/Hatzis*. The misunderstanding has been corrected."

Had it? she asked herself in the darkness of her dream. Consciousness was calling, and although she fought it, she could feel it looming inexorably closer. Whatever was happening to her wouldn't wait. She couldn't put it off to another version of her, like Ueh could. For a moment, she envied him.

The way he regarded his life unnerved her. Continuity of identity underlined so much of human nature that to deal with aliens who didn't value it was to risk persistent misunderstanding and confusion. Future consequences of present actions took on a whole new light when a different person might have to deal with them, not oneself. She couldn't help but wonder what crime she might commit if she knew *she* wouldn't have to pay the price.

But that wasn't so different, she supposed, to the engram situation. What would one Axford or Hatzis do in the light of the knowledge that others existed to pick up the pieces—or to carry the torch, if things went truly badly? Thor patently wasn't the same as the other Hatzis engrams, but she still shared a sense of kinship. She wasn't a clone, sister, or child of the original Caryl Hatzis; the bond between them was something much stranger. Perhaps, she thought, it would have been stronger under other circumstances.

Consciousness came closer, bringing with it pain and fear. Yet some relief, too. The thought of spending any great length of time in the darkness of her mind made her uncomfortable. The overwhelming slab of Sol's past sat heavily, weighing her down. Keeping herself busy was one way to avoid confronting the burden of it all, but that was impossible while she was asleep. The gunshot still echoed. . . .

Besides, if something had gone wrong, she needed to be awake to deal with it. She was the leader; the team was her responsibility. She couldn't sleep while the mission went to hell in a handbasket.

She woke feeling as though her head had been split open like a watermelon under a sledgehammer. Her eyelids fluttered weakly, and she tried in vain to sit up. Most disorienting of all was the fact that, although she knew she was awake—the intensity of the pain dispelled all doubts of that—and her eyes definitely were open, she still couldn't see anything.

"Hello?" The weak cry came from somewhere on Alander's left. "What's going on? Where are the lights?"

"Try switching to IR," Alander replied, unable to keep the wince out of his own voice.

"Shit." He heard scrabbling from where Thor was lying. Her body moved, sat up. She wavered for a moment as though considering passing out again. The hand clutching her head suggested that she had the same headache as him. "Sorry," she said. "I'm not thinking straight."

He didn't have the heart to make her feel worse than she already did. "We're the only ones awake. But the others are alive." He glanced at where they lay sprawled where they'd fallen, vivid blotches of heat against the hole ship's cool background. "I'm assuming that the jump did this to us," he went on. "Whatever method the cutters use to get around, it clearly doesn't agree with us."

"We could have been hit with some kind of weapon," she said.

"And lived?" He shook his head slowly, gingerly. "It wouldn't make sense to just knock us out."

"When has anything they've done ever made sense?" she muttered. "What does *Eledone* say?"

"*Eledone* isn't saying anything," Alander replied, his voice grim. "The hole ship isn't answering us."

"Fuck." She swore with little energy.

He had nothing to add. The obvious was better left unsaid for the time being. If *Eledone* had been more than just knocked out like its passengers—if it was dead—then that left the team in a very bad place.

One by one, the others stirred. Alander noted the order with which they woke. He and Thor had been first. Next were Gou Mang and Inari, closely followed by Cleo Samson. Sol and Axford were the last to struggle back to consciousness and their sluggish irritability demonstrated how much pain they were in.

A flicker of light came from the walls, overlaying the IR view with a brief flash of white. His thoughts froze in midbeat. He looked around in anticipation of it happening again.

"*Eledone*? Was that you?"

"Yes, Peter."

It was still dark, but the level of illumination in the cockpit gradually returned, brightening like a winter dawn until he made out the wary expression on Gou Mang's android face.

"*Eledone*," Thor called, rising to her feet. "Are you fully operational?"

"I apologize for my dysfunction," returned the voice of the alien AI. Alander couldn't remember the last time he'd felt so relieved. "I have sustained damage."

"What sort of damage, exactly?"

"My primary systems have been disrupted, resulting in substantial loss of ability. I am currently operating on thirty percent capacity."

"Give us the details," Sol requested.

"Forget details," said Thor. "Can you tell us where we are?"

"Not at present. I will within one minute, however."

"What about motive power?" asked Samson. "Can we go anywhere?"

"I will soon be able to restore limited NRT capacity."

"Ftl? Can you get us back to Rasmussen?"

"I will be unable to accommodate that request."

"Why not?" Samson pressed. "Your drives don't work? You don't know the way? What?"

The AI hesitated before answering. "My systems are not isolated. There is much overlap, and damage has been extensive. All systems have been affected."

"But you're fixing yourself, right?" said Samson. "I mean, you've fixed yourself this far. When your repairs are complete, will you then be able to get us out of here?"

"No." The single word echoed flatly in the cockpit. "I will need additional resources to effect such repairs."

"What sort of resources?" asked Sol.

"I will require access to a Dry Dock."

"Like the gifts have?"

"Yes."

Thor laughed humorlessly. "So we need to get you back to Rasmussen in order to get you fixed, but we *can't* get you back to Rasmussen because you need to be fixed. That's just great."

"We're trapped," said Samson dully.

"Somewhere," added Gou Mang, looking around at the dead screens.

"Do you have any sensory capabilities back yet?" asked Sol. "Are you able to look outside, at least?"

"Yes, Caryl, in some frequencies." Around them, the screens flickered to life. "I have been attempting to locate any of the probes or navigational beacons. At present, none appear to have survived. I will advise you if I receive a transmission, but I will not broadcast anything myself, as per your original instructions."

"Good," said Thor. "Keep it that way until I tell you otherwise."

"Yes, Caryl."

The self-repaired AI was having trouble distinguishing one Hatzis from another. Alander noted the fact, assuming it was a symptom of the hole ship's reduced capacity, while his attention turned to the screens and what they revealed about *Eledone*'s environment. The interior of the crippled cutter was still a raging turmoil of heat and energies. Surface temperature readings brought back peak figures in excess of several hundred degrees as gases and molten compounds roiled around the hole ship. *Eledone* advised that it was allowing itself to tumble with the chaotic flow of superheated fluids buffeting it. No motion was apparent from inside the hole ship, a fact for which Alander was extremely grateful.

"Do we know where exactly inside the cutter we are?" Thor asked.

"I am unable to determine that without using active sensors," the AI replied. "Doing so would reveal our location."

"What about the probes you brought with you? Are you able to use them?"

"Three probes are functional and ready to launch."

"Then send one. There's not much we can do until we know where we are."

"Yes, Caryl."

"What caused the damage, *Eledone*?" asked Axford calmly from one side.

"The disruption resulted from an unexpected hyperdimensional translation."

"The cutter drive, in other words," Axford said. "It wasn't a deliberate attack."

"That would be the most likely assumption, given that I appear not to have been harmed since."

"That's very reassuring," said Inari bitterly. "I, for one, think it's good to know we're lost in the middle of this thing and can't get home."

"We'll find a way," said Thor.

"How? Call for help? Even if our transmitter works, that'd make us sitting ducks. Remember where we are, Thor. We're inside the cutter!"

Thor glared at her. "Do you have any ideas yourself?"

"No, but—"

"Then please don't criticize others for not having anything to offer."

"All I'm saying is—"

"I can get us out," interrupted Axford.

Everyone faced the ex-general.

"You heard me," he said in response to Thor's unspoken question. "If I have to, I can get us out of here. But only as a last resort, when there's no other choice."

"How?" asked Thor.

"I prefer not to say at the moment."

She sighed. "Then for the moment, the information really isn't that helpful."

"If it means that we can forestall a petty squabble," Axford returned, "then I'd say it *is* helpful, Caryl." He faced Inari. "Based on my assurance that I can get us out of here, would you be happy to drop the matter for now?"

Inari hesitated before nodding. Her expression wasn't a trusting one. "I guess so."

"Then that's sorted." Axford turned back to Thor. "Maybe you lot can calm down now and get something constructive done."

"Probe away," announced *Eledone*, sending the equivalent of one full hole ship off on an exploratory mission. "I have instructed it to let our courses naturally diverge for one minute before activating its internal propulsion and moving farther away. It will commence surveying our location in five minutes."

"Out of curiosity, *Eledone*," said Axford, "just what self-defensive capacity have you managed to retain?"

"Ten percent."

"And how much offensive capacity?"

"None."

Axford nodded as his gaze swept the room to address them all. "Which means we're *already* sitting ducks, people. If that probe gives us away, we're as good as dead. Just thought you might like to know that."

"What makes you think the probe will give us away?" asked Samson. "There's nothing to lead it back to us."

"We just launched it, remember?" he said, explaining as though to a child. "It's not traveling ftl because we no longer have that ability. It's going to be using NRTs, and I don't think giving it a minute is long enough. *Eledone* should have consulted us before making that decision."

"It's not the ship's fault," said Thor tightly. "It was acting in accordance with operational guidelines. We told it before we left what provisions to take. It didn't need to consult us because it already knew."

"And *you* knew—how?" Axford snorted. "We have no idea what the Starfish can do or see in here. Who's to say that some automated system isn't watching us right now, just waiting for us to do something exactly like this?"

"What's your point, Frank?" said Thor irritably.

"My *point* is that I think we're being careless. I don't believe that operational parameters laid down before we started this mission should be allowed to dictate what risks you take with my life now."

"It's not just your life," Thor reminded him.

"Which only makes my point even more valid, wouldn't you say?" Again, Axford looked around the room, as though for support.

Alander asked, "What do you suggest we do?"

"We should divide the ship," Axford said, facing him. "That way we can maximize our chances of survival."

"I don't think that's such a good idea." Sol stepped between them. "Not right away, at least—not until we know where we are and what our options might be. After all, should we go our separate ways, we might not be able to contact each other again."

Thor looked grateful for the support but disgruntled that Sol had offered it without being asked. "Does that sound reasonable to you, Frank?"

"Reasonable enough." He scowled at both of them. "But I don't want to have this discussion again. Any decision this hole ship makes from here on in is to be done only after input from the rest of us. We've got just one shot at this. Let's not screw it up."

"All right." Thor conceded the point with some grace and instructed *Eledone* to advise them of all the details of future actions. The hole ship acknowledged the order without apparent rancor.

"I have incoming data." *Eledone*'s screens rearranged themselves to accommodate the information. From radar, lidar, and other active means of exploring around itself, the probe was building a much more detailed picture of its environment. It appeared to be the interior of a flattened tube approximately thirty meters across. The walls were curved and folded, as though crushed by great pressure, leaving a narrow channel that was ten times as wide as it was high and an unknown distance long. Gases and molten metals surged along that channel in turbulent streams, with the probe tugged along for the ride.

Alander noted that none of the superheated fluids raging around the probe were pooling or gathering at any point along the channel. It was probably designed that way, he supposed, like the chambers of a heart. What looked deformed or dysfunctional to a human eye was simply efficient, almost organic in nature. A vein, he thought.

Beyond the vein itself, there was nothing else to see. With no risk-free way to talk to the probe, they had to wait for it to move at its own schedule on to other means of gathering data. The picture that emerged was of an increasingly perplexing environment, one that had an analogue in neither biology nor machine.

The vein slid and kinked through a region comprised of rigid, load-bearing structures, each a long strut that was oval in cross-section. The struts seemed almost haphazardly arranged between undulating floor and ceiling, crisscrossing like the wires on a mesh fence, although never actually touching. The space around the struts was filled with an inert foamy material, nearly transparent to radar but riddled with vacuum-filled bubbles that cast back sparkling reflections. Probably insulating material, Alander decided, with the foam filling the gaps between floor and ceiling, as well as the larger spaces beyond.

The picture from those larger spaces was patchy and incomplete. Each successive increase in observational range increased the odds of the probe being seen, and it was programmed only to take chances at irregular intervals. Two enormous chambers abutted each other, almost touching but for the wall keeping them separate. What was in those chambers, exactly, was difficult to see. Vast, shadowy structures, neither rigid nor fluid, loomed at the fringes of the probe's sensors. Some were angular and asymmetrical, others flowing with an eerie grace. They could have been radar artifacts, shadows thrown by indistinct surfaces just out of range, or they could have been distinct things moving through those cavernous spaces. Whether they were machines, life-forms—perhaps even the Starfish themselves—it was impossible to tell. Alander regarded them with awe, feeling like a virus caught in a human body, wondering at the scale of the organs around him.

He cautioned himself to resist the biological metaphor. It had some value—for putting his size in perspective, if nothing else—but he was wary of jumping to incorrect conclusions because of it. The cutter within which they had stowed wasn't a human, and indeed might not be in any sense of the word alive. It was a space-faring vessel of war. The interior was a mess of tubes, chambers, and solid forms that didn't immediately succumb to his desire for symmetry, form, and function. The shadowy shapes he glimpsed could have been weapons systems, stirring restlessly, ready for combat—but what he perceived as purposeful and ordered was just as likely to be the exact opposite, and vice versa. He couldn't let his assumptions color the data lest he miss a crucial point.

The probe, growing bolder, cast the edges of its senses as far as it could. Distant outlines of the cutter began to take shape, revealing that the vein it was following was approximately one-third out from the cutter's central hub and slightly above its horizontal midpoint. The direction of the fluid was roughly clockwise around the hub and seemed to be spiraling inward. The cutter itself was still docked to the two that had rescued it, and all residual rotation had been completely dampened. Outside it was as still and quiet as a grave.

Within, Alander searched for some sense of structure to the cutter. It didn't help that the damage from the attack had laid waste to large regions of the craft. Burst veins pumped fluid en masse into chambers that might otherwise have been empty; load-bearing structures hung slumped and disconnected spearing painfully through softer foam and "muscle." The smoothly defined, sharp edge of the cutter was itself warped in places,

lending the entire thing a twisted, warped look. That it would
ever fly again, he sincerely doubted.

There was nowhere that he could immediately see that
looked like a centralized command area, analogous to a brain,
or the equivalent of a bridge, where living officers might con-
gregate to command the giant vessel. There had to be such a
point, and automatic assumptions sent him to the center of the
craft, looking for a spine connecting the poles or some sort of
interior disk from which such an operation might be coordi-
nated. But nothing leapt out at him. There, as everywhere else,
he saw only a tightly compressed tangle of spaces and structures, profoundly knocked about by the stresses of battle.

"Something up ahead."

Samson's voice wrenched his attention back to *Eledone*. At
first he thought she meant that something was approaching
them, but she was watching a different aspect of the probe's
telemetry than he was. She was pointing at the region ahead of
the probe, in the vein. The turbulence was increasing steadily,
and radar showed the edges of what might be a tear in the vein
wall ahead.

"It's being sucked in," she said.

"Can't it fight the flow?" Alander asked.

"Fighting the flow would draw more attention to it than
simply going with it," Thor replied. "There's no evidence to
suggest that following it would be dangerous."

"Personally," said Sol, "a change of scenery would be good.
I think it's learned as much as it's going to where it is."

Alander nodded, although he felt uneasy about the change
of environment. Thus far, the probe hadn't been attacked in the
vein, and it had managed to supply them with some excellent
data. It would be a shame to lose that advantage too soon.

As the probe drew nearer the tear, telemetry brought back
glimpses in visible frequencies of another chamber beyond.
This one had been breached and hung open to vacuum. The
superheated fluid filling the vein sprayed in a violent stream
from the tear, filling the vacuum with crystalline particles and
cooling plasma. Shadowy, insubstantial wisps hung around the
tear, drifting like seaweed with residual momentum. Again
Alander couldn't make out if they were actual *things* or artifacts

of the radar. Strange electromagnetic emissions growing stronger around the probe didn't provide an answer either way.

The turbulence increased as the probe was caught by the current pouring through the rent, and Alander found himself briefly reaching out to balance himself as the ragged walls fell by in a blurred and giddying rush. Then they were past, and the probe was tumbling in free fall through a glittering vacuum, gathering a dizzying view of the space around it. He glimpsed dark, ribbed, cathedral-like walls slumped in alien angles under a ceiling of spikes and hooks, many of them melted or shattered. He received the distinct impression of myriad eyes gleaming back at him from the dark spaces of that crowded, complicated topography, although he was sure he had to be imagining them. There was no sign of the vast, hanging things that he'd glimpsed on radar, but there were several floating structures that hung independent of the walls in the center of the space. Like elongated, lozenge-shaped barges, they extruded hairlike structures that glinted at their tips, seeming to signal in alien frequencies with unimaginable rhythms.

He switched from the radar to the visual view, letting his eyes digest the scene more naturally, but a bright flash on the radar drew his attention back. When his gaze had settled there again, the source of the flash was gone.

"Did you see that?" asked Gou Mang.

"I'm not sure," said Alander. "I think—"

He stopped when the flash came again: a hard, well-defined image that appeared in an instant, then disappeared as quickly, leaving an echo behind it like the afterglow of phosphor dots.

"What the fuck is it?" Thor muttered after the thing appeared a third and fourth time, on each occasion in a different part of the probe's field of view.

Almost as though it's circling the probe, thought Alander.

"This doesn't look good," said Axford.

"I'm inclined to agree with you on that one, Frank," said Thor.

"Is there any way to call the probe back?" asked Samson as the hard echoes increased in frequency. The glimpses were beginning to overlap, creating the impression that the probe was surrounded by myriad strange, bright points.

Thor shook her head. "Not without giving ourselves away."

The probe obeyed its internal instructions as best it could. When allowing itself to tumble innocently didn't divert attention, it fired its NRTs to move away from the mysterious objects. The glimpses followed it, seeming, if anything, to become more urgent and more closely defined. Alander began to feel distinctly threatened on behalf of the probe. Hard and metallic, the flickering shell was unlikely to be a welcoming party.

The end, when it came, was sudden. Two hard echoes jumped progressively closer to the probe, as though testing for a reaction. There was little the probe could do to defend itself. When attempting to run away failed a second time, the hard echoes contracted around the probe in an abrupt, bright rush, then the feed went dead. Every screen in the hole ship froze at the last recorded frames, then slowly faded to black.

"Damn it to hell," said Thor. She sounded more resigned than angry.

"What were those things?" asked Samson.

"Let's take a closer look," said Sol. "*Eledone*, replay those final images."

The hole ship obliged, bringing the screens back to life. Alander studied them with the others, puzzling over the sharply defined radar echoes. Images in other frequencies were less clear. Some showed faint patches that might have been evidence of camouflage against the chaotic background; others showed nothing at all. Most enigmatic was deep infrared, which revealed strange, three-dimensional, crosslike shapes rotating slowly in the distance, apparently unconnected to the radar ghosts but made significant by the fact that they appeared at no other frequency. *Hidden watchers?* Alander wondered. *The minds behind the radar weapon?*

"*Eledone*, what was it exactly that killed the probe?" Axford asked.

"I have insufficient data to answer that question," replied the hole ship, scrolling technical information down a screen for anyone who wanted to see. "I can, however, tell you that the hull interface was breached in three places shortly before transmission ceased. A massive invasion followed, compromising all systems."

Alander pointed at a screen showing the path followed by the alien weapons. "That looks like the way crystals grow through a supercritical solution." Damage spread in straight lines from each puncture point, dividing and dividing again until everything in their path was overwhelmed. "I'm guessing nanotech."

"Not the usual Starfish MO," said Axford knowingly.

"Maybe the yellow dots and blue lances are too energetic for in here," said Inari.

"In *this* raging soup?" Axford indicated the vein with its gases and molten metals through which *Eledone* was still tumbling. "I doubt they would make any difference whatsoever."

"Then what does all of this tell you?" asked Thor.

Axford 1313 shrugged. "I'll let you know when I've made up my mind."

"I suggest you do it quickly," said Sol, nodding at the screens showing the demise of the probe. "Because that hole the probe went through lies ahead of us, if we keep going with the flow, and presumably whatever killed it is still there. Unless we want to end up the same way, I suggest we figure out just what we're going to do about it—and *soon.*"

"How long before we reach the tear, *Eledone*?" Thor asked the hole ship.

"Unless we use our NRTs, approximately three hours."

"That's not very long," Inari pointed out unnecessarily.

"Which is all the more reason to not waste time dwelling on it," said Thor. "Inari, I want you and Gou Mang to go over the telemetry, find anything we missed. Frank, Cleo, take a closer look at that attack data; if we can work out exactly what it is, maybe we'll find a way to combat it. Sol, Peter, you might be able to find something we haven't considered. And I'll try to shift this bloody ship without getting us all killed." Her gaze swept around the cockpit, taking in every member of the crew. Alander felt a shiver run up his spine at her sudden resemblance to Sol. "Any objections?"

No one spoke.

"Right. Let's get started and see if we can't find a way out of this goddamn mess."

2.1.3

"Go on, Rob. Tell me more about what you've found."

Lucia was only half listening to Rob Singh as he burbled on about his research. The rest of her was concentrating on building herself a new body—and, perhaps, a new mind into the bargain.

"Well, it's not as though I've actually found anything, per se," he said. "It's just an idea. All I did was ask for blueprints of the gifts from the Library. Now, normally, the Gifts are as stubborn as the UN Security Council when it comes to giving out secrets. Or rather as stubborn as the Security Council *used* to be, anyway."

She detected a note of both sadness and incredulity in his tone, and she sympathized with him. It didn't seem real to her at times that Earth had been destroyed, and not by the Starfish, either. Humans and their AI descendants had been the ones who had brought about the planet's destruction, crushing it to dust and then sweeping it away as though it had never even existed. All that remained of humanity was a few creaky engrams struggling to survive in an exceedingly hostile universe.

"What was so different about this time?" she asked as the Surgery continued to follow her detailed instructions.

"This time I asked for blueprints of individual sections of

the gifts, spindle by spindle," he said excitedly. "And the Library quite happily gave them to me. You can call up schematics of the layout in here, for instance, or the Gallery. If you wanted to know the exact placement of every chair in the entire installation, the Gifts will provide it. It's only when you ask for technical information about sensitive areas that they clam up."

His telepresence robot rolled across the floor, flexed its limbs, and hopped up onto an examination table. Lucia was watching from a point low in the opposite wall. The robot, like a strange, skeletal dog, appeared to be looking straight at her.

"We could have done this ourselves, of course," he went on. "But no one bothered, I guess, because we just assumed it wouldn't tell us anything. But I did it anyway, out of curiosity. Sometimes you only find new things by looking at the obvious in a new light. It sounds trite, but it's true."

"And what did you find, Rob?"

"Hidden spaces," he said. He paused for effect, and she thought she could sense the hint of a smile in his voice. "Great big chunks of *nothing* that we never suspected were there. I know we always knew there were things we didn't know about the gifts, physically speaking, but we didn't think any farther than that. I mean, consider the hole ships. They have ftl communicators, and they don't need a structure like this to contain them. They have AIs, too, without having to devote an entire spindle to their operation."

"There's an awful lot of space for so little equipment, in other words."

"Exactly!" The robot hopped down from the table and began to trundle around the room. "This spindle, for example, contains the Surgery—but what else? Sweet effay, that's what. And those blank spots comprise no less than *eighty percent* of the spindle's total volume. That's a whole lot of nothing, Lucia. If you're anything like me, then you can't let go of the idea that there has to be *something* in all that space."

"Such as?"

The robot effected a shrug. "I don't know. The Gifts refuse to talk about those spaces, and I sure as hell can't find a way into them. But just knowing they're *there* tells us something, don't you think?"

The Surgery chose that moment to advise her that the building of the new body was complete. Rob's robot rolled to the middle of the room, directing its attention to the opposite wall, where a door was opening.

Lucia changed her pov to allow her to see it, too, although she didn't raise her hopes too high. It was a long shot at best, albeit one worth trying. She wasn't sure she'd understood half of what the design interface was telling her, or even begun to grasp the ramifications of the changes she'd suggested.

All reservations disappeared, however, when the door was fully open, revealing a small alcove and the newly designed I-suit floating in it.

"Fuck me, Lucia," Rob muttered in amazement. His voice sounded breathless over the telepresence link. "You did it!"

The I-suit looked like nothing so much as a thick-skinned soap bubble, discernible only as a vague shimmer in the air. Faint rainbows danced across its surface as Rob's robot rolled closer and raised camera stalks to view it more closely.

"Wait until the others find out!" he exclaimed. "None of us even considered creating *another* I-suit—"

"I'd prefer it if the others didn't find out just yet, Rob," she cut in.

His camera stalks raised and twisted around the equivalent of a frown, she guessed. "Why not?"

"I'm not ready yet." She regarded the I-suit with apprehension, unable to shake the idea that maybe she'd got something wrong. But she knew she couldn't hold back indefinitely. There was only one way to find out if it truly worked or not. "I'd like to test it out first."

Exercising pathways through the gifts she'd become increasingly familiar with, she sent her pov through the walls of the Surgery and into the I-suit enclosure. She felt links reach out to touch the new structure, its arcane nature bending to approximate new forms, new pathways. She'd tried to program the process as precisely as possible, but without knowing the medium she was working with, it was hard to predict what the result would be. What were the I-suits made of, exactly? Were they matter, energy, or pure information? No one knew, and that ignorance was dangerous, especially when her very life might be on the line.

She pushed forward, tentatively. There was no resistance. Suppressing the misgivings stirring at the back of her mind, she abandoned all caution and plunged in, mentally keeping her fingers crossed.

There was a wild, disorienting moment when she seemed to exist in two locations simultaneously: in the strange, semantically real but purely hypothetical spaces of the gifts and at the same time in an entirely different place. Sensory information bloomed in her mind, bringing her a flood of sights, sounds, and sensations. She felt as though she was expanding, inflating like a balloon, and for a moment the notion of bursting terrified her.

"Lucia?" Rob's voice seemed to reach her through new channels now, and she opened her eyes to see the robot staring up at her its posture one of almost comical surprise. "Is that *you?*"

She took a step forward, her new body moving with perfect ease. She felt warm, physical, *complete.* Her "skin" felt the movement of air around her; the soles of her feet registered her weight and adjusted automatically to keep her balance, and the index and middle fingers of her left hand were crossed, just as they had been mentally.

She brought them up in front of her face, staring at the shimmering, transparent reality with something approximating awe and amusement. She was actually *inside* the I-suit! At her instruction, it had molded itself to take her form without requiring an actual body to do it. She was a thing of energy, or exotic matter, or woven energy, or whatever the hell it was the I-suits were made of. She found herself not caring about the details. All that mattered was that her mind had a home!

"It's incredible," said Rob. "How do I get one?"

No doubt, she thought, that was what everyone would ask. But she didn't like the thought of throngs of people queuing up for their new bodies, especially when at the moment at least, she was the only one who knew how to operate the I-suit creator. She had other things to do—escapes to plan.

"I still don't want anyone knowing just yet, Rob," she said. "Let's just wait until we've finished exploring, okay?"

"Come on, Lucia! This is too damned important *not* to tell anyone!"

She felt a pang of guilt for wanting to protect her privacy, but she couldn't help it. "At least let me build you one first, and show you how it's done. That way you can show the others yourself."

She could sense his hesitation in the awkward stiffness of the robot. "That wouldn't be right," he said eventually. "There are people who should go ahead of me. Thor and the others— they should have had new bodies like this before they left."

"They already have I-suits. And the Hatzises who stayed behind and all the others who tell us what to do—most of them have I-suits, too. It's people like you and me who don't have them, Rob." She noted the revolutionary edge creeping into her words and forced herself to tone it down. "Let's hold onto this just a little while longer, okay? I don't want to feel like a circus freak when word gets out."

His hesitation was longer this time. She thought he might actually agree. A superfluous pilot forgotten upon the arrival of the Spinners, his only raison d'être now was to explore the mysteries of the gifts, and it must have been frustrating for him to have to do so via the clumsy medium of a telepresence robot, enduring slight communication lags and other inconveniences. How much easier, he must have been thinking, to actually *be* there, touching things with his own hands.

Whatever his answer was to be, though, she never got to hear it.

An earsplitting siren suddenly filled the halls of Spindle Four. Lucia in her new body and Rob in the robot both looked up in surprise.

"That's the Starfish alarm!" Rob's voice was filled with disbelief. "But they're not due here for another day!"

"Then they've obviously come early." Mortified at the thought of alien destroyers about to rain destruction down upon them, she had to force herself to think clearly. This wasn't the time for panic. If she was going to survive, she would have to be cool and resourceful.

But what could she do? What resources did she really have to defend herself against such an enemy? She hadn't worked on how to make or steal a hole ship yet, so she had no means of escaping from the system.

She mentally shucked off the defeatist thought. She wasn't

about to give up. Her head might have been on the chopping block, but she would not concede defeat until the ax itself had fallen. There *had* to be a way out of this!

The gifts, she thought, wildly. *I still have them! There must be* something *they can do.*

"Come on!" She grabbed the robot by a bundle of limbs and tugged it along after her. Her I-body ran smoothly and naturally, without tiring.

The instantaneous transfer point linking Spindle Four to the Hub wasn't far from the Surgery, but she didn't know how much time she had. For all she knew, the Starfish might already be on top of the gifts, snapping their skyhooks to drop the wreckage down upon Rasmussen's surface. The clock of her doom was ticking, and there was nothing she could do to stop it.

There has to be a way. . . .

Lucia repeated the mantra in her head over and over as she ran, half expecting with each footfall for the world to crumble into ruins around her. She reached the door leading to the Hub with Rob's robot still in tow, firing concerned questions at her, all of which she ignored. She plunged through the door, and within a heartbeat found herself in the Hub. Only then did it occur to her that she might have been leaping straight into a ruined spindle, and therefore to her death. But there wasn't time to dwell on the morbid. She needed to act fast.

To do what, though? she wondered. Looking around at the circle of doors, she realized she had no idea where to go next. There was nothing for her in the Library, the Science Hall, the Map Room, or the Lab, and the Surgery was about as useful as the Gallery. The Dry Dock was still empty—she ascertained this by reaching out with her I-body senses to touch the gifts, and realized instantly that no hole ship had arrived since last she'd checked—and the Hub itself was nothing more than a gateway. That left only one door.

"Lucia!" The telepresence robot struggled in her hands as the slight lag of the *Marcus Chown*'s transmitters caught up with its new location. "My God, Lucia! They're—!"

With that, the robot went limp and silent. Far away, through her alien senses, she felt the *Marcus Chown* die, its engrams with it.

Fear struck her, then, deep and energizing. She'd never felt anything like it before. Adrenaline she knew she didn't possess seemed to course through her new, electric body. Her thoughts flew at unprecedented rates. Whatever alien processor was now running her engram, it had considerably more power than anything UNESSPRO could have built. Time seemed to freeze as all the possibilities passed before her a second time, and death grew nearer by the nanosecond.

She faced the door that was her one remaining option. Black and peeling in places, it was a door she'd sent her mind through many times before, although she had never physically crossed its threshold.

She thought of shadows—the shadows that stirred in the deep places of the gifts, places even she had barely touched.

She asked herself where shadows might live, where one might go to join them.

She knew instantly what she had to do.

Abandoning the inert robot, she quickly made her way to the pitch-black door and reached out for the handle. It felt decidedly strange to see her hand moving out before her, barely visible apart from the faint gleaming of the waterlike surface.

A ghost before my time, she thought bleakly as her hand gripped the handle.

Would there be anything for her when she stepped through? She could sense the malignant alien forces gathering, building up like a thunderhead, preparing to sweep her presence from the universe. But she couldn't hesitate. For better or worse, she opened the door and plunged into the Dark Room.

There was nothing to greet her but a dark emptiness. She bodily threw herself deeper into the room, risking directions she had hitherto feared to travel. The blackness was an abyss, and its depths held things beyond her comprehension. Always before she had stayed near the room's the entrance, wary of going too deep and never being able to find her way out again. But now it no longer mattered. Now she welcomed the unimaginable depths of the impossibly black void.

I'm here, she called into the darkness. Dark shapes began to swirl around her, one moment like mist, the next like the coils of giant snakes. Deep in their heart she thought she detected eyes gleaming out at her.

The world around her shuddered violently as the Starfish destroyed one of the neighboring spindles. The shock wave rang along the superconducting cable connecting all the alien stations. The end had begun. Within moments, she knew, she would be staring into a void of a different kind altogether.

Can you hear me? she called into the dark. *Can* anyone *hear me?*

Silence.

Listen to me! It's time to move on!

She felt despair, then, at the thought that her instincts had been wrong, that the strange illogic that had led her here had been as flawed—as human—as all the others who had attempted to pierce the veil of mystery surrounding the gifts.

Another shock wave rocked the spindle. She felt like weeping, but her new body didn't have the capacity for that. She was shaken, rattled, gripped by pressures she couldn't begin to fathom.

Help me! she cried.

As the Starfish closed in on her refuge, alien weapons poised to erase her from the universe, a voice spoke to her out of the darkness:

"THIS IS THE FINAL GIFT WE BRING."

Something dark and unfathomable thrust itself into her mind, and time stopped.

2.1.4

"Fifteen minutes." Thor's voice rang out in the cockpit.

Sol glanced up, then returned to the task at hand, desperately searching for a way out of the fix they were in. At many times her normal clock rate, it seemed as though days had passed since Thor had given them their deadline. In that time, she and Alander had considered all manner of exotic possibilities. The radar ghosts were presumably some sort of seek-and-destroy countermeasure to prevent intruders from wandering freely through the cutter. That they were still functioning despite the centralized failure of the giant vessel wasn't so far-fetched: the only way to regulate such a structure would be to allow some systems a measure of autonomy. The radar ghosts could be a localized chapter of a global system that staggered on while the cutter died around it. That could take days, perhaps even weeks. While there was still energy in the system—as was evidenced by the veins of molten metal roiling outside *Eledone*—many of its subsystems could still function.

Sol had no doubt that they were dealing with the bottom of the security chain. She was equally aware that, in order to complete their mission, they would have to find a way to the top of that chain, and that meant not only surviving this challenge but also using it to their advantage. Security wasn't just about eliminating threats but gathering intelligence, as well. They had come bearing information that could benefit the Starfish; if they could find a way to communicate with the radar ghosts, then they might just be able to take that first step along that security chain. The trick, of course, was staying alive long enough to do that.

"What about neutrinos?" said Alander. "They're hard to detect; they'd make a good security medium."

"Good thinking," said Sol.

Together they trawled through the data from the probe. While neutrino emissions weren't something it had been programmed to note, its detectors did register a strong flux in the chamber on the other side of the breach. The exact source was hard to pin down, though. It could have been symptomatic of any number of natural processes. Still, it was something.

"*Eledone*, can you produce neutrinos on demand?" she asked the hole ship.

"I am able to modulate some of my internal processes to facilitate such a request."

"How long would that take?"

"Approximately two hours."

Sol shook her head in frustration. Even if they determined that neutrinos lay at the heart of the ghosts' communication system, and if they decoded the transmissions and worked out how to convey the message they needed to get across, *Eledone* still couldn't give them a transmitter until well after the deadline.

Alander obviously shared her frustration. "We might as well just hold hands and think happy thoughts at them for all this research is achieving."

The levity provoked a pang of annoyance in her, but she didn't say anything. She couldn't really blame him. She herself had been fighting a sense of creeping despair for the last half hour. So far the mission had hardly been a success, and they still had such a long way to go.

"Okay, time's up," said Thor in a tone like a death knell. "What do we have? Gou Mang, you first."

"There's evidence of heavy camouflage in place around the ghosts as well as the things in the background," said the android without preamble. "We did manage to tease a few details out of the data and came up with a better model of what the ghosts actually look like." An image appeared in the screen behind Gou Mang. It showed a quicksilver shape oscillating between a lumpy sphere and a vicious, spiked ball. "The ghosts—and there *are* many of them, not just one jumping rapidly from place to place—appear to oscillate regularly between these two forms. We don't know why, though. And the oscillations don't appear to be related to the period of their jumping through unspace. We haven't been able to determine if they have centralized intelligence, or if they're just obeying simple flocking behaviors. That's all."

Thor looked to Axford. "Frank?"

"As far as the attacks go, we don't have much data to go on," he said. "The progress of the nanoagent through the probe does suggest a nanotechnological process, but without an actual sample we're working blind. We don't know what processes it uses to replicate, what might block it, or even what methods of attack it employs. *Eledone* has a number of antinano systems, but none of them helped the probe. It'd be a long shot going up against these things without more info."

Thor nodded with apparent satisfaction, but Sol could see the disappointment in her eyes. "What about you, Peter? Anything?"

Alander outlined what they'd considered, but in the end was able to offer little more than the others had.

After he'd finished, Thor sighed and offered a précis on her own findings. "Well, the best I could come up with was a way of anchoring the ship outside the breach. Given the lack of any other ideas, I suggest we go with that. At the very least, it'll give us a little more time to think."

"You're sure we can do this safely?" asked Inari.

Thor nodded in reply. "If we can get close enough to one of the walls, *Eledone* will be able to extend the hull to attach itself to it. The external boundary should be sufficiently malleable to get a grip. If we can do it without using the drives, we probably won't be detected."

There was a murmur of consent, but no one spoke. The atmosphere of the ship was grave at best.

"If there are no other suggestions," said Thor into the quiet, "then I propose we get to work. Time is short, as I'm sure you're all aware."

Everyone moved to their stations. Sol felt a terrible sense of futility that she found hard to shake—and if she felt it, then she had little doubt that the others did, too. Even as *Eledone* reported its successful rearrangement of hull boundary material as a rudder to divert its course slightly, aiming for a section of the vein wall a hundred meters ahead of the breach, she couldn't help but wonder why they were even bothering. In the long run, they didn't have a clue what to do. What if they couldn't work it out? Or worse: what if there was *nothing* they could do? She didn't know what was happening outside the cutter, but she wasn't about to delude herself into believing that the Starfish had magically halted their advance. For all she knew, they had already descended upon Rasmussen and put paid to yet another human colony.

"I have failed in my first attempt to secure us to the intended point of contact," *Eledone* reported blandly. "I will try again at the next suitable point."

The view through the screens spun dizzily as the hole ship tumbled through highly turbulent flows. Even at her highest clock rate, Sol couldn't tell exactly what was happening, but she hoped and prayed that the alien AI knew what the hell it was doing.

"How much longer to the breach?" asked Gou Mang. Her tone reflected the anxieties of everyone in the cockpit.

"Ninety human meters." It was Samson who answered her, her eyes never leaving the instruments on the command stalk as the rippling vein wall swept by in a blur.

Up close, the vein looked less like a lumpy, biological construct than a mat of metallic fibers coated in glass. *Eledone* attempted to obtain a grip a second time, but again failed to find purchase.

"Sixty meters," Samson announced.

Sol sensed a growing urgency to the superheated currents swirling around them as the hole ship rocked and spiraled like a rubber duck caught in a typhoon.

"Thirty meters," said Samson after a third failed attempt.

"Perhaps we should have had a backup plan before taking the risk," said Axford wryly. There was more than just an edge of unease in his voice.

"I'm still wide open to suggestions," said Thor hotly.

All eyes remained glued to the screens as the hole ship read-ied itself for a fourth and final grab; everyone knew they wouldn't get a fifth shot at it. If they missed this time, *Eledone* would go tumbling into the breach, and into clear view of the radar ghosts.

There was a wild, disorienting moment during which the information from the screens was completely at odds with what her other senses told her—that she was standing completely at rest inside the cockpit, not tumbling in a sudden jolt of chang-ing momentum.

Then, abruptly, all was still.

Everyone looked around in similar confusion, collectively holding their breath in expectation of something else happen-ing.

"We *did* it?" Inari sounded both surprised and relieved.

The view on the screen rocked for a second, then stabilized.

"I have successfully anchored myself to the vein wall," an-nounced the hole ship without any hint of satisfaction.

As one, everybody in the cockpit exhaled.

"Five meters from the breach," said Samson. She laughed, then, in obvious relief.

Sol didn't want to dwell on how close they'd come to slip-ping through. "How stable is this location?"

A quick sweep from multiple viewpoints revealed that the edges of the breach weren't widening in the direction of the hole ship. What caused it was impossible to tell, although Sol assumed it was a side effect of the *human/Yuhl* attack. Structural destabilization would have led to localized disruptions caused by metal fatigue or material failure. Given that the cutter had stopped rotating, such stresses, she presumed, would be signif-icantly reduced.

The breach itself looked like a giant wound in the vein wall, a jagged tear stretching into the distance. Roiling currents swirled around the edges, producing strange eddies in myriad brilliant colors. From their new position, the vein itself looked vast and convoluted, like the inside of a nightmarish conch shell, stretched and distorted as though made of taffy.

"Seems stable enough to me," said Inari.

Samson shrugged. "I guess we'll find out soon enough if it's not."

"We're safe for the moment," said Thor. "That's the main thing."

"But what happens now?" asked Gou Mang.

"Now we send out a reconnaissance mission," said Axford.

Thor turned on him with a scowl, clearly not impressed by him undermining her authority. "And I suppose you're volunteering for that, Frank?"

He nodded confidently. "The hole ship can split off a single or even a half ship big enough for me to pilot. Just give me navigation capabilities similar to *Eledone*, and I'm sure I can surf my way right through those things and out the other side without any problems whatsoever."

"And what good would that do?" asked Thor.

"Well, at least we'd know we wouldn't be stuck here until the end of time, Caryl."

"How would *we* know that, Frank?" Thor made no attempt to hide her cynicism.

"Because I'd signal you from the far side, of course."

Thor eyed him steadily for a few moments before shaking her head slowly. "That's the second time you've suggested splitting up from us."

"What are you saying? That you don't trust me?"

"Of course we don't, Frank."

He snorted a laugh at this. "I can live with your suspicions, as long as you admit that my plan makes sense. Just agree to it and let's get on with it, can't we?"

Thor opened her mouth to speak, but Gou Mang got in first.

"It might be too late for that," she said, pointing at the screen nearest her. "Check out the breach!"

Everyone turned at this to see what Gou Mang was indicating. A white lozenge-shaped object with black stripes had slipped through the breach, effortlessly defying the current. The impression of a zebra fish was strengthened when the thing "faced" them, revealing what looked like an open mouth. As it jerked in surges through the violent eddies, Sol glimpsed a tube through its center, giving it the look of an old aircraft jet engine.

"What the hell is that?" asked Alander.

"I have no idea," said Gou Mang. "But whatever it is, it seems to be—"

Sol cried out in alarm as, with a surprising surge of speed, the thing lunged, and its central tube opened to engulf them.

"Jesus Christ!" Alander cried. The hole ship jerked beneath him, throwing him off balance. He went down on one knee, clutching the wall for support as the zebra fish vessel struck and clung to the outside of *Eledone* like a lamprey.

"What's it doing?" Samson asked.

"Eledone, report!" Thor's voice called out sharply through the rising babble. Screens flickered, showing numerous views of the attack.

"I have been struck by an unidentified object," the hole ship replied calmly.

No fucking kidding, Alander thought. The zebra ship had attached itself to *Eledone*'s hull with its "mouth." Whatever it was doing, it was causing tiny tremors to run through the hole ship.

"Have you been breached?" asked Thor.

"I am resisting an attempted incursion."

"The same as the one that took out the probe?"

"No. This is—" The hole ship faltered. "I am—it—"

"Eledone?"

"We are—"

"Eledone, respond, for fuck's sake!"

Alander could well understand the desperation in Thor's voice. The mission had started off badly and was getting worse in rapid steps.

The hole ship failed to respond to her command, and for a timeless moment there was no sound at all to be heard in the cockpit. Alander stood up and looked around. The tremors had ceased also.

"It's too quiet," whispered Axford, staring up at the ceiling as if in expectation of seeing something there.

"Too quiet by far," Sol concurred.

Then a new voice issued into the cockpit. Loud and harsh, it caused everyone to wince when it spoke.

"Intruders, explain your presence."

Thor stiffened. "Who's speaking? Are you the Starfish?"

"The intruders must explain their presence," the voice repeated, its pitch and timbre such that Alander could feel it through the floor.

Thor hesitated, uncertainty naked on her face.

"What have we got to lose?" Sol asked. "This is what we came here for."

"We need to speak to whoever's in charge," Thor said, her lips pale. "We have information that we think could be of some use to—"

"There is no 'in charge,' " the voice interrupted emotionlessly. "You are inexplicable; how can such a thing be tolerated?"

"We *must* be tolerated. We have come here to help you. We know where your enemies are hiding."

"There are no enemies. Your presence is anomalous."

"The Spinners, the ones who drop the gifts—the ones you've been chasing through—"

"There is no chase. You are inexplicable. Can such a thing be—"

"You have to listen to us!" Thor's voice took on a more desperate tone. "You're destroying the gifts, and us along with them! If you don't stop, we'll all be killed! Our species will become extinct!"

"There is a multitude. The universe does not want for observers."

"I don't care about other observers! Right now I only care about *us!* If you continue this way, you'll be committing genocide. You *must* listen to us. We can give you what you seek!"

The voice fell silent for a time, and Alander waited uneasily for a reply. He could sense a terrible gulf in comprehension between Thor and the alien mind interrogating them—so much so that getting across what they'd come to say seemed almost impossible. And yet . . .

"Why haven't they destroyed us?" Samson asked softly, as if worried the alien interrogator might hear her. "And how can they be speaking English? It doesn't make any sense!"

"Actually, if you assume that *that,*" said Axford, indicating the zebra fish ship on the screens, "is our probe sent back to us, then it actually makes perfect sense."

Everyone turned to him in confusion, but it was Inari who spoke first.

"The probe? But it was destroyed. We saw it."

"No, we assumed it had been destroyed because we lost contact with it. But what if it was taken over instead? Analyzed, dissected, rebuilt?"

"My God," Thor muttered, facing the zebra fish ship on the screen again. "It's been sent back as a kind of message."

Axford nodded. "I think that's a distinct possibility, yes."

"What kind of message?" asked Gou Mang.

"A warning, perhaps," said Axford.

"Not necessarily," said Sol. "It could just be a simple enquiry."

"Either way," said Alander, "I'm sure we'll find out soon enough."

He stared at the zebra fish ship with renewed interest. Now that Axford had raised the possibility, he could indeed see how the black stripes might be evidence of intrusion through the hole ship's normally smooth and white hull boundary. It now appeared to him as though a malignant, black worm had burrowed into the probe and distorted it out of shape. Like wires wrapped around the branches of a bonsai tree, the black constrained the white, giving it a new form and function.

"The intruders' presence is anomalous," the voice returned. Strangely, Alander couldn't tell whether it was speaking to them or in reply to an unheard query from elsewhere. This was made even more confusing with its next words: "Their origin is ambiguous; your goals are undermined. There is no reason for your presence."

"I told you," said Thor. "We came here to offer you information. We came here to speak to you to try to get you to understand what you've been—"

"Speak." The single word boomed throughout the cockpit. Again Alander wasn't sure exactly what it meant or to whom it was directed. Was the alien mind inviting Thor to speak, or merely saying the word out loud in an attempt to grasp its meaning?

"But will you *listen?*" asked Thor. "Or have you already made up your mind to destroy us? I don't want to spend my last minutes pissing into—"

"No continuity exists between here and those that destroy."

"I think I'm beginning to understand," said Alander, stepping forward. "It's saying that it isn't one of the Starfish."

"He's right," said Axford. "The radar ghosts—or whoever controls them—aren't the ones we should be talking to. They're someone else."

Thor's frown became exasperation. "You can't be fucking serious. They're another alien species?"

"Why not?" said Axford. "Why should the Yuhl and the Praxis be the only aliens the Spinner/Starfish migration have happened upon down the eons?"

Alander nodded. "It's a possibility, Thor."

"But you're not sure?" She studied him closely.

He shook his head. "Not of this, no."

"There's also another possibility," put in Sol. Then louder, for the alien voice, she said, "You're telling us that you *aren't* the ones who've been destroying our people, right?"

"There exists a distinction," answered the voice.

"Then who *are* you, if not the Starfish—or rather, the destroyers?"

"We are the components of the instruments that serve those that govern the interspaces."

Alander's head reeled for a moment. *A component of an instrument of a servant* . . . Christ, the zebra ship represented possibly the lowest rung of the Starfish hierarchy ladder, yet it still managed to overwhelm their hole ship without so much as breaking a sweat!

"The governors of the interspaces," said Thor. "How can we speak to them?"

"You are anomalous," returned the voice with irritating repetition. "They will not hear you."

"Then you'll have to *make* them hear us!"

"They will not hear you," the voice repeated.

"But it's vital we speak to them," Thor pressed. "They'll understand as soon as—"

"Your argument offers no logic or clarity. They will not hear you."

"Fuck clarity and logic! We came here to talk to the Starfish, and we're not leaving until we've done just that."

"From which sector have you come?"

"We came from a system we call Asellus Primus," Thor said, "but we're originally—"

"Your statement offers no reference to the interspaces," the voice interrupted again. "The intruders' presence is anomalous."

"We're not from the interspaces," said Thor. "We come from one of the systems you've destroyed!"

"The interspaces have no systems; they are anomalous to those who govern the—"

"The systems aren't *in* the interspaces; they're from *beyond* the interspaces. Just check the data of the probe you've taken over. There'll be—"

"The data was not relevant to the interspaces. The data has been expunged.

The final word of the zebra fish ship fell into the cockpit like a lead weight. *Expunged.* The creature or AI addressing them neither knew nor cared about the systems the Starfish were systematically destroying. It had even gone to the effort of erasing its memory in order *not* to know. This led to a very disquieting possibility: if it found their presence in the cutter to be equally irrelevant, would it erase them, too?

"What is the function of those who govern the interspaces?" asked Sol after a moment's uncomfortable silence.

"The governors ensure integrity and fidelity," came the immediate reply. "The governors ensure continuity. The governors ensure order."

"But that order has been broken down, hasn't it? The interspaces have been damaged."

There was a slight pause—a pause Sol was quick to recognize as uncertainty and seize upon. "If you allow us to speak to another tool or component, then perhaps we could help restore that order. After all, we have information that might—"

"The intruders are anomalous," said the voice. "Your purpose bears no relation to the interspaces."

"But there *is* a relation," Sol asserted. She pointed at the screens. "If the governors' job is to maintain order in the interspaces—by which we assume you mean the chambers and linking tubes throughout the cutter—then there is a clear relation between us and them, because we were the ones that caused the damage in the first place."

"Careful, Sol," Thor cautioned uneasily.

Alander could relate to her apprehension. Maybe it wasn't such a good idea to inform the aliens that the order it valued so highly had been disrupted as a direct result of their presence.

Sol dismissed the warning with a shake of her head.

"That misconception was present in the data extracted from your vessel," said voice from the zebra ship.

"It's not a misconception, I assure you," said Sol. "It's the truth. If you hadn't expunged the other information, you'd realize that."

"The source of the damage was external," said the zebra ship. "You are internal."

"Yes, but the data would also tell you that we originally came from the outside. *That* is where our systems lie—beyond the interspaces."

"There is nothing beyond the interspaces," said the voice. "It is not necessary."

Alander sighed. "If you're not prepared to listen to what we have to say, then why bother questioning us at all?"

"Your origins must be known before judgment can be made."

A violent tremor through the vein wall cut short any further attempt to reason with the alien voice. The view through the monitors blurred with vibration. Everyone turned to the screens to see a long, slow ripple move along the superheated tube.

"What's that?" asked Thor.

The image of the breach showed the jagged lips twisting and writhing, while roiling fluids made chaotic patterns in infrared displays.

"Whatever it is," said Sol, "it's frightening our friend away. Look!"

Without word or ceremony, the zebra fish ship pulled away from *Eledone* and shot off into the distance. Its tubular, striped body flexed and twisted in the currents, arcing toward an apparently unremarkable section of the vein wall a hundred meters downstream. Then, suddenly, the vein wall ripped open and peeled like a zipper along its length. The zebra fish ship was sucked into a sudden outrush of gases that ripped still more of the vein wall away. The enormous gash sucked at the contents of the vein in both directions and prompted a violent inrush from the chamber on the far side of the original breach.

Alander stared, amazed, as a dozen new ships darted through the gash. Shaped like fat knife blades minus pommel and guard, they sliced through the fluid as though it wasn't even there. Alander couldn't tell what propelled them, but their movements were economical and graceful. Bright lines of energy played along their edges, as though they were limned in neon. Weaving and ducking, almost playfully, they cut a swathe through the current.

But the elegance and grace of their movements was deceptive, for their intentions were undoubtedly deadly. As the zebra fish ship came up to intercept them, the neon lines flashed, and it fell away in pieces, sliced into ribbons that disintegrated and dissolved in the superheated current.

Then, almost casually, they turned their attention to *Eledone*.

Thor felt like screaming. Why couldn't something just go right for her for a change?

"What the fuck is happening *now?*" she cried out, unable to keep the edge of panic from her voice.

The twelve blade ships arced toward them in a silvery rush.

But as they loomed closer, it became apparent that they weren't aiming for *Eledone* at all, but rather the nearby breach. And as they neared it, a bloom of radar ghosts rose up to greet them.

It was like watching coral growth in fast motion, she thought. A blade ship would encounter a faint, silver resistance, then suddenly it would be enveloped by a swarm of hard radar images that would overlap and multiply until the blade ship was invisible. The images *Eledone* cast for them of the strange encounters changed almost too quickly to follow. Clouds of radar ghosts blossomed and collapsed in series across the screens, flickering in and out of reality in discrete places but progressing in waves as the blade ships advanced. Unlike the probe, which had been completely overwhelmed by the radar ghosts, the blade ships were resisting each attack with apparent ease. Slowly, the number of ghost blooms faded, and the way into the breach became clear.

"I'm not sure who I should be cheering for," said Inari, shaking her head.

Again the blade ships approached, and Thor's anxiety rose once more. The blade ships were bound to notice *Eledone*, and when they did, it was very likely they'd destroy it with the same ease that they'd dispatched the ghosts.

"We need to transmit a message," said Alander unexpectedly.

All eyes came from the screens to look at him.

"A message?" said Thor. "To whom? Broadcasting anything now is only going to get us killed, Peter."

"I don't think so. I remember—I mean, the Praxis has records of ships such as these."

"What does the Praxis have to do with this?"

Alander's hand came up to touch his forehead. He looked confused, even more disoriented than usual.

"Speak to me, Peter. What the fuck is going on?"

"I don't know *how* I know, but I do. It's in my head." He looked at her evenly, then, pleading with his eyes for her to trust him. "I think I have the means to communicate with them."

Thor's attention was drawn back to the screens as something black and angular slipped through the breach. It looked like a chunky six-cornered jack, all right angles and stubby arms, and was so large it barely made it through the jagged hole. The blade ships squared off against it and seemed to mount a counterattack, although it wasn't immediately obvious as to how they were doing it. Tiny puffs of light seemed to flower on the arms of the new arrival, sending clouds of black material in waves down-vein. It seemed to pulse, like a tuning fork ringing in slow motion, and waves of invisible energy knocked the blade ships aside.

They regrouped as a second black craft edged its way through the breach. Subtle energies flashed through the roiling fluid, sending *Eledone* rocking. It was only a matter of time, Thor feared, before something hit the hole ship—whether by accident or design. If they were going to do anything, it would have to be soon.

She faced Alander again. "Did the Praxis put this knowledge in your head?"

"He must have. I don't know how else it could've got there."

"What *else* did he put in there?" asked Axford sourly.

"I don't care about that at the moment," Thor said without turning, "as long as Peter can keep us alive. *Can* you, Peter?"

"The Praxis—" He spoke falteringly, hardly inspiring confidence. "He has a great deal of knowledge concerning—concerning the races encountered by the Starfish and Spinner migrations. This is one of them."

"But what are they doing *here?*" asked Gou Mang.

"I don't know. But they're called—they're called the A/kak/a/riil, and they were presumed lost thousands of years ago."

"Well, they seem pretty active to me," said Samson dryly.

An invisible shock wave tore the breach a meter wider, bringing the nearest point that much closer to where they desperately clung to the vein wall.

"Okay, for want of an alternative, I'm going to give Peter free rein on this one." She waited for Axford to object, but for once the ex-general had nothing to say. "*Eledone,* are you back on-line?"

"I am here, Caryl."

"Okay. I want you to give Peter a broadcast line in the medium of his choice."

Alander fiddled with the command stalk for a moment, then went very still for more than a minute. Thor waited anxiously, wondering when he would begin and, more importantly, what the response would be. She didn't expect the mysterious aliens to want to help more than they already had, inadvertently, by taking out the zebra fish ship, but a better understanding of what was going on would be a step in the right direction.

Eventually Alander stirred. "I'm sending the message now. The A/kak/a/riil communicate via resonances only accessible in unspace. *Eledone's* limited transdimensional capability puts a considerable cap on this sort of communication, but I'm doing my best to overcome that problem."

"What have you said to them?" Thor asked, wondering if Alander had noted the change in his tone. His voice was richer, deeper, more formal.

"I've told them that we're on a diplomatic mission seeking information on the Starfish and that we request their assistance."

"Let's see what they say."

On the screens, a third black ship had nosed its way through the breach. Two of the blade ships exploded spectacularly as its weird vibrating weapons systems joined the attack of its partners. But the ground was soon lost as the blade ships managed to destroy the first black ship, quickly followed by the second. Crumbling black chunks drifted into the distance, leaving only the third black craft behind.

"The *A/kak/a/riil* have opened a resonant link with *Eledone*," said Alander finally. "We can talk freely with them now."

"Well, that's encouraging, at least," said Thor.

"They say that we are foolish and should leave immediately. The governors and their servants will soon be defeated. Afterwards the chamber beyond will be theirs."

She sighed. "That's *not* so encouraging."

"Why do they want it?" Samson asked.

"They say that the governors' function has been superseded," Alander explained. "They say that with the death of the cutter, all roles are rescinded."

"What roles?"

"I'm not sure I understand," said Alander, looking puzzled again.

"You know," said Sol thoughtfully, "I think I'm finally beginning to get a handle on what's going on here."

Thor looked over to her. "Mind filling the rest of us in, then?"

"In a second. Peter, ask them who the governors are."

"The race we were just talking to was once called the Pllix," he responded. "They have governed the interspaces for as long as the *A/kak/a/riil* have been part of the Exclusion."

"The Exclusion?" said Thor, frowning. "And that is?"

"I think you're mistranslating something there, Peter," said Sol. "Check again. I have a gut feeling that the word you're looking for is *ecosystem.*"

After some consideration, Alander turned to Sol. "I think you're right."

Thor shook her head in irritation. "Exclusion, ecosystem— it's all gibberish."

"Actually, it makes perfect sense." Sol's expression was one of delighted wonder, as though she'd turned over a stone and found a nugget of gold instead of the usual collection of bugs and dirt. "Don't you see? We've been assuming all along that there are only two options to choose from when the Starfish come by. We can either run, or we can stay and die. But there's a third option: we can do what the Pllix did and hitch a ride."

"Stow away?" Thor couldn't help her scorn. "That's preposterous."

"Why preposterous?" said Sol. "It makes perfect sense."

"Look at those things," said Thor. "It's not as if they can just slip into a corner unnoticed!"

"You're forgetting the scale of the cutters," argued Sol. "Not to mention the Trident. These things are *huge*. Who knows how many hangers-on they could support? Over the thousands of years within this cutter, the Pllix have been absorbed by the governors, policing the veins and chambers and making sure that nothing intrudes. They've managed to integrate themselves into the Starfish fleet."

Samson nodded enthusiastically. "It makes sense. Life survives and adapts wherever there's a niche."

"And there are bound to be niches aplenty here," added Gou Mang.

"There always are for collaborators," said Axford.

"What do you mean?" asked Alander.

"I mean, they're helping the very creatures that destroyed their homes."

"But at least they're still alive," said Sol. "Look, what they're doing is essentially no different from the Praxis—and us. They've just gone about it in a different way, that's all."

"I'm still not buying it," said Thor. "They managed to infiltrate the enemy's craft only to settle down there and make it their home? You'd have to be insane."

Sol shook her head. "Just desperate."

"Peter," said Axford. "Can you ask the *A/kak/a/riil* what their function is? If this is an ecosystem, can they get us any closer to the top of the food chain?"

"They say that their function is that of—" Alander paused, as if trying to interpret the response. "It's a strange word they're using. There doesn't seem to be any corresponding word in our language. It seems to mean both scavenger and beneficiary."

"Beneficiary of what?"

"Of the cutters," he said. "When one dies, it is returned to the Source of All to be reclaimed."

"That makes them demolition crews," said Sol.

"Or recyclers," put in Inari.

Thor suppressed a shudder. The way the damaged cutter had been removed by two of its "siblings" had touched an absurdly anthropomorphic part of her, but if Alander was right, then that impression was completely askew. They weren't taking it away to be healed but to be cannibalized.

"What about getting us to the top?" she asked. "Would that involve finding this 'Source of All' thing?"

"They say that the Source is unapproachable. The Exclusion has no known links to it."

"The Starfish don't actually tell them what to do?"

"They say that they perform their functions independently. They take orders from no one."

There is no "in charge," the Pllix had said. A shiver went down Thor's spine.

"Are they at least going to help us get out of here?" asked Inari. "Or are they just going to leave us here to die?"

"That's up to us."

"How?" asked Thor.

"They only attack the governor's servants, the Pllix, because they resist the demolition. If we do not resist, we are free to leave."

"Just like that?" said Thor. "No questions asked?"

"They assure me that they won't try to stop us."

"But they won't guide us, either, I take it," said Axford.

"No," said Alander. "That's not their function."

Thor thought of the wild, chaotic landscape of the cutter. She doubted, somehow, that it would be any safer while it was being torn apart by the *A/kak/a/riil*. In fact, if anything, it might even be more dangerous. And what if more than one species filled the demolition crew niche? The next one they encountered might not be so accommodating.

"Can they at least tell us which way they've come?" she asked. "If we knew the best way to avoid the governors, that would be something."

Alander nodded, closing his eyes again to concentrate.

"They'll give us that information," he said. "They don't see us as any real threat."

Something akin to relief rushed through Thor, then. She only hoped it wasn't premature.

"Tell them that we are grateful, and that—"

"They have supplied the relevant information," Alander cut in, opening his eyes, facing everyone. "They've gone."

On the screens the *A/kak/a/riil* were concentrating on the destruction of the last of the black Pllix ships. The chunky, squat construct fought valiantly, but to no avail. As it crumbled under the combined onslaught of the *A/kak/a/riil*, five of the blade ships swooped in to gather up the detritus, enfolding it in webs of silver energy that seemed to eat into it, compacting it down into a form that could more easily be transported.

Scavengers, she thought. *Just like the Yuhl . . .*

Was this, she wondered, to be the fate of humanity?

"The way is clear," said Samson. "Thor? What are your instructions?"

Without taking her eyes from the blade ships, Thor muttered, "Just get us the hell out of here, Cleo. I don't think I can look at this any longer."

UEH/ELLIL

The entrance to Ueh's private niche opened with a liquid sigh, and the human called *Caryl/Hatzis* stepped through it.

"I'm sorry to bother you, Conjugator," she said, standing awkwardly before him. The niche contained little more than an alcove for him to crouch in and tubes through which he performed ablutions. There was no room for her to sit. "If it's not convenient, I can always—"

"It is not inconvenient," he said, synchronizing both of his throats to speak in English. "I was not sleeping."

Which was true. He'd simply been huddling in his alcove, rocking back and forth on his long-toed feet, clutching his stomach and chest to himself. A narrow circle of fluorescent lights on the ceiling banished shadows from every corner.

The expression on the human android's soft, fleshy face sagged in such a way as to suggest that she was satisfied with his response. Bulging, moist, and endlessly mobile, human features fascinated and repulsed him in equal parts: nonverbal signals varied from face to face, asymmetry was the norm, not the exception, and the placement of so many vital sensory organs on the *outside* of the brain's skeletal case left them vulnerable to attack.

He waited quietly for the human to continue, distracted by the thing he could feel moving inside of him.

"I wanted to talk to you about the Spinner front," said *Caryl/Hatzis*. "We've been here three days now, and no one will tell us what you've found. We *know* what you've found, Ueh; we're not stupid. Why won't the Fit talk to us about it? I think we have a right to know what's going on."

Ueh stared at her, puzzled. Three human days approximated two cycles. He'd been in his room the entire time, completely cut off from the normal activities of the *Yuhl/Goel*. He couldn't help but be curious as to what he'd missed out on in that time.

His curiosity was matched, though, by a need to keep what he had done secret.

"Tell me what you know," he instructed her, hiding a full-body shudder by tightening his arms around his shins. His wing sheaths stirred weakly against his back.

If she noticed his discomfort, she didn't comment on it. "I know what we *should* have found. We've searched the Library data for intelligent life-forms in the Spinner path. There aren't any listed, so we've had to search in person. That's a lot of systems, but we've been as methodical as we can. We haven't picked up any ftl signals from the Gifts, and we haven't detected any—" She hesitated. "What do you call them?"

"*E'athra/kilar*," he supplied, working both his throats together.

She nodded. "That's it. One of your clastic-slash-scientists told us before we left that the Spinners leave beacons where they can't find intelligent life, hoping to lead civilizations across the gulfs toward each other. But they haven't done it this time. There's nothing. You know it, and we know it. Why the silence?"

He didn't know, but he could guess. "To my knowledge, this has never happened before. Therefore the Fit will be cautious before saying anything premature."

"Anything at all would be good. We're supposed to be *partners*," she protested. "They don't have to be cautious around us. Not about sharing data, anyway. We're humanity-slash-Goel now, aren't we? What are they afraid of?"

Change, he thought. *That's what they're afraid of!* Bad enough that they had new allies who had already proven to be unreliable. Bad enough, too, that the *Yuhl/Goel* had split in two. Attacking the Ambivalence had shocked many. Now that the forward, beneficiary front had failed to materialize, that would be taken as a sign that they had fallen out of favor with their dual gods.

Did the Praxis know this, he wondered, *when he chose me for his mission?*

"Why did you come to see me?" he said, turning from his reflection. "Why me? What is it you expect me to do?"

She seemed surprised that he should ask this. "Because you were *envoy/catechist*—"

"I no longer fulfill that function," he interrupted immediately.

"Yes, but you understand us better than the others. The Praxis changed you like he changed Alander. You've been designed to stand between our people and help us work together."

I once was, he thought. He wasn't entirely sure what his purpose was now. "If I understand you better," he said voicing the troubling notion that simmered beneath his thoughts, "does that mean I understand my people less?"

She shook her head. "You're still conjugator."

"Yes and I have duties to perform that bear no direct relation to the Ambivalence. What I am not required to know, *Caryl/ Hatzis,* I am not told."

"But surely you could ask and . . . ?" She trailed off in the face of his hopeless expression. He could see it reflected in her eyes. The stark black and white lines were a sharp contrast to her swollen, rounded curves.

If I took off my mask, is that *the sort of face I'd see?*

"You still haven't told me why you came to me," he said.

She frowned at this. "I thought I just did—"

"No," he cut in. "Why *you* specifically, and not one of the others."

She blinked wide, watery eyes. "I'm Yu-qiang, the only Hatzis in the mission. I'm not in charge, but I'd like to make sure everything runs smoothly."

"Your original told you to do this?"

"She didn't need to."

He nodded. The thing inside him wobbled on its axis, causing him to clutch himself even tighter.

"I wouldn't have bothered you," she said, looking at him with some concern, "except no one else will talk to us. Even the Praxis has gone quiet. If there's something wrong, I think we have a right to know."

"Very well," he said, wanting simply to be rid of her. "I will try, but I may not be successful. I am . . . distracted at the moment."

"Are you sick?"

"No."

"Are you—?" She hesitated, then forged on. "Are you *pregnant?*"

He barked a dissonant laugh, both throats ululating across slightly different pitches. The bitterness and scorn it carried was probably lost on human ears. "No, I am not pregnant. It is not the time."

"I'm sorry; that must have seemed a stupid question." Curiosity replaced the uncertainty in her eyes. "This is something we know very little about in regards to your race. We know you have the term bearer-slash-favored, but we don't really know what it means. Alander thought you might be bisexual and mate in triplets, but . . ." Her sentence ended in silence and a shrug.

She was clearly hoping he would enlighten her. "I'm sorry, Yu-qiang. I must ask you to leave, now."

"Of course," she said, backing reluctantly away. The door sighed open behind her. "Thank you, Ueh. We'd be grateful for anything you can find out."

He nodded again as she left. When she was gone, he was able to address the intense physical discomfort he felt as a result of the thing squirming in his belly. The muscles of his major abdominal chamber were spasming, flinching inside him. He opened his mouth as wide as it would go, but instead of a moan, three jets of black blood burst from within and splattered across the floor.

He cleaned himself up best he could and shuffled painfully to a private data access point. People stared at him but said nothing. He felt like a *prophet/pariah*: honored and rejected at the same time; feared and respected in equal measures. He felt his expression shifting and swirling in strange, chaotic patterns.

He literally collapsed when he reached the access point. Slithering, holding his guts in with one hand, he barely managed to haul himself into the chair. Exhausted, he let himself slump into its embrace, barely able to sit upright.

"I am Conjugator *Ueh/Ellil*," he told the access point.

"I know," said the smooth voice of the Praxis.

Ueh suppressed a shudder. He had expected an AI: safe, distant, uncomplicated. "You are here to answer my questions?"

"That depends on what you want to know, Ueh."

"I want to know where we are." That wasn't the first thing that came to mind, but it was what he'd gone there for.

"*Mantissa A* is in parking orbit around the star the humans call Alkaid. We have been here for a full cycle."

"What of the Spinners? Have we located the front?"

"Spinners?" The Praxis chuckled throatily. "You speak like a human, Ueh."

"You remade me that way, remember?" The discomfort gave his tone a disrespectful edge, but he didn't care.

"The Spinner front has not yet been located."

"What of *e'athra/kilar*?"

"None has been found as yet."

"What does this mean?"

"I do not know, Ueh." The Praxis spoke like an indulgent guardian, playing a game he saw through easily and wasn't terribly interested in. His amusement lay in observing the one he was playing against. "There is much speculation among the *Yuhl/Goel*, though. Some of the Fit believe that the Ambivalence has changed course, and we simply have yet to notice."

"But that would mean an enormous deviation, unlike anything we have ever seen before."

"Exactly. But it's still a possibility. Others naturally feel that they have incurred the wrath of the Ambivalence by taking part in the Battle of Beid. The fact that the gifts continued to arrive in human space after then makes no difference to them. Theirs is the voice of irrational fear."

"And what do the *rational* voices say?"

"Some say that we should wait to see what happens. The search continues apace. There are many systems to comb through, and many to revisit. The front may yet appear."

"If it doesn't?"

"A handful speculate that the Unfit have succeeded. If the

Ambivalence has been persuaded to attack itself, then the migration may have ceased. There will be no more gifts."

The ramifications of that statement were profound, and Ueh could well understand why the Fit were so reticent to discuss the matter with the humans. Salvation from destruction also meant the withdrawal of beneficence.

"What do transmissions from Surveyed Space reveal?" Ueh asked. "We are still in range, aren't we?"

"For the time being, yes. But the transmissions tell us nothing. There has been no news from the system called pi-1 Ursa Major. If nothing is heard soon, then *Mantissa A* will jump to 24 Canes Venatici."

Appropriate, Ueh thought, translating the human name of the constellation the A-type giant belonged to: *the hunting dogs . . .*

He changed the topic abruptly, as the thing inside him moved again. "What have you done to me?"

"I told you," said the Praxis. "I've given you something for the future."

"But what *is* it?" he persisted. "A seed? A spore? *What?*"

"Does it pain you?"

"Very much so."

"I am sorry, Ueh. I wish it could be otherwise." The Praxis did sound contrite. "The organ that made it is a part of me that I have not used for many thousands of years. It has grown distant, following its own imperatives. While it is true that this organ was once designed for reproduction, its issue no longer fulfills that function. I no longer reproduce. It has another purpose."

"And that purpose is?"

"To atone," said the Praxis. "You carry my Atonement within you."

"I don't understand."

"You will, soon enough—especially if events continue to unfold as they appear to be unfolding. Everything is proceeding as I both hoped it would—and feared it might."

Ueh's face took on jagged star shapes, the Yuhl equivalent of a wince, then dissolved into asymmetrical chaos.

"You will tell me no more?"

"I cannot, Ueh."

"Will you talk to the humans about the missing front?"

"It is not my function to dole out reassurances."

"That's not what they want to hear. They are *humanity/Goel* now. Surely they deserve to be taken into our confidence."

"They are *not humanity/Goel*, Ueh," the Praxis countered. "Nor can they ever be."

That surprised Ueh. "But they have joined the migration, they've *earned* the title."

"*Goel* is no mere honorific, Ueh. It once had meaning."

"I was taught that that meaning was *companion,*" he said.

"It has come to be regarded as such down the long cycles, but that is not its true meaning."

"Then what *did* it originally mean?"

But only silence followed, long and uncomfortable, made more so by the pain of Atonement in his belly. Eventually, when it became clear that the Praxis would speak no more, Ueh was forced to abandon his questioning and crawl back to his niche. Once there, he curled crouched in a tight ball, rocking back and forth in the vain hope of finding peace within himself.

2.2

THE JUDAS ALTERNATIVE

2160.9.30 Standard Mission Time
(3 September 2163 UT)

2.2.1

Lucia Benck woke bathed in the light of a new sun.

Her mind took some time to disentangle itself from the assumption that she should be dead. The last things she remembered were the Starfish coming to Rasmussen, the destruction of the *Marcus Chown* and the spindles, the deaths of Rob Singh and the others, and her desperate flight to the Dark Room. It was burned into her memory like some grim, ghastly snapshot of mortality.

But here she was, still very much alive, and most definitely somewhere other than Rasmussen. Rasmussen's sun, BSC5070 was a bright G-type star with eleven planets, whereas the system she was in now had seven worlds ranging from dense, rocky balls to vast, turbulent gas giants with impossibly fragile-looking ring systems. How she actually "saw" them, though, she didn't really understand. The knowledge was present in her mind like something she'd always known, like a memory of something familiar. And the more she thought about it, the more she came to realize that it *was* familiar—as familiar to her as her body had once been.

It was Sol System.

Something was different, though. Jupiter and Saturn and all

the outer planets were instantly recognizable, as were Mars and
Mercury. Most of the Kuiper bodies were exactly where they
should have been. The sun itself glowed a familiar blotchy
yellow, exhibiting all the sunspot activity Lucia would have
expected of neither a solar maximum nor a solar minimum.

There was, however, a huge gap between Mercury and
Mars, occupied by just one small world. It wasn't even a planet,
really. It was dead and lifeless, its surface littered with scorch
marks and newly formed craters. It took Lucia a long moment
to identify it, and she did so only by locating the site of the
old Chinese Yi Base on what had once been known as the small
world's dark side. Now all sides were dark, except for the one
facing the sun. Earthlight no longer shone on Luna, for the
Earth itself was gone.

Lucia had heard the stories from Thor and the others, but
the reality had never truly sunk in. Seeing it now with her own
eyes—or whatever it was she was seeing with—brought home
the terrible truth.

Home?

Home was gone, and would never be again. All the things
she recalled about it—her childhood in Dalarna, following the
Strzelecki Track, her selection to UNESSPRO and entrainment—it was all *gone.* As were her family and friends; as was
her original. Everything, everyone—really, truly gone.

All that remained were great clouds of dust from the massive
post-Spike construction the original Caryl Hatzis had referred
to as the Frame. The Starfish had reduced the lot back to atoms.
Not one self-replicating molecule remained to allow even a
token attempt at reconstructing her home.

Home . . .

She cautioned herself to stop thinking of it that way, for
although it would always be her point of origin, there was nothing of home about it anymore. The only artifact in the entire
system was a Yuhl grave marker in close orbit about the sun,
an almost insignificant reminder that once upon a time life had
existed here. Right now she was the only life in this dead system.

And she remained unsure, exactly, what she *was,* still.

That she remained Lucia Benck was indisputable, but her
exact *being* was unclear. She had no clear sense of a body. She

felt limbs when she moved, certainly, but they weren't remotely like her old ones. These were strange and entirely too numerous. Some of them stretched in directions that didn't exist in the real universe; others touched things that couldn't possibly be felt, like the heart of atomic nuclei, or the vacuum, rich in zero-point energy. She was like some arcane, highly evolved octopus, swimming in seas beyond comprehension.

What's happened to me?

Her voice echoed into the void, but was not answered. She felt a great emptiness settle upon her. Even tourists needed somewhere to return to—an anchor, a point of reference. But she no longer had that, and the absence of it was, in a way, far worse than losing the ability to travel.

Her attention was suddenly attracted to a disturbance in the empty system—a disturbance where just nanoseconds before there had been only inactivity. A point of light blossomed in the darkness. Feathery energy sprayed into the solar wind, causing strange ripple effects to sway and bend around it, like the corona during a total eclipse.

Recognition came with a thrill of fear. She had heard of such things. Kingsley Oborn, back on Rasmussen, had posted theories in the conSense discussion rooms concerning what he called the *fovea,* the forerunning spooks of the Starfish. Where the fovea came and saw signs of life, death soon followed.

Would this one see *her?* she wondered. She didn't know. She didn't know if she *could* be seen anymore. The last thing she remembered was pleading with the Gifts to move, and then hearing a voice. "THIS IS THE FINAL GIFT WE BRING."

What that meant, she had no idea at all. But it was the last thing she remembered, and for that reason alone it was probably significant.

The final gift . . . ?

I think it's time to get moving again, she said, feeling myriad mouths echo the words through her, broadcasting the message a thousand ways. *We've been rumbled.*

There was no answer. Unlike the last time she had called for help, there was no sense of eyes watching her, of vast intelligences lurking just beyond the edge of shadow. Now there was just her, alone but for the eye of the Starfish.

She could feel it drilling into her, dissecting her and analyzing her every detail. What was it seeing? she wondered. There was no way of knowing. But it knew she was there. Of that, at least, she was certain. And it was calling for the killers.

If you're going to do something, now would be the time, she nervously told the void, hoping that whoever had heard her pleas on Rasmussen would hear her now.

But silence again was her only response. If it had been the Gifts that had lifted her out of Rasmussen, then they hadn't really helped her at all by dumping her here in Sol System. Far from saving her, they'd just left her helpless in exactly the same situation she'd been in before. The only difference was the setting.

The fovea flickered and flared, the chaotic rhythms of its powerful glare seeming to taunt her.

Just wait a little longer, and your concerns will be over, it seemed to be saying. *Just a little longer, and we'll put you out of your misery.*

But I don't want to die! Her cry of defiance resounded through the nothingness surrounding her strange new body. *Not without knowing what I am!* If the Starfish were going to put a finish to the charade that had been her recent life, she at least wanted to see what it was they were killing.

With a small mental effort, she managed to persuade part of herself to disengage itself from "her" and leave, looking back as it did so. She wasn't entirely sure what was going on as she did this, nor even *how* she was managing to do it. Many conflicting senses vied for attention; information flowed into her in ways she had trouble understanding, let alone comprehending.

But when she saw what the sputtering fovea had noticed in the quiet ruins of Sol System—when she finally realized what she had become—she understood everything.

"THIS IS THE FINAL GIFT WE BRING."

Excitement and appreciation for her new self swept through her as she turned her attention to the fovea. It was still watching her. She wondered if it could sense her flexing her new wings.

Catch me if you can, she goaded it.

Then she disappeared from Sol System.

*   *   *

Her first jump took her back to Rasmussen, where the ruins of the gifts and the *Marcus Chown* still bloomed in infrared frequencies. Rasmussen's perfectly preserved ecosystem was in flames where orbital towers had crashed through the atmosphere and slammed into the crust. The Starfish weren't long gone, and she had no desire to attract their attention again. With the gentlest flex of her will, she moved on once more.

She was wary at first of wasting time. In the hole ships, faster-than-light travel wasn't instantaneous; a day's travel in the real universe corresponded to approximately eighty light-years, and two days' time relative to the passengers. She soon realized, however, that her new means of getting around was a *lot* faster than that. The journey from Sol to Rasmussen took barely an hour, real time. This alone was enough to dispel any lingering doubts she may have had as to the veracity of where she now found herself. Not that this made her situation any less incredible.

The mind that had spoken to her before the Starfish had destroyed Rasmussen was gone. All she had with her now were smaller subroutines and underlings designed to facilitate her will. She was barely aware of them, unless she really dug deep.

She worked outward from Sol, looking for survivors, tracing the terrible wake of the Starfish, and seeing for herself what they'd done. Groombridge 1830, lambda Auriga, Theta Perseus, and many, many others were all barren of life. The last segment of humanity's bold exploration of the space around its home was dwindling, almost vanishing as she watched.

An impulse took her to iota Boötis, where the colony had been called Candamius in honor of its rugged mountains. The Can, as she'd heard some of the colonists refer to it, had been a harsh world, not dissimilar to Peter's old home of Adrasteia, but people had lived and worked there for many years, nonetheless. The human compulsion to explore and make familiar, to *own,* had taken root there as firmly as anywhere else. And from there, too, it had been expunged just as ruthlessly as with every other colony.

A terrible fatalism swept over her then. *What is the point?* she thought. The Starfish were indefatigable. Whether the engrams stayed behind or ran, the Starfish would catch up with them eventually. There was no hope, no future. The history of humanity had come to an abrupt end—something that not even the terrors of the Spike had managed to achieve.

But she couldn't let go. Although theoretically she could have run at any time, she felt a kinship with the survivors. She had been plucked from death at the last moment; what they were facing, she had somehow endured—if only by being in the right place at the right time. She would rather ascribe her continued existence to luck than to any special quality within her. And even if it *was* just dumb luck, she couldn't walk away from it. It felt as though she should make it mean something.

She was supposed to be a tourist, but every tourist needed a home to return to, or else what was the point? Similarly, she was supposed to want to be with Peter, despite her decision to explore the universe without him. How could that definition of herself survive his rejection of her? She needed new definitions now, and she needed to find a way to write them into her old overseer. To do that, she needed other people; she needed alternatives.

The only alternatives open at the moment remained in the Alkaid Group, probably the last human-occupied systems left in all of Surveyed Space. Rasmussen was gone, but it was the closest of the five. The other four had two or three days left before the Starfish would reach them. She knew the order of them, as did anyone who had been on Rasmussen. After BSC5070 came BSC5423 and Zemyna, then HD132142 and Demeter. They were the next two in the firing line. After them came BSC5581 and Geb; then, last of all, BSC5148 and Sagarsee. Familiar names with familiar fates awaiting them. If she could replicate her success and offer them a way out of their predicament, perhaps they could help her find peace of mind.

With this thought, she jumped straight to Sagarsee, translating without effort into a polar orbit around its seething atmosphere, rich in protolife. She was scanned instantly upon arrival and felt alarms go off all around her. The colonists, having heard about Rasmussen, were understandably jumpy and regarded any unexpected arrival as a potential threat. The fact that she looked so familiar didn't ease their concerns.

Some of Lucia's new limbs reached easily into the command systems of the colony's survey ship, the *Frank Drake,* and shut off the alarms. With the sirens silent, a clamor of voices rose around her, wanting to know what she was and what she was doing there. She could understand their confusion; she didn't fully comprehend how she had come to be this way either.

Hole ships flickered in and out of real space around her, probing her, testing her defenses. She effortlessly kept them at bay as she pondered the best way to introduce herself. There were no easy options. Through their senses, she could see what she looked like to them: half a kilometer long, shaped roughly like a cylinder tapering at both ends, with tiny dimples and indentations dotted seemingly at random across her surface. She was gold in color, and an identical twin to another in geosynchronous orbit around the planet below.

She was Spindle Ten, the Dark Room. She was the final gift the Spinners had left for humanity.

2.2.2

An argument filled the cockpit of Eledone. *This was nothing* new, and Alander might have been tempted to switch himself off to it, slow down his clock rate until it was resolved and everyone could move on, had it not been for two important facts. The first was that there was too much to see: In the background, Cleo Samson was guiding the hole ship along the path given to them by the demolition crew, and the scenery was just incredible. The second was that the argument taking place wasn't among the usual suspects; it involved all four Hatzises, and that's what made it so compelling. Axford obviously agreed, as he sat off to one side, watching with a look of supreme satisfaction on his face.

"There are no obvious command structures and no clear lines of communication," Gou Mang was saying heatedly. "How the fuck are we going to talk to someone in charge if we can't even *find* them?"

"We've just been looking in the wrong places, that's all," Thor responded. Her expression looked haggard to Alander; beneath her anger lurked deep exhaustion. She was starting to show the pressure they'd all been under since the mission began.

"I don't think you truly comprehend the scale of what we're trying to do here, Thor," said Inari. "We're like microbes trying to flag down a fucking *whale!*"

"She's right," said Gou Mang. "We're never going to get them to notice us."

"Not like this, we won't, no," Thor agreed.

"Then why have you got us banging our heads against this brick wall? You're just going to get us all killed!"

"At least we will have died trying!" Thor glared at Gou Mang and Inari, livid at them for defying her. "But we are *not* going back until we've explored every option. I won't allow it."

"You won't *allow* it?" Gou Mang echoed. "And what gives you the right to make decisions that affect the rest of us?"

"You did, actually," said Thor evenly, "when you volunteered."

"None of us volunteered for a suicide mission," said Inari. "We came along because we believed we had a chance!"

"Which we still do."

"Not if you continue the way you're going."

Thor opened her mouth to speak, but then shut it again, biting down on her retort. She didn't have to say a word for Alander to know what she was thinking; it was right there in her eyes. She felt betrayal at the way her command had been questioned and fear that it had been so openly challenged. She might not call it fear but that was what it was. She had been fighting fear of substitution ever since Rasmussen, with her obvious successor only meters away from where she was now standing.

"I don't see what else Thor could have done," said Sol. Had Alander been in physical contact with her, he would have urged her to remain quiet, to let the others sort it out without her input. But then, silence wasn't the Hatzis way, as was evidenced by this ongoing debate.

"We knew before we went in that it was unlikely we'd succeed," Sol continued, addressing both Inari and Gou Mang. "I don't think you're being fair to Thor by recanting now."

"Things have changed," said Gou Mang. Sol's former second-in-command stared at her with uneasy defiance. "When we knew nothing, it was easy to imagine that we had a chance of succeeding. But we know more than we did back then! Continuing on now when we know what we're up against is both futile and counterproductive."

Inari nodded in agreement. "The only way we can make this mission count for anything is to return to the others and convey what we've learned."

"And what *have* we learned?" Thor asked. "That we found a couple of warring factions of other aliens existing within the cutter? What could they do with that?"

"They could decide to join them," said Gou Mang. "We could decide to find a niche of our own in a cutter just like the *A/kak/a/riil* and the Pllix did."

Thor shook her head as she laughed. "Just like that? We hitch a ride and everything will be fine?"

Gou Mang shrugged. "It's a possibility, at least. One that the others should be made aware of."

"And what do you think the others have been doing since we've been gone?" said Sol. "Sitting on their hands doing nothing?" She shook her head. "The Unfit will be looking for alternatives, in case we don't return. They might even attempt to send other missions to try to contact the Starfish. I don't think we should consider going back until we are absolutely certain that success is not possible. At least this way we save others the anguish and frustration of trying." She glanced at Thor, to all appearances wary of undermining the other's authority. "That's just my opinion, anyway."

Thor nodded slowly with weary gratitude. "We keep going. That's my *decision.*"

Gou Mang shook her head. "You're going to get us all killed, Thor. The Starfish may be the ones holding the gun, but you're the one hell-bent on pressing our heads against the barrel."

Gou Mang's normally olive skin was pale and blotchy, and Alander realized that she was terrified. Not that he could blame her. They'd seen nothing since the battle between the *A/kak/a/ riil* and the Pllix that could remotely be described as reassuring. The swathe of destruction left by the demolition crew in the vast body of the cutter led through chambers more enormous than anything humanity had ever managed to build. Roiling energies still surged through the chambers, pouring out of the ragged mouths of severed veins, but the closer to the exterior they moved, the more noticeably quiescent the craft became. They passed through layers of structural material, folded silver sheets stacked in layers dozens deep, shot through with bright blue threads as wide as tree trunks. Bundles of fibers that looked like optical information conduits—but which probably served a very different purpose—spewed forth washes of multicolored light where they'd been roughly severed. The charcoal remains of angular Pllix vessels could be seen everywhere *Eledone* passed. Perhaps as a result of the governors' destruction by the demolition crews, the hole ship wasn't challenged or intercepted again. As the *A/kak/a/riil* had promised, the way was clear.

But that still didn't make it easy. There were frequent hazards: dead ends where punctured chambers had begun to collapse; rivers of energy that even *Eledone* had to skirt, weird ripples in space-time that swept through the ruins as incomprehensible field effects failed. The last came and went like ghosts in a digital image, and were all the more startling for it. Thus far none had come too close. Alander was glad not to know what effects they might have on the damaged hole ship.

"Your point is moot, anyway," said Axford 1313, standing to address Gou Mang. "We don't have the means to go anywhere at the moment. We're stuck here whether we like it or not."

"That doesn't mean we can't at least *try* to find a way." Grim defiance carved her mouth into a sharp line. "We could hitch a ride with another cutter, perhaps, or convince the *A/kak/a/riil* to repair us."

Axford dismissed her comment with a self-righteous smirk and a shake of the head. "What makes you think we could succeed where others before us have clearly failed? They've kept to themselves for God only knows how many millennia; they're clearly not interested in being contacted."

"The Praxis knew about them," said Inari, glancing at Alander.

"All the Praxis knew," Axford said, "or thought he knew, was that the *A/kak/a/riil* had been destroyed by the Starfish. He obviously didn't know they'd survived; otherwise he would have mentioned them—right, Peter?"

Alander shrugged but didn't say anything. The fact that the Praxis had invaded his memories as well as his mind and body still unnerved him. There had been no subsequent revelations since his conversation with the *A/kak/a/riil*, and he had consoled himself with the thought that there might be no more until something in his environment triggered a match in the data he had been given. But just because he had been granted access to certain information didn't automatically make him an expert on what the Praxis did or didn't know.

What other surprises lurked inside him was of greater concern.

"This is the kind of knowledge that could come in handy for the others," Gou Mang insisted. "They should be told about it!"

A small silence filled the cockpit as Samson continued to navigate through the ravaged interior of the cutter.

"That, at least, I will concede is a valid point," said Thor after some thought. "But I'm still not prepared to give up on this mission just yet. While we look for some way to speak to the Starfish, we'll also look for a way to get back. That way, if the former fails, we can still have a shot at the latter. Is that an acceptable compromise, Gou Mang? Inari?"

The two nodded reluctantly, although Gou Mang was clearly not convinced. She might know when an argument was lost, but she was also a Hatzis. Alander had no doubt that the issue would surface again. He'd known Caryl Hatzis long enough to know that an argument was never lost completely, only temporarily.

"How close are we to the outside?" Alander asked Samson, filling the tense quiet.

"At this rate," she replied, "we should reach our destination in about one hour."

"Right, then I'm going to shut down for half an hour," said Thor. "Gou Mang, you're in charge until I wake up."

Gou Mang looked surprised at the request, but accepted the responsibility with a nod.

Sol came over to sit beside Alander, touching palms so that she could speak to him in private.

Clever, don't you think? she said. *Conceding command to Gou Mang doesn't give her anything, but it allows her to save face. I would have done the same thing, I think.*

Would you have pulled the plug on her if she'd decided to go back? he shot back.

I'm not sure. It would've been more interesting to see what Frank would do first. There's a whole heap of stuff he's not telling us—stuff I'm very keen to learn more about.

When do you intend to do that?

When everything is a little more quiet, perhaps. Or more dangerous still than it has been.

Alander looked over to Thor. *Do you think she's really shut down?*

Yeah, she's out, all right. Gone into fast mode to get as many z's as she can.

Alander nodded. *That's not a bad idea at the moment. We've no idea what we're going to find on the outside of this thing.* He was trying not to think that far ahead, but it was hard not to dwell on it. If the *A/kak/a/riil* had adapted into demolition crews designed to take damaged cutters apart, who were they working for? The Starfish themselves, or someone else higher on the ladder?

He assumed that they were about to find out and was unsure how he felt about it. When he thought about the possible roads the mission could take, he kept getting stuck on a terrible vision of them following a chain from species to species in a vain hope of finding one that might offer them a direct link to the Starfish, until one day a thousand years from now another species would stumble upon them, and they would have found their own niche in the world of the cutters, perhaps becoming a race known to others as the Seekers or something similar.

And what if there were no Starfish to find, anyway? What if the aliens had died out eons ago, and the destructive fleet they were exploring was advancing purely on momentum— machines programmed by designers long since extinct, inhabited by parasites, and now impossible to shut down?

Time would tell, he supposed—time that was passing all too quickly. If they didn't find an answer soon, it would be too late to make a difference in Surveyed Space, and what happened to *Eledone* and its crew would be irrelevant.

Sol withdrew her hand from his, perhaps sensing that he wasn't in the mood to talk. He felt disappointment for a moment, having taken some comfort from the physical contact, if nothing else, but didn't move to reclaim it. Whatever their relationship had been or was, just then was undoubtedly the wrong time to test its boundaries.

Alone in his mind, Alander settled back to sit out the hour in silence.

Eledone *passed through a region crowded with structures that* looked like purple stalactites and stalagmites. Giant interlocking cones stretched from floor to ceiling and back again, culminating in tapered, perfectly geometric tips. The tips of stalactites and stalagmites didn't match, however, so the peak of one formation pressed into the trough of another. To Sol, *Eledone* seemed like a bread crumb gliding through the teeth of unimaginably large beasts.

"There's less damage here than in previous regions," Alander noted.

Sol nodded in silent agreement. There was still the occasional molten blister bulging from the otherwise seamless surfaces, and even a few long, curling scars where energy weapons had been discharged, but they were indeed fewer in number than she'd seen in other areas. There was none of the roiling turbulence of the veins, either. Clearly, as they neared the outer layers of the giant vessel, the environment was becoming increasingly calmer.

"Check that out," said Axford, coming to stand beside her in the center of the cockpit.

Sol looked to where Axford was pointing. It was a dark patch off to one side. "It looks like an impact site," she said.

Axford nodded. "And it looks old, too—not fresh."

Inari came up alongside them also. "Which means what, exactly?"

"Even ships this advanced would have to get hit by space junk now and then," explained Sol. "If that is the site of such a collision, it means we really are getting closer to the outside."

She knew no more about their environment than any of the others, but the notion was a reassuring one, anyway, and she found herself embracing the hope, *wanting* it to be true. As to what they might find outside when they reached it, she had no idea. It could very well be a case of flying out of the frying pan and into the fires of hell.

They had passed through sections of the ship where giant portions appeared to have been sheared away and removed. Vast reefs of detritus marked their passing, but there was no indication of who had done the actual work. She didn't know if the A/kak/a/riil or some other, as yet unidentified niche dweller was responsible.

She was beginning to think of the cutter as less an animal and more a kind of cell. It was roughly the right shape, for starters, and lacked many of the things she would normally associate with an independent creature. The thought that various alien races might be absorbed into its functions was not so peculiar, given that her cells had absorbed other creatures during their evolution in order to function more efficiently. Whether it was gut flora or mitochondria, the absorption of the lesser into a greater whole seemed to be a biological paradigm.

She was certain, however, that she didn't want to be absorbed. Even in Sol, before the Starfish came, when she had been just part of the much larger mind that was Caryl Hatzis, she'd had a clear sense of her own identity, as a separate, independent being. Did the Pllix have that? she wondered. Or the A/kak/a/riif? She didn't want to find out the hard way that they were in fact slaves to the Starfish overmind—if such a thing existed.

"You really *are* keeping a low profile these days, aren't you, Caryl?" said Axford, looking sidelong at her. "Still, it was nice to see you back in the thick of things earlier. Just because Thor can manage on her own doesn't mean she should have to do it all the time."

She turned to face him and held for a beat, watching him. He looked back at her with a faintly amused expression in his eyes.

"Tell me, Frank," she said, ignoring his unsubtle stab at small talk. "How *were* you intending to get us out of the hole ship earlier? You never did explain."

"Because there was no need to," he said.

"Surely we have a right to know just what our resources are," she said. "What if something were to happen to you and—?"

"If something happens to me, then my hidden capacity is irrelevant, no?"

"Not to us, not necessarily. We might still be able to use it, so you should tell us. This is supposed to be a team effort." When he didn't respond, she pushed a little harder. "Come on, Frank. What is it? Are you packed full of antimatter explosives or something?"

He tilted his head to one side for an instant, then straightened again. "That's not it, Caryl."

"You could be lying."

"I doubt you'd believe me if I said I wasn't. In fact, were I to be completely honest, you'd still have your doubts. So, frankly, I don't see the point." Axford tapped his forehead gently. "My secret is staying right here until I'm ready to reveal it."

"Fine." She sighed with genuine frustration. What with Axford's hidden secrets and Alander's strange Praxis-given memories, it seemed like everyone had something to hide. "You win. But this isn't supposed to be a competition. Not between us."

He laughed. "That's exactly what it is, Caryl. That's what it will always be. You and I will never be able to comfortably cohabit. Trust me."

The bluntness of his words, and the apparent cheerfulness with which they were delivered, sent a chill down her spine. "Perhaps we won't need to," she said after a moment. "It's a big galaxy, after all."

"A galaxy that I intend to own one day."

"*Own*, Frank? Is that a threat?"

He shook his head. "No threat, Caryl. I'm simply telling you as I see it. And you of all people should be able to appreciate what I'm saying. That's what makes you simultaneously my chief competitor and my chief ally. We both know that the engrams are just a step up the ladder. It's what lies at the *top* of the ladder that is the prize. Together or apart, we might just get there one day."

They were speaking softly now, less by speech than by coded sounds too soft for the others to hear.

"I'd say the Starfish might have something to say about that."

"And perhaps this is what it's all about—all the destruction and hope dashing. The Spinners or their servants are blindly going about their uplift program while the Starfish blithely knock everyone back down again. Maybe there's simply no more room at the top. Maybe the Starfish are among the uplifted who don't want to share what they have. Who knows?"

"If that's the case," she said, "then what's the point of fighting?"

"Because this is our first test, Caryl. If and when we pass it, we'll be able to move on to the second test. And make no mistake, there *will* be a second test. It's only taken a few thousand years for the first test to stumble across us; think how quickly we might stumble across the next threat when we actually head out into the stars looking."

"You make it sound like we're in college or something."

He shook his head firmly. "Far from it, Caryl. This is evolution, red in tooth and claw. The Yuhl didn't pass the test; they're stuck in their Pax Praxis forever, unable to migrate or change. The Pllix and the *A/kak/a/riil* didn't pass the test, either; they're clinging like limpets to the underbellies of the Starfish pest controllers. If we are to survive, then we must be better than them. If we are to go up another rung in the great evolutionary ladder, then we're going to have to fight back with all our heart and willpower."

She thought about this for a moment, staring at the screens that depicted the almost dreamlike environment that they were navigating through. Then: "Tell me, Frank: what do *you* think is at the top of that ladder?"

He smiled at this and shrugged lightly. "I have absolutely no idea, Caryl. How could I? Does an ant about to be crushed underfoot have any concept of what a human foot might look like, let alone the entire being? We simply don't have the mental capacity to *imagine* what we might find there at the top."

"But that doesn't stop you from wanting to get there, does it?"

"Nor does it stop me from looking for allies to help me get there."

"You've got a strange way of going about it," she said.

"It doesn't come naturally. That I'll admit." He smiled, and for a brief moment some of his intensity seemed to boil off. "It might only be the fact that I've been abandoned here by the others—by the versions of me who've taken their chances with the Praxis—but at this point in time, anything is looking good. Even this motley bunch."

"But you're still not prepared to tell us what the ace up your sleeve is?"

A short, definite shake of the head. "A guy's gotta have some secrets, Caryl."

On the screens, the dense thicket of interlocked cones had thinned, opening up to form a wide, domed space that reminded Sol vaguely of the pocket immediately behind the cornea of a human eye. *Eledone* reported that they had entered a region of relatively clean vacuum, with low particle counts and very little stray energy.

"There must be a hull breach nearby," said Samson hopefully.

Thor stirred at this, quickly standing and alert. "We've found the way out?"

"It's possible," said Alander.

"This is your last chance to change your mind," Axford said to Thor.

"I'm aware of that." Thor didn't look as though the rest had moved her even remotely to changing her mind. Bald and lean, with a hungry look that Sol's other engrams lacked, her attention was firmly focused on the information displayed on the screens before her. "What's that up there?" she asked, pointing.

Eledone zoomed the view to reveal a twinkling point high on the giant cornea's ceiling. "I am detecting a scattering of laser light at that point," announced the AI.

"It looks like a tear to me," said Thor. "Head for it as discreetly as you can, Cleo. I know we're going to stand out in here, no matter what we do, but I think we can minimize the disturbance. Not too many g's; don't aim straight for it, bring us in on a wide spiral—whatever it takes. I'll leave the finer details up to you."

Samson gripped the command stalk, and *Eledone* swept off on an entirely new course. The twinkling point of light quickly resolved into a jagged line—a tear, just as Thor had proposed. As they drew nearer, Sol made out black points crawling and hopping along its inside edges. They became sharply defined, rounded shapes, like helmets with multiple legs. Whatever they were, they were clearly in the process of widening the tear, and they were doing so with both speed and ease. As each chunk of the translucent retinal material fell away, they scooped it up and stored it under their carapaces, opening winglike shells to expose cargo bays beneath.

Like black ladybugs, she thought. Only these ladybugs were equipped with cutting lasers and reactionless thrusters.

As *Eledone* approached in a lazy, nonthreatening arc, the black bugs scattered with lasers flashing, gathering a moment later at the other end of the tear.

"I am receiving a complex repeated signal," said *Eledone*. "The cypher employed is not one with which I am familiar."

Thor turned immediately to Alander. "Peter? Do you recognize these things?"

He glanced away from the screen to face Thor. "Nothing's coming to me," he said. "Sorry."

She sighed. "So starting up a conversation with them is obviously out of the question."

"At least they're not overtly hostile," put in Gou Mang. "Which makes a nice change."

The bugs appeared to be making a pyramid out of themselves as *Eledone* drew closer.

"Hey, look!" said Inari. "I can see stars through the tear!"

Sol peered closer at the image she indicated. There did indeed seem to be stars visible between to ragged lips of the tear, but they were shimmering as though viewed through exceedingly hot air. What was causing the effect, she couldn't tell. There might have been a field effect of some kind surrounding the breach, an antidepressurization system that had come into effect too late to save this area from evacuation. Or perhaps atmosphere boiling from the breached cutter had crystallized in the vacuum, clouding the view.

"Whatever they are, I don't think there's any point worrying about the bugs anymore," Thor said, watching the way they scrambled to link limbs and carapaces. It appeared as though they were trying to build a small, thick wall to keep the *Eledone* at bay. *Making themselves look larger,* Sol speculated. *Making themselves more threatening than they really are.*

"I say we go for it," Thor said.

"Once more into the breach, eh?" said Axford, grinning.

"Something like that," said Thor. "Take us through, Cleo."

Samson straightened *Eledone*'s course and accelerated for the stars. The bugs reacted instantly, flexing their stubby black legs and causing the wall to contract into a solid structure. A squat bug squeezed out of the middle, its forelegs raised high. Blue sparks crawled across gleaming carapaces, tickling antenna and glinting eyes.

This doesn't look good, Sol thought.

Barely had she finished the thought when a bright flash filled the screen, followed a split second later by *Eledone* bouncing in midflight.

"Eledone? What the fuck—?"

Another flash cut Thor off in midquestion. Sol felt Alander's hand grip her shoulder, steadying himself against the resulting disturbance. The source of the attack was clearly the central bug in the combined alien assembly. Its forelegs spat densely woven bullets of energy that were powerful enough to make even the hole ship think twice.

"I am sustaining damage," *Eledone* announced in a deadpan tone.

"Can we ride it out?" Thor asked as a third bolt blinded all the screens simultaneously. When they cleared, the distance between the tear and their former location had halved.

"There is a chance that we can get through intact," said Samson.

"But there's also a chance we won't," said Axford, bracing himself against a wall as the hole ship rocked again beneath another attack.

"Just do your best, Cleo!" Thor called out with a grimace. "Everyone else, hang on!"

The bugs spat again. The intensity of each shot increased as the distance separating them decreased. Sol fell to her knees on the fifth, and thick webs of energy filled the air as *Eledone*'s less subtle safety measures came into effect. She could move only in slow motion, as though caught in gel.

Her eyes stayed fixed on the screens as the bugs fired again. The distance between them was shrinking rapidly, as evidenced by how violently the cockpit shook. There was time for maybe two more shots before they reached the tear. Alien faces molded out of gleaming black shells glared alarmingly at them from the screens.

"Almost there!" groaned Thor through the anti-impact field. The team members were liberally scattered through the cockpit now, some touching the ground, some suspended in midair. Sol had just enough time to think how ridiculous they must have looked when the final shot hit, and every screen around them went white.

There was a moment of disconnection as *Eledone* rocketed through the tear with considerable momentum, flashing past the bugs and through any field effects that might have tried to impede them. Sol was frozen, unable to move and helpless to assist in any way. The hole ship was flying blind, the last shot having left its instruments dead. She could only pray that the effect was temporary.

Soon the anti-impact field eased enough for Sol to turn her head and look at Thor.

"Eledone," Thor ground out through clenched teeth. "Report!"

"I have sustained damage," replied the AI, its voice more wooden than normal. "Repairs are under way."

"How long until we can see again?"

"Ten seconds."

Sol anxiously counted them down, living ten seconds for every one. It seemed to take forever, but at the end of it, *Eledone* was as good as its word, and the screens flickered back to life.

Sol strained against the anti-impact field, not immediately comprehending exactly what she was seeing. Images in numerous frequencies conveyed strange, contradictory impressions that, when combined, made her dizzy. There was something that looked like a planet; at least, it was as big as two Earths combined, but in some frequencies it was riddled with holes, and in others it seemed to balloon outward in a massive torus. Tapering filaments stretched across the sky, which was rippling just as it had been when glimpsed through the tear.

Camouflage, Sol thought, wondering what the effect looked like from the outside.

A shape reminiscent of the Trident hung superimposed

across the rippling starscape, lit from below, with streams of ships flowing to and from it. Three more of the giant vessels were visible in the distance; one appeared to be hunchbacked, sporting two extra horns or tines midway along its spine. There were other things Sol couldn't immediately identify: a blowing plasma bubble that oscillated every two or three seconds, sprouting numerous thin, elongated arms that whipped out to touch passing vessels; a net of stressed space-time that filled the bubble of space contained by the camouflage field, giving the vacuum a wavy, gridlike aspect unlike anything she'd seen before in the natural universe; a liberal dusting of hyperdense objects that darted to and fro under impossible accelerations; a distant point of light that looked like an artificial star sending vast, looping magnetic field lines across everything.

Like a God bestowing benedictions, she thought with a shudder.

It looked like chaos to Sol, but she knew instinctively that this wasn't the case. It was just beyond her understanding. She had no doubt that she was seeing just the tip of the iceberg, and that there was much more taking place out there that she wasn't able to see. That she was seeing the Starfish fleet itself she could only hope was the case, because if this wasn't it, then the scale of the actual thing would have been something a mere human could never hope to grasp.

What astonished her more than anything, though, was the fact that this fleet must have been moving every day or so to keep up with the front. Her mind boggled at the thought of the energy that such a maneuver would take.

Alander was studying the view behind them. The cutter was floating alone in space, disconnected from the siblings who had brought it home. It had puffed up and split radially in numerous places, bursting like an overripe mango. Energy and matter poured through the splits, sucked or propelled outward by shepherding points of light that were, Sol assumed, yet another species caught in the Starfish biosphere. The intensity of their industry appalled and amazed her. An undertaking like this would have taken even the Vincula months to accomplish; here, the Starfish scavengers were taking the cutter apart in just days. What they would do with the raw materials when it was gone, there was no way of telling—and she hoped Thor wasn't thinking of sticking around to find out. She didn't want *Eledone* to be mistaken for a floating piece of space junk and recycled.

"What now?" asked Gou Mang as the cutter was left behind them and the anti-impact field receded.

Thor tore her eyes away from the screens. "Now we try to find someone in charge."

"And hope we don't fall foul of the local security forces," said Axford.

"Any idea how we do that?" asked Gou Mang.

Thor shrugged as she looked around at everyone in the cockpit. "All suggestions are welcome."

"I still say we should try to get back to Rasmussen," said Inari.

"Yes, well, until we stumble across a working ftl drive, then I'm afraid that idea will have to go on the back burner." Thor cast a dismissive glance at Inari. "Anything else?"

"First things first," said Sol. "If we're going to try to speak to the Starfish, then we're going to need to find some sort of command nexus or communications conduit. If we can tap into either of those without getting ourselves killed—"

"Too late for that," said Axford, nodding at one of the screens.

Sol turned to see what he was looking at. At first she couldn't see anything out of the ordinary, but then she caught it: a black shadow sliding across the stars—a gnarled branch of something much larger, looming hard over the hole ship.

"Cleo, get us out of here!"

Samson obeyed Thor instantly, twisting the control stalk and sending the hole ship away from the shadow, hard and fast on an invisible wake of energy.

The shadow responded equally fast. Clutching branches twisted across the rippling stars, expanding and stretching to engulf the sky. Sol felt like a mosquito about to be swatted by a giant hand as the branches edged closer, blocking the view of the Starfish fleet. Blackness swallowed them—complete on all frequencies.

"Are we still moving?" asked Thor, staring numbly at the black screens.

"We appear to be," Samson answered, but her face was a tangle of conflicting emotions. Clearly she wasn't sure.

"*Eledone*, I want you to broadcast the following message on all frequencies, including ftl," said Thor. Her lips were white. "This is Caryl Hatzis of the United Near-Earth Stellar Survey Program Mission 154, *S. V. Krasnikov*, to HD92719. I am the leader of a diplomatic mission to the race we refer to as the Starfish. We have tactical information for you regarding the people you're following. They're hiding in a system among the ones we have surveyed. If you are prepared to speak with us, we will give you this information. All we ask is that you stop killing our people! Please respond!"

"Message sent," *Eledone* said.

"Do you really think that will do it?" asked Gou Mang.

Thor's eyes didn't leave the blackness filling the displays. "I have no idea," she said. "But what else can we do?"

"There's something coming," said Inari. A screen zoomed to show a thin sliver of white moving at an incredible speed and headed straight for them. Within a matter of seconds, the sliver had grown impossibly large on the screen.

Thor spun around to face Samson. "Cleo, what—?"

But that was all she got to say as the hole ship lurched beneath them, throwing them into the air. The anti-impact field caught them and held them suspended above the floor.

"I am sustaining damage," said *Eledone* unnecessarily as, with a scream of energies, something long, perfectly straight, and gleaming silver stabbed through the cockpit wall and skewered Thor right between the eyes.

2.2.3

Lucia walked among the engrams as an angel would among mortals. And yet, even in the seemingly magical garment of her I-body, she felt flawed, fragile. The limitations of her mind were severe. Until she escaped the confines of her engram, and of her original, she would never be free.

I feel more like a golem than an angel, she thought. *A creature of dust and clay, animated by words alone.*

There was little time for introspection, however. She had four colonies to save, the last four in Surveyed Space: Zemyna, Demeter, Geb, and Sagarsee, due for extinction in that order.

"You're asking us to leave everything we've built here and take a chance on you," said Vince Mohler, civilian supervisor of the *James J. Funaro,* the mission sent to Zemyna. "It's a big ask."

"It's either that or die," countered Ali Genovese, military supervisor from Demeter.

"I know, but—" Ali's civilian counterpart, Owen Norsworthy, sought the words to express his confusion. "It just seems so *wrong.*"

"It runs counter to programming." Lucia said, stating the truth bluntly. All the mission supervisors had dedication to their missions programmed into them. They were bound by a powerful and partly artificial sense of duty to ensure that the missions ran according to the rules. That meant not abandoning them until a threat was clear and unavoidable and not even the certain knowledge of the destruction of every other colony was enough to satisfy those constraints. Until the Starfish actually appeared and began reducing the gifts to rubble, the mission supervisors were bound by their programming to try to keep things running as they had to date.

She had only noticed this on convening the meeting of the surviving mission supervisors. Earlier, after the mass gathering in Rasmussen, she had wondered how Sol had managed to convince so many of the remaining colonists to stay, while most of the survivors from destroyed worlds had chosen to leave. Why hadn't it been the other way around? Surely those who stood in the firing line would be most likely to feel the threat, while those who had suffered losses would be most interested in staying to take revenge? It hadn't made sense.

But now, watching the mission supervisors balk at abandoning their posts, even though they knew that death awaited them if they didn't, the reasons were obvious.

"It runs counter to programming," she repeated, "and that programming will kill you if you let it."

"And how can we be sure you won't run like you did in Rasmussen?"

Lucia turned to Cleo Samson, civilian supervisor of Sagarsee, who had voiced the challenge that must have been on all their minds. She wasn't offended by the question—in fact she had anticipated it—but she doubted her transparent features would have conveyed that.

"You can't," she answered simply and honestly. "Nor can I guarantee that I won't. Which is why I will need your help to ensure that I don't."

She had thought it through very carefully, analyzing her feelings during and after the attack of the Starfish and her awakening in Sol System. Just because her mind had a new home didn't mean she wasn't subject to the same programming as the other engrams. In principle, she was as much a machine as they were, driven by desires and needs that were hardwired directly into her mind. Her needs were different, that was all.

"Help you?" Cleo echoed dubiously. "How?"

"I need to know if a hole ship called *Klotho* was among of the survivors of Rasmussen," she answered.

"Sol's ship?" Cleo frowned. "We're still cataloguing the survivors, so I can't say for certain. What with the Unfit still gathering here and the stragglers coming in from other colonies, it's something of a mess right now."

"What do you want with *Klotho*?" asked Donald Schievenin, Cleo's military counterpart.

"I *don't* want it," she replied. "I want something that's *in* it." Her shrug was an attempt at nonchalance intended to hide a deep desperation. "If it didn't survive, there might be another way. But I'll talk about that only if I need to."

The gathered mission supervisors, android bodies with barely anthropomorphized faces, stared at her with wary expressions. She wanted to reassure them, but she wasn't willing to expose her vulnerability any more than she had to. They were a war council united more by frailty than strength. They were the scarred survivors of a horrific extermination campaign, but they were also the victims of necessary pragmatism. UNESSPRO had used every trick in the book to ensure that their missions succeeded; the fact that many missions hadn't succeeded, even before the arrival of the Starfish, suggested that maybe their extreme means had been necessary.

There was no point taking the discussion any further. Until they trusted her, it was just air.

"Get back to me regarding *Klotho*," she said, "then we'll talk some more. You know what I'm proposing. The offer will remain open."

"We haven't heard from Thor yet," said Cleo Samson.

"The Starfish are due at Zemyna within twenty hours," said Vince Mohler. The nervousness he felt for his colony—and the conflict that caused within his programming—showed openly on his face. She felt sorry for him, even if she couldn't help him.

"Then you'd better think fast," she said, getting up and walking soundlessly from the room.

Her plan was simple. Ever since she'd awoken inside Spindle Ten, she had been struck by its superiority to the hole ships. It was larger and faster by far than the relatively tiny bubbles on which the engrams wafted between stars. It was not, however, as flexible in terms of size and shape, and it was clearly not designed for fighting. It had no built-in defensive systems, and she doubted that the Libraries would tell her how to equip it with such. The Tenth Spindle wasn't a warship by any stretch of the imagination, but it could, she thought, make a perfectly good ark.

This was where the mission supervisors balked. Why should she succeed where other similar missions had failed? Numerous hole ships had been expended on attempts to jump past the Starfish wake in all directions. None of them had ever returned.

That was because, she countered, the hole ships were like ants trying to outrun stomping feet. It simply wasn't feasible. Spindle Ten might not be even remotely close to the Starfish's capabilities, but it *did* improve their chances of survival, and that was all that mattered. It had enough room for everyone, including the Unfit. If they could dodge the fovea for long enough, they could escape the deadly wake and return to Sagarsee when it had passed. With the Starfish gone, there would be nothing left to fear. They would be free to begin the recolonization of any star system they chose.

"That's *if* it works," said Rob Singh, with whom she'd shared her thoughts on the matter. Speaking through a telepresence robot similar to the one around Rasmussen, the local version of him had joined her at her request in the halls of Spindle Ten, which was currently docked near Sagarsee's Hub.

"You weren't invited here for your pessimism, Rob," she responded, watching him through the eyes of her I-body. Although her engram was still running somewhere in the Dark Room, she was able to project her pov through any available source.

"Why *did* you ask me here, anyway?" he asked, glassy, penetrating eyes swiveling to watch her transparent face.

"For company," she said. "And because I feel bad about what happened to you in Rasmussen."

"That wasn't me," he said. "It was *another* me."

"You know what I mean. Besides, you all seem the same to

me. You're even *doing* the same things. You're poking into the gifts, right? Looking for discrepancies?"

"Just like the one of me from Inari, yeah." Spindly arms twitched. "And look where that got him."

Killed, she remembered, in the fall of Sothis. "But he didn't die *because* of that, Rob. And neither did the copy of you in Rasmussen."

"It didn't help, though, did it? I'm beginning to think I've—*we've* been wasting our time. Even if there are any more secrets here, if the errors I've found aren't just mistakes, then there simply isn't time to work it all out. What's the point?"

"There's always a point, Rob," she said. "The more we learn, the better our chances are. If you throw the towel in and concede defeat, then we *will* die. If you keep looking, keep fighting, we *might* survive. That slim hope of continued existence is worth fighting for."

He though about this for a moment, the telepresence robot completely motionless. Then: "You do give me hope, Lucia. I'll grant you that. I'd volunteer for one of the Dark Room missions myself, if only Donald would let me."

"I've already put in a good word for you."

"Yet here I remain. Tumbling sidekick to—well, whatever it is you are now. No offense, Lucia, but I know where I'd rather be."

As they spoke, in Sagarsee and all the remaining colonies, attempts were under way to explore the other remaining Dark Rooms. If there were others who could liberate more of the Spindles, then that increased the carrying capacity of Lucia's ark plan, and that had to work in their favor.

She didn't let the fact that no one had so far been successful in this venture dampen her enthusiasm.

"Can I ask you something, Rob?" She didn't wait for his permission. "You've looked into this more than anyone. How do you suppose the Gifts knew what language to use when they first came to us? They addressed us in English, and the Unfit say that they spoke to their ancestors in *their* own tongue."

"We assume they scanned the early probes for information on our culture before making contact."

"Which would suggest they must have been watching us before revealing themselves, right?"

"Maybe, but probably not. Christ, Lucia, these beings are so much more advanced than we could ever hope to be. I suspect they'd be able to understand a culture in less time than it took me to say a single sentence."

She nodded. It was a scary though but a believable one, given everything she'd seen.

"That must be how they knew about Peter," she said. "Why they always choose him, if they can, to be the interface between us and them."

"It seems logical," he said, "although we still have no idea *why* they choose him. Why pick someone who can barely think straight to stand between you and the ones you're trying to help? I know he was a generalist and might once have been the obvious choice, but now . . ." The robot paused thoughtfully. "It's almost like they *want* to make things difficult for us."

"Maybe they do," she agreed. And that did seem all too plausible. If the Spinners could learn the English language in barely a handful of seconds, then it didn't strike her as likely that they'd make such a simple mistake when it came to choosing their spokesperson. "Maybe it's a test: when we fixed Peter, they'd talk to us properly."

Eye stalks swiveled. "An interesting notion."

She thought so, too. It made a kind of sense, and it connected with other data that had been bothering her.

If pi-1 Ursa Major really was a Spinner hideout, and had been for forty or more years, then why was *she* still alive? The Spinners had destroyed the colony founded by her fellow colonists there; they had responded to every attempt to explore the system since with extreme force; yet they had let her pass through the system unscathed, only interfering with her primitive camera in a way that was almost guaranteed to arouse suspicion. It didn't seem likely to her.

The trouble was, the alternative was even worse. A picture was building in her mind of a species toying with the junior races it found. She and Peter were united by complex webs of causality just as they were united by the urges of their originals. Was it a coincidence that she had survived both pi-1 Ursa Major and Rasmussen and emerged fused with Spinner technology? Was it also a coincidence that Peter had survived

Adrasteia and Beid and been himself changed in the process? The Spinners knew both of them intimately: they had scanned her long before meeting Peter, and could have known about him well in advance. Was the lesson here not so much to survive as one was, but to give up everything one had once held dear?

She and Peter were still linked by more than the strictures of her engram. He might think that he had slipped free of his noose, but she knew better. They were as entangled as ever, and would remain so until death—or the engram equivalent.

She had tried using the new tools at her disposal to change the strictures of her engram. She had attempted to copy herself, intending to edit the copy and then set it running, ultimately erasing her original. But she hadn't been successful. The copy hadn't functioned properly, juddering to a halt within seconds.

But that was okay, she told herself. In this brief window of time before the Starfish came, she still had options. She was sure she could work things out.

Rob and her I-suit representation walked the corridors of Spindle Ten—corridors she had already explored in great detail, but which she'd wanted to show him anyway. As well as companionship, she wanted his perspective. As someone who was firmly convinced that the Spinners were hiding something, his take on things was slightly different than the others'. They tended to take their alien benefactors for granted. To them, once the gifts had been deposited, the Spinners were out of the picture. But Lucia was reluctant to make such assumptions. To do so could be dangerous, if not potentially fatal.

They completed the tour without finding any new spaces or any ways into the spaces Lucia knew were hidden. Even from her privileged perspective, there were still things she couldn't see or gain access to, but that she *knew* to be there.

"Lucia?" The voice, speaking to her via conSense, belonged to Cleo Samson. "We've found *Klotho*. The Unfit commandeered it in the evacuation of Rasmussen and merged it into *Mantissa B*."

"Where is it now?"

"Dry docked."

"I'll be over right away."

"Can I come?" asked Rob, eavesdropping on the conversation with refreshing openness.

She hesitated before answering, but only briefly. "Sure. Why not?"

They retraced their steps to the door leading out of the Spindle. The Gifts around Sagarsee wouldn't talk to her, but they had let her connect to the local instantaneous transfer network. Sagarsee's Hub now had eleven doors, hers being a portal of dark frosted glass she remembered from UNESSPRO's central admin building. They stepped easily across space to the Hub, and from there to the Dry Dock, via similar doors to the ones in Rasmussen. Here, as there, the doors had been plucked from the mind of Peter Alander, his engram in both colonies frozen in brainlocked hell.

Klotho looked no different from any other hole ship. It's white, fat, spider egg–like main body dominated the chamber, lacking the slightest surface feature to tell whether it was rotating or not. The cockpit was just emerging from its side, sliding smoothly around the main body's equator like an expanding black blister. It swelled into a hemisphere, then became more clearly a second sphere sliding out of the first. Its rotation slowed as it separated completely and came to a halt next to the ingress ramp. Lucia and Rob walked briskly to meet it, traversing the long distance around the enormous dock in silence.

It was strange, she thought. To someone from Earth in 2050, when the UNESSPRO missions had left, the scene would have been utterly fantastical: a shimmering woman seemingly composed of water and a clumsy telepresence robot dwarfed by a machine that looked more like a giant chemistry model than a faster-than-light spacecraft. Yet to Lucia such scenes were becoming commonplace. She had to stop to remind herself that, despite their growing familiarity with such objects, neither the Yuhl nor the engrams actually knew how the machines at their command worked.

The oval entrance was open when they arrived, so she walked straight in. The interior was similar to the other hole ships she'd been in before: the central cockpit with its couch and screens, and one small stateroom off to one side. She could easily have transferred her pov to its AI banks and explored from there, but that wouldn't have enabled her to take what she wanted from within it. For that she needed a body.

"Where are the personal effects of Peter Alander and Caryl Harzis?" she asked the AI.

"They are in storage," it replied. "As per the instructions Peter—"

"Release them to me," she cut in impatiently.

The machine obeyed without protest, as she'd expected it to. The gifts were lax on privacy and security, except when it came to their creators. Then their mouths were sealed and their secret places locked tight.

A closet opened in one wall, revealing a small amount of effects: some clothes, a replica book, and a sample from the Lab. As soon as she found the solid-state data storage unit Peter had once shown her, she picked it up and instructed the AI to put everything else away. The SSDS seemed ridiculously primitive compared to everything around it, but it had the advantage of being both tangible and private. It was something she could hold and keep to herself if necessary.

"That's it?" Rob asked, his robotic eyes peering up at the object in her hand. "That's all you came here for?"

She nodded. "That's it."

"So what's on it?"

She clutched the SSDS to her chest as though it was a gift from a lover. In a very real sense, that was exactly what it was, and as such she was reluctant to explain even to Rob what she wanted it for.

"Just some old records," she said evasively. "I need to cross-reference something."

The robot's anemone eyestalks wiggled at her as he followed her out of the hole ship. "You know, you're starting to sound just like them."

She glanced down at the robot trundling along in time to her smooth and silent steps. "Starting to sound like who?"

"The Gifts," he said. There was a hint of amusement to his tone, but there was also an edge of seriousness, too.

She couldn't really object to the accusation, as it did hold a grain of truth. In a physical sense, she *was* more like a Gift than she was a human, running on alien processors and embodied within a bubble of energy. But she was still Lucia beneath all that. That was the very problem she was attempting to solve.

She was spared having to reply to Rob's comment, though, by the electric tingle of an incoming ftl message registering in the distant Spindle Ten. How she knew the message was going to be different from the others that came from patrolling hole ships in far-off systems, she didn't know, but she stopped to listen anyway.

"This is Caryl Hatzis of the United Near-Earth Stellar Survey Program Mission 154, *S. V. Krasnikov*, to HD92719. I am the leader of a diplomatic mission to the race we refer to as the Starfish. We have tactical information for you regarding the people you're following. They're hiding in a system among the ones we have surveyed. If you are prepared to speak with us, we will give you this information. All we ask is that you stop killing our people! Please respond!"

She felt everything in Sagarsee come to a halt around her. Engrams, Yuhl, androids, telebots: they all froze to hear what happened next. This was the first they'd heard of Thor since the team had left to try to contact the Starfish. No one had been certain if they'd even survived beyond stowing away in the cutter in Asellus Primus. That they had was a huge relief. For Thor to break ftl silence now, the mission had to be close to its goal. And if that was the case, then the next thing to come through could well be something from the Starfish themselves.

As the seconds dragged into minutes and nothing came, Lucia felt the anticipation of all those around curdle into frustration. Then frustration became disappointment, disappointment became hopelessness, and hopelessness ultimately became despair.

Hearing so little was somehow worse than if they'd heard nothing at all. What the fuck had *happened?* Had Thor been successful, or had she and the others been swatted out of the sky for exposing themselves so openly? There was simply no way of knowing. They couldn't even trace the signal back to its source so they could at least locate the Starfish fleet; only the Starfish themselves had that technology. All they knew was that Thor had been within the effective range of the local ftl receiver when she'd sent the message. That put her somewhere in a bubble 200 light-years across, centered on Sagarsee.

"Do you think—?" Rob began, breaking the silence with a hesitant whisper.

"I'm trying not to think, actually," she cut him off. Then, wheeling around and moving off in the direction of the Dry Dock's door, she said, "Come on, Rob."

Rob's robot rolled after her. "Where are we going?"

"Back to the Hub," she said, walking with determined strides. "We have an ark to prepare."

2.2.4

WHO ARE YOU?

The voice spoke to her out of blinding pain and seemed to take on some of its characteristics. Teeth like broken glass cut the words into tiny fragments that stabbed her eardrums; the tongue that shaped them snapped like a whip, leaving her flayed and exposed; the breath that carried them dripped tiny droplets of acid that burned her skin.

WHAT IS YOUR NAME?

Then she felt the voice, and the associated pain, recede, and suddenly around her a familiar world formed. She smelled apples, felt wind on her cheeks, and saw slender, sinister branches overhead casting shadows across the sky. The promise of the voice's return lingered in the air, giving it a dense, powerful sense of foreboding. When she looked down she saw grass beneath the bare, human feet that had once been hers.

"Where am I?"

A BETTER PLACE, returned the voice. This time there was no pain; the words came to her on a sweet cider–perfumed wind. A PLACE WHERE WE MIGHT TALK.

The orchard was as familiar to her as home, compared to the things she had recently seen, but it didn't soothe her: Memories of old betrayals and murder haunted her.

"Who are you?"

THAT IS UNIMPORTANT. YOU MAY CALL ME THE NEXUS.
THAT IS AS GOOD A NAME AS ANY. I CHOSE THE NAME BECAUSE
OF THE CONVERSATION YOU AND YOUR COMPANIONS WERE
HAVING IMMEDIATELY BEFORE MY ARRIVAL.

"You were listening to us?"

YES.

Her face felt rubbery, distant. "It *is* important who you are,"
she insisted. "I want to know who I'm talking to."

THAT KNOWLEDGE WOULD NOT HELP MATTERS.

"Why not?"

IT IS A PROBLEM OF PRESENTATION. THE FACES WE WEAR
REFLECT THE WAY WE WISH TO BE SEEN, AS WELL AS WHAT
WE ARE. WE DEPICT OURSELVES, AND DO SO PROGRESSIVELY
MORE SO THE MORE INTELLIGENT AND CAPABLE OUR CULTURE
BECOMES. THE WAY I CHOOSE TO DEPICT MYSELF WOULD NOT
BE COMPREHENSIBLE TO YOU, AND I WOULD NOT LIKE TO DE-
PICT MYSELF IN TERMS YOU *COULD* UNDERSTAND. IF YOU ARE
ANYTHING TO GO BY, I WOULD NOT LIKE TO BE BOUND BY
YOUR CULTURE'S DEMEANING NOTIONS OF IDENTITY.

She bristled at that. "What do you mean? What's wrong with
us?"

THIS IS THE POINT I WISH TO RAISE WITH YOU. WHAT IS
YOUR NAME? WHY ARE YOU HERE?

"You can read me my mind, access my memories. You tell
me."

THAT IS NOT THE POINT OF THIS EXERCISE. I AM QUESTION-
ING YOUR MOTIVES. I DON'T THINK YOU TRULY KNOW WHAT
YOU'RE DOING, WHY YOU ARE HERE.

"I'm here because . . ." She hesitated. "I'm here to try to
save the survivors. We have to stop the Starfish or they'll kill
everyone."

IS THAT SUCH A BAD THING?

"Of course it is, if you're one of the ones being killed."

SURVIVAL IS ALL, THEN.

"Not *all,* obviously, but under these circumstances I think
it's a justifiable goal."

TELL ME YOUR NAME, the voice insisted.

She looked around at the illusion of the orchard. The lines
of trees seemed to stretch off to infinity, and she had no doubt
whatsoever that she would not leave that illusion without the

help from the owner of the voice—and that meant cooperating with it in its games.

She sighed. "Very well. My name is Thor."

NO, IT'S NOT, said the Nexus. A strong wind blew through the orchard, bending all of the trees back and forth in a gentle fashion. ACCORDING TO YOUR MEMORIES, YOUR NAME IS CARYL HATZIS.

"Yes, but I'm not *the* Caryl Hatzis. I'm an engram—a copy. There are lots of us, so we differentiate by naming ourselves after the colony we come from. That's why I'm called Thor. The same with Gou Mang, Inari, Yu-qiang . . ."

She trailed off, sensing that her answer was failing to satisfy the Nexus.

"Only the real Caryl Hatzis can use that name," she said.

YES.

Silence followed the simple affirmative. She waited uncomfortably for the Nexus to say something else, but there was only the wind through her hair and the sound of wood creaking.

"Well?" she said. "So what? Whatever this means to you, it's not exactly a great revelation to me. Sol is the template on which all her engrams were based; she had the name first. Big deal. That doesn't mean she's the best of us, or that she should automatically be in charge."

OR THAT SHE *deserves* THE NAME.

She opened her mouth, then closed it. FUCK YOU, she thought. I KNOW WHERE YOU'RE GOING.

IF YOU KNOW WHERE I'M GOING, the Nexus asked, blatantly reading her mind, WHY DON'T YOU ACKNOWLEDGE IT TO YOURSELF?

"Because it's not important!" Her rubber cheeks felt hot and suffocating; she wished she could tear off the mask and be herself.

AH, BUT IT IS IMPORTANT, the voice argued. COMMUNICATION DEPENDS CRITICALLY UPON INITIAL CONDITIONS. I CHOOSE TO KNOW WHAT THOSE CONDITIONS ARE BEFORE I BEGIN THE PROCESS OF SEEING WHERE THEY LEAD. IF YOU CHOOSE TO OBFUSCATE THEM, THEN I WILL TERMINATE THIS DISCUSSION NOW.

Thor bit down on an angry retort, even though it didn't matter anyway. The Nexus could read her every thought as it happened, so there was no hiding what she wanted to say. And somehow, realizing that, she was put at ease. There was nothing she could hide from the Nexus, and therefore there was no shame in admitting what it already knew.

"My name is Caryl Hatzis," she said. "And if truth be known, I wish I was the only one."

A warm breeze rustled the leaves of the trees around her.

THE DETERMINATION TO be CARYL HATZIS IS VERY PROMINENT IN YOUR SUBCONSCIOUS THOUGHTS, said the Nexus. WHY DO YOU THINK THAT IS?

Thor shrugged. "I guess I'm just programmed that way. The engrams were written with a strong sense of self, to counteract programming fudges. We believe we are who we're told we are because to believe otherwise might tear us apart." She thought of Alander and the identity breakdown all of his engrams had suffered. "Sometimes it causes problems."

THE ALGORITHM IS UNSUBTLE BUT EFFECTIVE IF YOU ARE NOT EXPOSED TO OTHERS OF YOUR OWN KIND, WHO ALSO SHARE THE SAME DELUSION. CONFLICT IS AMELIORATED BY THE EXISTENCE OF YOUR TEMPLATE PERSONALITY, BUT IT IS KEPT MERELY LATENT AND CONTINUES TO ERODE BENEATH THE SURFACE. IN TIMES OF STRESS, IT MAY RISE TO THE FORE. OR IT MAY RESULT IN UNPREDICTABLE BEHAVIOR. THE FACT THAT YOUR ORIGINAL HAS TAMPERED WITH YOUR PROGRAMMING DOES NOT HELP.

A new anger abruptly washed through her. "She's *what*?"

THE ORIGINAL CARYL HATZIS HAS SUBTLY ALTERED A HANDFUL OF YOUR OPERATIONAL PARAMETERS, the Nexus casually explained, THUS ALLOWING YOU SOME SMALL FREEDOM FROM PERSONALITY CONSTRAINTS. YOU ARE FLEXIBLE IN WAYS YOU WERE NOT DESIGNED TO BE. GIVEN THE RANDOM NATURE OF THESE ALTERATIONS, I SUGGEST THAT THEY WERE MADE HAPHAZARDLY, PERHAPS ONE OF MANY SUCH CHANGES ENACTED ON ALL YOUR FELLOW ENGRAMS. THE ORIGINAL CARYL HATZIS MAY BE SEEKING TO EXTEND YOUR WORKING LIFE BY INTRODUCING THE EQUIVALENT OF MUTATIONS AT THE MOST BASIC LEVEL.

Most of what the Nexus had to say wasn't even registering. "She's *changed* me?"

CHANGED THE WAY YOUR OVERSEER BALANCES YOUR IM-

PERATIVES. IN YOU, YOUR DESIRE TO BE CARYL HATZIS IS STRONGER THAN IT SHOULD BE. THIS RESULTS IN A POWERFUL DRIVE TO SUPPLANT THE OTHERS, WHICH MANIFESTS AS HOSTILITY AND AMBITION. THESE ARE ARGUABLY BENEFICIAL TRAITS IN TIMES OF CONFLICT, BUT THEY ARE NOT CONDUCIVE TO COMMUNICATION. The Nexus paused significantly. I AM MERELY POINTING THIS OUT. I DO NOT THREATEN YOUR IDENTITY NOR YOUR RELATIONSHIP WITH YOUR TEMPLATE PERSONALITY. I WISH TO CONVERSE WITH YOU IN A RATIONAL WAY, WITH NO CONFUSION OVER YOUR MOTIVES.

She was unable to speak for some time. Thoughts swirled through her mind like storm clouds in fast motion. She felt as though the soft underbelly of her psyche had been laid bare and poked with electrodes. Yes, she resented Sol for being the one to whom everyone aspired, and for making her feel second-rate and inadequate—and she could live with that. But to find out that it was Sol herself who had made her feel that way—who had reached into her mind and fucked around with her operational parameters, the very processes that made her *her*—that made her sick to the stomach. What had Sol done to her other engrams? To everyone? Were they all just marionettes dancing for her amusement? Was Sol setting herself up to become like the Praxis, a supermind surrounded by slaves attendant to her every desire?

"What about *your* motives?" she asked the Nexus, seeking a way out of the turmoil filling her mind. "If we're going to communicate, shouldn't we start talking about *you* at some point?"

I AM NOT THE SUPPLICANT IN THIS RELATIONSHIP, it said dismissively. I AM NOT COMING TO YOU FOR SUCCOR. I HAVE THE UPPER HAND IN THIS SITUATION, AND I DO NOT INTEND TO LOSE THAT BY DIVULGING INFORMATION TO YOU. MAKE NO MISTAKE, CARYL HATZIS: WE ARE NOT EQUALS, NOR SHALL WE EVER BE.

"Then what is this? Are you just toying with me? Killing a little time?"

ON THE CONTRARY. I AM LEARNING MANY THINGS ABOUT THE WAY YOU OPERATE THAT I COULD NOT FROM TAKING A STATIC SNAPSHOT OF YOUR MIND. NO MATTER HOW SUPERIOR I AM, THERE ARE DETAILS OF PROCESS THAT CAN ONLY BE OB-

SERVED, NOT PREDICTED. THE EVOLUTION OF THINGS IS THE
ULTIMATE STUDY FOR ANY INTELLIGENT LIFE-FORM. WHAT YOU
HAVE TO OFFER ME IS FAR LESS INTERESTING THAN THE WAY
YOU OFFER IT. IF INFORMATION DOES NOT FLOW, IT IS DEAD.
DO YOU UNDERSTAND ME?

She thought she might be beginning to. No matter how far
advanced a mind could be, no matter how much it knew about
the way things were, it could still be interested in the unfolding
of things. In the narrative, in the story. In *her* story . . .

YOUR STORY HAS COME TO AN END, CARYL HATZIS OF THOR.

"Don't write me off too soon," she said defiantly. "I'm not
dead yet."

THAT IS EXACTLY WHAT YOU ARE. YOUR BODY IS NO LONGER
FUNCTIONING, AND WHEN THIS CONVERSATION IS OVER I WILL
ERASE YOUR PATTERN FROM MY MIND ALTOGETHER. YOU WILL
CEASE TO EXIST AS A CONSTRUCT OF THIS VIRTUAL WORLD.

"Cease . . . ?" Her stomach sank at the words. "But why?"
she asked feebly. "What have I done to make you want to kill
me?"

YOU HAVE DONE NOTHING, CARYL HATZIS, replied the
Nexus. YOU HAVE DONE NOTHING, AND YOU ARE NOTHING TO
ME. YOUR FATE IN NO WAY CHANGES WHAT I AM OR WHAT I
MUST DO, AND I HAVE NO COMPUNCTION ABOUT KILLING YOUR
BODY TO ACCESS YOUR MIND. YOU ARE BUT AN INSECT AT-
TEMPTING TO ALTER THE MOTION OF CONTINENTS. NO MATTER
HOW MUCH YOU STRAIN AND PUSH, YOU WILL HAVE NO EFFECT
WHATSOEVER.

"Butterfly wings," she said, desperately trying to think of a
counterargument. "Small things *can* make a difference."

CHAOS CANNOT BE CONTROLLED. THE BUTTERFLY CANNOT
KNOW AS IT BEATS ITS WINGS THAT IT WILL CREATE A STORM
ON THE OTHER SIDE OF THE WORLD.

"But it can try!" She struggled to think past the fact that her
life hung in the balance. "And if it tries in an interesting way,
doesn't that count for something? Doesn't its narrative become
interesting?"

OF COURSE. THIS IS WHY I QUESTIONED YOUR MOTIVES EAR-
LIER. I MIGHT BE INTERESTED IN HELPING SOMEONE WHOSE
MOTIVES ARE MORE THAN JUST ASPIRING TO BE THE TOP OF

HER PRIVATE HEAP, BUT I HAVE NO INTEREST IN MEDDLING IN INDIVIDUAL VENDETTAS.

"Then why are you still talking to me if you have no interest? Why haven't you erased me already?"

I AM NOT UTTERLY WITHOUT WHAT YOU WOULD CALL COMPASSION. THERE REMAINS A SHRED OF INTEREST IN YOUR FATE AND THE FATE OF YOUR COMPANIONS.

Thor felt infinitely weary and utterly drained. What did the Nexus want of her, for fuck's sake? She had been more honest with it than she was with anyone—perhaps even herself. It could read her mind itself rather than drag her through this ridiculous charade. Why didn't it just decide and be done with it, and put her out of her misery?

"Look, who *are* you?" she asked after a few seconds. "Can't you at least tell me that much, before you're done with me?"

WOULD IT MAKE A DIFFERENCE?

"Of course it would! If you're one of the Starfish, then you already know what I came here to tell. At least I could die knowing that I got the message through. But if you're not, if you're just another underling getting in the way, then . . ." She halted, unsure what to say.

THEN YOU'LL BE ANGRY AND FRUSTRATED, the Nexus finished for her. AND YOU'LL STILL BE UNABLE TO ACCEPT THE INEVITABLE.

That seemed to sum it up well enough. But again the feeling of pointlessness to the whole conversation rose up in her. Why use words when the Nexus knew her thoughts as they occurred to her?

THERE'S ALWAYS A POINT, CARYL HATZIS. YOUR BEING HERE HAS A POINT; MY TALKING TO YOU HAS A POINT. THAT POINT IS AN INTERSECTION, A LOCUS OF CONNECTION. THE DYNAMICS OF EXCHANGE ARE VERY DIFFERENT TO THE IMPOSITION OF ORDER. BY GIVING YOU THE OPPORTUNITY TO CHANGE MY MIND, I FEEL THAT I HAVE AT LEAST ACTED FAIRLY, IN ACCORDANCE WITH THE NATURAL PROCESSES OF LIFE.

She shook her head, feeling very much out of her depth.

"And *have* I changed your mind?"

NO, YOU HAVEN'T.

"So this was nothing more than a diversion for you, then,

before you go off and destroy another of our colonies. Is that it?"

She thought she almost heard a sigh in the brief silence that followed. LISTEN TO ME, CARYL HATZIS, the Nexus said finally. THE INFORMATION YOU HAVE GIVEN ME MAY BE VERY IMPORTANT. THE CONCLUSION YOU HAVE REACHED — THAT THE SYSTEM YOU CALL PI-1 URSA MAJOR CONTAINS SOMETHING ANOMALOUS — SEEMS INESCAPABLE IN THE FACE OF THE DATA YOU HAVE COLLECTED. MUCH OF IT IS CIRCUMSTANTIAL BUT PERSUASIVE NONETHELESS: AN ENIGMATIC FLYBY DECADES AGO, SEVERAL SCOUT VESSELS DESTROYED IN MORE RECENT TIMES. IT INDICATES A CHANGE OF TACTICS ON THE BEHALF OF THOSE WE FOLLOW, THE ONES YOU CALL THE SPINNERS, AND THAT, IF TRUE, IS A MOMENTOUS DEVELOPMENT. WE HAVE BEEN LOCKED IN AN EMBRACE THAT BEGAN LONG BEFORE YOUR RACE EXISTED. CHANGE IS SLOW AND SUBTLE, BUT ONCE BEGUN CAN UNFOLD IN AN INSTANT. YOU MAY BE A CATALYST OF A KIND WE HAVE NOT SEEN FOR MANY TENS OF THOUSANDS OF YEARS.

"Then . . . you *are* one of the Starfish?"

NO, I'M NOT.

Despite the coolness of the thoughts that flowed directly through her mind, it did little to sweep aside her confusion.

BUT I AM CLOSER TO THEM THAN ANY OF THE OTHERS YOU ENCOUNTERED BEFORE. THERE IS, AS ONE OF YOUR NUMBER SURMISED, A RICH ECOLOGY OF LIFE CLUSTERING AROUND THIS GREAT MIGRATION. THERE ARE NUMEROUS CONNECTIONS AND LEVELS: IT IS A MAGNIFICENT ENVIRONMENT FOR ONE SUCH AS MYSELF, WHO THRIVES ON PROCESS. THOSE PROCESSES GOVERN MY EXISTENCE HERE: I EXIST TO FACILITATE INFORMATION FLOW. IN THAT SENSE YOU ARE FORTUNATE. HAD ANOTHER NICHE DWELLER FOUND YOU, YOU WOULD HAVE BEEN DESTROYED OUT OF HAND.

"So you're saying we happened across the right person to help us?"

I AM INTERESTED IN YOUR STORY, CARYL HATZIS, BUT I HAVE MY OWN NEEDS TO SERVE. I CAN ASSIST YOU, OR I CAN DISMISS YOU, KILL YOU. THOSE ARE MY OPTIONS. IF I DO NOT REGARD YOUR QUEST TO BE WORTHY, THEN I CAN HARDLY LET YOU WANDER AROUND UNCHECKED.

"Then why not help us? If you can read my thoughts and

have already been listening in on my crew, then you already know that our quest is worthy."

BUT IN ORDER TO HELP YOU, CARYL HATZIS, I MUST FIRST KILL YOU.

A protest rose in her thoughts, but the Nexus caught it before she had even uttered a single syllable.

PLEASE, LET ME FINISH. YOU MUST HEAR ME OUT BEFORE I DECIDE. THEN IT WILL BE YOUR TURN TO MAKE THE DECISION. YOU THINK YOU KNOW THE STARFISH AND THEIR MOTIVATIONS. YOU TELL YOURSELF THAT YOU CAN'T POSSIBLY KNOW, BUT YOU BELIEVE THAT YOU DO, REGARDLESS. YOU ARE AS INCAPABLE OF KNOWING THEM AS I AM, AND I AM THE MOST ADVANCED INTELLIGENCE YOUR SPECIES HAS EVER ENCOUNTERED, INCLUDING THE ONES YOU CALL THE GIFTS. THE ASSUMPTION THAT YOU KNOW THEM IS BLINDING YOU, CRIPPLING YOU. YOU MUST SEE WHAT I SEE BEFORE YOU CAN PROCEED.

THOSE YOU CALL THE STARFISH ARE UNKNOWN TO ALL WHO TRAVEL WITH THEM. I HAVE SERVED THEM FOR MANY THOUSANDS OF YOUR YEARS, AND I AM NO CLOSER TO KNOWING THEM THAN YOU ARE. THE ONLY ADVANTAGE I HAVE OVER YOU IS A SIGNIFICANT AMOUNT OF EXPERIENCE WITH THEM: OBSERVING THEIR WAYS, THEIR PATTERNS, THEIR METHODS. WHAT GOES ON BEHIND THOSE FACTS, WHAT PROCESSES DRIVE THEM, IS A MYSTERY WE MAY NEVER ANSWER. FOR ALL WE KNOW, THEY MIGHT NOT EVEN EXIST ANYMORE: THE MIGRATION COULD CONTINUE WITHOUT THEM QUITE EASILY, FOR WE NICHE DWELLERS CAN CARRY OUT OUR TASKS FOR CENTURIES WITHOUT REQUIRING INSTRUCTION OR DIRECTION.

WHAT HAPPENS AT THE TOP OF THE CHAIN IS A MYSTERY. I HAVE DEALINGS WITH BEINGS HIGHER UP THE ECOLOGICAL LADDER IN THE MIGRATION, AND THEY TOO REPORT THAT THEY HAVE NO CONTACT WITH THE STARFISH. PERHAPS WE *ARE* THE STARFISH OURSELVES: ALL THE NICHES COMBINING AS ONE TO FORM A SYNERGISTIC SOCIAL ORGANISM THAT SOMEHOW RETAINS COHERENCE AND STABILITY DESPITE ITS MANY DIVERSE COMPONENTS. I DON'T KNOW, AND MY IGNORANCE IS AS GREAT AS YOURS IN THESE MATTERS.

AND AS SUCH, I CANNOT TELL YOU WHAT THE STARFISH WILL THINK OF THE INFORMATION YOU WISH TO GIVE THEM. I CAN ONLY HELP YOU DELIVER IT.

"But you must have an opinion on it."

Jagged branches swayed against a wintry sky for a few moments, as if the Nexus was considering her comment.

IF WHAT YOU SAY IS TRUE, it said eventually, AND THE SPINNERS HAVE INDEED HIDDEN THEMSELVES IN PI-1 URSA MAJOR, THEN YOU MAY WELL ACHIEVE THAT WHICH YOU SET OUT TO DO. THE SPINNERS MAY BE DELIBERATELY CHANGING THEIR TACTICS NOW UNDER THE ASSUMPTION THAT THE STARFISH, AFTER SO LONG, WILL NOT NOTICE. AS THE SPINNER WAKE MOVES, WE FOLLOW; AS WE ACCELERATE, THEY PULL AHEAD. LULLED BY THIS ROUTINE, PERHAPS WE WOULD NOT HAVE NOTICED ONE SMALL DEVIATION, WERE IT NOT FOR YOU. THIS DEVIATION WILL BE A WELCOME CHANGE IN ROUTINE FOR SOME AND A THREAT TO THE ESTABLISHED ORDER FOR OTHERS. WHAT HAPPENS IF THE SPINNERS ARE DESTROYED? WILL THE MIGRATION DISBAND? OR WILL WE BE DESTROYED ALONG WITH IT, NO LONGER NEEDED? AGAIN, WE CANNOT POSSIBLY HOPE TO KNOW.

"But *will* you pass on our message?" she asked, sensing an offer of assistance in the Nexus's tone. "Can you tell those others higher up the chain so that the Starfish will eventually find out?"

NO. I CANNOT IN GOOD CONSCIENCE DO THAT. THERE ARE THOSE WHO WOULD RESIST THE MESSAGE, PERHAPS EVEN EXPUNGE IT FROM EXISTENCE, ALONG WITH ALL OF THOSE WHO HEARD IT. I COULD NOT RISK THAT. I ENJOY THE PROCESS OF MY LIFE TOO MUCH.

BUT LISTEN TO THIS, CARYL HATZIS, FOR IT IS PERHAPS THE MOST IMPORTANT THING I WILL TELL YOU: YOUR RACE HAS MADE ASSUMPTIONS. I HAVE TOLD YOU THAT ALREADY, BUT I HAVEN'T TOLD YOU ALL OF THEM YET. THERE IS ONE MORE THAT YOU MUST CONSIDER. IF YOU ARE RIGHT ABOUT THE SPINNER TACTIC, THEN YOU ARE POTENTIALLY COMMITTING A GREAT CRIME AGAINST THEM. THEY ARE, AFTER ALL, SELFLESS PROPAGATORS OF KNOWLEDGE, PROVIDING A GREAT SERVICE TO NEW CIVILIZATIONS AND CULTURES WHEREVER THEY TRAVEL. AND YET YOU WOULD BETRAY THEM SIMPLY TO FURTHER YOUR OWN EXISTENCE. WHO WOULD BELIEVE AN EMISSARY FROM SUCH A TREACHEROUS CULTURE?

"It's the *only* way we can get your attention," she defended quickly. The moral question of her mission had never been satisfactorily resolved beyond the kill-or-be-killed argument. "If we don't, then—"

PLEASE, the Nexus cut in. ALLOW ME TO FINISH. YOU REGARD THE STARFISH MIGRATION AS A GREAT DESTROYER, SWEEPING ALL LIFE BEFORE IT. DO YOU THINK THAT THIS IS HOW WE SEE OURSELVES? YOU HAVE REASONS FOR WANTING TO BETRAY A BENEFACTOR: PERHAPS WE HAVE REASONS, TOO.

"But you said you didn't know what the motives of the Starfish were."

WE DON'T. BUT WE CAN SURMISE: WE CAN PROJECT. AND WE CAN PROPOSE NEW THEORIES AND TEST THEM AGAINST NEW DATA, AS I HAVE DONE WITH THE DATA YOU HAVE GIVEN ME. WHAT YOUR DATA HAS TOLD ME DOES NOT CONTRADICT THE STANDING MODEL OF OUR SUPERIORS' BEHAVIOR, EVEN THOUGH THAT MODEL STANDS IN CONTRADICTION TO YOUR OWN. PERHAPS I AM GUILTY, AS ARE YOU, OF CHOOSING MODELS THAT SUPPORT MORAL DECISIONS I MUST TAKE IN ORDER TO SURVIVE. THIS IS A REAL POSSIBILITY. BUT I OFFER YOU AN ALTERNATE MODEL FOR YOUR APPRECIATION. THEN I WILL GIVE YOU YOUR CHOICE.

A chill wind swept through the orchard. She hugged her arms around herself. The idea of what her choice might entail made her uneasy.

THE GALAXY IS AT WAR, the Nexus said. IT IS A PLACE OF CONSTANT CONFLICT ON A THOUSAND FRONTS BETWEEN MILLIONS OF SPECIES. YOUR SPECIES IS FAMILIAR WITH WAR; YOU HAVE AN APPRECIATION OF THE WASTEFULNESS OF IT, OF THE CHAOS THAT ATTENDS IT. IT IS FREQUENTLY POINTLESS, DESTRUCTIVE, AND TIME-CONSUMING—BUT AT THE SAME TIME IT CAN GENERATE CHANGE, DRIVE EVOLUTION, AND ENCOURAGE PROGRESS. IT IS A DOUBLE-EDGED SWORD THAT BALANCES HUNDREDS OF BILLIONS OF STARS ON ITS POINT. IT IS THE ONLY UNIVERSAL BEHAVIOR THAT WE HAVE DISCOVERED.

I THINK, THEREFORE, THAT YOU WILL APPRECIATE THE PROPOSAL I HAVE FOR YOU. I WANT YOU TO IMAGINE A RELATIVELY SMALL SKIRMISH IN AN OUT-OF-THE-WAY CONFLICT. WHO THE ANTAGONISTS ARE IN THIS SKIRMISH IS UNKNOWN TO US, NOR IS IT IMPORTANT WHO WINS. BUT ALL IS NOT LOST FOR ONE COMBATANT. SHE BREAKS AWAY AND FLEES. SHE MIGHT BE THE

AGGRESSOR IN THE CONFLICT; SHE MIGHT BE THE VICTIM. EITHER WAY, SHE RUNS. ONE OF HER ENEMIES FOLLOWS, SEEKING TO BRING HER DOWN. THE CHASE IS LONG AND HARD. THEY RUN THROUGH TANGLED FORESTS, ACROSS BLASTED BATTLEFIELDS; THEY SKIRT OTHER CONFLICTS AND NEVER RETRACE THEIR STEPS. THEY ARE LOCKED IN A CHASE TO THE DEATH. ONLY ONE WILL RETURN.

THIS, THEN, IS THE SPINNER/STARFISH MIGRATION — THE AMBIVALENCE, AS THE CREATURES YOU CALL THE PRAXIS AND THE YUHL REFER TO IT. THEIR NAME IS A GOOD ONE. IT SUMS UP THE UNCERTAINTY OF OUR POSITION WELL. TO YOU THE STARFISH ARE VICIOUS PREDATORS, INTENT ON THE DESTRUCTION OF ALL THE SPINNERS' GOOD WORKS. TO US, THE SPINNERS ARE FUGITIVES FLEEING JUSTICE, TO THE QUEST OF WHICH WE DEDICATE OUR LIVES. WHICH OF US IS RIGHT? WE MAY NEVER KNOW.

"This doesn't make sense," she said, holding a hand to her forehead. "Why would the Spinners help us if all they want to do is get away?"

THEY'RE *NOT* HELPING YOU.

"But the gifts—"

—ARE DIVERSIONS SOWED BY THE FUGITIVE TO DISTRACT HER PURSUER. SHE GIVES YOU JUST ENOUGH TO ATTRACT OUR ATTENTION BUT NOT ENOUGH TO DEFEND YOURSELVES OR EVEN UNDERSTAND YOUR FATE. WE CANNOT IGNORE YOU BECAUSE THERE IS AN OUTSIDE CHANCE THAT THE SPINNERS WILL ONE DAY FALL BEHIND, INTO OUR PATH: SHE COULD MASQUERADE AS ONE OF YOU, IF WE CHOSE TO BE LENIENT. SHE SLOWS US DOWN BY FORCING US TO BE THOROUGH, TO LET NOTHING PAST US. THE SPINNERS HAVE USED YOU, CARYL HATZIS, AND BETRAYED YOU TO YOUR DEATHS.

"Why would they waste so much energy on us?" she asked softly. "It doesn't make—"

YOU ARE THINKING ABOUT ENERGY FROM YOUR OWN NARROW DEFINITIONS. WERE YOU THE FUGITIVE, YOU WOULD EXPEND A LITTLE ENERGY IN STOPPING TO AGITATE AN INSECTS' NEST, INCITING THE COLONY INTO A FRENZY TO DISTRACT THOSE FOLLOWING.

Tears of frustration sprang to her eyes as images of burning colonies filled her mind. The sound of excited scientists switching on their ftl communicators for the first time and inadvertently igniting a conflagration that would eventually consume the human race . . .

IT IS AN OBVIOUS TACTIC, the Nexus went on, BUT AN EFFECTIVE ONE. IT IS HOWEVER, NOT AS ELEGANT AS HIDING OUT IN ONE OF YOUR EMPTY SYSTEMS AND MASQUERADING AS DEAD AS THE STARFISH SWEPT BY. FOR TENS OF THOUSANDS OF YOUR YEARS THEY HAVE CONTINUED ALONG ONE PATHWAY, SO MUCH SO THAT ONE MIGHT BELIEVE THEY WOULD CONTINUE THIS WAY ALWAYS. BUT NOW THEY HAVE CHANGED, AND BY A CURIOUS TWIST OF FATE—AND INDEED LUCK—YOU HAVE NOTICED THEM DOING SO. THEIR TRAP TURNS AGAINST THEM: THE INSECTS RISE TO BITE THEM AS THEY HIDE. The voice of the Nexus took on a rising pitch. THIS IS INFORMATION THAT COULD WORK TO OUR ADVANTAGE; IT IS INFORMATION THAT NEEDS TO BE FORWARDED SO THAT OTHER NICHE DWELLERS MIGHT HEAR AND APPRECIATE IT.

She took a deep breath. "This is where I have to make a decision, I guess."

YES, CARYL HATZIS, IT IS, said the Nexus. YOU SEE, THERE IS ONLY ONE WAY I CAN BRING THIS MATTER TO THE DIRECT ATTENTION OF THE ONES YOU SEEK. CENTURIES OF EXAMINATION OF THE MIGRATION HAVE CONVINCED ME AND OTHERS OF THE IMPORTANCE OF THE PLACE THE NICHE DWELLERS REFER TO AS THE SOURCE OF ALL. YOU HAVE SEEN IT; YOU THOUGHT IT WAS A SMALL STAR. IF THE STARFISH REMAIN AMONG US, THEN IT IS IN THERE THAT THEY RESIDE.

"So what do I have to do to get their attention?"

NO ONE KNOWS THAT. ALL I CAN DO IS GET YOU THERE. A warm light blossomed at the end of the row of apple trees beneath which she sat. It seemed for a moment as though the sun was rising. But this sun was smaller, denser, hotter, its light was hard and piercing. She braced herself as it rose higher in the sky, but there was nothing she could do to withstand its heat. Beneath her, the grass browned and withered; leaves and fruit fell like ash to the ground. Her nostrils filled with smoke, and it took her a second or more to realize that she herself was burning.

NO ONE HAS ENTERED THE SOURCE AND RETURNED, the

Nexus continued. IF YOU DECIDE TO GO, YOU WILL MOST
LIKELY NOT COME BACK.

"So if I go, I'll die," she said. "But if I stay, you'll deactivate
this illusion, and I'll die anyway. Not much of a choice, really,
is it?"

There was no pain, but she could feel herself being consumed, millimeter by millimeter. She did not resist. There
didn't seem any point.

THAT ISN'T THE DECISION I ASK YOU TO MAKE, said the
Nexus. THE DECISION YOU MUST MAKE IS THIS: I CAN SEND YOU
INTO THE SOURCE AND TO YOUR CERTAIN DEATH, OR I CAN
REACH INTO THE MINDS OF ONE OF YOUR COMPANIONS, PUT
YOU IN THEIR PLACE, AND SEND THEM INSTEAD.

Her breath caught in her throat, not just from the heat. "Inari
or Gou Mang, you mean? One of the engrams?"

NOT JUST THE ENGRAMS: I COULD PUT YOU IN *ANY* OF YOUR
CREW. I COULD MAKE YOU PETER ALANDER OR FRANK AXFORD.
I COULD MAKE YOU CLEO SAMSON. AND I COULD DO IT WITHOUT
ANYONE KNOWING. EVEN THE ONE YOU CALL SOL.

The fire of the Source licked at her bones as she considered
her options. Near-certain death at the hands of the Starfish, or
the chance to live inside the body of someone else. And more
than that: a chance to become the original Caryl Hatzis, the one
everyone looked up to and admired, and to whom they turned
to for leadership and advice. She could be the one person in
the universe she wanted to be, just by telling the Nexus that
that was what she wanted.

But even as she considered the possibility, she doubted that
it could be so simple. Why would the Nexus go to so much
trouble just to soothe her ego? Wasn't it more likely that this
was some sort of elaborate moral test designed to see which
way she'd jump? If she made the wrong choice, she would be
unworthy of any help at all, let alone the attainment of her
overseer's deepest desire.

Perhaps, she thought, the entire mess was part of the test.
What if everything from the Spinners to the Starfish was nothing more than a deadly filter, a wringer through which new
civilizations were squeezed to see if they'd make it out the far
side—a cosmic litmus test designed to weed out the weak? That
the final outcome of that test might crucially hinge on the de-

cision she now had to make left her feeling more than a little
uncomfortable.

The Source rose over her until it seemed to hang directly
overhead. She wasn't sure if she had a body in the illusion
anymore. She was aware only of the Source and a vague impression of creeping branches around the edges, as though a
forest were overtaking the orchard. Her mind was perfectly
clear, though. She couldn't claim disorientation as an excuse
for whatever decision she wanted to make.

Was the alien mind laughing at her as she wrestled with the
decision? She didn't want to die, and she *did* want to be the
superior Hatzis. But at the same time she was the leader of
the team sent to save humanity. How could she turn her back
on that mission, on her duty and her crew? What right did she
have to shun that responsibility and send another in her place?

She remembered the conversation from which the Nexus
had chosen its name. *"We're going to need to find some sort
of command nexus or communications conduit,"* she had told
Inari. *"If we can tap into either of those without getting ourselves killed . . ."*

As always, it was the last part that was proving the most
difficult. But it wasn't impossible. With the Nexus's help, she
could become that conduit. And who knew? Maybe she
wouldn't die in the process. Or maybe it was craven to hope
for life when the lives of so many others were at stake. But she
had to give herself some chance. Otherwise the decision was
literally taken out of her hands. The mental model that Sol had
given her—the sense of self that craved originality and perpe-
tuity—simply would not let her kill herself.

But if on such a craven decision the worth of humanity
hung, then she couldn't find it in herself to think that a bad
thing. Humanity wasn't noble or proud. It would happily sell
out its benefactors in order to stay alive even a day or two
longer. It would accept a halfhearted sacrifice, made under extreme duress.

"Very well," she said. "I accept your deal. What do I have
to do?"

NOTHING, CARYL HATZIS. IT IS BEING DONE TO YOU AS WE
SPEAK. YOU WILL HAVE A CHANCE TO EXPLAIN TO THE OTHERS

WHAT IS HAPPENING, THEN YOU WILL BE ON YOUR WAY. BUT MAKE IT BRIEF, CARYL HATZIS. TIME IS OF THE ESSENCE.

The faintly amused tones of the Nexus carried her down a slippery slope of unconsciousness. The branches closed around her; darkness spiraled inward. Barely did she have time to be afraid when *she* was gone and only the conduit remained.

2.2.5

The rapier-thin, silver skewer slid through Thor's head as cleanly as a hypodermic needle. Alander could only stare in shock, trapped as he was in the anti-impact fields and half-deafened by the sound of *Eledone*'s electronic screams of protest at the intrusion. A fine mist of blood erupted from the entry and exit wounds, spraying the cockpit and those around. The impossibly sharp tip of the skewer glinted evilly in the white light of the cockpit, wavering slightly as Thor's body spasmed and flailed as though receiving a powerful electric shock.

Then, as suddenly as it had come, the skewer withdrew and disappeared through *Eledone*'s hull boundary. The hole in the wall quickly sealed, but Thor wasn't so lucky. Blood and gray matter bulged out of her head wounds, kept grotesquely in place by her I-suit. Everyone stared helplessly at the android as her eyes rolled back and her limbs sagged limply at her side.

"Eledone!" Sol yelled. "Let us go so we can help her!"

The keening hole ship obeyed, although it shuddered around them as though revolted. Thankfully it had the presence of mind to keep Thor afloat as the rest of them dropped to the floor. She hung between them, to all appearances dead. Alander approached her warily, aghast at Thor's bloodied head and face. The lightning-fast plunge and retreat of the skewer had the

same callous impetus as someone testing a roast turkey to see
if it was done.

The screens around them began to flicker. The hole ship
was slowly recovering. The images were still hazy and ill defined, but he could make out the branchlike appendages of the
attacking ship retreating. The warped stars reappeared, the light
of alien suns returned.

"Is she—?" Gou Mang's eyes were wide, unable to look
away from the blood bulging from Thor's forehead, held back
by invisible forces.

Sol reached out to touch the android's throat and shook her
head. "Her heart's still beating."

Thor didn't respond to the touch.

"I can't believe this is happening." Cleo Samson eyed the
walls as though expecting another spike at any moment. "This
is insane."

"Insane or not," said Inari, "the fact remains that it *is* happening. And unless we want to end up dead like her, then I
suggest we try to figure out—"

"Look at Thor," said Axford. "Something's not right."

"Yeah, she has a hole through her fucking head," snapped
Gou Mang. "That's about as far from being right as you could
possibly—"

"Look *closer*," Axford cut in again, angered by Gou Mang's
hysteria. "Something's happening to her!"

Alander peered curiously at what Axford was indicating.
The skin looked perfectly normal at first, until he realized that
it was shifting and changing in minute increments. Freckles
were drifting; veins were stretching. It was like watching a wax
model melt in free fall: there was no dripping or gross defor-
mation, just a slow, subtle mixing.

Everyone stepped back when they noticed minutely thin filaments begin to stretch outward from the surface of her skin,
swaying and reaching for open air.

"That's nanotech!" Inari gasped. "She's been infected with
something!"

"The I-suit is keeping it in," said Sol, although she, too,
took an extra step back, just to be on the safe side.

"For how long, though?" asked Gou Mang. "That thing

pierced *Eledone*'s hull like it was nothing more than a balloon. How can we be sure this won't do the same to the I-suit?"

"She's right," said Axford. "We should eject her from the ship before she has a chance to infect us all. The farther away from me she is, the better I'll feel."

"No one's getting ejected," said Sol firmly. "She's *hurt,* for crying out loud! She needs our help right now."

"For all we know, she could already be dead," Axford argued. "They could be keeping the body alive until they've fully taken it over."

"I don't care, Frank!" Sol returned, wheeling on him. She was passionate, determined, but Alander could hear uncertainty behind her words. "We aren't abandoning her until I'm convinced we have no other choice—not while she's still got a heartbeat! *Eledone*? I want Thor isolated from the rest of us. Is that understood?"

"Yes, Caryl."

Sol and Alander were pushed aside as a bubble appeared around Thor's floating body. The bubble merged with the cockpit walls and then withdrew. It took only a second for the wall to heal behind the bubble and for the space between Sol and Alander to be cleared again. There was a slight vibration through the floor as part of the hole ship split away from the rest.

"I have separated into two unequal sections," explained the AI. "I have given Caryl Hatzis her own life support and environment protection."

A screen opened behind Axford, showing the interior of the excised hole ship. In it was visible, from several angles, Thor's body.

Sol took a deep breath. "Okay, now that's been taken care of, maybe we can look at the situation more rationally." She looked meaningfully at Axford. "Any suggestions?"

"Yeah," said the ex-general. "I want the air in here scrubbed, and I want every surface renewed. I don't want any chance of us getting infected also."

"That task has already been performed," said *Eledone.* "There exists no locus of infection by the invasive agent."

Happy with the AI's diagnosis, Alander returned his attention to the screens depicting Thor's body. It was now as smooth and colorless as a lump of white cheese. Even as he watched he could see the blood that had pooled around her wounds turn a deep black and retreat inside her.

"What the hell *was* that thing?" he muttered. "What did it do to us?"

"It was a sort of anti-intrusion response, I think," said Axford. "Analogous to an immune system. An intruder is noted and injected with a pathogen designed to destroy it. If we hadn't isolated the pathogen so quickly, we might all be in the same situation as her right now."

"Wouldn't it have been easier to just destroy us outright?" Alander asked.

"Not if it wasn't in their interest to do so. It might attract too much attention—or there might be delicate regions nearby."

"This is sounding less and less like ecology," said Inari, "and more like biology."

"The perils of analogy," said Gou Mang. Her face was pale and shocked, making the rhyme obscenely incongruous. "It singled out Thor as though it knew she was our leader—and *that* scares the crap out of me."

"*She's* the only thing that scares me at the moment," said Axford, his eyes still on the monitor. "And I'm not about to let myself believe this is over until she's a long way away from me."

"That's only part of the problem," said Sol. "If that thing notices that its plan hasn't worked, it could come back and pick another one of us and do it all over again. How do we prevent that from happening?"

"Any volunteers for the boss's job?" joked Samson grimly.

On the screen, Thor was turning a milky color. Her I-suit ballooned outward. Strange flashes came from random points across her skin, as though the nanotech that had infected her was scintillating. The only thing that identified her as even remotely human was her shape. Everything else—mission uniform, features, hair—had been absorbed.

"I'll do it," said Sol after a few moments of silence. "I'll take Thor's place—at least until we have a better idea of what's going on."

No one objected. Alander put a hand on her arm and gripped

it tightly, reassuringly. Her brief smile told him she appreciated the gesture.

"Maybe it's time we reconsidered going home," she said. "We're completely out of our depth. There's nothing we can do here except get ourselves killed. That we haven't yet speaks more about our luck than our skill. Sooner or later, that luck is bound to run out."

"We've already had this discussion," said Axford.

"Things have changed, Frank. When we—"

"Wait a minute," Gou Mang interrupted. "Check this out, everyone."

She indicated the screens showing views of the Starfish fleet. The alien vistas were ever-changing, magnificent, and mysterious. The fiery sunlike object appeared to be in the grips of a magnetic storm. Vast tendrils of plasma looped up and out around its equator, falling back down half a turn or more later. The strange arcs overlapped, rising and falling, so that it looked like the object was trying very hard to create a ring system like Saturn's, but failing due to its high gravity.

Trident ships wove through the rings, almost as though shepherding them. The massive vessels were accompanied by types Alander had never seen before: rippling deltas; curved cylinders; structures like old atomic models, composed of rods and spheres in haphazard clumps. He couldn't tell if they were habitats or vessels in their own right.

As he watched, the backdrop of stars, distorted as though by heat haze, suddenly shifted to new configurations. The fleet, and *Eledone* with it, had moved.

Inari laughed humorlessly. "This just keeps getting better and better."

Her words fell into a frustrated and frightened silence. The enormity of what they were attempting was finally sinking in. The Starfish were so far advanced that any hope of communicating with them seemed ludicrously naive. Sol was right; they were way out of their depth.

"It's just one surprise after another," said Gou Mang.

Alander shook his head. "I think I'm beyond being surprised."

Barely had he finished saying this when Thor sat up and looked at them from the screen.

*   *   *

Sol hadn't been watching the screens on that side of the cock-pit. Her attention was focused on the sunlike object. The plasma loops seemed to be settling down now that the Starfish fleet had completed its jump. Activity was increasing across the strange collective.

It was only when Alander cried out in surprise that she turned to see Thor moving. The infected android was resisting the restraining fields and trying to stand. For a moment, she struggled ineffectually, then appeared to give in.

"Yes, Caryl." *Eledone*'s voice startled everyone in the cockpit. Then, on the screens, they saw the fields holding Thor in place relax and place her gently on the floor.

"*Eledone*, no!" Sol barked. "Disregard any orders—"

"Do not be alarmed, Sol." The voice boomed through the hole ship cockpit, filling it like water. On the screen, Thor's body straightened, facing them emotionlessly.

"Thor? Is that—is that *you?*" said Alander.

"I was Caryl Hatzis," said the voice. Thor's nanofactured flesh swirled like the atmosphere of a milky gas giant. "Now I am the conduit."

"The conduit?" asked Sol. "What does that mean?"

"I am to stand between you and the Source of All. I will convey—" Just for an instant, the creature before them seemed to fumble for words. "—Your message."

"Convey our message to what?" Sol stared at the screen in something very much like despair. She wasn't used to being so far out of her depth like this. It was frightening.

"There is no time for explanations," Thor went on. "I must leave now."

"But will you return?" Sol asked.

Thor didn't respond. Instead, she raised an arm to point at one of the walls of her habitat. It shot out like a spear, fingers stretching to a fine point and piercing the wall with no apparent effort. Thor's body collapsed to a ball that flowed like liquid through the hole in the wall and was gone in an instant. The screen shifted to an outside view showing the much smaller sphere of the habitat. An elongated milky smear moved rapidly against the backdrop, darting away from the habitat at first, then looping back to engulf it, ballooning outward in an impossibly large mouth and enclosing the habitat completely. The balloon collapsed, leaving a fat ovoid in its wake. A hole puckered open at one end, and strange energies suddenly stirred the vacuum.

Blurring with speed, almost too fast for *Eledone* to follow, the thing that had once been Thor jetted away from them. Telemetry followed it against the inconstant backdrop. Sol watched, stunned, as it performed a smooth course correction, sending it on a collision course with the fiery object at the heart of the fleet.

"Where the fuck is it taking her?" Gou Mang asked weakly.

"To the Source, I guess," said Sol.

"Two minutes to impact," *Eledone* announced.

"What do we do now?" asked Inari.

She shrugged. "I suppose we sit and wait."

"But how will we know whether she's succeeded or not?" said Gou Mang.

"If the Starfish stop wiping out our colonies, then I guess we can assume she got through to them," said Alander.

"I don't know about you guys," said Axford, "but I, for one, don't like the idea of sitting here out in the open waiting to see if she succeeds or not. Personally, I'd rather move and wait elsewhere."

Sol nodded. "I'm inclined to agree. *Eledone*, take us away from here. Nothing too conspicuous, okay?"

"Understood, Caryl."

The hole ship moved off on a curving course to one side of the injured cutter. Forgotten in all the drama, the mighty ship was looking decidedly threadbare. Its skeleton was visible in some places, while in others great gouts of outrushing gases obscured everything. Intense magnetic fields spun around both poles, sending auroras rippling down its flanks.

"One minute," said *Eledone*.

Thor had vanished off the screens, but passive detectors still picked up a trace of her on more exotic frequencies. Her passage appeared to be slowing as she approached the sunlike object, but Sol knew that to be an artifact of relativity. She was traveling so fast that she would arrive at her destination before the radiation she emitted would reach the hole ship.

Eledone plotted a projected course for the others to follow and maintained a countdown based on the assumption that her course wouldn't dramatically change.

"Ten seconds," said the AI. Then, following a slight pause: "Three, two, one . . . contact."

"That's it," said Sol when the symbol representing Thor reached the edge of the sunlike object.

"And now what do we do?" asked Inari.

"We wait," said Sol. "Just like I said."

"For how long? It could take hours, days."

Sol faced Inari. "Unless you've got a better—"

A blinding white light silenced her. She reeled back, covering her eyes. It didn't do any good; the light was blazing from all around her, even *inside* her eyelids as though every nearby atom was pouring out photons by the trillion.

Then the coruscation was gone, and normality returned.

"I think we just had a visitor," said Sol, stepping up to the center of the cockpit. "Look."

She indicated one of the screens on which three words were written: *You may witness.*

"Was that—?" Gou Mang started, but clearly didn't know how to finish the sentence.

Sol shook her head. "I don't know what that was."

"Do you think it means it worked, though?" asked Samson.

"Already?" asked Inari in amazement.

Sol shrugged, her attention returning to the screens. The Starfish fleet seemed to have been seized by a sudden rush of activity. Everything had begun to move simultaneously, as if at the bidding of some ftl signal.

Energies whipped; strange shapes stirred. Sol sensed an increased blurring of the stars, as though space itself had become agitated. Alien vessels darted from quarter to quarter; many vanished and didn't reappear, while others emerged from nowhere—although whether they were emerging from camouflage or unspace was impossible to tell.

Another flash made her wince, but this time it came from outside the hole ship. The Source was flaring. Tremendous ribbons of energy detached from the equatorial ring and spun off into the vacuum, where they scintillated into nothing. The glowing streaks could have been weapons, vessels, bizarre forms of communication, even living beings. Sol felt like a savage trying to understand a jet airliner as it flew overhead, craning openmouthed at something utterly beyond her comprehension.

"Something's coming our way," said Axford, pointing at a blip on one of the screens that was arcing to meet them.

"We are receiving a hail from an outside source," said *Eledone.*

There were a few seconds of silence as Sol waited for a response, until she realized that this response needed to come from *her. I'm in charge again,* she thought wearily. *Fuck it.*

"Okay, let's hear it," she said finally.

A smooth, genderless voice spoke dispassionately in English: "Do not be alarmed."

Everyone in the cockpit looked at one another and frowned. "That's it?"

"Yes, Caryl," *Eledone* replied.

"Can we get a visual on that blip?" she said, alarmed despite the advice.

A shaky blur appeared on another screen. What it showed looked like a ring seen hole-on, with a perfectly geometric web stretched across it. The strands were fuzzy-looking, but she couldn't tell if that was an artifact of the long distance or representative of the object's actual appearance. There were no signs of drive emissions or space-time wake.

"The rate of acceleration is increasing," said the hole ship. The image didn't become any clearer as the object drew closer. "Estimated time of arrival is twenty seconds."

"How much is it going to miss us by?" asked Sol.

"It's not going to miss us at all," replied the AI.

"Don't be alarmed, my ass," she muttered irritably. *"Eledone,* try hailing them in return. Ask them what the hell they're doing!"

"There is no response, Caryl," said *Eledone.* "Five seconds. Four—"

The web in the middle began to glow a dull yellow when it was two seconds away. Sol sped her processors up to their maximum rate and watched in horrified amazement as the craft powered in to intercept them. Only at the last moment did she revise her impression of it from a web to a net.

With barely a jolt, they were scooped up by the thing and propelled on their way at a rate of acceleration that she had hitherto thought impossible.

I guess the waiting has ended, she thought, watching the blurring screens with more than a little trepidation.

Someone was shaking him.

"Ueh?"

"Conjugator *Ueh/Ellil?*"

"Is he dead?"

Ueh wished the people around him would just go away and leave him alone. He was tired and in pain; he didn't need this right now. But it was obvious that the clamor of voices wasn't about to let up. He forced himself to move in an attempt to respond to them. It was difficult. The barest effort of raising his head was almost too much for him. His limbs felt distant, as if belonging to someone else. Nevertheless, his efforts were clearly noticed by those gathered around him.

"He moves!" he heard one say.

"Thank the Ambivalence!"

"What's wrong with him?"

"I am—" Both his windpipes were raw. He pushed probing hands away and blinked at the bright lights. "There's nothing wrong with me," he lied. The truth would only cause them more concern. He must have collapsed onto his side in his alcove and, judging by the way his limbs felt, lain there for some time. His skin felt inflamed from the slow soughing of dead pigment scales as he slept. His face felt rubbery, and his insides—

He clutched at the massive wound that the Praxis's remade

reproductive organ had left in him. It was still incredibly tender but thoroughly sealed. He mentally probed at his abdominal cavities. They were thin-walled and wasted like the rest of him.

Atonement was still inside him, quiescent but very much alive. It was perceptibly larger and seemed to be spreading. He sensed tendrils reaching up his spinal passage and down his thighs. They were stiff, like scars, only *inside* his body. What they were doing, he had no way of knowing.

With the help of those attending him, he managed to get himself up into a more comfortable crouching position. He felt light-headed and strange, as though he had woken from a dream that had been almost—but only *almost*—identical to reality. The disorientation persisted when he managed to focus on the people crowding into his alcove. One was all smooth angles and subtle shades.

"What are you doing here?" he asked Yu-qiang.

"*I* came to see you," said the android-embodied engram of *Caryl/Hatzis*. Her expression was one of concern. "I was worried about you. When you didn't answer, I called for help."

"Why?" Her concern puzzled him. "Didn't the Praxis talk to you?"

She nodded. "He told me that you had interceded on our behalf—and for that we are extremely grateful, Ueh."

"Have you succeeded in finding the Spinner front?"

"No, and that is becoming increasingly strange."

One of the other figures crowding the entrance to his niche spoke up in fluent Yuhl and edged Yu-qiang aside to tend to the conjugator. The tones of his native language were rich and complex to his ears but entirely too much for him to follow at the moment. He was used to seeing the world in superposition, just as all binocular creatures assembled single three-dimensional models from two flat retinal images. The Yuhl saw the world in *every* way from dual viewpoints. But he wasn't Yuhl anymore—not solely Yuhl, anyway. And because of this, he found himself thinking linearly. Seen that way, the world was a disturbing place indeed, full of misleading perspectives and odd associations.

He let himself be tended to but immediately regretted it. Strong hands eased him gently from the niche, forcing him to stand. Expressions flashed in bull's-eye circles of surprise at the sight of his wound. Yu-qiang's eyes, too, widened in shock.

"What the fuck—?" She rounded angrily on the attendants.

"*I/we were unaware* of his condition *was not reported*," said one of the attendants in halting English. "*I/we* have not seen—"

Yu-qiang turned away, leaned in closer to Ueh. "How did this happen? Who *did* this to you?"

"The wound is of no consequence," he said. "It is superficial."

"It looks infected." She grabbed the attendant who had spoken and pointed. "Is that supposed to be that color?"

Ueh waved her and the attendants to silence. "There is nothing wrong with me," he insisted. "Please, I need to rest."

"You can't expect us to leave you like this, Ueh," said Yuqiang. "Christ, you could die!"

It was unlikely he would, but he could appreciate her concerns. The wound did look extremely nasty. Nevertheless, he didn't have the energy to argue the point; he just wanted to be alone, so he repeated his request with more control, hiding the pain he was feeling behind a mask of calm.

"I must ask you all to leave me in peace," he said.

The attendants had no choice but to obey his wishes, and withdrew reluctantly, bowing in apology and respect as they retreated. *Caryl/Hatzis*, however, was not bound to obey his order and refused to go. She clearly felt she had a duty of care.

"No way, Ueh," she said. "Someone has to keep an eye on you."

"Very well," he said after the attendants had gone. He rubbed his face and felt flakes of white and black shiver to dust under his fingers. "You alone may stay."

She helped him back into his alcove, then. "Are you sure you don't want any treatment?"

"My body is treating itself."

Yu-qiang could accept that, albeit reluctantly. The humans knew about the Yuhl's extensive history of biomodification. She leaned against a wall, watching as he tried to find a more comfortable position, perching himself on his long-shinned legs. Once such a position would have been the most natural thing in the world to him, but now it just felt awkward.

She waited him out, watching him with wary, suspicious eyes.

"I am sorry," he eventually said, realizing he hadn't found out why she had come to his niche. "What are you doing here, *Caryl/Hatzis*?"

"I came to thank you for talking to the Praxis on our behalf, that's all."

He employed the human headshake to demonstrate that he didn't believe her. "That is not the only reason. There is something else."

She looked like she might deny it for a moment, then capitulated. "Okay, I came because I thought you should know that we're getting signals from Sagarsee. Not directly, we're way out of contact now. But there are relays filling in the gaps, keeping us informed of anything they overhear."

"And what is it they hear?"

"There's activity in pi-1 Ursa Major. Something's going on there, but we don't know what yet. There was a transmission from Thor, though; she was trying to talk to the Starfish." Yuqiang shrugged. "There's a chance she might have gotten through to them."

His image of her seemed to split in two, then came back together again. "I see," he said, although he didn't really. "And this is important?"

"Is it *important?*" she echoed, incredulous. "Of course it is! If she managed to get through to them and convinced them to stop wiping out our colonies, then we should be able to go back!"

"And why would we do that?" he asked, genuinely perplexed. "Why would you want to?"

"Well, because—" She was clearly confused that she'd been asked the question in the first place." "Well, because it's *home*, Ueh."

"Your home is gone," he pointed out. "Earth was destroyed by your own people when—"

"That's not the point!" she interrupted. "It's where we *came* from. We belong there! Wouldn't *you* want to go back to your home if you could—the system where your people were born?"

He didn't know how to answer that question. Return to the home worlds? The possibility had never occurred to him before.

He had been hatched, cocooned, and raised in the *Mantissa*; he'd never been anywhere else for longer than a partial cycle at a time.

"The urge to do so is not strong in me," he said. "In *us.*"

"But the Species Dreamers—"

"The Species Dreamers want a new world, *Caryl/Hatzis*, they don't want the old one back."

"What about the Praxis?"

He couldn't help a flicker of complicated emotion showing on his face. "You would have to ask him what his thoughts were on such matters. It would not be appropriate for me to answer on his behalf."

"But would he—?" She hesitated, and Ueh sensed that at last he was getting to the real reason why she had come to see him. "Would he *let* us return, if we wished to do so?"

He didn't know how to respond to that, either. The request certainly sounded reasonable enough: if the Ambivalence could be halted, there was no reason to keep running; the humans could return to the systems they'd once inhabited. But they had cast their lot with the Praxis and the *Yuhl/Goel*, and their fates were now linked. If the Praxis chose to keep moving, whether the Ambivalence was present or not, he might not pause to let them remain behind. He might not want to lose the hole ships and other resources, especially if the Spinner front would no longer replenish such losses. Never before had the Praxis been faced with such a decision.

"Again I would suggest you ask him yourself."

"I've tried," she said. "But he won't answer unless I agree to be eaten. This is something my original wouldn't countenance."

"Then I don't see how I can help you." He shifted in his alcove restlessly. "I am tired, *Caryl/Hatzis*. I need to rest."

"That's okay," she said, offering a faint and disappointed smile. "I don't mind waiting here with you. We can talk later, perhaps."

He frowned. "Why would you do that? There is no need."

"I don't want anything happening to you in my absence," she said. And although she did her best to avoid looking at it, he knew her concern stemmed from the wound she'd seen running the length of his abdomen.

He started to protest but then thought better of it. If she wanted to stay, why not let her? He may well need the help later on. He didn't know what the Praxis's Atonement was doing to him, after all. It could kill him while he slept. He was sure it was keeping him alive only so long as he was useful. What happened after that period, though, he didn't dare think.

Yu-qiang waited as he settled himself down and prepared for sleep, still balanced awkwardly on his feet. He felt her stare upon him, assessing him, monitoring him for any adverse changes. But he didn't mind. He was tired, and he needed to rest, and the silence that had settled around them in the alcove allowed him to do just that. . . .

He dreamed of the Praxis's mutated reproductive organ. Whatever its original function had been, its purpose was plain. It gutted Ueh with all the precision and brutality of a primitive medical machine. His screams were ignored as tubes, blades, and clamps worked feverishly inside him, reorganizing him, restructuring not just his physical form but his hormonal balance as well, making his interior a suitable environment for the thing he had been chosen to carry.

When the time came for it to be inserted, he was almost beyond noticing. He had vague memories of curved, slender arms emerging from the chamber walls, bearing something smooth and white in their embrace. Bean-shaped and half as large as Ueh's head, it slotted neatly into the new place inside him. He remembered the soundless slicing and cauterizing as the reproductive organ worked to seal him up with the thing inside him. Weak, deep in shock, he had been expelled from the chamber, sliding down a chute slick with gore to a ramp deep in the heart of the *Mantissa A*. From there he made his own way back to his private niche.

Ueh had never been part of a breeding trio. He knew how they worked, though. All Yuhl carried sperm and eggs, and all had wombs. When the time came to reproduce, sperm from one combined with the egg of another in the womb of a third. In order that the fertilized egg could be carried to term, the immune system of the bearer had to be suppressed by the donating parents. The process was invasive and painful, involving secretions from thorny organs under the wing sheaths. One donor held down the bearer while he was impaled by the other donor, then the donors swapped roles. Usually, afterward, the bearer was more often than not insensate, drugged by powerful hormones, his entire body ravaged by the demands of reliable procreation.

Fortunately, pregnancy rarely lasted longer than a human month, during which time the bearer hovered in an almost comatose state. The donor parents worked in shifts around the clock to tend to the bearer's every need and to maintain the hormone imbalance permitting the unchecked growth of the fertilized egg. Birth involved a relatively uncomplicated removal procedure, followed by the usual cycles of nonconscious larval growth and pupa. An emergent Yuhl adult had no memories of his birth yet maintained close contact with all three parents throughout his early life.

Ueh knew that humans did it differently, and while their method seemed strange to him, he could accept it. Every sexual species he had encountered through his long life had had some element of parasitism in its mating procedures. From the outside, what looked normal could seem utterly shocking. But he had never encountered a successful, intelligent life-form that reproduced without regard for the one carrying its children. He suspected that there was a natural law preventing such amoral species from acquiring the cooperation necessary for true civilization.

What the Praxis had done to him, then, wasn't likely to be reproduction. The Praxis had told Ueh that he might well die from the procedure he had agreed to endure, but he hadn't said anything about being the host for a malignant fetus. Nevertheless, Ueh still had his doubts. They manifested in the form of nightmares involving him giving birth in a violent and bloody fashion as humans did. And when there weren't the dreams, there was always the Praxis whispering to him in his sleep.

He wondered how it must feel to be the sole representative of one's kind left in the known universe. Did the Praxis feel lonely, vulnerable, guilty? What, exactly, could the Praxis possibly have to atone *for?*

When he woke—gently this time, to no harsh surprises—

Yu-qiang was still there, watching him patiently via the alcove's reduced light.

"Sleep well?" she asked.

He didn't answer, recognizing the question for what it was: a meaningless pleasantry.

"Where are we?" he asked instead. "Have we moved?"

"We're in a system called Hipp66486," she said. "K-type star—the sort you lot like—with a few planets. There are some G-types not far away that look almost homey."

"What sort of planets?" he asked, feeling curiosity regarding the outside world for the first time in cycles.

"Two gas giants out deep, three regular balls close in. None inhabited."

"Habitable, though?"

She shook her head. "One primordial, one freeze-dried, one rocky lump."

He shifted position in a disturbingly humanlike shrug. Atonement was everywhere inside him now. He could feel its tendrils in every part of his body, spreading and curling like roots, turning back only where they encountered skin.

"Any word from Sagarsee?" he asked.

"Very little. We're down to our last colonies. If Thor doesn't do something fast, there'll be none left to save."

He straightened now, curious about the emotion evident in Yu-qiang's tone. "You have regrets, don't you. You wish you had stayed behind to help."

She didn't answer immediately. "Even if I did, I know there wouldn't be anything I could have done."

"Except die with them."

She sighed. "Do you really think it'll come to that?"

He studied her as best he could through eyes that were determined not to focus. "What if it does? Will your people resign themselves to their fate, then? No more questioning our ways and dreaming of returning home?"

"Humans don't do resignation well," she said, smiling faintly. "Even when they say they do, there's always a small part of them that hopes something will come along to change their situation." She paused thoughtfully. "I guess things would be easier if we could find the Spinner front. We're stranded at the moment, in limbo."

He knew that feeling well: part human, part Yuhl; caught between his old life and whatever the Praxis had in store for him.

Shifting position again, he realized that for the first time in a while he was restless, wanting to move. He was tired of being cooped up like a prisoner in a cage, a pupa in its cocoon.

He reached for Yu-qiang's hand. Startled at first, but quickly recovering, she helped him out of the alcove and to his feet. He stood unsteadily for some time, recovering his balance and letting his muscles stretch. The scar reaching from his throat to groin was stiff and inflexible, but it had lost its terrible viciousness. Atonement's fine tendrils tingled inside him. Their presence was not debilitating. He felt drained by their presence but was no longer in any discomfort.

"Are you okay?" asked Yu-qiang, holding him steady with one hand.

He nodded in response to her question, but his mind was focused on the new sense of urgency that was building inside him. "I think I would like to go for a walk."

The door sighed open at his mental command, and she guided him through it. Noise and light assailed him. The everyday life of *Mantissa A* was something he had not experienced for several cycles; he'd grown unaccustomed very quickly to the never-ending bustle that filled the corridors. He moved slowly along the corridor, feeling his way more than seeing, as he adjusted to the expanded world around him. Attendants and colleagues offered greetings in his native tongue. He offered only the most cursory response—a word or two, a halting expression.

"Observation deck," he said. His domed head felt strangely light, and he found himself leaning more heavily on Yu-qiang than he would have liked. "That way."

Once there, Yu-qiang helped to steady him as an observatory intestine descended from the ceiling to smoothly engulf him. He welcomed the warm and familiar embrace.

The universe opened up around him, dazzling him with its beauty. The multitude of stars shone brightly; not dimmed in the clever illusion by the flare of a nearby sun. Yu-qiang had called it Hipp66486, which seemed an ugly name for something so beautiful. He imagined that he could feel that sun's warmth on his skin, making the backs of his legs glow and his wing sheaths flex in satisfaction.

"What are you feeling?" asked the Praxis.

The mellifluous voice didn't make him shudder as it once had. He noted, however, that the Praxis had asked him *what* he was feeling, not *how*.

"I feel—" He fumbled for the human word; there was no equivalent in the language of the Yuhl. "—*homesick*."

The Praxis didn't comment, and for a moment Ueh thought he might have said something stupid. Certainly the yearning feeling filling him was unfamiliar and unsettling, one he had never experienced before. Was it because of his conversation with Yu-qiang? he wondered. Had she put the thought in his head?

With a noise like a soft exhalation, the engram of *Caryl/Hatzis* appeared beside him in the illusion of the universe outside. They stood together, staring at the vistas of space, basking in the light of the nearby star.

"We used to think it was lonely out here," she said. "Now we think it's not lonely enough."

"Everything is relative," he said.

"I suppose. I guess it's going to seem lonely for you guys if the Ambivalence *has* been stopped."

He scanned the sky, searching for the planets she had mentioned. He found them easily enough: five bright points standing out from the starscape. He zoomed in on each in turn. They were exactly as Yu-qiang had described. Not one of them was habitable, but they weren't without promise.

The promise of what? he wondered. Had he been swept up in the human ideal of a home?

"I have commandeered you a hole ship," said the Praxis. "It is ready to leave whenever you are, Ueh."

The suggestion that he might need a hole ship startled him— no less because he realized only then that he *did* want to leave *Mantissa A*. Getting out of the niche wasn't enough; that wasn't from where his restlessness stemmed. He wanted room to breathe, to *be*—and the Praxis seemed to know this.

"The third planet," Ueh said, indicating a primordial world in the view below him, gray green in color from the vantage point of space. Its hot, turbulent atmosphere was inhospitable but well within the tolerances of an I-suit. "That's where I'm going."

Yu-qiang stared at him in astonishment. "You can't be serious, Ueh. You can barely walk, and you want to go exploring?"

"You can come with me, if you wish."

"Of course I'm coming. I wouldn't let you go wandering off on your own—not in your condition. But I still think you're crazy to be attempting this right now."

He slipped out of the simulation, sagging as his full weight returned. Yu-qiang was there to support him, though. Then, following his directions, she helped him to nearest docking point.

"What if the rest of the Yuhl leave you behind?" she asked as they walked.

"They won't."

"They'll be off the moment they find the Spinner front, Ueh. You know that."

"They won't," he insisted with growing urgency.

"Crazy," she muttered again as they continued along the narrow corridors, attracting puzzled looks wherever they went.

Inside him, Ueh could feel Atonement shift restlessly with every step he took. It could feel its impending freedom, he was sure.

[faded text from previous/adjacent page bleed-through]

2.3

THE LAW OF HYBRIDS

2160.10.1 Standard Mission Time
(5 September 2163 UT)

2.3.1

"Hello, Peter. Can you hear me?"

"Lucia?" At first, the image of Peter Alander from Athena—as she remembered him, not the new, bearded, more youthful creature fashioned by the alien called the Praxis—appeared perfectly firm in conSense. Lucia had found him in the files of frozen memory that Peter had called the Graveyard. He had been designated by mission number only—512—and came complete with a detailed case history of early senescence onset and brainlock. The clarity of his image made a lie of the diagnosis.

"Is that really you?" he asked her, eyes widening.

"Yes, Peter." Her heart warmed at the sight of him and of his obvious delight in seeing her. She reached out in the virtual space to take his hands, her flesh touching his with all apparent solidity. His skin was as warm as his gaze.

Then his smile slipped and he looked down at their linked hands. "I don't feel real," he said, puzzled. "I feel like a fake."

"You're not a fake, Peter. You're the real thing."

"You said I'd feel that way before we left, that *all* the engrams would think they were real. What if I'm just a fake programmed to lie to itself?"

That's exactly what we are, Lucia wanted to respond, but she refrained, knowing it was the wrong thing for him to hear right now.

"Peter," she cooed, gently squeezing his hands. "None of this is important. You are who you are, not what you're made of. Intelligence and personality transcend the hardware. You can be yourself."

"That's all well and fine, Lucia—but who *am* I?" His gaze skated over hers, filled with desperation. "And come to that, who are *you?* How can I know for sure that—"

"Peter, stop and think *who's* asking that question!"

His image began to shake, as though he was trembling. The image flickered like a television transmission under poor conditions. Static snapped across his features. He stretched, twisted, juddered.

"L-Luc-cia!"

The despairing cry fragmented, cut short on the final vowel.

Then his image froze altogether, and she was forced to shut him down. Peter Alander 512 joined 154 from Thor, 44 from Geb, 919 from Ilmarinen and 755 from Rama. She had more than a dozen left to test and she wasn't sure if she had the stomach for it. Nevertheless, she knew she had to go on, if only to remain focused on the job at hand.

She needed him as badly as the survivors needed her.

The mission supervisors of Demeter and Zemyna, the two colonies under imminent threat from the Starfish, had finally bowed to public pressure and allowed their nonessential crew to leave in advance of the inevitable attack. With Thor's plea to the Starfish unanswered, there was no concrete reason to hope that the alien advance had been in any way slowed. Given the choice between pretending, in accordance with programming, that everything was going to be just as it had always been, and taking sensible precautions, a large amount of data and personnel were evacuated to Sagarsee. Lucia helped in those efforts, both as transport and facilitator. She could move larger amounts of mass more quickly than the hole ships, and that left them free for scouting and other tasks. The sight of the tame Spindle also proved to be reassuring, as though the Spinners themselves were complicit in humanity's attempts to survive.

Lucia wasn't so naive as to believe that. The Spinners had

given her one more tool on a whim. It could have been a random act of charity or offered in accordance with an unknown agenda. Either way, she didn't feel terribly reassured.

Sagarsee's resources were soon stretching. In the six years since the *Frank Drake*'s arrival, the young colony had built a number of bases on the ground as well as the beginnings of an orbital installation. All were part of a scientific infrastructure, not a holiday resort. Disgruntled engrams were forced to share processing power with many more than the system had been designed for, necessitating simplified conSense environments or frequent slow-mos. From the virtual halls of BSC5148, Lucia detected rumblings of discontent as limited resources were gobbled up by the pressing situation. Fovea tracking and high-level planning took up great chunks of the operating capacity.

Lucia found time around her twin roles as ferry pilot and symbol of the resistance to address her own needs. Operating at extreme fast speeds, she rummaged through the Graveyard, looking for signs of hope.

"Hello, Peter. Can you hear me?"

"Lucia? Is that really you?" Peter Alander 400 from Eos looked exactly the same as the others and would, no doubt, respond to the same stimuli in exactly the same way.

"I *think* I'm me," she said. "I feel like I'm Lucia Benck. I look like her, and I act like her. Does that make me her, do you think?"

He frowned, coming closer, almost warily, to study her face. In the virtual environment, his skin was a beautiful human color; his eyes were impossibly clear.

"You're an engram," he said. "You're an engram like me."

"Yes, Peter, I am." There was no point skirting the issue. She didn't have time for the embodiment therapy that Peter from Adrasteia had gone through. She needed to find a quick and effective way to keep him talking to her. "You and me, we're just pretending to be human, even though we're not really. We both have shortcuts in our personalities that cause us problems. You don't feel like yourself, but I need you to keep me here. It's either that, or I run. Do you understand, Peter? Do you understand what I'm saying?"

"Tourist and truth seeker," he said, referring as he often did to their last conversation on Earth—or rather the last conversation on record between their originals before their engrams were activated and launched into space. She, too, remembered it well.

"The truth seekers are supposed to ride on the impetus of the tourists," she said. "But it's the other way around now. Without you, Peter, I'm going to break down. You have to help me."

His face threatened to collapse into the now-familiar mask of confusion and existential angst. "I remember—" He faltered, recovered. "I remember the Gifts, the Spinners . . ."

She clutched on that detail. "That's right! You were woken up when the Spinners arrived on Eos. They brought you back to talk to the Gifts."

"I—I—" He gripped her hand and held it tight. "They said you hadn't made it. You weren't there."

"But I'm here now, Peter. I came back for you."

A small lie, but she hoped it would bolster his self-esteem.

That wasn't the problem, though. She understood it as soon as his face fell. The *esteem* he felt for himself was irrelevant when he had no clear sense of *self* at all.

"But who *are* you?" he asked. "Who am *I*? If we're not us, then—"

"We *are* us, Peter. You're Peter, and I'm Lucia. We were together, and part of me wants us to be together again. I can't run anymore; I can't leave these people behind. You have to be my anchor."

His image twisted, snapped back into shape. "I can't tell—who—I—"

"Peter, no!"

But it was no use. He froze like a statue in midsentence. His face became flat and inanimate, a cardboard cutout of a once-living man. All of the subtle processes that made him who he was seized up in midbeat, and he was gone.

She dismissed him despairingly, wishing she could swear like Caryl Hatzis. She wanted to scream into the void and curse UNESSPRO and all the engram engineers who were responsible for what had become of herself and all the others. How could they have designed the engrams so effectively for the short term, and yet screwed up so badly for the long term? She wondered, if they had known they were building people who would ultimately be the last humans alive, whether the designers would have been so careless?

She turned from the thought. It was pointless wasting time on speculation. She had half a relative hour to kill before arriving back at Sagarsee, so she decided to try one more. Calling up the engram from mission 17, to chi Hercules, she prepared herself for yet another emotional roller coaster ride.

"Lucia?" Peter's engram said upon seeing her.

"Yes, it's me." She couldn't hide the weariness in her voice. "And you're you. I should have that inscribed on tablets and hung about our necks."

"I wasn't expecting you to be here when I woke up." He looked around at the neutral environment she had conjured for his reactivation. "I wasn't expecting to wake up at all, in fact. I chose the dark."

His image flickered but didn't freeze.

Her curiosity snagged upon his words. "The dark? What do you mean by that?"

"He gave me a choice, and that's the one I took. I told him to say hello to you from me."

"Told *who?*"

Peter's image flickered again. "The other me; the one at Sothis."

Lucia thought quickly, not knowing where this conversation was going. It was different from the others. She'd been to Sothis; it was a smoking ruin, thanks to the Starfish. This version of Peter must have been there prior to the attack. And for him to have spoken to another version of himself there, there must have been another version working at the time. The logic was as inescapable as it was exciting.

"He called me a cripple, a wounded creature. He told me it wasn't Caryl's fault. He told me—"

"Which one was he?" she asked. "Where was he from?"

"Upsilon Aquarius," he replied. "He said—" The flickering was more persistent, the third time, but he returned and remained stable for longer. "He said I might not come back, but I chose to be shut down anyway. It was better than the alternative."

"What alternative?" Her excitement had abated on learning that the one this Peter had spoken to was the same one who had rejected her; nevertheless, she was still interested in what had happened.

"To join with him, to become—something else." Peter grimaced. "I may be sick, but I know who I am. Who I *was,*" he corrected. "Who I'm *supposed* to be."

"He wanted you to merge with him?" The idea was strange, more the sort of thing she might have expected of the original Caryl Hatzis, judging by what she'd heard from Rob Singh.

"Yes, but he'd changed. He wasn't me anymore. How could I not be who I am? That would be suicide."

She thought this through, wondering if she'd found the key to keeping Peter animated. By threatening to take away his fragile sense of self entirely, the other Peter had managed to make this one cling more tightly to it. But was it stable, or just a temporary fix?

The only way to find out was to keep him talking.

"You don't have to choose the dark anymore, Peter. I can keep you running as long as you want."

He shook his head. "I'll only start looping, and I don't want to go through that again. I'll end up shutting down altogether."

"But I—" She stopped, unwilling to admit her vulnerability to him. He was more his old self than any of the others had been. His confident, almost arrogant sense of his own rightness made her afraid to look *wrong.* "We need you."

"I can't make a difference, Lucia. You're up to your eyeballs with alien AIs and worse. What can I do about them?" He snorted as if in amusement. "Christ, according to me, they shouldn't even exist in the first place!"

That's right, she thought, remembering how Peter had famously announced to the scientific community in the 2010s that humanity should be alone in the universe, if certain quantum mechanical assumptions held true. That the UNESSPRO missions had initially found only single-celled and other equally primitive life-forms had initially borne his opinion out. But now . . .

"The Spinners must have come as a shock," she said.

He bristled slightly at that. "They don't prove my theory wrong, if that's what you're implying. They could be non-conscious AIs. If they perform no truly observational act, and if their makers died out before complex life on Earth evolved, it could all still be just as I said."

"What about the Starfish?" she said. "Or the Yuhl? Or the Praxis?"

"The Starfish could be AIs, too. As for the others, I don't know anything about them."

"They're flesh and blood. I've seen them."

He faltered only for a moment. "There are possible explanations. If the Spinners and the Starfish are universe-hopping, looking for intelligent life in each, they could be picking up passengers as they go. The Yuhl could be from a completely different continuum than ours; their evolution would have had no effect on the way we evolved."

"That's one possible explanation," said Lucia. "But not a very likely one. I think you're clutching at straws here, Peter."

"Is it any more unlikely than this entire situation?" He seemed very much alive and stable in the grip of an intellectual debate. "And I can think of a second explanation, if the first isn't good enough for you. The Spinners and Starfish could be riding a reverse time flow from the future, bringing conscious aliens back with them. Have we ever spoken to them, interacted with them face-to-face?" When she shook her head, he seized that admission as proof. "That would be because our notions of causality are fundamentally different. We may not be *able* to interact, except via intermediaries, because their arrow of time is opposite to ours. We're riding a wave of expansion out from the big bang, while they're coasting inward to the big crunch. If they evolved in the future, they would, again, have had no influence on our own evolution."

She thought about this for a moment. "Actually, that's quite an interesting theory," she said, meaning it. "But does it help us at all? Can it keep us alive any longer?"

He shrugged. "That's up to you. Understanding the problem is just the first step."

"Which is why we need you, Peter, to take the next step. You have to stay with us." *With me,* she added silently. "Can't you at least try it?"

His stare tightened, and he seemed to stick for a second, as though tripping over his thoughts.

"I chose the dark," he said. "It was the only choice I could make."

"But you have more options now!"

"You misunderstand me, Lucia. It was the only choice I could make. *This* me, not the other one, or my original. *Me.* I know I'm a faulty program; I know I can't work on my own; but this is something I have that's *mine,* and I'm clinging to it. Unless you can offer me a foolproof way to keep me awake while retaining *my* mind, then . . ."

The unfinished sentence lingered, an unspoken question: *Could* she do this? After a few seconds she sighed and shook her head; there was no way she could guarantee that this would be possible.

"Then I afraid I'm going to have to insist you shut me down. I'll take my chances. The dark will part again, one day. Maybe then there'll be a solution."

She looked away as his image began to flicker again. He almost certainly didn't have much time left before he froze like the others, but he had been the best to date. She didn't know what gave him the edge—meeting the other Alander, or having been forced to confront his condition and make a life-or-death choice—but she was reluctant to let all hope slip through her fingers.

"And if there is no solution?" she asked him solemnly. "If you die?"

"Then that solves all my problems, I guess."

He looked apologetic and uncharacteristically fragile as she instructed the overseer to bring his simulation to a halt. Her virtual environment fell silent. She fought a sense of pointlessness that threatened to overtake her. The temptation to give up and run was too strong, she couldn't trust herself not to give in to it if she gave it the slightest encouragement. Living longer was all very well, but she didn't want to do it with a guilty conscience.

For the first time, she wondered how long she could live inside Spindle Ten. If she found a way to circumvent her programming and her engram didn't seize up, might she be risking immortality by staying with the other survivors? She could see no real reason why not. She was just a tangle of electrons—or some other means of carrying information—swirling around the innards of the Spindle. If nothing destroyed the mainframe or the software, a program could run forever.

Unless, she thought, there was something else the Spinners hadn't told them.

The thought of a gestalt Peter Alander made up of all the Graveyard engrams running parallel, the group propping itself up even as they individually stumbled, had just begun to seem vaguely workable when she arrived at Sagarsee with her refugees in tow. The first thing she noticed was an unusual degree of activity around the planet's gifts; hole ships were coming and going at a rapid rate. The second thing was the intense level of ftl communications flowing through the system. Information was flooding in. Even as her charges began to stir in their electronic bunkers, she was dipping into the stream in an attempt to work out what was going on.

What she found was disturbingly familiar.

"Lucia, thank God you're back," said Cleo Samson when her presence had registered on the *Frank Drake*'s sensors. Her voice was urgent. "We need you immediately."

"Why? What's happening?" she asked. "All I'm seeing is pi-1 Ursa Major and flashes of something else." Something much like ball lightning encircling the sun, thousands of tiny, fiercely radiant points strung out in curving lines, moving at an appreciable fraction of the speed of light.

"We can't get close enough to figure it out right now." Cleo's face in conSense perfectly mirrored the anxiety she was feeling. "Three scouts have already been taken out by whatever's going on in there, and I don't want to risk any more."

"So what is it you want me to do?" Lucia asked.

"You can move faster than the hole ships; you might be able to get in and out before anyone sees you."

And if I can't? she wanted to ask, but instead said, "I'm not designed for combat, Cleo."

"No one's expecting you to fight, Lucia. We just need to know what's going on. If it's the Starfish, then maybe Thor achieved what she set out to do. But if it's not . . ."

Cleo didn't need to finish the sentence. Pi-1 Ursa Major was the great unknown. If it wasn't the Starfish, there was no telling what it could be instead. The engrams were like a child poking at the lid of a trap-door spider's lair. If something unexpected came out, they might not be able to put it back in.

"Okay," she said, even as she fought her reservations about returning to the system where, apart from herself, everyone on her survey mission had died. "But I'm not going until I've unloaded my passengers."

Cleo nodded. "Reconnect with the Hub and send the refugees through, then go straight to pi-1 Ursa Major and see what you can find out. Come back to us afterward or transmit the information via ftl; either way is fine. I really don't want you to take any chances, Lucia, so don't be afraid to pull out if things get hairy in there. We're going to need you here to help us put things back together, afterward."

With that, Cleo's image blinked out.

Lucia shook her head in the emptiness of her virtual world. *Put things back together,* Cleo had said. Not *escape.* The strictures of her programming were still limiting her decision making and planning. But there was nothing Lucia could do about that, except hope for the best that Thor had indeed done what she'd set out to do.

Resigned to taking a more active role than she'd intended, she quickly busied herself by emptying her corridors and rooms of everyone who had left Zemyna. Then she put one graveyard aside in order to possibly head directly into another.

2.3.2

Axford turned from the screen and looked at Caryl Hatzis. "I'm going out there."

Alander knew Sol was going to let him before she'd even opened her mouth. She nodded after a few moments' consideration and said, *"Eledone,* I want you to divide yourself into two distinct habitats. One for myself, Inari, and Cleo, and the other for Peter, Frank, and Gou Mang." Her eyes met Alander's briefly. "I want you to allow the second habitat a discrete personality, answerable to Peter."

"Yes, Caryl."

He moved to stand with Axford and a disgruntled-looking Gou Mang just as a wall of energy split the cockpit in half. The transparent boundary retreated around the edges, shrinking rapidly into a window, then a porthole, then closed entirely. Alander watched Sol as her half of the hole ship went its own way. There was a look of weary unease on her face, and she offered no expression of reassurance or encouragement as she disappeared from view.

Nor should she, he thought. Although the Gatherer—the AI that had collected from the vicinity of the damaged cutter and brought them to the Trident—had reassured them that they would be perfectly safe, there were no guarantees. His understanding of *safe* didn't include being sealed up in a chamber with apparently no exits and told to wait.

"Still doesn't trust me, does she?" Axford said when Sol was out of sight. His tone had a hint of amusement to it.

"Maybe she has no reason to," said Gou Mang.

"My behavior on the mission so far has been exemplary."

She snorted. "*So far* being the operative phrase."

Axford shook his head in mock disappointment. "I'm surprised at your lack of forgiveness, Caryl. This is a war zone; you have to learn to accept help when it's offered."

"And what exactly is it you're offering?" Alander piped in.

"I really can't tell you that," said Axford, sounding genuinely regretful. Then he smiled. "You see, I don't particularly trust you, either."

It was Gou Mang's turn to shake her head. "Let's just get on with this, can't we?"

Alander let them fall into a sullen silence. Their irritation was borne as much out of tiredness as anything else, he imagined. That made it understandable, if not excusable. He couldn't decide if Axford was trying to pick a fight or had some other agenda. He'd been trying to divide the already fractious team ever since they'd set out from Asellus Primus. Perhaps, Alander thought, he was just getting cocky at having achieved a measure of success.

A ring of new screens appeared around them. They showed the same view visible through *Eledone*: a bone-colored, curved chamber large enough to hold several cathedrals.

"Hole ship? From now on you'll answer to the name *Selene*," he said, choosing the name of one of *Eledone*'s component vessels. "When we're completely separated, I want you to set us down by the edge of the chamber. We'll want to disembark there."

"Yes, Peter."

"Is it safe?" asked Gou Mang.

She asked Alander, but *Selene* answered: "Conditions outside are within tolerance levels of your I-suits."

Gou Mang chuckled. "Actually, that's not what I meant."

"I can only provide you with the information at my disposal. I no longer have sufficient resources for speculation."

Alander nodded. He'd never known the hole ships to speculate much anyway, before or after the sort of damage *Eledone* had received.

The hole ship coasted smoothly to the point he'd indicated. The chamber was truly enormous and bulged around them like a hollow pumpkin. Its shape was distinctly organic, but its smoothness suggested that it had been made. Once again the comparison with biological systems was easy to make but probably misleading.

The airlock irised smoothly open in one wall of the cockpit. There were no telltale air currents to indicate that the hole ship was open to the alien atmosphere outside; a thin skin of energy still maintained a barrier between them. Feeling nervous, Alander preceded the others along the short corridor to the egress airlock and stepped outside.

There was no sense of resistance as he stepped through the meniscus, nor did he feel the I-suit tighten around him in response to the alien conditions. In Upsilon Aquarius, he had leapt into a vacuum protected by nothing but the I-suit, and he'd been fine. If the hole ship assured him that he was safe from the elements, then he had no reason to doubt it.

He walked several paces across the bony floor. The surface was hard beneath his feet but, like the walls of the chamber, perfectly smooth. There were no breaks or seams, no edges anywhere. The nearest wall sloped steeply upward, then curved over him, culminating in a domed ceiling. At the center of this was a circular depression. A forest of slender cylinders dozens of meters long hung suspended from the depression, looking like dangling tree roots. According to radar, these "roots" were solid and unmoving, showing no evidence of any degree of swaying whatsoever, regardless of the motion of the Trident around it.

Axford and Gou Mang joined Alander outside, taking positions on either side of him.

"So now what happens?" asked Gou Mang. Her voice rang clearly in his ears; he couldn't tell if it came through the air across the distance between them or if there was some sort of linkup with the I-suits. "Is this a visitor's lounge or a holding cell?"

He took another look around but didn't answer, assuming

that she hadn't really expected one. Meanwhile, Axford had wandered off to examine the rising curve of the wall.

"Is anyone here?" Alander called. There was no reply, but he couldn't help the feeling that they were being watched. "Hello!"

There was a tearing sound, as though the air around them had been ripped aside, and abruptly he found himself face-to-face with a gray sphere half as wide across as he was tall, floating in the air four meters away from him. He jumped back a step in alarm, as did Gou Mang. The side of the sphere facing him was etched with deep gouges in an intricate but apparently random pattern.

"Hello," it said, and promptly disappeared.

Axford looked up sharply. "What was that?"

Gou Mang had a hand on her chest and was looking around wildly. "Never mind that! Where the hell did it go?"

"Are you okay out there?" asked Sol from *Eledone*. The hole ship was hanging safely in the distance like a milky soap bubble.

"You saw it, too?" asked Alander.

"Very clearly. Radar picked it up, so it wasn't an illusion. *Eledone* thinks it's hollow."

"Is it still here?" asked Axford. "Hidden perhaps?"

"No. According to the information we have, it's definitely gone."

"So what's the point of saying hello and then vanishing like that?" asked Gou Mang.

Axford chuckled uneasily. "Maybe we frightened it when—"

He called out in alarm as the thing reappeared as suddenly as it had before—and in exactly the same spot. All three jumped back from the mysterious sphere.

"I desire to communicate," it said. Its scarred face rotated once, as though turning to look at them in turn.

"Okay," said Alander, taking a deep breath to steady his pounding heart. "But what's your name, first? And who sent—?"

With the same tearing sound as before, the sphere disappeared again.

"What the—?" Gou Mang looked around, wide-eyed and confused. "Where the fuck has it gone now?"

Alander shook his head, casting his gaze around also. Then, to the chamber in general, he said: "You said you wanted to communicate!"

"The facilitation of communication is my primary objective," said the sphere, appearing at a point closer to him this time. Alander started again, but this time he didn't retreat.

"Then why don't you answer us?" he asked.

It was silent for a beat, then disappeared again.

"It's playing with us," said Axford.

Alander nodded in agreement. "Either that or it's stalling."

"I am conversing according to my operational parameters," the sphere assured him, popping into existence close by his side. The gouges were deep and shadowy, possibly bottomless. He thought for an instant that he could smell iodine.

"And what exactly *are* those parameters?" he asked. In the second it hesitated, Alander knew what was about to happen, so before it had a chance to disappear, he quickly tried another tack: "If you explain those parameters to us, maybe we'll be able to communicate properly. Otherwise we might as well just give up!"

"My parameters reflect those of my maker," said the sphere, "as do yours."

"Who is your maker?" asked Gou Mang.

The sphere didn't respond, and as it disappeared for the fourth time, Alander thought he might be beginning to understand.

"We are copies of our original," he said. "We are flawed, but we function well enough."

The sphere returned. "I represent an aspect of my higher self—one of many dispatched to facilitate various duties."

"I'm going to assume, then, that everything we say is being reported back to that higher self."

"All data is collated and analyzed for meaning."

An interesting way of putting it, Alander thought. He nodded. "My name is Peter Alander."

"I am called the Asteroid."

"The Asteroid?" Gou Mang asked. "What sort of name is that?"

The sphere rotated as though to look at her, then disappeared.

Axford laughed out loud. "Good work, Peter. I think we're finally getting somewhere."

Gou Mang looked suspiciously between them. "What are you talking about?"

"The Asteroid only responds to statements," Alander explained. "Specifically, statements about us that it can reciprocate about itself. It ignores questions."

"Looks like we've got the lion by the tail," said Axford smugly.

"By a hair of the tail, perhaps," Alander corrected him. He was reluctant to start feeling cocky too soon. "The head is still a long way off."

"Whatever," said the ex-general. "Head, hair . . . The main thing is that Thor must have managed to get *someone*'s attention."

"We don't know that," said Alander.

"He may be right, Peter," said Sol. "*Asteroid* is actually a synonym for *starfish*. It seems unlikely that this is a coincidence."

"A synonym, not *one* of them," said Alander, looking around the immense chamber. It was lifeless and empty, but again he felt as though they hadn't been abandoned. He sensed minds infinitely larger than his contemplating them, wondering what do next.

"We're here to talk to the Starfish," he said. His voice fell echoless into the vast space.

"I am here to talk to you," said the Asteroid, popping smartly back into existence.

"We have given them information." Alander recalled what Thor had called herself before firing herself bodily into the sunlike body at the heart of the Starfish fleet. "The Conduit conveyed our message to the Source of All."

"You were brought here to witness."

"We're not seeing much at the moment," said Axford.

"The information you provided has not yet been verified."

The chamber *was* a holding a cell, then, Alander thought. "We'd like to know what's going on, though."

Instead of responding, the Asteroid vanished again.

Axford sighed. "Just when I thought we were starting to get the knack—"

He was cut off as the walls of the chamber disappeared. For a moment everything was utterly black. But not only had the chamber disappeared, but so, too, had *Selene, Eledone,* and the others. Alander was alone, hanging in a terrible, silent void.

Then, suddenly, the tail end of a question from Gou Mang came out of the nothingness:

"—is everybody?"

No one answered, they were too busy staring in breathless awe at the sight before them. They were surrounded by stars, floating apparently naked to the void.

"That's pi-1 Ursa Major," said Axford, pointing at a bright sun directly ahead of them. He was a starlit figure to Alander's left.

"Are we actually there?" Alander asked. "Or just *seeing* it?"

"Just seeing it," said Sol from *Eledone.* "We haven't moved."

"Could the whole Trident have moved?" asked Axford.

"If it moves the same way as the cutters, then we would have felt it, I'm sure," said Alander.

"Either that or we're shielded inside it." Axford waved the issue away as irrelevant. "Whatever. The main thing is that there's the target. We *are* witnessing after all."

Gou Mang laughed. "Witnessing *what?* We're not exactly being swamped with details here."

That point Alander had to agree with. "Asteroid, we can't see anything."

The scarred sphere appeared next to him. "This view is not ideal."

"We could see if our point of view was closer."

"I see from the point of view of my maker."

"You could see better if your maker's point of view was closer."

The sphere rotated once.

"Your statement wasn't about you, so it's not going to respond," Axford diagnosed. Then, for the Asteroid: "We are in a hurry, but we'll be patient until your maker's point of view improves."

"Time is irrelevant."

"To you, maybe," said Gou Mang. There was no hiding her

frustration. "But our people are going to die if you don't get a move on!"

"Your people are of no consequence."

"Well, they damn well should be!"

Again, the sphere ignored a general statement. Alander rubbed at his temples, feeling his head beginning to ache. He thought carefully about his next words, making sure they would result in a reply.

"Asteroid, this system has proven extremely dangerous to scouts we've sent to investigate it," he said. "I hope your maker is being careful."

"My maker has many ways of minimizing danger to itself."

"We believe that whoever's hiding in here is your enemy, the ones you've been chasing."

"My makers are attempting to ascertain the truth."

"It is our hope that, if it does prove true, your maker will cease the attacks on our colonies."

"I cannot speak for my makers."

"But you discuss their capacity happily enough. How—?" Alander reminded himself to keep his comments specifically tailored to himself but also phrased to get an informative response. "We—my people speak in terms of questions and answers. I find this manner of conversing difficult."

"I am programmed to communicate within strict confines regarding the dissemination of information," said the sphere. "Data must be traded; information must flow equably."

"I'd assumed that you'd read our minds. Your makers could probably do it without even thinking."

"You're assuming a little too much, there, Peter," said Axford. "They probably obtained English from Thor, when she spoke to them. Even if they could read our minds, why *would* they? It's arrogant to assume that we are worthy of their regard."

He nodded. The sphere had turned to Axford at the sound of his voice, then rotated back to Alander. While there was in no sense a face on the scarred sphere, its movements did suggest the turning of attention to one person or another.

He wasn't expecting the sphere to respond to his previous question/statement, so was surprised when it said, "Reading minds is not my function. I exist to facilitate the process of ascertaining your nature. Few come before my makers and are regarded. Those who make the decisions do not have time to perform such tasks."

Alander was trying to work out what tack to try next when the view shifted. There was no sense of motion or transition; suddenly he was seeing from a different viewpoint, one much closer to pi-1 Ursa Major. The effect was dizzying, and for a moment he lost his balance.

"*That* wasn't there before," said Gou Mang, pointing at a glowing ring surrounding the star.

"It's new," agreed Sol from *Eledone*. "Asteroid, what we're seeing doesn't match our astronomical data."

"The phenomena you are witnessing is the work of my makers."

"I can't tell what they're doing," said Alander.

"Much of my makers' works will no doubt seem mysterious to you."

Alander nodded. "There is an awful lot of information we'd like to trade for. Is there any other way we can do it than this?"

He mentally kicked himself when the Asteroid spun once and disappeared.

"I'm wondering," Sol jumped in quickly, "if your makers aren't deliberately making it harder for us to work out the truth."

The Asteroid returned. "I am under no compunction to stop you from wondering about my makers' motives."

Axford barked out a laugh as the viewpoint shifted again. This time they were hanging from a point above the ecliptic, looking down on the sun and its new ring. Dark sunspots swirled in the solar atmosphere; magnetic field lines flexed and snapped, sending great gobbets of energy aloft in the deep gravity well. Alander had never seen such an amazing sight before.

The ring of lights resolved into purple-hot balls of light trailing glowing tails, moving at speed around the star's equator, their spiraling wakes twisting and turning around each other. The star's atmosphere was responding, bowing under invisible energies and forming a shallow trench girdling the star, as though it had tightened its belt.

The Asteroid, which had vanished during the short silence,

reappeared. Still slightly giddy, Alander almost imagined it to be a distant, battered world orbiting pi-1 Ursa Major rather than a small object at close quarters.

"My makers have found no evidence of that which your emissary described."

It took Alander a moment to realize that the Asteroid was referring to Thor. "Our hole ships were attacked when we came here," he said.

"My makers have found no evidence—"

"But Lucia reported that she saw evidence of activity on a massive scale. That's what we came here to tell your makers."

"There is evidence of past activity," the Asteroid said.

"Then the Spinners must have left," said Gou Mang.

"So it would seem." Axford's voice had lost all trace of humor. "Maybe your friend Lucia scared them away."

The thought struck Alander as ridiculous enough to be true. If the Spinners were completely paranoid about their security, they might have left as soon as she happened by. But why then destroy the more recent hole ships? Why not destroy her as well?

"I can't believe there's nothing here," he said to the slowly spinning Asteroid.

"There is something," it said. A rapid sequence of images flashed by, appearing in windows against the starscape, then sliding away into black. They showed hole ships materializing out of unspace, taking the barest glimpse of the system, then disappearing. The extrusions were impossibly small, just centimeters across, barely enough for sensors to take the slightest reading, but they were there. It was incredible that the Starfish fleet, even as advanced as it was, could notice such tiny invasions in the incomprehensibly huge volume of a solar system.

Yet they had, and the fact added credence to their statement that there was no sign of the Spinners. If they could spot a tennis ball–sized dot from millions of kilometers away, then they could surely spot an alien fleet, no matter how well hidden.

"They're from our people," Sol said. "They've noticed your presence here."

"My makers have made the connection between them and you. Their presence here is a distraction."

"We can tell them to leave, if you'd let us. We're jammed in here, as I'm sure you realize."

"It is not necessary for you to communicate with the others of your kind. They are being deterred."

"You're attacking them?" The question escaped Alander's lips before he could stop it. The Asteroid disappeared once again.

"Shit," Sol cursed.

"You can say that again," said Gou Mang. "We fucked up. If we'd come in time, maybe we could have done something, but now . . ."

The dull resignation in her voice was awful to hear.

"Not necessarily," Alander said.

She turned on him, her android face ugly with despair. "How can you say that? Didn't you hear what the floating rock said? The Spinners have *gone,* Peter! The Starfish aren't going to stop looking for them. In fact, they're probably going to look even harder, now they know the trail is hot. I'd say our chances of surviving something like that are even closer to zero than they were—"

"They're not zero," Axford interrupted. "We can still run."

"Yeah, *if* they let us go," she said. "And *if* we can fix the hole ship. And *if* we can find the Praxis without bringing the Starfish down on it, too. If, if, fucking *if!*"

Gou Mang shook her head and went to walk back to *Selene,* striding surreally across empty air through the illusion of pi-1 Ursa Major.

She hadn't taken ten paces when the Asteroid reappeared unprompted.

"There is something," it said, as it had before. A new image appeared in the void. It was blurred and glowing with wild energy flows, as though caught in the act of some powerful transformation while hanging above the world that the colonists who had traveled to pi-1 Ursa Major had called Jian Lao. Despite the blurring and the discharges, it was instantly recognizable.

Alander stared at the golden spindle in confusion. "I don't know how that got here," he said, respecting the Asteroid's protocol for information exchange.

"My makers recognize the architecture of this artifact as a product of those we seek."

"Absolutely," he said. "We call them the Spinners. They were the ones who built these things and gave them to us. We call them the gifts."

"If you've found one here," said Sol, "then surely that vindicates us."

The sphere rotated to face her. "This artifact is not indigenous to this system."

Gou Mang returned to Peter's side. "Not indigenous?" she whispered to him. "That can't be right."

He shook his head and addressed the Asteroid again: "We've never known the gifts to move of their own volition before."

"This artifact is radiating in frequencies you use for communication purposes," said the Asteroid.

"What's—?" Alander stopped to rephrase the question as a statement. "We'd very much like to hear what it's saying."

A new voice filled the void around them. That it was one Alander knew well rocked him to the very core of his being.

"This is Lucia Benck of the UNESSPRO Mission 391 hailing the visitors to this system. Please respond. I repeat this is Lucia Benck of the United Near-Earth Stellar Survey Program Mission 391. Please respond."

Lucia? He felt dizzy for a moment. The presence of the spindle was a great enough mystery on its own, but that it was broadcasting Lucia's voice was an even greater one—one he couldn't immediately get his head around. How had she persuaded one of the mighty spindles to break orbit and travel to pi-1 Ursa Major? What the hell had happened since they'd left the Alkaid Group?

The view shifted yet again. They were hanging near one of the inner worlds. Four massive Trident ships were visible at varying distances and attitudes, silhouetted against the sun. There were myriad other vessels gleaming in the bright light. The ring around the star continued to bind its waist tight, although the effect was less visible from a distance. The only obvious symptom was a flaring of coronas from the poles. Vast feathers of multicolored energy stretched with deceptive laziness out of the stellar atmosphere, reaching for the stars.

"My makers are concerned," said the Asteroid.

"We've given them no reason to be concerned," assured Axford.

"There is reason to suspect that we have been misled."

"We haven't misled you!" Gou Mang's expression was one of outrage.

"I can see why they might believe we have," said Axford, half-turning to address her. "We tell them the Spinners are here in pi-1 Ursa Major. We send them god knows how far to investigate, and there's nothing here. Then a spindle shows up, trying to hail them. That creates a connection between the Spinners and us that already existed before—on all the colonies they've destroyed."

"They think *we're* the Spinners?" said Gou Mang, her tone caught between incredulity and amusement.

"Probably not." Axford shrugged. "But we could be evidence of something more than just coincidence."

The Asteroid spun back and forth for several seconds. "My makers' suspect you have led us into a trap."

Alander shook his head, a feeling of unreality creeping over him. "That wasn't our intention, I assure you."

"We're just trying to save our people," said Sol from *Eledone*.

"My makers were lured here."

"We didn't *lure* them anywhere!" Alander could feel the situation quickly slipping out of their hands.

"If you believe that we did," said Gou Mang carelessly, "why don't you just leave and be done with it?"

The Asteroid promptly disappeared at the question, leaving Alander to supply the obvious answer.

"Because the makers don't see any real threat here."

"None they can't handle," added Axford. The ex-general indicated the incredible view. It was shifting with increasing frequency, taking in all the major worlds and many of the Lagrange points. There were cutters and Tridents everywhere, mingling among ships of an infinite variety of shapes and sizes. It seemed inconceivable that such a fleet could ever be seriously threatened by anyone or anything.

The changeable view made Alander feel light-headed and uneasy.

"Asteroid, you said there was nothing in the system," said Axford, his voice seeming to come from a great distance away.

The Asteroid returned but, strangely, didn't respond.

"I wonder if you've considered threats from *outside* the system," Axford pressed. "That strikes me as an obvious source of attack."

The Asteroid spun as though seeking a response to a dialogue it wasn't designed to pursue.

Behind it, the viewpoint of the Starfish returned to pi-1 Ursa Major's primary, the blinding, yellow-hot star and its belt of lights. Energy streamed from the poles in gouts of blue and green. Whatever the Starfish were doing, it was going to have a lasting effect on the sun, its magnetic properties, and the flow of its solar wind. The rounded, stubby prongs of a Trident vessel hung silhouetted against the fiery atmosphere, moving slowly across the view.

Alander knew something was going to happen seconds before it did. He could feel it in his bones, in the instincts his engram was supposed to have left behind with his original body on Earth. The engram entrainment program was supposed to have been the final proof of the nonexistence of the soul, of psychic phenomena—for how, the researchers had said, could they re-create human minds with such accuracy and verisimilitude out of nothing but numbers if the originals they were copying consisted of anything more than that?

And yet, Alander *knew*.

He opened his mouth to shout a warning, but it was too late. Behind the Trident, the sun swelled like a dumbbell-shaped balloon, impossibly fast, swelling out and around the ring of lights about its waist and sending two enormous globes of novalike energy exploding across the system. The Trident silhouetted against it vanished in a wave of energy, and the viewpoint of the Starfish shook violently.

"What the fuck—?" Gou Mang exclaimed, staggering back from the blaze of energy.

"It has begun," said the Asteroid.

2.3.3

The explosion of pi-1 Ursa Major took Lucia completely by surprise. She had just arrived at a new location, almost directly above the sun's north pole, and was marveling at her new perspective on the system. There wasn't time to sightsee, though. Her ftl "ears" were still ringing with the destruction of Zemyna, which had been hit by the Starfish within an hour of her arrival at pi-1 Ursa Major. Jumping backward and forward in an attempt to avoid the Starfish defenses, she'd been doing her best ever since both to hail the aliens and warn them off.

What more did they *want?* She felt powerless to express her anger and frustration. Dodging the furious energies flung at her consumed most of her concentration, but she still had time to wonder at the motives of the twin forces squeezing humanity to destruction between them. Why weren't the Spinners reacting to the presence of the Starfish, as they had to humanity's hole ships? And why weren't the Starfish calling off their advance while they checked the Spinners' hideout?

Her first clear glimpse of the band tightening around the sun had given her reason to pause and wonder. She had no idea what it was, either. A power source? A defensive mechanism? Some sort of AI architecture? It was impossible to say.

Then, suddenly, the north pole of the sun had expanded to almost fill her field of view. Her first panicky thought was that the sun itself was moving, coming right at her. Only when she leapt to a safer spot, with virtual heart hammering, did she see that it wasn't the star moving at all. It was blowing into two halves, sending two bulging hemispheres of stellar material boiling up and over the ecliptic with impossible speed. Even at her fastest clock rate, and even though the gas was confined to sublight speeds, the rate at which it was expanding was absolutely terrifying. Main Sequence G-type stars just weren't supposed to behave like that!

The Starfish fleet close in to the sun vanished into the boiling plasma. Radiation swamped whole electromagnetic bands, blinding her in some senses. She shied away from the billowing shock waves, jumping down into the ecliptic, where the solar winds were less affected by the sudden turmoil. As the explosion ripped the star apart, a fiery ceiling and floor spread out over the system. Within hours, the stellar storm would render the system completely unrecognizable—and uninhabitable for anything unprotected by advanced technology.

She didn't know what effect the sudden discharge of matter would have on the orbits of the planets, but Jian Lao would never again be the paradise she had imagined. Its atmosphere would boil away if the fiery clouds came too close, or it would freeze if its orbit shifted too far out and the stellar remnant—if any would remain—cooled. The dream of her and Peter standing together on some gently rolling hills watching the sunset would be lost forever.

"This is Lucia Benck of the United Near-Earth Stellar Survey Program Mission 391. Please respond." She kept up the beacon, hoping against hope for a reply from either the Starfish or Thor. "I repeat: this is Lucia Benck of the United Near-Earth Stellar Survey Program Mission 391, hailing the visitors to this system. Please respond."

Silence was her only reply. What had happened to the mission sent to contact the Starfish remained a mystery. But for Thor's ftl message and the fact the Starfish had arrived at pi-1 Ursa Major, she would have felt safe assuming them dead. There had been no transmissions since, and no sign of any kind to suggest they were alive.

She jumped at random around the ecliptic, dodging cutters and Tridents and the weapons they sent after her. She saw no sign of the hole ships that the Unfit and the mission supervisors back at Sagarsee were surely sending to keep an eye on things, but she was diligent in reporting to them by ftl. The continued silence suggested that the entire system was somehow being jammed. That the Starfish were responsible for this, as well as the detonation of the sun, seemed the logical assumption. The ring they had put around the sun's waist had already altered its chromosphere immediately prior to blowing up. Perhaps they had suspected the Spinners to be sheltering deep in its core— an amazing thought, but again not out of the realms of possibility for these beings—and blowing off the outer layers was intended to flush them out.

She did her best to record what happened, knowing that the astronomers among the engrams would never forgive her for missing such valuable data—if they survived long enough to study it. It was easy enough to chronicle the unfolding of the polar nebulae, although much harder to see through them to what lay within. She detected shapes lurking in the billowing clouds, strange shadows flashing in and out of space-time, sending great bubbles of gas collapsing and expanding. It was impossible to tell what they were. Some looked like Tridents or other Starfish vessels; others were lumpier, more organic in appearance, with sweeping fins and winglike appendages. *Exactly like starfish,* she thought, *designed to surf the atmosphere of stars.*

When a second star blossomed in the ecliptic, just outside the first gas giant's orbit, she wondered if she was getting a little out of her depth. Then all hell broke loose, and leaving wasn't an option she could seriously consider anymore.

Sol had entertained an uneasy suspicion about the location of the Starfish point of view with respect to their own position in the scheme of things. That was confirmed when the roiling bubble of the nova clouds hit their apparent position, as surrounding them in the Trident. Barely a second after everything lit up around them, a faint tremor rolled through the walls, floor, and ceiling of the concealed space containing them.

"Damn them," she cursed through gritted teeth. "We're on the fucking front line!"

The view changed, not, as she had previously supposed,

reflecting a shift in perspective to another viewpoint but probably, she now realized, indicating a *real* shift in location. The Trident carrying them dropped down into the ecliptic, where space was relatively clear, then up again, into the shock wave's leading edge. Magnetic field lines snapped and twisted with incredible ferocity as the star came apart from within. Plumes and jets of tortured gas rose and fell around them, as though they were standing on the lip of an active volcano. The Trident rocked as its massive cross-section rode the wave of energy with ill-designed grace. Its distinctive back-scratcher shape, tens of thousands of kilometers long, wasn't intended for such an environment.

"Asteroid," she heard Alander calling. "We want to know what's going on!"

The sphere didn't reappear or respond. A sudden, more energetic jolt was followed almost immediately by a jump to another part of the system. The light there was different: cleaner, more intense than that of the billowing star.

"That's the Source of All!" Samson exclaimed, pointing out the hard white, sunlike object blazing to one side.

"What the hell's *it* doing here?" asked Inari.

The Trident jolted again as something flashed across the field of view—a lime-green, tapering triangle with a glint of silver at its aft end. The thing appeared to be traveling backward.

"Peter, get yourself back in the hole ship," she said.

"Way ahead of you," said Alander. She could see now that all three of them were already moving.

Alander stumbled as the floor shook beneath them. Under fire, the Trident jumped yet again, to a point far from the Source. It joined a swarm of cutters and other Tridents gathering near Jian Lao, the planet that would have been the colony world for the *Andre Linde*. Ghostly webs of energy enveloped the giant ships, glowing like marsh light in the glare of the nebulae. Sol found it almost impossible to make out exactly what was happening.

"Who blew up the sun?" Inari asked.

"Your guess is as good as mine, at this stage," said Sol. "*Eledone*? Any readings?"

"Passive sensors are not detecting anything beyond the walls of this chamber."

"I think it's time we started using active sensors again." She eyed the view with a feeling of deep misgiving. "Whatever's going on out there, I want to know about it before it hits us."

"Surely we'd be safe in here?" said Samson. That she phrased it as a question indicated her doubt. Sol had no reassurances for her.

More of the green triangles swept into view, trailing white points of light that scattered and vanished then reappeared in waves aiming for the gathering of Starfish vessels. A responding wave of red darts, blue whips, and other exotic weapons rose up to meet them. Space knotted and writhed as the two waves collided, tangling vicious energies in a multicolored, almost beautiful display. The arena was large enough for light-speed lags to have an effect on how it was reported. Explosions that might originally have occurred simultaneously seemed to come in waves: craft appeared out of unspace apparently seconds before they'd moved, in response to distant events that weren't yet visible.

Sol did her best to follow it all. The triangles were being picked off with relative ease, but there were many of them. She looked around, trying to locate their source. None was immediately obvious. As dozens of cutters spun to join the attack, the Trident they were in jumped to the outer system, where in frosty darkness a new battle line was forming. The antagonists this time were snakelike threads of a shimmering gray many hundreds of kilometers long that spat bolts of energy from their ends. They looked impossibly thin but were in actual fact dozens of meters across. When severed, they disintegrated into showers of debris loaded with nanotech mines and other traps. Sol saw Starfish vessels explode from the inside out as the mines spread exponentially through them, others flew sluggishly, their guidance systems disrupted and proving easy picking for the green triangles. As more and more of the gray threads were destroyed, the fragments reassembled to replace them, snapping unpredictably out of debris clouds.

Alander reported from *Selene*. The three of them had reentered the cockpit and were rotating to merge with the main body.

"We're ready to leave whenever you are," he said, his image in the foreground of the view on one of *Eledone*'s screens.

"We wouldn't last a second out there," Gou Mang argued from behind him, looking nervous.

"There's no time for a discussion on the matter now," she said. "Merge the ships, and we'll talk about it afterward."

"Merging is a bad idea, Caryl," said Axford. "If things get ugly, we'll need to watch each other's backs."

"Nothing we're carrying could possibly hope to make a difference in all of this."

"Still, I insist you consider it."

"I *have* considered it, and I say merge the fucking ships!" Sol tensed as she issued the challenge. "Do you have a problem with that, Frank?"

"As a matter of fact, Caryl, yes, I do."

Behind Alander and Gou Mang, Axford raised his left hand. It was dripping a dark fluid and seemed to be broken. Before Sol could ask what was wrong, there were two sharp, earsplitting cracks, and Alander and Gou Mang were punched to the ground. The view went dead on Axford just as he was turning away to talk to *Selene*.

"Peter!" Sol reached to help without thinking, a sickening sensation in her gut. She knew the sound of a PEP discharge when she heard one. "Peter—talk to me!"

Selene's cockpit spiraled into the heart of the hole ship, and Sol's calls went unanswered.

Alander, too, knew what a lethal PEP sounded like, albeit from fictional dramas and documentaries. His original had never had one fired at him before. Nothing in his hand-me-down memories could have prepared him for the sheer physicality of the experience.

The flash and the sound came simultaneously with the impact. He felt as though a cannonball had hit him in the back of the neck. His I-suit absorbed the energy that would have otherwise turned his hair, skin, and an inch-deep patch of muscle and bone into plasma, but there was still enough punch remaining to knock him off his feet. As the air behind his head exploded, he was flung forward into the wall, hitting it solidly and sliding bonelessly to the ground.

For a long moment, he couldn't move, nor could he see or

hear. Pain testified that he was still alive, but he couldn't determine where that pain was coming from. His entire body seemed to be hurting, and it was so intense that he was barely able to think straight. What few thoughts he had he directed toward figuring out what the hell was happening. Clearly he'd been shot from behind, and the fact that Gou Mang had been in eyeshot the whole time meant that Axford must have pulled the trigger. But where had Axford come by a PEP gun, for God's sake? And *why* had Axford shot him?

He forced himself to open his eyes. At first, all he saw was red. Then his eyes focused, and he realized that what he was seeing was blood: a spreading pool of it all over the cockpit's floor. In the middle of it lay Gou Mang. She wasn't moving.

He winced. The first PEP shot must have been aimed at him, for he hadn't heard a second aimed at her. Although he couldn't immediately see how badly she was wounded, the sheer quantity of blood indicated that it was serious.

Axford 1313 strode into view, and Alander saw where the blood was actually coming from.

Axford's lower arm had burst open to reveal not just a stubby PEP weapon at the base of his wrist but several other new limbs that unfolded like legs from an insect's carapace. Axford knelt on the floor at the center of the cockpit and thrust the ruin of his arm, with the mess of slender, new limbs fully extended, before him. Strange digits slid with surgical precision into the floor. Alander heard the ex-general grunt, followed by a strange sighing sound. When Axford stood again, his arm was part of the hole ship. The floor stretched up with him like white molasses, forming a perfectly geometric line. Knobs and protrusions grew at seemingly random points, and these extended into branches that Alander recognized. Axford had grown himself a control stalk.

Arm and stalk separated with a sucking sound, and blood dripped to the floor from both. Axford seemed in no way inconvenienced by the wound; his face was set in concentration as he worked.

Alander considered his options. Axford obviously wasn't expecting him to wake so soon, or he would have taken more precautions. That gave him the edge of surprise, if he wanted to take it. But physically overpowering Axford wasn't something Alander wanted to try in a hurry. He assumed there were more tricks hidden in the ex-general's body, some perhaps more lethal than a PEP gun.

He could try talking Axford out of whatever he was doing, but his unprovoked attack on Alander and Gou Mang suggested that a verbal approach would be pointless. He clearly wasn't in a talkative mood.

Alander lay still, trying to work out what to do. If he could access the hole ship, he would be able to wrench control from Axford. But there was no way to access the AI without speaking and thereby giving himself away.

He had to do something soon, though. Gou Mang still wasn't moving, nor did she appear to be breathing.

"I am receiving a communication from Caryl Hatzis," the hole ship announced in a voice identical to *Eledone*'s.

"Ignore it," Axford said. "Give me manual control."

"I am authorized only to obey only Peter Alander."

"Well, Peter's dead, so stop being a pedant and give me control of the ship. I can't run everything on my own."

"You are mistaken," *Selene* cut in. "Peter Alander is not dead. He is perfectly conscious."

Axford's eyes snapped to where Alander lay on his side in the spreading pool of blood. The gory crystal eye of the PEP gun came up again, aimed directly at him. Alander lifted and rolled, not fast enough to avoid the shot. It glanced off his shoulder with sufficient force to spin him into the wall, but it lacked the surprise of the first shot. He was only stunned, not knocked out again, as Axford would have no doubt liked.

Smoke boiled from where the deflected energy boiled blood to plasma. That gave him a second to recover before Axford tried again. The laser pulse would be less effective through smoke, and his aim would be impaired. Alander shook his head and told himself to stand up while he had the chance.

He lifted his eyes just as another shot cracked out of the smoke and knocked him back down. He blinked a few times, trying to lose the stars that were blurring his vision.

"Jesus Christ!" he gasped, raising a hand in a vain attempt to ward off another shot. "Enough, already!"

"Then stay the hell down!" Axford loomed out of the

smoke and pressed the muzzle of the PEP gun against the back of Alander's head.

"Listen to me," Alander started, but stopped when the gun was pushed harder against him.

"You've nothing to say that could possibly interest me, Peter."

The world turned white with pain as a noise like thunder sounded in Alander's ears. The acrid smell of burning blood filled his nostrils.

Is that mine? he wondered. *Have my brains been charbroiled?*

He would have laughed at the idiocy of the notion had he not been in so much pain. Of course it wasn't his brain. The fact that he could think at all should have told him that.

He opened his eyes, and through the intense pain he saw Axford turn and move away, grunting with satisfaction.

"You're going to have to do better than that," Alander managed. His arms flailed for purchase on the slippery floor as he forced himself upright.

Axford 1313 swiveled. The eye of the PEP gun fell on him again, but this time it didn't fire.

"That's not possible," the ex-general said. "I designed this to punch through the I-suits. There's enough residual kinetic energy in each shot to turn your internal organs to jelly. Like hers!"

He kicked Gou Mang's android body where it lay on the floor by his feet. She didn't respond.

"She's dead?" said Alander, freezing in the act of trying to stand.

"Of course she's dead! I couldn't afford to have her getting in the way—no more than I can afford to have *you* getting in my way, either. Now do me the favor of *staying down!*"

The eye of the PEP flashed in Alander's face, and the sudden impact of the blast snapped his head back. He felt the crunch of vertebrae in his neck, tasted blood in his mouth. To his amazement, though, he didn't fall back down. He'd withstood the shot.

Something was happening to him. He could feel it in his arms and legs. There was something crawling under his skin, twisting into knots and then untangling. He felt his back hunch, then straighten. He blinked and shook his head as if to dispel a dream.

"Looks like you're going to need a little more firepower," he said, climbing cautiously to his feet.

"Clearly." Axford was watching him without fear. His expression was one of wary assessment. "What am I going to do about you, Peter? I could keep shooting you, but I'm not one for pointless gestures."

Alander felt strength flowing through him, invigorating him. He fought a sense of invulnerability. Just because he could resist PEP bolts at extremely close range didn't mean he was indestructible.

"If it's pointless, Frank, why don't you lower the gun?"

"As a deterrent, it still has some value. Remember, while your body has unanticipated reserves, so does mine. I'd advise against coming any closer."

Alander paused. The two of them faced off against each other with blood-smoke swirling around them.

"Okay, Frank," he said. "It's over, either way. *Selene*, open a line to Caryl Hatzis."

"Peter!" Sol's reply was instantaneous. "What the hell's going on over there?"

"It's Axford," he said, adding with a shake of his head, "Again."

"Jesus, Peter," said Sol. "What happened to you?"

He realized only then how he would look to her eyes: blood-spattered and knocked around by too many PEP shots. "I'm okay, but Gou Mang's dead. Axford went off the rails there for a while, but I think everything's under control now." He looked at Axford again. "*Is* it, Frank?"

The ex-general shook his head as though disappointed. "You're letting yourself be dragged down by her, Peter. I thought you had more sense than that."

"Well, I guess we're both full of surprises today, aren't we? *Selene*—uh!"

That was all he managed to get out. Axford lunged at him with his many-tooled arm; wickedly sharp instruments stabbed with gleaming precision. Nanodrills and cutting lasers flashed. Backed up by the flash and grunt of the PEP weapon, Axford threw himself physically forward, a lethal monster masquerading as human.

Alander felt himself move with near impossible speed. He leaned to his left at the same time as his right forearm came up to deflect the bulk of the attack. They were moves his original had learned in a self-defense course, decades before entrainment, and they'd been instilled in him along with everything else. He had never used them before, yet he moved now with a finesse and ease that suggested he'd practiced the moves every day of his life.

The PEP gun flashed again. It knocked his left shoulder back, nothing more. Whatever was happening to him, it was advancing at a rapid rate. Axford 1313, murderous yet blank-faced, seemed to hang motionless in the air as Alander pivoted around his center of gravity and eased aside the arm with its deadly cargo. His left leg kicked up and out, striking Axford firmly in the chest. The blow wasn't intended to injure the ex-general, just to ward him off. Nevertheless, there was a loud crack of bones as his foot connected.

Alander's foot crumpled along with Axford's chest, and the two of them rebounded apart with surprising force. Alander fell to the floor, the pain in his foot hurting more than all of the PEP shots combined. Axford had seemed to weigh *tons*.

"Christ!" he cried out, rolling away.

As time returned to its usual rate, he clutched his injured leg and wondered at the burning sensations racing along his limbs.

"I'm merging the two ships," he heard Sol saying somewhere beyond the pain.

"No, wait," Alander said. He wanted to make sure the ex-general was no longer a threat to the others and their mission before the ship conjoined again. "Give me a second, Caryl."

Axford had fallen face forward to the floor. Alander slid painfully away from him, wary of his shattered foot, expecting the man to get up and attack again at any moment.

"Selene—" He hesitated on the brink of ordering the hole ship to eject Axford 1313 from the ship. Instead, he clambered onto his one good leg and limped to where the man lay. He squatted next to the ex-general and reached out to prod his

shoulder. There was no response, so he rolled Axford onto his back.

Or tried to, anyway. Axford weighed considerably more than he should. Alander had to brace himself firmly and heave before the body rolled.

That Axford was very dead was obvious once he'd managed to get him onto his back. Where his foot had struck, there was a deep impression left in staved-in ribs and internal armor. Neither skin nor I-suit had been punctured, but the damage couldn't be hidden. Axford looked as though he'd been crushed by a falling pylon.

How the fuck did I do this? Alander asked himself. *What in God's name* am *I?*

He moved back from Axford's body. Dead he might be, but Alander still didn't trust the man. "*Selene,* I want you to isolate him from the rest of us. Don't let anything in or out unless Caryl Hatzis or I specifically tell you to. Is that understood?"

"Yes, Peter."

The boundary was already forming when he turned to check Gou Mang. As Axford had said, the PEP blast had killed her—or at least stopped the android that she occupied from working. If the organic circuitry running the android wasn't too badly damaged, there was a chance her engram could be recovered.

"Peter?" Sol's voice broke into the cockpit quiet. "Is it safe to merge yet?"

"Yes," he said, feeling numbness settle over him like an anesthetic. "I guess so."

Alien technology flexed around him, but he barely noticed. Slumping back on the floor, he felt all his new strength drain out of him. Whatever the Praxis had given him—and it had to be the Praxis—wasn't permanent. That was abundantly clear. Also clear was the fact that it hadn't solved anything. Yes, he had survived Axford's attempted mutiny, but what surety did that give him? His crushed foot was healing itself practically before his eyes. He didn't need to look at the screens around him, at the fight in pi-1 Ursa Major heating up, to realize that he had never been so far away from home as he was at that very moment.

2.3.4

Lucia dodged a wave of green triangles. Deceptively small from a distance, they had turned out to be half again as long as she was. They tended to ignore her, angling for larger game unless she blundered across their path—which she was careful to make sure she didn't. A very small fish in a very crowded ocean, she was doing her best to keep a low profile.

All around her, on every bandwidth, in every form of radiation known to her, pi-1 Ursa Major teemed with emissions. Explosions rocked space-time as exotic weapons found their mark. She was buffeted by forces she was unable to comprehend. Dazzled, frightened, feeling depths of ignorance and danger in equal measures opening up beneath her, she fought a growing sense of certainty that her luck had to run out soon.

She should have fled when she had the chance, she told herself—before the sun blew, when she was blithely wasting time trying to contact the Starfish. Christ, they didn't care about her or humanity. She knew the only way to survive was to run, and to *keep* running.

But she also knew that this was just her programming talking. It supported any excuse to run. That she agreed with it this time didn't change the selfishness behind the urge—and neither did it mean that she could actually do it. All her ftl capabilities had been disrupted following the explosion of the sun. Flexures of space-time such as that must surely, she assumed, have an effect on *something*. She could no more leave now than she could turn back time, and the ftl bands were still full of garbage. She'd seen too many other vessels disintegrate while attempting an ftl jump to attempt one herself.

That the Spinners might have blown up the sun simply to give them an edge in the battle was a notion almost too large to comprehend. Blowing up stars as a tactical maneuver? The idea made her feel even more small and inconsequential than she already did.

Keeping her new senses peeled for any sign of Thor's mission, she dodged on reactionless thrusters past a conflagration involving a cutter and what looked like a giant squid made from glowing rings. The rings pulsed in waves down to the tips of kilometer-long tentacles, sending lances of purple energy into the cutter's spinning hull. Most of these were deflected, although enough struck home to paint bright red streaks that spewed gas and debris into the vacuum. It dodged and swooped, but there was no escaping the energy squid. Finally it disintegrated into an expanding disk, sending trillions of highly energetic fragments slicing across the system. The squid was torn apart, exploding an instant later with a dazzling, nova-like flash.

Lucia outran both explosions to take refuge near one of the system's less noteworthy asteroids. Not that she felt any easier there. While she wasn't likely to be targeted if she kept out of the way, she could still be killed in the crossfire. The system was full of combatants, their weapons, and the spillage from those weapons. All it would take was one clumsy move, and she could kiss existence good-bye.

With survival in mind, she activated the engram of Peter Alander 17. She didn't feel happy about doing it, but she was rapidly running out of options.

"I don't understand what you think I can do," he said when she had apprised him of the situation. His image was fragile in the face of the alien battle. At least she hadn't had to explain who she was again; he remembered her well enough from their previous encounter.

"You can help me think of a way out of here," she said.

"How? I know less about the Spinners than you do. You're practically one of them, now."

"Hardly." She felt herself withdraw from the accusation, even as it provoked a strong sense of wonder in her. "All they've done is toss me a glass bead, and it's about as useless in the face of a missile."

"But you've got hybrid vigor, Lucia."

"I've got what?"

"Hybrid vigor. Mixing two things can sometimes result in a new thing that's stronger than the two you started with."

"You're talking about synergy?"

His image shook. "Don't write yourself off just yet, that's all I'm saying. You have an opportunity, here. Don't waste it."

He froze in midframe.

"Peter?"

But the engram didn't respond. She quickly erased it from the overseer, then tried reloading it and starting again. It wouldn't take. Garbage and memory fragments were all that issued from the conSense interface.

> //tangled in the metaphysics//
> How could I not want that?
> //swallowed by the sea//
> Right here in this moment, Lucia, you and I are—

Remembering the end of that sentence, she killed the garbled simulation. Nonexistent tears pricked the eyes of her persistent self-image. She was a ghost haunting an empty alien tomb. She wasn't *real*. She was as dead as Peter Alander 17 seemed to be now—as *all* the Peter Alanders were. They simply had the good sense to know when to lie down and accept the fact.

With his passing, her confidence and sense of self were severely undermined.

Hybrid vigor, my ass, she thought.

A ping on the spindle's equivalent of sonar brought her out of her funk. The spindle's sensors had detected a hole ship nearby. Rousing herself, she sent her attention outward, to where the ping had returned from. There was a Trident heaving to nearby, its deceptively slender cross section and three curving tines crawling with electrical discharges of some kind. The ping was coming from the base of the center tine, where the long body swelled and divided. It was coming from at least two hole ships.

Thor, she thought. *And maybe the others . . .*

Something black oozed across the star field and touched the Trident along its extended tail. What it was she couldn't tell, but the effect was immediate. The Trident buckled and began to fold into two pieces. Ponderous mass responded to irresistible forces. Gas and debris spewed into the void.

The dark shape withdrew, presumably to strike elsewhere. Lucia didn't know whether to thank it or damn it as it went. Her friends were in the crippled ship somewhere. But at least, she told herself, it had solved the problem of how she was going to get inside.

*Sol looked up from the merger of the two hole ships as the Star-*fish display outside winked and fizzled out. The view of the battle vanished, and they were suddenly back in the bonelike chamber.

One of the views from the hole ship was directed up at the ceiling. Sol couldn't feel it, but the "chandelier"—the dangling arrangement of slender, strawlike threads that might have projected the illusion—was trembling.

"I think we might be in trouble," she muttered uneasily.

"Seismic readings are up," said Samson. "There was a hefty jolt a few seconds ago. I'm guessing we've been hit."

"The question is, how badly?"

The meniscus separating the two cockpits peeled back, and the smell of burnt blood rolled over them. Sol didn't flinch from the gore. She hurried to where Alander sat, propped against the couch, staring at his leg. His skin was ruddy under his beard and hair, his gaze focused on a point slightly above his exposed ankle.

"Peter?" she said, putting a hand on his shoulder and bending into his line of sight. "Are you all right?"

The intensity of his expression dissipated. "Yeah, I'm fine. Check Gou Mang."

Sol went to where Inari was already inspecting the body to see if anything could be done for the android. Gou Mang's neck had been broken by a close-range PEP shot. Her I-suit had protected her from the heat and the laser itself, but it had only absorbed a proportion of the impact. The shock wave had spread up into her brainpan and down her spine. There wasn't much left, but Sol did her best.

Putting a hand on still-active infrared ports scattered across the android's skin, she accessed emergency preservation systems. A snapshot of every independent engram was stored in nonvolatile memory, deep in each android's thorax. The miniature SSDS system was shaken, but it did still contain data. Lacking the time to check it in detail, Sol uploaded it into her considerably more sophisticated data storage systems. She would examine it later to see how much had survived.

Either way, the body itself was a write-off. As was Axford's. Through the membrane keeping him at a distance from everyone else, she could see the hunched posture of the body where Alander had collapsed its rib cage. Its shoulder had pulled in, as though guarding a secret.

"I'll lay odds that the son of a bitch isn't really dead," said Samson from behind them.

"I'm inclined to agree with you," said Sol. She turned away, grimacing at the blood. "*Eledone*, I want this mess cleaned up immediately. Then I want to find a way out of this fucking place. Cleo, will you look into that?"

Samson nodded and went back to her post at the command stalk. Sol returned to Peter's side; he was staring again at his leg.

"Peter? Are you *sure* you're okay?"

He looked up, a bemused expression on his face. "What am I, Caryl?" He indicated his ankle. "This thing crumpled when I kicked Frank, and now look at it—it's *fine*. You've seen his chest, what I did to it. Christ, he shot me god knows how many times, and yet it took just one shot to kill Gou Mang. What the fuck did the Praxis *do* to me?"

The question came with such emotion that she felt almost guilty that she couldn't give him an answer. "I honestly don't know, Peter," she said, standing.

"I'm different; he *changed* me. I'm not who I was when . . ." He trailed off uncertainly.

"None of us are the same as we were in entrainment camp," she finished for him.

"That's not what I was going to say." There was a weariness in his eyes that hadn't been there before: the weariness of a man struggling with his own identity and maybe growing tired of the fight. "I'm not the same as I was before he *ate* me. He made me into flesh and tissue, Caryl. He said he was remaking me in my own image, but I think the fucker threw some of himself into the mix, too." He stood up with surprising speed and flexed the leg. It moved with both strength and grace, causing him to laugh uneasily. "Jesus, I've almost forgotten what it was like to be *me,* you know?"

That surprised her. "That's a good thing, isn't it?"

He shrugged. "The old me would've had an opinion on how best to get us out of here. And he probably wouldn't have cared too much if you made it out with me or not."

She smiled at this. "I'd happily take the new you over the old you, any day."

He came closer and put a hand on her upper arm and squeezed. She was wary of his new strength but forced herself not to flinch.

"Thanks, Caryl."

"There's no need to thank me, Peter. We're both monsters, you and I. Sports." Her smiled tightened. "We'd make a good pair, under happier circumstances."

He smiled awkwardly and took his hand away. She felt a sadness she hadn't expected.

"I'm not finding anything," Samson interrupted. Sol broke away from Alander's stare and faced her.

"You've looked everywhere?"

Samson nodded, then shrugged. "There are no breaks or seams, no unexplained bulges."

"What about up there?" She pointed at the bone straws overhead.

"Nothing. Look for yourself, if you want."

Sol rejected the offer with a curt shake of the head. "Then we'll just have to try cutting our way out. *Eledone.*" Sol studied the screens before her. "Take us to this point, here." She randomly picked a point where the floor swept up to become a wall. "See if you can cut through it."

Light flared on the screens as one of the hole ship's more exotic tools sliced into the smooth surface. Crystalline streaks of light ricocheted in all directions.

After almost a minute, Sol asked. "Is it making any progress?"

"There is a soft inner layer that is easily penetrated," said the hole ship. "Beyond that, however, is a tougher core through which I do not seem to be making any progress."

She cursed under her breath. "Then try somewhere else. There has to be a weak point *somewhere.*"

The hole ship shifted to a new location of its own choosing and tried again. Sol knew, though, that there didn't have to be a weak spot at all. If the Starfish were proficient at matter transmutation—which, given their other capabilities, seemed extremely likely—they could simply build a new hatch out of nothing and blend it seamlessly with the wall after they had passed through it. If something serious had happened to the Trident, Sol feared that they could be stuck in this chamber forever.

That's not *going to happen,* she vowed. She hadn't come this far only to die in some obscure nook.

"What about calling for help?" suggested Inari. "It's not as though we have any reason to hide anymore. The Unfit might have sent someone to see what's going on. If we can contact them, they might be able to jump in here and get us out."

Sol nodded, liking the suggestion. "Cleo?"

"Ftl is still out," came the instant response. "This isn't just the damping effect the Starfish put on us before. Something's getting through, but it's garbage. Static."

"What about other ships?"

"I tried searching again, but *Eledone* gave me the same response. Apart from the seven hole ships we have configured here, there are none in the vicinity."

"We can keep trying, anyway. Send a message detailing our situation. If anyone's listening out for us, they might hear us through the noise. We can't assume they won't hear us just because we can't hear them."

The hole ship jetted up to the base of the chandelier and started slicing in a new spot.

Third time lucky, Sol thought to herself hopefully.

"Hold on a second," said Alander. "How many hole ships did you say that *Eledone* had identified?"

"Seven," Samson replied. "That's right, isn't it? We brought eight, and lost one probe to the Pllix."

"But what about Thor? She took one with her when she left, so there should only be six."

"But *Eledone* says there's seven."

"Then there must be someone else." Sol looked around the screens at the chamber containing them, wondering if rescue was just on the other side of an impenetrable wall.

"Either that or Thor survived," said Inari. "Maybe she's come back for us."

Sol and Alander exchanged glances, and in that moment she knew that Alander was thinking the same thing she was.

"What's wrong?" asked Inari, obviously noticing their concerned looks. "That would be a good thing, wouldn't it?"

"That would all depend on what she came back as," said Alander.

"Mayday, mayday. This is Cleo Samson of Rasmussen hailing all UNESSPRO *or Unfit personnel near pi-1 Ursa Major on behalf of Caryl Hatzis of Sol. We have an emergency situation and require immediate assistance. Please respond."*

The light ebbed slightly, giving the words space to sink in.

Mayday, mayday . . .

Thoughts moved sluggishly at first, gaining momentum only gradually. Key concepts settled back into place; mental subroutines locked together, began to turn like cogs in a complex machine.

This is Cleo Samson of Rasmussen . . .

She knew that name, and the voice. What she didn't know or understand was who *she* was and why she was hearing these words. She felt as though she had returned from a place far away, a place that had been so full that there had hardly been any room for herself. She had felt squeezed, crushed to the

verge of oblivion by nothing more substantial than thought itself.

. . . on behalf of Caryl Hatzis of Sol . . .

Her sense of self seemed to explode at the sound of this
name, and suddenly she knew who she was again.

Please respond . . .

Respond, yes, Thor thought as memories rushed to fill the
gaps. But *how?* It was all very well to know who she was again,
but that didn't tell her where she was or *what* she was, for that
matter.

She remembered the Nexus and the mission it had sent her
on, to the Source of All. She remembered her transformation
into the Conduit and the strange new understandings that had
come with that. She remembered her wild flight into the Source,
feeling as though she was diving into a sun, as though something more powerful than gravity had gripped her and was pull-
ing her in, sucking her down, tearing her apart. . . .

Beyond that, though, there was nothing.

Mayday, mayday . . .

Cleo Samson's message began to cycle through again. She
and the others were in trouble—but that they were alive at all
was a good sign. The Starfish could have killed them all out
of hand, had her mission gone disastrously awry. She considered this for a moment. Did this mean, then, that she *had* been
successful? That she had achieved what she'd set out to do? If
so, then that meant the mysterious aliens had listened to what
she'd had to say and had come to pi-1 Ursa Major to deal with
the Spinners and halt their advance.

This more than anything convinced her it was time to move.

She tested her limbs for a response. Sensation flooded in
from nerve endings throughout a body that, until she tested it,
she wasn't even sure she had. The whiteness ebbed, and she
felt cool smoothness under her. She was lying on her back,
staring at the bright ceiling of a hole ship cockpit. She flexed
her fingers, raised her knees, turned her head; when she knew
that she could, she carefully climbed to her feet.

Her android body raised itself off the ground and stood, as
easily and calmly as though nothing had ever happened to it.
That disconcerted her more than anything else. Was she to

emerge from her experience completely unscathed? Had anything happened at all?

"Hello?" she ventured. Her voice, too, sounded the same as ever.

WELCOME BACK, CARYL HATZIS, said the Nexus. TEMPORARILY.

Both hope and fear faded, then.

"This isn't real, is it?" she asked.

NO, IT'S NOT.

"Then am I . . . *dead?*"

I DID WARN YOU THAT YOU MIGHT NOT SURVIVE THE EXPERIENCE.

"Yes, I know, but—" She fell quiet, resisting a headache threatening to blossom in her temples. "But if I am dead, then what am I doing *here?*"

I HAVE BEEN SENT TO INTERVENE, came the reply. YOUR SITUATION IS COMPLEX ENOUGH TO MAINTAIN THE INTEREST OF THOSE HIGHER UP THE LADDER THAN ME. THEY FIND YOU AN INTERESTING CASE.

Thor repressed an angry retort. She resented being regarded as some sort of bug on a microscope slide.

"And meanwhile my friends are still in trouble."

WHAT WOULD YOU DO WERE I TO RELEASE YOU? AND WHY WOULD YOU DO IT?

"Do we have to play this fucking game again?"

YES. The answer was simple and blunt.

She sighed, throwing up her arms in resignation. "Okay, but can we at least keep it brief this time?"

THAT IS UP TO YOU, CARYL HATZIS.

"What I would do is try to help my friends. And why? Because it's the right thing to do, of course."

HOW WOULD YOU HELP THEM?

She shrugged. "How do you expect me to answer that when I have no idea what has happened to them?"

WOULD YOU GIVE YOUR LIFE TO SAVE THEM?

She couldn't resist a snort of derision. *"Again?* I thought I'd just done that."

THAT WAS FOR THE GOOD OF ALL THE SURVIVORS. BUT WHAT ABOUT THE HANDFUL YOU CAME HERE WITH? WOULD YOU DO IT FOR SOL?

Thor fought briefly with conflicting emotions. Resentment of Sol warred with deeply ingrained self-interest. Conscious of the Nexus watching every second of the struggle, she tried as hard as she could to be honest, and to come to the conclusion she needed.

"Yes," she said. "I would give my life for Sol. It's important that she gets back to the colonies. They need her."

COULDN'T YOU OR ONE OF THE OTHER CARYL HATZIS EN-GRAMS DO THE JOB EQUALLY WELL?

Her jaw muscles clenched on the answer she hated to give, but knew was the truth. "No, we couldn't."

THERE IS NOTHING QUITE LIKE A SURE KNOWLEDGE OF ONE'S LIMITATIONS AS A STARTING POINT FOR EVERY VENTURE. The Nexus paused as if in thought. YOU MAY RETURN TO THEM AND DO WHAT YOU CAN. WE WILL NOT MEET AGAIN.

"Wait." She stepped forward, frustrated that there was no apparent focus for the Nexus. It was everywhere and yet nowhere simultaneously. "Tell me what happened between me and the Starfish. Do you know?"

DON'T YOU?

"No. I don't remember anything."

I'M SORRY, BUT I HAVE NO ACCESS TO SUCH INFORMATION. The Nexus sounded almost resentful. THERE ARE THINGS WE LOWER BEINGS SIMPLY CANNOT GRASP FOR VERY LONG. SOME-TIMES THE STONES OF KNOWLEDGE ARE TOO HOT TO HOLD ONTO; THEY BURN THE LIKES OF YOU AND I. SOMETIMES IT IS BETTER TO JUST BE CONTENT WITH WHAT YOU KNOW AND WHO YOU ARE, CARYL HATZIS.

The illusion of the cockpit began to fade, and Thor felt alien thoughts creep into the back of her mind. She clung to the memory of who she had been as the insidious tide rose up and over her, and she became, once again, something else.

*Lucia raced a pack of tenacious, clawlike creatures along a se-*ries of tubes wide enough to stack ten spindles identical to hers one on top of the other. Giddying eddies and whirlpools buffeted her from side to side. Wild surges of energy distracted her senses. As shock waves rolled back and forth along the massive vessel, its interior was becoming an increasingly dangerous place to be.

Its many denizens weren't helping. Reacting to the attack in a thousand different ways—some steadfastly trying to repair the damage as it spread, others determined to keep further incursions at bay—they swarmed in her path like so many hyperevolved insects. Lucia didn't know if any of them were the Starfish, nor did she care right now. She was simply doing her best to stay out of their way while trying to reach the last known location of the hole ships she had detected.

She came to a massive junction, a chamber large enough to hold a small moon with dozens of tubes leading in every direction. Cables stretched across the chamber like strings of melted cheese, crisscrossing madly in her path. She dodged and wove through them, pushing her navigational abilities to the limit. At the speeds she was flying, her old probe, *Chung-5*, wouldn't have stood a chance. It would have been diced and sliced in an instant like a boiled egg through a tennis racket. Although larger, the spindle had every benefit of advanced alien technology to make it more maneuverable as well as more resilient.

Her flying wasn't perfect. Once she brushed against one of the cables and sent it twanging across its length. One of the clawships chasing her mistimed its passage and was neatly bisected; it evaporated in a blast of energy that was powerful enough to send the cable and its neighbors vibrating violently. In the chaos, Lucia managed to duck into a nearby tube and race away.

"Mayday, mayday. This is Cleo Samson of Rasmussen hailing all UNESSPRO or Unfit personnel near pi-1 Ursa Major on behalf of Caryl Hatzis of Sol. We have an emergency situation and require immediate assistance. Please respond. Mayday, mayday—"

Cleo's voice emerging from the electromagnetic chaos that was pi-1 Ursa Major sent her hurrying forward, hoping the tube would keep taking her in the right direction.

"Cleo, can you hear me? This is Lucia."

There was a slight pause as the emergency recording shut down.

"Lucia?" came Sol's voice in its place, full of surprise. "Is that really you?"

"It is," she replied. "I'm on my way."

"We can only just hear you, Lucia. You must've just come into range. Where are you, exactly?"

"I'm heading your way as fast as I can," she said. "The Trident's not in good shape, in case you hadn't already guessed. We need to get you out of there—and fast! What's your situation right now?"

"Not good. We're trapped inside a chamber without a working ftl drive. We've tried looking, but we just can't find a way out of this goddman place. It's a nightmare."

"Ftl is down right across the system, unfortunately. Just hang in there, though, okay? I'm picking up readings from your hole ships and triangulating on your location. I'll see what I can do when I get there."

There was another small break. "Was that you we saw before?" asked Samson. "In the spindle?"

Lucia realized only then that her transformation postdated the departure of the Starfish mission. "It's a long story. Is Peter there?"

"I'm here, Lucia."

Relief flooded through her—and a welcome sense that she was doing the right thing.

"Peter, I—"

She didn't finish the sentence. Something large and powerful on the far side of the tube wall destructed in a series of explosions, sending waves of energy and matter across her. She tumbled, disoriented, as the tube unraveled around her. Her senses dissolved to static as she fought to right herself, clutching at the distant ping that was the cluster of hole ships belonging to Sol.

I'm coming, she recited to herself. In the chaotic wash that disrupted every attempt to communicate, the mantra helped her focus. *I'm coming, Peter. . . .*

*Harsh static cut Lucia off in midsentence. No matter how Sam-*son tried, she couldn't reestablish contact.

"At least we know she's out there," said Inari. "She might be able to help if Thor can't."

Eledone was still attempting to slice a way out of the chamber, but with no luck. Whatever material the walls were made of, it was far too tough for the hole ship to penetrate.

"No sign of Thor yet?" asked Sol.

"She's not showing on anything *Eledone* is giving us."

"Yet *Eledone* still says she's there?"

"It seems so. We're getting a count of seven hole ships, which suggests she is."

"I'd like to see what *Eledone*'s seeing."

Alander observed from the side, where he was monitoring vague reports of the *Trident*'s growing distress. A new display opened filled with complex schematics and several bright points. *Eledone* was a bright, overlapping cluster in one corner of the 3-D image; the chamber and its walls were shadowy ghosts beyond which lurked dark spaces and ill-defined shapes. There were no other bright points beyond *Eledone*.

Sol zoomed in closer to study the layout of the hole ship. Alander could practically hear her counting under her breath. Ever since they'd lost Thor, *Eledone* had been traveling in the form of two triangular arrangements stacked on top of each other, slightly rotated so that the upper layer nestled into the gaps of the lower layer. There was simply no room for another hole ship in the arrangement.

"Expand it further." Sol's command was instantly obeyed by the hole ship. The bright points swelled into a sphere, not dissimilar to how the hole ships looked in actuality. They bulged from the screen like a strange bunch of grapes.

"You consist of seven ships, right, *Eledone?*"

"That is correct, Caryl."

"That's what I thought," she said. "So, call me an idiot, but I can only see *six* hole ships."

"There are seven," *Eledone* insisted.

"Okay, so where *is* the seventh? Why can't I see it?"

"I do not know, Caryl."

She sighed. "I'm too tired for fucking riddles and games. Just show me where it is, will you?"

The screen returned to its former appearance and the image zoomed in on *Eledone*.

"Goddamn it, *Eledone*." she cursed in frustration. "This is what I was looking at before. What am I supposed to be seeing here?"

"The seventh hole ship, Caryl. It is there."

"Okay, okay. Zoom in on it for me, will you?"

The image ballooned.

Sol shook her head. "I can't see anything. Zoom in closer."

The "grapes" expanded until their edges leaked out of the window.

"What the fuck is going—"

"Wait a second, Caryl," said Alander, leaving his station to step up to the screen. He pointed at something in the image. "*Eledone*, what's that?"

Tucked into the join between two of the spheres, almost invisible in the overlap, was a round, white circle.

"That is the hole ship you are seeking, Peter."

"It's *part* of you?"

"No, Peter. It is an independent vehicle."

"Then where *is* it? If it's not part of you and yet it shows up on this view, then it must be in here with us."

"Hands up all of those who can see a suspicious looking sphere floating around in here," Sol said, her frustration emerging as sarcasm.

With a sinking feeling, Alander turned to look at where Axford's body hung contained in its separate section of the cockpit. "Oh, shit . . ."

Sol followed his gaze. "What? What is it?"

Alander moved over to the boundary that separated the ex-general from everyone else. *Eledone* created an opening in the containment field, which he stepped cautiously through. He winced as the smell of blood immediately accosted his senses.

"Peter, what are you doing?" said Sol, moving to the boundary also, but stopping at its edge. "We don't even know if he's dead yet!"

"It's in him, Caryl."

She frowned, shaking her head. "What is? The *hole ship?*"

Alander nodded. "Remember, they can shrink a long way down when they want to. God only knows what he's filled it with: weapons, sensors, all sorts of stuff."

The others joined Hatzis now, all staring at Axford's inert body. "He'd be just crazy enough to try something like this, too," said Samson.

"When he said he could get us out of *Eledone*," mumbled Inari, "I never imagined *this.*"

"None of us did," said Alander. "But if the ship wasn't activated when *Eledone* was damaged, then there's every chance its ftl drive might still be working. All we have to do is get it out."

"Be careful, Peter," said Sol. "Let *Eledone* do most of the work. He—*it* could still be booby-trapped."

Alander acknowledged her caution with a grim smile. That was indeed a strong likelihood, given Axford's nature. The ex-general would have a contingency plan for virtually every possible outcome of a situation, he was sure.

Axford's body appeared unchanged from when it had been contained, but he treated it warily all the same. The insect-leg tools where Axford's hand had once been hung limp and sinister in a tangle. Extending a toe, Alander touched the body gently at first, then more firmly when there was no response.

Again he noted a strange sense of resistance. The body wasn't moving quite right, as though it weighed far more than it should.

Hardly surprising, he thought, *given that there's probably an entire hole ship buried in there.*

He pushed harder, noting how the body listed slightly around a point low in its abdomen. He jumped back slightly when Axford's head lolled to one side, as if turning to face him. But the android's eyes and expression were free of accusation; the look of surprise for when Alander had caved in Axford's rib cage remained frozen on his face. The movement had simply been a result of the body shifting.

He took a deep, calming breath before addressing the hole ship. "*Eledone*, I want you to cut into Frank's body. I don't care how; use a field effect or something."

"Where would you like the incision to be made?"

"Above the waist of his uniform," he said, pointing. "Just along the seam there."

Something shimmered in the air as an invisible blade sliced along where Alander indicated; everyone watched on in silence as the thick, black material parted and peeled back. The skin of Axford 1313's body looked little different than that of any other android, but Alander watched it warily all the same. An incision yawned on the dead man's belly, opening like a lipless mouth. There wasn't much blood; Axford had been dead long enough for it to settle. Alander stared in mute fascination as *Eledone* cut smoothly through fat and abdominal muscle to the gut.

"I have encountered an obstruction," the hole ship said after a few minutes of cutting.

Alander leaned closer. "Wipe the mess away. Let me see."

Gore parted to reveal a gleam of white that clearly wasn't bone.

"I don't believe it," breathed Inari from behind him. "The bastard could've taken us home at any time."

Alander pointed. "*Eledone,* I want you to remove that object—the hole ship—from Frank's body. Can you do that?"

"Yes, Peter." Shimmering forces enfolded the corpse as the gash across its midsection widened. A matching incision formed a cross down its belly. Axford's body bent backward. A thick layer of tissue folded neatly away. Like a surreal caesarian section, a white sphere bigger than an adult human's head and slick with gore bulged out of the cavity. It popped free with a hideous squelching sound and hung motionless in the air.

Behind it, Axford's body straightened and slid to one side, no longer relevant.

Alander walked around the mini–hole ship. It was hard to believe, close up, that he was standing in front of the entrance to an ftl vessel. It looked like nothing more than an oversized marble spattered with red paint. He was at a loss for a moment to know how to get inside it. If he convinced it to expand to its normal size, it would blow their cockpit to pieces.

The solution, when it came from Sol, was so obvious that he was annoyed for not having thought of it himself.

"*Eledone,*" she said, "is it possible for you to merge with Axford's hole ship while it's in this state?"

"Yes, Caryl."

Alander glanced at Sol, who simultaneously shrugged and nodded, as if to say: *What have we got to lose?*

He acquiesced with a nervous sigh. "Okay, *Eledone*, do it—but make sure you keep its interior separated from ours."

Alander stepped back as the miniature hole ship drifted toward the outer wall of the chamber. A dimple puckered up to meet it, swallowing the blood-smeared globe with a single gulp. He felt a soft vibration thrum through the deck beneath his feet, but there was no other indication of what was going on out of sight. Powerful technology flexed, twisting matter into unusual shapes and sending energy coursing along new pathways.

Silently, a door appeared in the wall opposite him. Oval and opaque, it awaited his approach.

"Open it, *Eledone*."

There was a slight puff of air as pressures equalized. Alander stepped forward to peer up the short corridor leading into Axford's hole ship. He couldn't see anything untoward, but he stepped through the door with caution, nonetheless.

The floor jolted beneath him. He stopped to steady himself, and glanced questioningly over his shoulder at Sol.

"External," she assured him. "The Trident must be really be taking a hammering."

He nodded, relieved that he hadn't triggered some mass-destructive device but concerned also that they weren't making any real progress toward escaping. Taking another deep and tremulous breath, he continued into the hole ship, walking forward into the cockpit where he was hoping he'd find something that might be of use to them.

The cockpit turned out not to be the usual white space he'd expected. The walls were lined with glass-covered alcoves and frosted storage containers. He had to think hard before he remembered where he'd last seen anything like them. Their lines were harder, metallic, not the smooth roundedness of the Spinner tech. They had an almost military air. That they were of human origin, not alien, seemed obvious.

There was a line of nine white spheres along one wall, each identical to the one Alander had found in Axford's gut. His mind reeled at the implication. *Hole ships within hole ships within hole ships*, he thought. The chain could go forever with just one entrance to the "real" universe.

He tried to open one of the alcoves, but it was firmly sealed shut. Through the frosted glass he could make out a faint shadow, a vaguely human form, but he couldn't discern the face. The alcoves were linked by cables to a bank of SSDSs covered in flickering displays. They moved rhythmically, hypnotically.

As he bent down to examine the cables, the purpose of the alcoves came to him. They were android breeders, sometimes referred to as ovens among nanotechnicians. He hadn't seen one since entrainment days, although each survey mission had one built into the core vessel. But he'd never seen so many in once place before!

"Why the hell would he . . ."

Before he could finish the question, the answer had already occurred to him.

"Peter?" Startled from his thoughts, Alander wheeled around to see Sol standing in the entrance. She came forward when he faced her. "I didn't hear anything dramatic happen after you came in, so decided it must be—"

She, too, stopped to stare at the ring of android breeders. There were twenty in all, each containing half-grown androids. Alander didn't have to check to know whose androids they were.

"So much for weapons," Sol said, looking slightly pale.

Alander could understand her discomfort. "He wasn't along to help us at all, Caryl. He never even thought we stood a chance, right from the start. That's why he was constantly trying to get away. That fucker was here to *colonize*."

Sol shook her head. "But for you, he might've gotten away with it, too."

"I still might," said a voice from behind them.

They spun around together to find Axford standing between them and the doorway.

Sol took a surprised step back. "But you're *dead*," she said.

Alander looked past him, up the short corridor leading outside. Axford 1313 was visible, still splayed where he'd left him.

"Thirteen-thirteen is dead," Alander said. "This is a different one. Right, Frank?"

Axford affected a relaxed smile, belying the functionally vicious handgun he was pointing at them. "I'm 1041," he said. "Nice to see you again, Caryl."

"You've been here the whole time," she said. "Thirteen-thirteen was just the courier. You're the payload."

"The seed, if you like. I was watching through his senses

when you killed him. I thought about revealing myself then, but I figured it was safer to wait. You might not have guessed the truth. If you hadn't, I would have been free to leave whenever the ftl environment had settled down."

"You're not going anywhere now, Frank," said Sol.

"I don't think you're really in any position to threaten me, Caryl." Ten-forty-one looked down at his handgun; then, surprisingly, he tossed it aside and faced Alander. "I know that I probably can't kill you now, but I have a feeling you're going to let me go anyway."

"You're very much mistaken, I'm afraid," he said.

"Maybe." Axford glanced at Sol. "But I don't think so."

"What makes you say that?"

"You still think you're going to succeed, Caryl," he told her. "You might be right, you might well survive. But me, I *know* I'm going to survive, here and in many, many other places. We're all going to meet up eventually and begin expanding." His voice was cold. "I told you once that it's a big galaxy, that we could coexist peacefully. I wasn't lying, either. But it doesn't have to be that way. Treat me badly, and it'll be *your* worlds I colonize first." He shrugged. "The choice is yours."

Alander stepped forward, fists clenching.

"I'm warning you, Caryl," said Axford, backing away. "Call off your pet freak right now."

Alander laughed. Physically attacking the ex-general had never been his intention; he was just going for the weapon Axford had discarded. He picked it up and hefted it in one hand.

"What's this?" he asked. "A PEP gun like 1313 had?"

"Much the same."

Alander looked at Sol. With one smooth motion, he raised the gun and aimed it at Axford. "What do you think, Caryl? Should we lock him up, or just shoot him now and be done with it?"

"He has a point," said Sol with an uncomfortable reluctance. "We're not in a position to make enemies of him, Peter."

"Don't let him intimidate you," he said. "He may be able to breed, but so what? We can breed, too, and there are more of us than him. Remember, we have the advantage of a wider gene pool. It takes more than determination to survive. We have the breadth of experience. We have hybrid vigor."

Axford smiled. "Maybe so. But that's not enough, either. It's a dog-eat-dog universe out there, and you have to be the dog that bites first, or you end up getting bitten. Personally, I don't think you have what it takes."

Alander tightened his grip on the weapon. He could feel the floor of the hole ship shaking beneath him. Whatever was happening to the Trident, it was only getting worse. They didn't have all day to stand around arguing about who deserved to survive in the long term.

Are we immortal, Lucia had asked him once, *or destined to die a thousand times?*

Alander fired. He wasn't an expert shot, but at such close range, it was effective enough. The noise was deafening, the flash of light blinding. He barely blinked, and Axford was on the floor, a bloody mess contained by his I-suit where his head had once been.

"Jesus—!" Sol flinched from the violence. "My God, Peter. You killed him!"

"That was the idea." He lowered the weapon, aware of sweat on his palms, weakness in his knees, and a tremor all down his gun arm. He didn't feel sick, and he didn't feel guilty, but he was immensely relieved that he didn't feel powerful, either.

She went over to check Axford for a pulse. Like Alander, she obviously wasn't prepared to take any chances when it came to the ex-general.

"Two down," she said, standing. "God only knows how many more to go."

Alander couldn't take his eyes off the gruesome pulp bubbling beneath the invisible skin of the I-suit. He lowered the weapon, shaking his head. "This morning, I'd never killed anyone before. Now I've killed two people."

"The same person, twice," said Sol, stepping up and taking the gun from him. She still looked a little pale. "If it makes you feel better, Peter, don't think of him as a person. He's a plague. You did the right thing."

She didn't sound completely convinced.

"I'm not much of a person, either," Alander said. "Part human, part Yuhl, part Praxis."

"We become what we have to in order to survive. That's the rule, isn't it? And if we're not who we intended to be when we set out, if we don't like what we are—" She shrugged. "I suppose extinction is still an option."

"Sol!" Inari's voice echoed down the corridor. "You need to see this!"

Her face set in worried lines, she took a second longer to check on Alander. "Are you going to be okay?"

He nodded, surprised to be so certain. Killing was not something his original would ever have countenanced, under *any* circumstance, yet he felt okay with what had happened. There had been no alternative.

"Good," said Sol, stepping past him. "We'll clean up this mess later."

He followed her slim, posthuman lines up the corridor to *Eledone*'s cockpit where, on all the screens, they saw a glowing circle widening in the chamber's wall, red gold around the center and blinding white in the middle.

"Rescue?" said Sol hopefully.

"There's no response on any of the bands." Samson shrugged nervously. "Whatever it is, though, Sol, it's a hell of a lot more powerful than we are."

Alander fought an encroaching sense of numbness as everyone stared mutely at the screens, waiting for the next surprise.

2.3.5

Since the explosion that had almost claimed her and an am-
bush sprung by a swarm of red-edged disks as vicious and fast
as the much larger cutters. Lucia had continued her journey
with extreme caution. The urgency with which she was driven
to reach Peter hadn't faded, but she couldn't afford to be reck-
less. Getting herself destroyed wouldn't do anyone any good.

She guided the golden spindle through buckling tubes and
between crumpling bulkheads. The I-suit she had built to contain herself had contracted into a gelatinous sphere, its base
state when not occupied by her thoughts. It was as useless to
her in the Trident's inferno as an umbrella would have been in
a tidal wave.

The sonar ping drew inexorably closer. Despite dead ends
and the growing threat of demolition, she wound her way to
an area dominated by giant pumpkin-shaped vessels. Each was
roughly the same volume as her spindle and was connected to
its neighbors by glassy threads, many of which had shattered
under stress. Among the glinting fragments and the groan of
tortured matter, the ping continued to sound, weak but steady.

Working her way through the giant vessels, she soon managed to isolate which one Peter and the others were trapped in.
But then another problem presented itself: How the hell was
she meant to get them out? There were no obvious signs of an

opening anywhere to be seen, and she possessed no weaponry of any kind, nor was she equipped with tools advanced enough to cut into anything harder than aluminum. Her frustration mounted. To be so near to Peter and yet—

Light suddenly flashed behind her—extremely white and extremely hot. She turned instantly, terrified by the realization that she had let her guard slip. She was still very vulnerable in here; if she was to get the others out of this situation, as well as herself, then she needed to keep her wits about her.

Before she could flee, something brilliant and white swung around one of the pumpkin-shaped vessels and came to an abrupt halt directly in front of her. Rays of coherent light radiated out from it like halos in a spiritual vision, almost as if searching the space around it, roaming and tasting it in the way that an ant's feelers tasted everything they touched. The powerful beams passed over the surface of her golden spindle, and she felt herself physically flinch.

But the beams of light ignored her, swinging forward instead to concentrate on the side of the vessel containing Peter. Merging as one, the beams pumped inconceivable levels of energy into the side of it until the dark material began to glow.

"There are people in there!" Lucia cried, pushing herself forward to intervene.

"I know, Lucia," replied a voice in heavy, hard-pitched English. "I can help them."

A dizzying sense of unreality swept over her at the sound of the voice. *"Caryl?"*

"I am Thor."

"You're—? But—"

"We are not so different, Lucia."

Actually, she thought, realization of what must have happened sinking in, *that probably couldn't be farther from the truth.* If the Starfish had given Thor something similar to what the Spinners had given her, then they were staring at each other from completely opposite sides of the fence.

The ship before her was football-shaped, with a hole at one end, and barely half as large as she was. The coherent glare seemed to come from the skin itself. It radiated an organic sheen, as though in constant motion even when floating motionless. That gave it a slightly blurred edge, as though it wasn't quite all there.

Nevertheless, a common past did unite them; they had both been humans first, before circumstance had led them astray. Underneath the gold Spinner shell and the cold light of whatever Thor had become, they were undoubtedly human still.

The vessel containing the hole ships she'd been chasing was beginning to heat up, an orange glow growing brighter where Thor's beams converged. The glow spread until its center was too white to look at. Harsh electromagnetic noise filled Lucia's receivers, sounding so loud that she began to worry that it might attract attention.

"Are you sure you know what you're doing?" she asked.

There was no reply from Thor. Half the vessel was glowing now, and still the barrage didn't let up. Lucia wondered what the chances were of inadvertently cooking the hole ships contained within. How much heat could *they* take?

Without warning, Thor's beams suddenly spread apart, and the blasting of the vessel ceased. Lucia's senses took a second to recover from the glare, but once they did, she saw that the vessel now looked uncannily like an eye painted in garish false color; the brightly glowing patch surrounded a circular black hole where the exotic material had failed.

"Come out while you are able!"

"Thor?" Sol's voice was filled with surprise and reservations. "Is that you?"

"There is no time. we must leave now."

"She's right," put in Lucia. "The Trident isn't stable. It could blow at any time."

"*Lucia?*" It was Peter's turn to be surprised.

"It's good to hear your voice," she said, feeling a surge of relief. "But we'll have to save the pleasantries until later. We need to get you out of here before anything else goes wrong."

"This is a matter of high priority," said Thor.

Space-time shook around them as something massive exploded farther down the spine of the Trident. Gravitational shock waves stretched the matter around them, tugging symmetries askew, then snapping them back into place.

A seven-sided hole ship emerged from the gap in the side

of the vessel, its whiteness in stark contrast to the blasted matter surrounding it.

"Follow me," Thor instructed them. With a swirl of light beams, she spun on her axis and accelerated into the distance. The multiple hole ship followed as best it could, looking decidedly clunky in comparison. Lucia brought up the rear, unwilling to stray too far from her charge as they made their escape from the disintegrating ship.

"Who's boss now?" asked Samson wryly as she piloted Eledone in Thor's wake.

"I'd say *she* is," Sol said, pointing at the screen. "I mean, look at her. She's—"

Words escaped her.

"Changed?" supplied Alander.

She nodded. "Yes, changed."

The truth was that she felt humbled. She had assumed all along that engrams were incapable of change. Even when she tinkered with them, meddled with their operating assumptions, they were still hampered by the overseer that ran them, constantly bringing them back into line when they strayed. She had hoped to find a way around these restrictions but hadn't yet managed to do so. It had taken alien intervention to achieve it with Alander first, and now Thor.

Exactly what had happened to Lucia, she didn't know, but the way the liberated spindle was dogging *Eledone* and the tone in Lucia's voice when she had asked about Peter suggested that she hadn't so much changed herself as changed her home.

Still, hybrid vigor, as Alander had suggested, might well be what they needed to survive in the short term as well as the long. And right now, she was quite happy to clutch at whatever life raft came her way.

Temperatures skyrocketed as they wound along narrow passages and through folding chambers. Conditions were soon as bad as they had been in the wounded cutter. There was no hope in this case, though, that the disintegration was self-inflicted. No recycling for the mighty ship, she assumed. There was no sign of the Pllix anywhere. The Trident was a victim of the laws of physics.

She hadn't seen physics in action like this since Sol System had been destroyed. Great rents opened around them, sending fragments of wall and ceiling flying like ashes in a bonfire. *Eledone* bucked as it rode the explosive flow. The white point of Thor vanished in a howling, rumbling shock wave that gradually overtook them and shook them like a die in a cup. She could hear the battered hole ship's voice, barely audible over the noise, complaining of damage, and beyond that a deep moaning sound that issued from God only knew where. For all she could tell, it could have been the dying groan of the Trident itself.

The shock wave dispersed around them as it expanded, and Thor reappeared, glowing like a sun through clouds. The rumble faded, and *Eledone* ceased its litany of complaint. The moan ceased, also, its origins never determined.

As *Eledone*'s sensors recovered, what remained of pi-1 Ursa Major took shape around them.

"Oh, my God," Alander breathed.

Sol silently echoed the sentiment.

The system's primary was spent. Its remains consisted of two expanding sheets of gas and energy, sandwiching the ecliptic all around its equator. Some of the expelled matter had cooled, lending a mottled, blotchy appearance to the debris. The rest burned with a reddish, angry glow, except for two striking, blue-yellow jets emerging from where each pole had been, half-visible through the murk.

Sol's first impression of the system was how much darker it appeared to be. With the primary sun destroyed and its energy spread out over a vast volume, the amount of visible light was limited. That, however, only cast the ongoing battle into sharp, shadowless relief. Violent flashes and streaks still flickered from hundreds of locations, blue- and red-shifted by extreme velocities and exotic warps in space-time. The extended flash that accompanied the final breakup of the Trident falling rapidly behind them was barely enough to illuminate vast clouds of gas and debris around it, even for a second. Similar clouds bubbled everywhere Sol looked, expanding and merging wherever hostilities had broken out.

And the planets! She shook her head, disbelieving her eyes. Even after the death of the sun, she still had trouble accepting the scale of this battle. Stars were violent places, by nature turbulent and changeable, but planets didn't normally blow up or expel vast chunks of their atmosphere in energetic plumes.

Yet they, too, were gone. The Earth-like inner world, Jian Lao, had been reduced to dust. The atmosphere of the bigger gas giant had been stripped away and its core broken up into millions of jagged and treacherous chunks. Trails of molten debris and plasma marked the locations of the remainder of the planets. Once-molten cores were reduced to glowing cinders, while ring systems and moons were indistinguishable from the rest of the rubble filling the system.

Pi-1 Ursa Major was essentially dead, but the fight between the two super-races carried on regardless.

"I can't get my head around this," Inari said tonelessly. Her eyes were glazed as she stared at a view of the Source of All in the middle reaches of the system, just outside what had once been the habitable zone. Its sunlike appearance was gone. Now it looked like a flickering fluorescent tube tied in a knot around something dark and sinuous that coiled in and out of its glowing folds. A luminous mist enshrouded it, making it hard to tell what precisely was going on. Sol was reminded of a human zygote, its cells dividing, growing, then dividing again.

"Where are we going?" asked Samson into the hushed cockpit, piloting the hole ship with the control stalk.

Sol shook her head. "I have no idea, but keep on Thor's tail as best you can."

Thor arced smoothly until she was pointing up into the northern plume of gas and stellar debris. Accelerating at many dozens of g's, the three vessels were soon moving at an appreciable fraction of the speed of light. Debris rained on shields that had never, to Sol's knowledge, been used for such purposes. *Eledone* was used to traveling through unspace, not the real universe, where at such velocities a single molecule could tear an unprotected ship apart.

"She's taking us out of the zone of interference," Lucia reported. "We're unable to use ftl here, in the light cone of the explosion. We can't escape until we get outside it."

"But how are we meant to get outside the light cone when we can't travel faster than light?" asked Samson.

"The disturbance is not symmetrical in space," Thor replied. "There are irregularities."

"And we're heading for one of those?"

Sol waited almost thirty seconds before it was clear that Thor wasn't about to answer.

"She seems more and more like you every day, Sol," Samson commented.

"What good will getting out of the light cone do us?" asked Inari. "We don't even have a working ftl drive."

"Yes we do," said Alander. "Axford's hole ship is merged with *Eledone*, so we'll be able to use his."

Inari nodded but only looked partially convinced. There was still a faraway look to her eyes, as though she'd long since passed the point of being surprised. She was coasting, now, in shock; it would probably take hours, maybe even days, to recover.

They entered the glowing clouds, blue-shifted to higher energies by their velocity. Stellar detritus enclosed them, and strange high-pitched noises came to them through *Eledone*'s walls as particles ricocheted off the shields.

The battle between the Starfish and Spinners vanished into redness behind them. Sol's last glimpse was of the corrupted Source of All writhing like a nest of snakes as alien ships of wildly different shapes and sizes converged from all sides. The system was alight with the fire of battle. On top of the infrared wash from the explosion of pi-1 Ursa Major, there were thousands of points of higher-frequency light winking on and off in time with the ongoing fight.

There was no sign of pursuit, though and for that she was profoundly grateful.

Then something loomed at them from the radiant clouds: the hulk of a cutter kilometers long. Craters gaped in its hull. Cold and dead, it fell instantly behind without incident.

It wasn't enough to make her relax, though. Tension filled the cockpit as the convoy sped on, constantly accelerating through the stellar debris. It was hard to believe, Sol thought abstractedly, that the molecules they were colliding with had, just a day ago, been in the heart of a star. And strangely, that thought brought with it a glimmer of hope. With the Starfish taking such a beating, for the first time in a long time, survival didn't seem so bleak.

Whether or not it was enough, of course, she wouldn't know until they were within ftl range of the colonies. The mission had cut it horribly fine. Zemyna and Geb had passed their deadline by some hours. If the fovea had arrived even slightly ahead of schedule, Sagarsee could have been attacked, too. The idea of returning to nothing but burning wreckage where the last of the UNESSPRO colonies had been founded chilled her to the core.

In silence they continued to accelerate through the clouds. Gradually these began to thin, and through them brighter stars appeared. Inari openly wept at the sight of them. Sol kept her feelings close to herself, standing apart from Peter and the others, not daring to look away even for a moment.

Then out of the ether came the crackle of human voices:

". . . reporting from Demeter that . . ."

". . . fovea sighted at 0920 . . ."

". . . decrease in overall activity but hot spots . . ."

". . . no joy . . ."

"Hail them," said Sol quickly. "Tell them we're coming!"

"This is *Eledone* in pi-1 Ursa Major calling all human vessels in the vicinity. Can you hear us?"

"*Eledone?*" came the instantaneous response. "Where the hell did you come from?"

"A long story," said Sol. "Who are we talking to?"

"This is *Faridah*," came the reply. "Christ, we thought you guys were dead!"

"Far from it, *Faridah*. We're heading home, if there's still a home to return to."

No joy . . .

"The circle is closing in, but we're hanging in there. Welcome back—and watch out for signal hunters. They're all around here."

Right on cue, something angular and silver appeared alongside Thor. Whips of crimson energy lashed out at her shining hull, tangling themselves in stabbing beams of light.

"Sagarsee," said Thor, and with a flash she disappeared.

The angular signal hunter turned its attention on the next ship in line. Golden light met crimson as Lucia pushed herself forward between them. Red whips coiled around the spindle and dragged it in.

"*Eledone*," said Sol, "take us to Sagarsee. Lucia, we'll meet you there, okay?"

"I'll leave once you're gone."

The energy whips were scoring Lucia's golden hull. Sol bit her lip, realizing only then that the spindle was defenseless against the alien signal hunter. Mentally she urged *Eledone* to hurry, not wishing to sacrifice Lucia just so their escape could be facilitated. Not for the first time she cursed the blind obedience to ingrained behavioral rules that so often drove engrams to their deaths.

The view winked out, and unspace enfolded them. Instantly, she felt as though the walls of the cockpit were closing in on her.

"We made it," said Inari, expelling a sigh that was part laugh. "We actually made it!"

"So it would seem," said Samson. Her own relief seemed more cautious.

"I wouldn't get too excited too soon," said Alander with annoying practicality. "We still don't know what we're flying back to."

Sol nodded, sympathizing with his unwillingness to celebrate while the events of the previous days were so fresh.

No joy . . .

The words rang through her thoughts. Ramping her clock rate right down, she took a seat and waited out the trip home in frozen silence.

2.3.6

They came out of unspace over Sagarsee's north pole. After the close confines of *Eledone* and the chaotic madness of pi-1 Ursa Major, the simple, uncomplicated sunlight of BSC5148 was like a visual breath of fresh air. Sagarsee hung bold and blue beneath them, its clouds swirling in a thick spiral over ice and frozen seas. The stars above were clear and unobstructed by stellar debris or the detritus of warfare. It wasn't Earth, but for Alander, it was the next best thing.

Barely had they reentered the real universe when voices clamored for their attention.

"Sol! You made it!" Cleo Samson looked up wearily from her position by *Eledone*'s command stalk at the sound of her own voice and the appearance of her own face on one of the screens.

"We made it," Sol confirmed, stirring from her position on the couch. "As did you, obviously."

"Only by the skin of our teeth." The mission supervisor of the *Frank Drake* suddenly lost all sense of relief, and her expression became serious. "We lost Zemyna and Demeter and the last we heard was that Geb was under attack. But Lucia tells us that the Starfish are getting their collective ass kicked in pi-1 Ursa Major, so all of this should stop now, right?"

Alander studied the vessels clumped around Sagarsee's gifts.

There were dozens of hole ships in various configurations; the larger were most likely craft belonging to the Unfit, combined to form traveling habitats. Orbiting close to the Hub was Lucia's spindle. She must have made the jump much more quickly than *Eledone* to have already secured an orbit.

"Let's hope so," said Sol. "Thor could probably tell you more, though."

"She's here," said Samson. There was a look on Samson's face that suggested she wasn't too sure about this new, improved Thor. "Somewhere, anyway. The last we saw of her, she was scouting the edge of the system. God only knows what she's looking for. She never explained—"

"Can we talk about this later?" Sol cut in tiredly. "I need to get out of this fucking tin can."

Samson nodded and offered an apologetic smile.

"Sure. Just give us five minutes to clear the Dry Dock, and it's all yours."

Samson closed the line then, and Alander watched the screen in anticipation, waiting for the face he *knew* would appear there next.

He didn't have to wait long.

"Hello, Peter," said Lucia. In the screen she looked the same as she had more than a century earlier, back on Earth. Her deep brown eyes stared at him with warmth and playful intelligence. It was like watching a photograph come to life.

And just like a photograph, he sensed the two-dimensionality behind it. She was an image beginning to lose her resolution from being copied too many times. Despite everything that had happened to her since leaving Earth, she was trying to be exactly the same as she used to be, and looked strained because of it.

"Hello, Lucia," he said. "I'm glad you made it out okay."

She smiled. "I didn't think I was going to for a while there."

"None of us did."

A fleeting look of anxiety crossed her face, then vanished. "Who would've thought that we'd end up here, eh, Peter? We've done things our originals could never have imagined in a thousand years."

"And then some."

She smiled again, this time more naturally, as if relaxing into the conversation.

"I guess it's something to be proud of, anyway," she said.

He nodded. "It is."

She hesitated, and Alander sensed her attention shifting. "I was talking to Thor," she said. "She told me I should speak to Sol."

The original Hatzis stepped up beside Alander. "I'm here, Lucia."

"I—" The anxious look returned.

Hatzis glanced at Alander, then back to the screen. "What is it, Lucia?"

She seemed to steel herself then against her uncertainties. "I want to change, Caryl."

Hatzis frowned. *"Change? In what way?"*

"Thor said you could help me like you tried to help her."

The corners of Sol's eyes tightened fractionally. "What did she tell you about that, exactly?"

"Just that you were reprogramming all of your engrams to make them more flexible."

Sol didn't react to a sharp look Inari cast in her direction. "That's not entirely true, Lucia," Sol said. "I've introduced a few random changes to the parameters to see if any of them helped, certainly. But that's about it. I'm not sure I have the know-how to rewrite everyone from the inside out. I'm hoping I'll find something simple that will keep you all together longer. If I can't—" She shrugged, glancing around the cockpit. "Well, I guess it'll get kind of lonely around here in a few years."

"I *want* to change, Caryl," Lucia said again. "The spindle can keep me alive forever, but what's the point if I simply vegetate in here? Peter's Graveyard—" Her eyes flicked to him with something akin to apology. Then she sighed. "All the Peters are gone, I'm afraid."

Alander frowned. "What do you mean, they're *gone?"*

"They're all frozen," she said. "I'm sorry, Peter. It's just that I needed them. I needed their company, I needed . . . *you."*

A strange feeling swept through Alander, as though someone had, quite literally, walked over his grave. Lucia had drained the last few moments of coherence from the fading echoes of him like some bizarre sanity vampire. Part of him wanted to be angry, but a bigger part didn't see the point. Those other versions of him weren't him anymore; not really. They were just faulty reflections of his original; copies that had lost their resolution in much the same way that he regarded the image of Lucia staring back at him from the screen now. The fact that he had once been one of them didn't necessarily make him feel any closer to them. He could only empathize with what they'd been going through.

Still, the desperation in her to do something like that . . .

"I don't know how to fix them," Lucia was saying with growing panic. "Or even if they *can* be fixed. And I don't want to run away now just because I can't stop feeling the way I—"

"It's okay, Lucia," Sol cut in. "We understand what you're saying. And I'm happy to try to help you, but I can't make any promises."

"If you like," said Alander, "I can come across and be with you in the meantime."

Her virtual image expressed clear relief. "That would be . . . appreciated, Peter. Thank you."

Alander caught a sharp look from Sol. He wondered if she thought he was reverting to his own old routines, now he had the chance. If challenged, he could honestly say that he wasn't. He was helping Lucia because he wanted to, not because he had to. When he looked into himself, he saw only himself, not the bones of a long-dead man.

And the Praxis, he reminded himself. His limbs had reverted to normal once his foot had healed. There was none of the strange tingling that had followed the attack on Axford 1313. He could almost pretend that nothing had happened. Almost . . .

Hatzis nodded, either in resignation or acceptance, and looked away. Her eyes were red, and her face had lines that hadn't been there days earlier.

Cleo Samson of Sagarsee broke in to announce that their berth was ready. Cleo Samson of *Eledone* acknowledged and smoothly took them home.

The gifts of Sagarsee weren't full, but they were definitely crowded. A large number of Yuhl were present in the flesh, coordinating the activities of the Unfit with the makeshift engram infrastructure. Most of the humans weren't physically present, but the airways were thick with conSense transmissions. Numerous oddly shaped telepresence robots scurried, rolled, climbed, or even flew through the corridors. The return of Thor and her mission to the Starfish brought last-minute preparations for evacuation to a halt. The members of the mission split up almost immediately, heading for numerous debriefing sessions.

Alander, however, pleaded senescence in order to avoid all the meetings. For all that he'd done in recent weeks, he was still looked upon by many as something of a washout. The stigma of so many breakdowns was hard to erase, and for once he was happy to use it to his advantage.

Jumping through the Hub to Lucia's spindle, he sank gratefully into silence.

"Hello, Peter," she said immediately upon his arrival, a liquid shimmer casting rainbows out of thin air.

He didn't jump, but the urge to do so was strong. "Hello again, Lucia." He squinted at the half-seen shape before him. "Is that what I think it is?"

"An I-suit." She opened her arms as though showing off a new outfit. "Would you like one, too?"

"Would I—?" He stopped, staring at her ghostly image. "You can actually do that? You can make them to order?"

"The gifts are more complex than you could possibly imagine."

That I can believe, he thought.

A small silence fell then, with Alander not knowing what to say. He longed for the ease with which he'd once been able to speak with her, but that was in the past. He wasn't that person anymore; his feelings had changed, become something very different from what they'd once been. Her feelings for him, however, hadn't changed, but he suspected they hadn't been that strong in the first place. He was sure she could live without him as long as she had the stars to keep her company. He had struggled just to live.

Standing there before her now, he could see how different they really were. His body was a continuing mystery to him; hers was even more bizarre. What would happen, he wondered, if they tried something as simple as a kiss? Would her I-suit body feel like a human's, or would it be cold and slippery like plastic? He was in no hurry to find out, and that fact only reinforced how much he had changed. There had once been a time when he would have given anything just for the chance to press his lips against Lucia's.

"I'm monitoring the feeds around us," she said. "If you like, we could listen in on what's being said right now."

He sensed that she was feeling awkward, too, which wasn't surprising. The last thing he wanted to do was watch a bunch of people—and nonpeople—arguing over politics, but it had to be better than this awkward silence.

"Sure," he said. "Why not?"

He thought she smiled, but he couldn't be a hundred percent sure.

"This way," she said, turning to move in the direction of the Dark Room.

He followed her gossamer form down familiar corridors to the blank space in which he'd once recuperated. Blackness enfolded him, and he sank into it as he would a warm bath. The thought made him think of the bath he'd tried to take on Adrasteia, the day the Spinners had come, and that thought gave him an oddly disquieting feeling.

Strange, he thought. *It seems like a million years ago.*

The first time he'd been in the Dark Room, he had been completely alone. This time, however, Lucia was with him. And while he couldn't see her, he could certainly sense her presence and feel her thoughts and emotions coiling around him like a fine mist.

Images and words spilled out of the darkness, entering his mind via conSense pathways, but without the usual jarring disorientation. Lucia's hand was sure and gentle, interfacing with his senses with far more ease than reality itself.

"The Unfit have sent several hole ships ahead to find the Praxis," she explained, showing him navigation charts pinpointing the locations or destinations of numerous hole ships, scattered across Surveyed Space and beyond. "We don't know where he's gone, though. It's been seven days since he and the others left, and in that time they could have traveled three hundred light-years or more, putting them well outside the ftl communication bubble."

"Maybe that's what Thor is looking for," he said.

"Maybe." He sensed a shrug to her voice and understood that, even from her privileged point of view, there was no way of telling what Thor was doing.

"What about the Unfit?" he asked. "Do they think the Praxis will return if he hears of Thor's success in contacting the Starfish?"

"That would depend on how the Starfish react, I imagine. It's possible, if everything goes well. But even if he didn't, even if he decides to keep going, I'm sure some of the Yuhl would return."

Alander nodded. "What about Geb? Any news from there?"

"Yes, and it's not good." She called up reports from scouts sent to the stricken colony. The data showed the Starfish destruction conducted in the usual style: brisk, methodical, remorseless.

"I don't understand why they still did this," said Lucia as Alander studied the data. "Thor told them what was going on, so they know we're innocent now."

Like everybody else, she was clinging to that one simple thought, and he didn't want to disabuse her of the notion. Nevertheless, he did outline what the Asteroid had said upon seeing Lucia in the vicinity of pi-1 Ursa Major, shortly before the star had exploded. She needed to know his worst fears, in case they came true.

There is reason to suspect that we have been misled.

He remembered the spindle shining against a deep and hostile black backdrop.

My makers suspect you have led us into a trap.

"You think—" she began, then stopped, obviously considering what he was telling her. "You think they're coming after us, don't you? That they blame us for what happened to them in pi-1 Ursa Major."

"Lucia, I honestly have no idea *what* these beings think," he said. "But yes, it's a possibility."

She was silent for more than a minute as she thought about this some more.

"It doesn't bear thinking about," she said eventually, quietly.

"No," he replied. "No, it doesn't."

He remembered how it had felt when he'd learned that he was responsible for the destruction of Sol System, that he had

inadvertently called the Starfish down on the last true humans
by careless use of his hole ship's ftl communicator. At first the
feeling of guilt had been overwhelming. It didn't matter what
he told himself, that there was no way he could have possibly
known what would happen. No one even knew about the Starfish at that point, let alone that using the Spinner technology
could incur their wrath. He had been like a minnow taken from
his small, freshwater pond and dropped into some vast ocean,
rejoicing in his newfound freedom until the inevitable shark
appeared.

Time, though, had brought the realization that all he'd done
was precipitate Sol System's destruction, not been the cause of
it. The Starfish would have reached Earth soon enough, as they
swept through Surveyed Space. A few days' notice wouldn't
have made any difference to the final result whatsoever.

Maybe, he pondered, it would be different to be the one
who had brought destruction down upon the last human colony.
Then again, these wouldn't be the last humans. There were still
others out there somewhere, jumping from star to star on the
Praxis's back. And then, of course, there was always Axford.
No doubt he was out there somewhere, too, continuing to
spread through the galaxy like some malignant cancer.

Alander and Lucia continued to eavesdrop on the others in
silence. They listened in on discussions ranging from long-
range policy to everyday trivia. Coordinating the activities of
several hundred traumatized engrams called for the sort of leadership and infrastructure that the UNESSPRO survey missions
hadn't been designed to accommodate. Various improvisational
methods were springing into being, often revolving around
identical engrams from different missions. A surly collective of
Otto Wyras wanted an increased allocation for scientific processing, especially in the wake of the pi-1 Ursa Major nova.
Others sought solace and therapy in discussions with themselves or in groups comprised of just two or three templates. It
was common to see the same associations repeated everywhere:
if overseer rules stated that Owen Norsworthy and Nalini Kov-
istra should be friends, then so they would be, always. Rifts
formed along ancient fracture lines, tracing enmities laid down
on Earth and propagated to the stars.

It was amazing, Alander thought, that the engrams had made

it as far as they had. Given the odds stacked against them, they should have all turned out like him. The whole project should have fallen flat on its collective face before any of the missions had even left Sol's neighborhood.

After a while, the wash of information became oddly soothing. Floating in a sea of faux humanity, his mind began to wander, his thoughts slowed, and he gradually drifted into sleep. It was hard to differentiate between the darkness of the Dark Room and unconsciousness, so sliding from one to the other was easy. Nor did he fight it when he realized what was happening. He just accepted it, allowing himself sink even deeper into that sleep, drifting with the babble of all the streams of conversation taking place around Sagarsee.

"Sleep well, Peter," was the last thing he heard before unconsciousness claimed him completely.

He didn't dream.

"If we have been saved," a voice said an undetermined time later, "then the work is only beginning. We're pretty much all that's left of humanity, so where do we go from here? Where do we live? How do we even govern ourselves? Christ, how are we going to make a viable society out of the same sixty-odd people repeated over and over again?"

Alander vaguely recognized the voice but couldn't quite place it. He blinked into the darkness, clutching for reference points. He could make out an open door in the distance, and leaning through it a spindly, matte-gray creature, glass eyes gleaming.

"That's what people are trying to work out right now." There was no mistaking *that* voice: it was Lucia. "Perhaps you should be out there talking with them instead of in here talking to me, Rob."

The mention of the name helped Alander place the voice: Rob Singh. He was one of several mission pilots disenfranchised by the arrival of the Spinners and their hole ships.

"Politics isn't my bag," said Singh. "I'm more interested in finding out *why* all of this had to happen. Just because the problem might have gone away doesn't mean that we should stop trying to pick at it. All of the questions we've found in the gifts still haven't been answered. The Spinners are just as much a mystery as they ever were."

"What's going on?" Alander asked finally.

"Oh, I'm sorry, Peter," said Lucia. "We didn't mean to wake you."

"That's all right," he said. "How long was I out?"

"Not long," said Lucia. "Only about an hour."

"Is that all?" He had the mental equivalent of a creased face from having slept in an awkward position; nothing was quite lining up yet. "I think I'm going to need at least a week before I'm fully rested."

"You're not the only one," said Singh via the telepresence robot.

Alander tried to shake the sleep from his thoughts. "What's happening in pi-1 Ursa Major?" he asked. "Does anyone know yet?"

"It's still impossible to get in close enough to tell," said Singh. "The light cone of the explosion is expanding, keeping our scouts a fair distance from the center. There's still fighting going on in there, we know that much—although who's actually winning we have no idea. Would you believe, though, that some are quibbling over naming what's left of the star?"

Alander smiled weakly. Sadly, he could well believe it: it was just the kind of petty-minded nonsense that invariably occupied people's thoughts.

"And yourself?" asked Alander. "What have you been doing while you wait?"

"I've been going over the mission reports filed since you got back. They're quite fascinating, you know. We've all learned a lot in the last few days."

"I glanced at them, too," Lucia said. "I found them more confusing than anything."

"Maybe," said Singh, "but there are some answers to be found if you're prepared to look." He was sounding pleased with himself. "I was reminded at one point of a conversation you said you had with one of Peter's engrams. The one from chi Hercules."

Alander remembered that engram. He had tried to convince him to merge his memories with his, but he had refused. Now, presumably, his last moments of life had been sucked dry by Lucia. "Why? What did he say?"

"He talked about his theory, the various ways the Spinners and Starfish could have evolved without affecting our own evolution—quantumly speaking. One of the theories he raised was that they're moving in a reverse time direction to us, heading for the big crunch rather than the long cold or big bang or whatever lies ahead."

"Mind games," said Lucia. "He was just following his operating parameters."

"That doesn't mean the thought doesn't have merit," said Singh. "Do you remember the Asteroid? The way it only spoke in statements?"

Alander did: the strange, spherical creature that had claimed, or at least implied, that it was a close link to the Starfish. He couldn't imagine how it related to the stuttering thoughts of his failed copy, though. "Yeah. So?"

"Did you ever work out *why* it did this?"

Alander hadn't. "You have a theory, I take it."

Singh's robot shifted position at the door. "I believe it was only able to speak in statements because the normal conversational rules didn't apply to it. More specifically, because the progression of question and answer wouldn't work—not if its superiors were viewing time in reverse. How could the Asteroid provide an answer before it had heard the question? Or better yet, why would it bother asking a question when, from its point of view, you'd already answered it?"

"I don't understand," said Lucia.

"I think I do," said Alander. He moved toward the doorway where the robot twitched and whirred. "Rob's saying that conversation between beings in opposite flows of time is *only* possible by statements."

"Exactly," said Singh. "It was an interface between two completely contradictory ways of being. Or might have been."

Alander thought back to the strange and awkward conversation, and recalled wondering at the time why beings as advanced as the Starfish would have trouble communicating with them. Singh had come up with a possible explanation, and if he was right, it opened a whole new can of worms.

"That could make things terribly complicated," said Lucia.

"It would mean that they see a universe of decreasing entropy, right? Where things become more ordered with time, not less?"

Three eyestalks on the robot rotated as if to examine the darkness of the room. "That's the gist of it, yes. As bizarre as it may seem, they may come from a time beyond the universe's turnaround point, when the arrow of time swings back. To them, they're still traveling forward, into their future, and it's the rest of the universe that's traveling backward."

"So from their point of view," she went on, "they're not destroying the gifts at all—they're *building* them. To the Starfish, it would be the Spinners who are destroying them!"

"It's possible," he said. "But we don't know if the Spinners are following the same time arrow as the Starfish. If they're not, it gets even more complicated."

"Jesus wept, Rob," said Lucia. "Is this even possible?"

"Technically. There was a theory put forward once that reverse time flow could account for some of the dark matter we still haven't found; it could be material from the distant future, traveling back to the big crunch. Really, though, I'm just throwing ideas around here, trying to see which way up they land."

"And interesting ideas they are, Rob," said Alander, easing his way out of the shadows of the Dark Room to stand over the telepresence robot.

"So where would they come from?" asked Lucia. Her tone was unashamedly skeptical. "How far in the future are we talking about?"

"Current estimates put it at fifty billion years or so to the turnaround."

"That's a hell of a long time," said Lucia.

"But not impossible."

"In order to maintain their arrow of time," Alander said, mentally dusting off theories he hadn't read about for years, "they'd have to stay at a distance from the rest of the universe. They could interact, but only weakly; otherwise they'd risk flipping their arrow of time over to ours."

"What would that do?" asked Lucia.

"I don't know." Alander struggled with an image forming in his mind. "What if the Starfish or the Spinners or both are from the future, traveling back to our past, but everything we've seen so far is from our universe, from *our* arrow of time, grown up around them like coral?"

"That's precisely what I've been wondering," said Singh. "It seems so strange that the Spinner and Starfish migrations have always been there, locked in time like a thread, while other life-forms have grown around that thread to make it their home. In a sense, they *have* lost their arrow of time, because causality has become so tangled in the thread that it doesn't have much meaning anymore. Did the Starfish or the Spinners make the gifts? Did the Starfish or the Spinners destroy them? It depends entirely on how you look at it. Did we trigger the battle in pi-1 Ursa Major by going to the Starfish, or did we finish it? Did the Spinners arrive in pi-1 Ursa Major forty-three years ago, or was that when they left? Perhaps, from their point of view, they're only just arriving there now."

"Or perhaps they've always been there," said Alander.

Lucia's skepticism was an almost physical presence in the Dark Room. "Personally, I prefer the other theory doing the rounds."

"Of course," said Singh, "because it's easier to accept. But that's why I distrust it. If the Spinners were giving us the gifts to distract the Starfish while they got away, then that would make *them* the bad guys—and that conveniently absolves us of our guilt, doesn't it?"

"Guilt for what?" asked Lucia.

"For handing them over to the Starfish, of course," said Singh. "I'm sorry, but anything that makes the universe seem so neatly comprehensible, while at the same time makes us feel better about our actions within that universe, strikes me as being unlikely."

Alander didn't know if he wholly agreed with that, but he had to admit that Rob Singh's theory was intriguing. The image of a thread curling through space-time, causally locked between its endpoints, was a strange but seductive one—as well as terribly fatalistic. He was starting to see it less as a coral around which a rich and varied ecosystem had built up, rather than a strip of flypaper, trapping everyone that came too close. And once caught in the tangled web of causality, there might be no escape; the thread would be unbreakable. Only at the end-

points—at the beginning and end of the intertwined timeline—
would the chance to slip through appear.

The question, therefore, was: where in the future *was* the
endpoint? Was humanity—or what was left of it—trapped for
millennia, like the Yuhl, or was the end in sight?

"Perhaps the Praxis can help resolve this," he said after
some thought. "If they've encountered more Spinner drops
ahead, then we'll know the migration is continuing, regardless
of what's happened in pi-1 UMA."

"I'm sure someone will ask," said Singh. "Once they find
him."

"*If* they find him," Lucia added gloomily.

Alander couldn't stay hidden forever and he knew it. Eventually,
following increasingly annoyed summons from Sol, he did reluctantly emerge to offer his version of events. He wasn't sure
how seriously his viewpoint would be taken, but he could accept that his role in the killing of two Axfords and the destruction of the android breeder factory was pivotal and warranted
at least a personal statement after the fact.

Lucia accompanied him in her I-body form first to the Hub,
then to the Library, where the inquest was being conducted. He
related what had happened to a panel of mission supervisors
with as much accuracy and objectivity as he could manage.
The events of the previous two weeks were hard to view with
complete detachment, however, and he found his palms sweat-
ing as he related how he had subdued Axford 1313. The sensation of ribs breaking and organs collapsing under the force
of his blow was still horribly vivid. The smell of blood, he
feared, would never leave him.

After this he went to the Surgery for a detailed examination.
The instruments in Spindle Four were considerably more advanced than anything he'd ever seen on Earth, and he dreaded
what Kingsley Oborn—the closest thing to a medic from a
thousand missions containing no actual bodies—would find. He
gritted his teeth as arcane scanners swept up and down his
body, while strange nanotech-laden fluids flowed through his
tissues.

Oborn's conclusions were nebulous at best. There was evidence of extensive change on a cellular level throughout Alander's body, but exactly what those changes meant could not be determined without more comprehensive tests.

"I'm working on a new android design," said the biotechnician, stroking his chin where a beard would normally have grown. "If there are changes we can incorporate based on the work the Praxis did on you, then that might give us a more robust start, at least."

"Which mission are you from?" Lucia asked him.

He eyed her modified I-suit with naked fascination. "Ten Taurus. I'm looking forward to going back there when all this is over."

"To live?"

The biotechnician shrugged. "I'd like to, but I know that if we all split up, nothing will get done. We have to stay together to work things out. Later, once everything has settled down, we can talk about resettlement."

"In your new android bodies."

He beamed at her. "Of course. Who'd want to stay a con forever, right?"

Alander had never heard the expression before, and his confusion must have showed. Lucia explained it to him as they left the Surgery.

"That's *con* as in conSense," she said. "Some of the droids tend to look down on those stuck in VR, even though conSense is often more comfortable and flexible than life in the flesh. The reverse is also true, of course: cons sneer at droids for being clunky and slow."

Alander grunted, wondering if he was seeing the beginning of a new culture clash. Was this how the future was going to shape out, as a conflict between those in the flesh and those without? He wondered where people like Lucia would fit in, straddling the divide.

"You can take the engram out of the ape," he said, "but you can't take the ape out of the engram, eh?"

"Perhaps," said Lucia, walking ahead of him like some shimmering ghost. "Although I'm sure someone's working on that even as we speak."

* * *

In the strange, virtual landscape of the Unfit, Alander heard the cautious celebrations of an alien race that had been running for as long as most of them could remember. Of those who had chosen to stay to pursue the Species Dream, only a handful had been alive when the Spinners had first arrived in their home system. Their memories were faded and confused. Given the plasticity of the Yuhl brain, all of them had been cognitively recast many times since their escape from the Starfish.

"We lost everything," said one of the elders, accorded no special status by virtue of her survival but allowed to speak as one who had dreamed of regaining her freedom. "Billions died in the hive moons. Fire spread through the weave, undoing everything we had built. The Ambivalence didn't heed our pleas. The Praxis made himself known to the few of us who escaped, and our fate was sealed."

Alander listened to the litany of recollections with interest, wondering at how it must feel to have ended a millennia-long emigration. He wasn't certain that the inbuilt ability to understand the Yuhl's speech, granted to him by the Praxis, was translating accurately, but he thought he sensed a certain sadness in the telling as opposed to relief. Had the survivor of the purging of the Yuhl home systems hoped for death rather than freedom? Perhaps in the Yuhl's eyes, one release was as good as another.

The concept of the Ambivalence—that Starfish and Spinners were facets of the same manifestation, rather than two independent migrations following one another—dovetailed neatly with Rob Singh's speculations. Alander wondered if the Yuhl's innate sense of symmetry gave them an edge in understanding the phenomenon they had been caught up in, or whether centuries of being around the Praxis had simply given them access to his own insights. The fleshy alien had been trailing the Spinner front much longer than the Yuhl, after all, and would therefore have a better understanding of the superpowers—an understanding that less knowledgeable races could only benefit from.

"This is the dawning of a new time," said Sol, her voice ringing out clear and strong through the minds of the Yuhl and engrams assembled. Alander knew she had doubts as to her role among the engrams, but it didn't show. "What future lies ahead for our two races is unknown, but if we face it with determination and dignity, then we—"

"Yes, let's face it, Caryl," a familiar voice interrupted. "I guess you'll face it in exactly the same way you've faced everything else: incompetently. In fact, I'd be prepared to lay odds that you won't see out another year."

A wave of shock spread through the gathering. "Frank?" called Sol. "How the hell did you get—?"

"It doesn't matter *how* I got here," Axford cut in again. "That I *am* here is all that matters." His voice was full of amused contempt. "You know, Caryl, I hear you talk about dignity and determination, but it's just your usual rhetoric, isn't it? All I see is a bunch of submissive fools sitting around in desperation waiting for the heel to come and crush them."

"Whereas you'd be making plans and exploring options, right?" said Alander disdainfully. "Why don't you save us the self-congratulatory rant, Frank, because we've heard it all before."

"Ah, Dr. Alander, I presume?" returned Axford. "The Praxis's pet experiment. Tell me, how does it feel to be part of the freak show? As your humanity sloughs away, do you even care about what you did back in Sol? Do you ever grieve for the millions of deaths you were responsible for simply because you are unable to string two coherent thoughts—"

Alander's laugh cut him short. "You might have been able to bait me once, Frank, but not anymore. Once upon a time I was probably intimidated by you, but now I can't even muster the enthusiasm to pity you."

"I'd be mindful of that hybrid tongue of yours, Peter."

"You accuse us of rhetoric, but you're just as guilty of it. If you have more than words to threaten us with, then you wouldn't be wasting your time here with us now. And this *is* time wasting, Frank."

There was a feral edge to Axford's voice when he replied. "Maybe you should talk to that freak girlfriend of yours, Peter."

Then he was gone, the presence of his mind vanishing into the morass of other thoughts, roiling and clamoring at his invasion. Alander didn't stop to discuss the intrusion or the meaning of Axford's words. He quickly retreated from the gathering and rejoined his body. With a squelching sound, he pulled his head from the organic helmet that linked him to the Unfit. A Yuhl attendant was on hand to wipe him clean of slime, but he pushed the alien away, looking for Lucia.

Her I-body lacked the nerve endings required to join with the Unfit, so she had waited patiently by his body for his mind to return.

"What happened?" he asked, taking her translucent hands in his. They were shaking.

"He came to me," she said. "Frank the Ax. He tried to get inside of me, to take over the spindle."

Even written in fields barely more visible than air, her distress was obvious. It was in her posture and hinted at in her ghostlike features. For a person composed entirely of mind, with no body to call her own, android or otherwise, Axford's invasion must have constituted something close to rape.

"Did he succeed?" Alander asked uneasily.

She shook her head. "The Dark Room wouldn't let him in— not down deep where I live. I'm the only one who can go there. But he tried, and when he failed, he tried to hurt me."

"You're okay, though, right?" He studied her I-body for injuries, even though rationally he knew it would look perfect no matter what had happened to her spindle-bound mind.

"I'm fine." Her disposition lightened at this, appreciating his concern. "But I'm glad he's gone. I think Thor made a big mistake doing a deal with him."

He nodded in agreement, even while acknowledging the help that Axford had at times given them. That help might have been undermined by betrayals, and may never have been unselfishly offered, but it *had* helped them. He had alerted them to the Yuhl, shown them how to merge hole ships, given them tactical advice when they most needed it, and consistently tried to educate the scientists and administrators chosen by UNES-SPRO to survey the stars that the universe was a very hostile place—a place where it was becoming more and more apparent that only the most brutal would survive.

Lucia suddenly released Alander's hands, her head tilting in a manner that suggested she was listening to a sound that she alone could hear.

"What is it?" he asked, seeing her expression become one of concern.

"It's Thor," she said. "She's back."

"And the Praxis? Is he with her?"

"No. Listen." Lucia reached out and took Alander's hand. He was instantly plunged into a conSense view of the system. Thor shone like a many-tailed comet in close orbit to Sagarsee.

"—Have returned," she was saying, "and I bring bad news."

Alander fought disorientation. "What sort of bad news?" he asked, not unsurprised to hear his voice over the simulation. "Didn't the others make it?"

Thor didn't answer his question. "You must leave here."

"Leave here?" said Cleo Samson from the world below. "But why? I thought we were safe now."

There was a flicker in the sky behind Thor's radiant beams of light as a new star blossomed in the sky.

"No," said Thor, "you are not."

"Oh, fuck," said one of the engram Hatzises as the conSense view zoomed in on the new light. It was feathery and brilliant and seemed to be moving in its heart. "The fovea . . ."

"My God," Sol mumbled. There was no mistaking the disillusionment in her voice, the hopelessness, the futility. Every syllable was steeped in it. "You know the drill, everyone. Evacuation stations—*now!"*

"But where are we to go?" asked one of the other engrams. "There's nowhere left to run!"

Sol didn't answer immediately, and the silence became tense as the gathering waited to hear what advice the last true human alive had to offer.

"I'm going back to Sol," she said finally. "The rest of you can do what you want."

"Sol?" someone cried out. "But—"

Sol didn't give the person time to finish.

"I'm not going to keep on running like some goddamn animal," she said. "If I have to die, then it's going to be on *my* terms, not theirs." She hesitated only fractionally before adding, "If I'm going to die, I'm going to do it at home."

Alander was torn between weeping and cheering as, with a click, Sol exited the simulation, leaving the engrams in an uproar behind her.

2.3.7

A sense of mortal dread washed over Lucia upon seeing the fovea. Her first instinct was to flee along with all the others. Although she was tired of running, she knew she could outpace the fovea easily enough. If she kept moving, it wouldn't keep up with her.

Dread turned to horror, however, when she remembered that Peter wasn't physically with her. He was on *Mantissa B,* two jumps and a hole ship journey away from safety.

That horror was only compounded by Sol's announcement. *I'm not going to keep on running like some goddamn animal.* If Peter went with Sol or Lucia was unable to rescue him, she would be cut free, adrift. Lost. Time seemed to slow as she confronted the difficult decision of what to do next.

She didn't have time to dwell on it. Her attention was drawn back to the panic consuming Sagarsee. The airwaves were cluttered with shouting voices, a crazy mix of questions, suggestions, and recriminations. There was a terrible edge of desperation to the voices, too, that Lucia could all too well relate to. Predominant was disbelief at the impending attack from the Starfish. What had happened to the reprieve? Despite the sense of uncertainty Thor and the others had brought back with them, the remaining engrams had thought they were through the worst of it. But now . . .

Through the panicked cries flooding the airwaves, Lucia noted that Frank Axford's name was being mentioned a lot. It was hardly surprising, given how he had called in the Starfish back at Beid. He wouldn't think twice about betraying putative allies if it suited him, and that the Starfish were about to come down upon Sagarsee so quickly after Axford had made an appearance would have only confirmed this suspicion in people's minds.

But despite these feelings, Lucia knew that in this case, at least, Axford wasn't to blame. There had been no ftl transmissions from anywhere near Sagarsee. And if the Starfish *had* called off the attack on human colonies because of Thor's message, then it didn't make sense that a simple communication would prompt them to start up again on their genocidal rampage.

Lucia felt herself dithering, even as the need to make a decision became increasingly urgent. Her I-body ran with Peter as he hurried to the visitors' evacuation point. A crowd had already gathered there, pressing forward to take the next available hole ship. *Mantissa B* was beginning to break apart into clumps, shedding smaller hole ship configurations like a vast flower dispersing pollen to the solar winds. An alternative rendezvous point was touted for those who didn't share Sol's suicidal imperative. Alkaid itself, the "chief of mourners," would be where survivors would regroup to discuss further options. At a distance of one hundred light years from Sol, it was farther than most of the remaining engrams had ever traveled.

On my *terms, not theirs . . .*

Sol's decision cut a swathe through the panic. She, at least, offered a resolution to the situation. As terrible as the prospect was of simply resigning oneself to the Starfish's wrath, at least it would bring an end to the uncertainty and fear. And judging by the clamor of voices Lucia could hear, a lot of people were tempted to follow Sol's lead. Many had already committed themselves to the journey and were calling on others to join them. In the waiting area on *Mantissa B,* lots were being cast to decide where the next evacuating tetrad would be going.

Lucia's I-body watched with impotent despair as Alander voted for Sol, and the motion passed.

"What's going to happen to them?" she asked Thor. The

shining hybrid vessel hadn't fled yet. It seemed to be holding
back, helplessly observing the frantic evacuation, its radiant
beams picking out fleeing hole ships as they disengaged from
each other and vanished into unspace. "Will the fovea follow
them?"

"Individually, their wakes will be difficult to trace," Thor
replied, "But en masse it is likely that their destination will be
pinpointed."

"And what about you, Caryl? Are you going to run, or will
you make a stand with Sol?"

Lucia read the silence that followed as uncertainty. But she
knew they would have to make a choice soon. It never took
the cutters long to appear after the fovea arrived.

Frustration and apprehension sent her into the pov of her
I-body as it followed Peter—along with dozens of other android
bodies—into the cockpit of the evacuation tetrad assigned to
go to Sol. Even through his hair and beard, Lucia could clearly
make out his haunted expression.

"I can't let you do this," she said to him.

He faced her with a shake of the head. "It's not up to you,
Lucia."

"This is the wrong decision, Peter! You know that!"

"Right or wrong," he returned, "it's *my* decision."

"But—" She choked on the words. *But what about the
stars?* she wanted to say. *What about us?*

The image of the two of them holding hands on Jian Lao
was still strong in her mind, even though her survey mission's
colony world had been destroyed along with pi-1 Ursa Major.
There would be no sunny future as she imagined it, but that
didn't mean they had to abandon hope, too. She had yet to give
up the inbuilt need for that.

As the tetrad detached from *Mantissa B* and prepared to
jump to Sol, she decided to take drastic action. She couldn't
stand by and do nothing while Peter killed himself. Moving her
I-body closer to his, she put a translucent arm on his shoulder.
Forces flexed, and the I-body lost its shape. Flowing like a
raindrop down a pane of glass, it swept over him in a single,
smooth rush, quickly covering him and his own I-suit.

"What—?"

She flexed again, applying pressure to clamp his mouth shut.

Her mind stretched out, reaching for and finding the hole ship's AI. Its core persona belonged to a hole ship christened *Huang-di*.

"Open the inner airlock door," she commanded. Ignoring Alander's protests and the confused stares of the other refugees, she marched Alander through the short corridor leading from the cockpit. "Close the inner airlock door."

Choking noises emanated from Alander's clenched teeth. She let up on the pressure slightly to allow him to speak. "Lucia, you can't do this!" he groaned. It sounded as though his voice was coming from inside her head. "Let me go, for Christ's sake!"

"*Huang-di*, evacuate the airlock."

Background noise faded to a faint murmur communicated only through the soles of her feet. Peter's voice, however, was still loud.

"I might not be able to fight you, Lucia," he was saying, "but I can refuse to talk to you! I can slow my thoughts to nothing; I can shut myself down entirely! What use would I be to you, then?"

She hesitated, but only slightly. If she forced him to survive, at least there'd be a chance he might change his mind. But if he was dead, there was no hope at all. It wasn't a difficult choice to make.

"Open the outer door, *Huang-di*."

The last vestige of air tickled by as it rushed into the void. The burning light of the fovea greeted her as she folded Alander's resistant legs beneath her and hurled both of them out into space.

She jumped pov to the spindle. Huang-di *was a tiny dot against* the starscape, and Peter an even smaller dot drifting away from it. Firing up her reactionless thrusters, she sent herself careering through the chaos of hole ships just as a cold blue flash heralded the arrival of the cutters.

Panic reached a fever pitch among humanity's survivors, and Lucia heard desperate entreaties, hollow threats, even prayers hurled at the Starfish—all, of course, to no avail. The last complete set of Spinner gifts gleamed in golden sunlight as razor-edged destruction hurtled toward them. Lucia knew, as did everyone, that there was nothing that could be done now to make a difference. All anyone could do was try to stay alive.

Energy fields with the thickness of butterfly wings and the strength of titanium snatched at Alander and the encompassing I-body as the spindle swept by. Lucia gathered him up, drawing him into her sanctuary. Where exactly she was going to go, she still hadn't decided. Without knowing what had happened to the Praxis, she couldn't automatically assume that jumping ahead was the best option. But there had to be *some* direction she could jump that would be safe. At some point, there had to be a boundary beyond which the threat of destruction dropped to zero.

Almost in response to her quandary, Thor suddenly announced: "I HAVE DECIDED. I AM GOING TO BSC5581."

Her voice came to Lucia as more than half of the remaining refugees fled in one sudden wave, *Huang-di* among them.

"Why?" Lucia asked, but the bright point that was Thor had already vanished.

The cutters swooped low and fast over Sagarsee, snapping towers as easily as if they were little more than twigs. There wasn't time to think; she just had to act. Like a signature, each of the alien ships had a different way of bending space—the cutters, the Trident, and the more exotic Starfish craft. The strange creature Thor had become was no exception, and as she moved through unspace, she left a distinct ripple in the hyperspatial continuum, making it easy for Lucia to follow her, just as she had from pi-1 Ursa Major.

"I'm sorry," she said to Peter as they traversed space-time's more subtle geometries. "I had no choice."

"Spare me the apologies, Lucia." he snapped. Free of her I-body, he was still trapped in the spindle. She gave him full access to her telemetry, but he wasn't interested. "You don't give a damn about me, so you can quit with the bullshit!"

"But I *do* care—" she started.

"If you did," he said, "you wouldn't have taken me against my will. And don't give me any of that crap about how you did it for my own good, or for the good of the others. I'm not buying it. You only did it because you need me to keep you going."

The accusation stung because it simply wasn't true. But there was no time to reason with him. They had emerged from unspace in BSC5581. The world called Geb was still burning. Alander fell silent, reminded perhaps that there were bigger issues to worry about than his own personal liberty.

Lucia and Thor were alone, the only ships in the system. If any survivors had followed, they had yet to arrive, hole ship propulsion being considerably slower than the means she and Thor enjoyed.

"Now what?" she asked.

Thor said nothing. Instead, she sent out bright white beams across the ruined world below them, testing its smoky atmosphere. Lucia thought of insect antennae again and wondered if she would ever know what Thor was thinking.

Then a light blossomed high over the ecliptic, and Lucia's heart sank. The fovea had followed them.

Thor didn't waste time on discussions.

"HD132142," she said. Before Lucia could comment, Thor had already gone, leaving Lucia's spindle alone under the harsh, cold glare of the fovea.

"If we're going to follow her," said Peter after a few heartbeats, "then I don't recommend you pause for thought, Lucia."

Still lacking a viable alternative, Lucia did as he suggested. Before the cutters had chance to slice their way into the real universe, she was once again trailing Thor at a discreet distance.

When she arrived at HD132142, she found it empty apart from Thor hovering over another destroyed colony. The fires were cooling, but smoke still cast a thick pall over the world's surface. Gloom would reign for months yet, maybe even years.

Within moments of her arrival, the fovea burst over the clouded world like a new sun.

"BSC5423," Thor said, and vanished again.

This time Lucia didn't hesitate. Deep in Thor's unspace wake, she followed.

"This is getting us nowhere," Peter said. His tone was resentful, but at least he was talking to her without anger. "Keep going like this and you're just going to end up back at Sol anyway. We might as well get there early and avoid all of this jumping around."

Lucia had noted Thor's progression, too. HD132142 was the system containing Demeter, the third most recent colony attacked by the Starfish. Zemyna, the next in the series, was in BSC5423. Thor was clearly working her way backward through the chain of colonies. But *why?*

Soon after they arrived at the ruins that had once been Zemyna, the fovea appeared again. Thor was gone in an instant, and Lucia was close on her tail, heading for Rasmussen in BSC5070.

"What the hell are you doing, Caryl?" she asked Thor immediately upon their arrival. "What are you trying to achieve?"

"Symmetry," came the reply.

"Symmetry? What the fuck does that—?"

But the fovea's arrival cut short the conversation, and Thor disappeared again.

Lucia followed; she had no choice. If there was a purpose to Thor's movements, then she wanted to know what it was.

"What do you mean by symmetry?" she asked again in lambda Auriga.

"Every thread has two ends," Thor said, then was gone once more.

In Theta Perseus, Lucia tried again. "Are you talking about Rob's causally locked thread?"

"Your lexicon is insufficient."

Peter chuckled bitterly to himself on the way back to 10 Taurus, the next system on the roll call of the dead.

"She always was an arrogant bitch," he said. "But if she thinks the Starfish are going to follow her back the way they came—"

"I don't think that's what she's trying to do," Lucia cut in. She had difficulty even considering the possibility that had occurred to her. Thor was only half-right. It wasn't just the English lexicon that was lacking; Lucia's mind simply didn't have the capacity to contain such thoughts.

Presumably, Thor's did. Under the reddish light of Luyten's Star, Lucia watched as Thor jumped closer to the fovea, braving its intense radiation. The fovea flared brightly, threateningly, and then Thor was on her way again to the next system. Lucia followed, with the fovea close behind her.

At Groombridge 1830, Thor tried again and was similarly rebuffed; in iota Boötis, she seemed to get a little closer before being forced away; at chi Hercules, the fovea came out almost on top of Thor, forcing her to retreat before making the attempt. And so it continued. It was like watching a strange kind of game, Lucia thought, a game of hopscotch conducted across solar systems with the threat of the cutters never far behind.

"What *is* she up to?" Alander asked on the way to the next system. "Trying to *merge* with it, for Christ's sake?"

"That would be taking hybridization a little too far, perhaps," said Lucia. "But I don't think that's what she's doing. The fovea probably isn't even the kind of thing you *could* merge with."

"What do you mean?"

"Everything has its own signature when it jumps through unspace. Everything except the fovea. The fovea doesn't leave a wake of any kind. There's no sensation of it traveling at all; it just *appears.*"

"What are you saying?"

"I'm saying that I don't believe it's a ship."

Alander frowned. "Then what is it?"

"I think it's the mouth of a wormhole."

In beta Cane Venatici they watched as the fovea blossomed over another dead world. Now that the idea had occurred to her, it seemed obvious: why send ships to investigate systems when peeking through space-time would be enough? Given the other wonders of the Spinners and the Starfish, wormhole technology wasn't too much of a stretch for the imagination. If the Starfish didn't want to get too close, for whatever reason, all they had to do was open a hole in the system they wanted to examine, see what awaited them there, then send in the cutters if necessary. The radiation was simply a by-product of the hole, like blood from a wound.

The question was: what was on the other side of that mouth? Where did it lead? And what did the intelligences watching through it make of Thor's strange dance?

They passed Vega and Sothis, two sacrifices of the Battle of Beid. Axford and Sol had both lost their headquarters in the fallout of that skirmish—a minor one in what, to the Starfish, was a much larger war. Or so Lucia imagined it. But the fovea showed no sign of recognition as it passed by the ruins, and the dance continued, with Thor edging closer and closer to the mouth of the wormhole as though daring it to swallow her.

"Wormhole or not, I don't see the point of all this," said Alander. "Once the fovea reaches Sol and the others, the cutters will come, and that'll be the end of it."

Lucia agreed, and she suspected Thor did, too. As they swept through systems and Sol came ever closer, the dance took on an urgent note. Constantly testing the perimeter around the wormhole mouth, Thor no longer paid Lucia and Alander any attention at all. She ignored Lucia's questions and simply assumed that she would be followed. Lucia felt like a spectator, a witness to something she could never hope to understand.

They arrived at HD92719, a system that at first seemed no different than the others: alien worlds turned under an alien sun, and ash darkened the face of the one planet most like Earth.

Then, unexpectedly, Thor spoke.

"I am home," she said in the few seconds before the fovea appeared. "Here is where it begins."

Lucia didn't understand what Thor meant by "home" until she checked the UNESSPRO records. HD92719 had contained the colony after which Thor was named.

"What do you mean, Caryl?" asked Alander. "This is where what begins?"

Thor had no time to reply, if she had ever intended to. The fovea opened up above them, blazing like a supernova. It loomed over them, taking up a quarter of the sky. It seemed larger than it had before, and at first Lucia thought that this was just an optical illusion. But then she realized that it actually *was* expanding.

"Holy shit," Alander muttered, noticing it, too.

Thor vanished with a flash of white light as the edge of the fovea swept nearer. Lucia was ready to follow to the next system, but according to Thor's wake, that wasn't where she was headed. The ripples in unspace denoting her passage were aimed directly into the heart of the wormhole.

Radiation boiled through vacuum as the fovea swept outward, its roiling surface tearing and bursting. Lucia's Spinner-enhanced senses caught glimpses of arcane geometries and tortured space-time. The interior of the wormhole seemed almost alive, rippling with symmetries she wasn't equipped to comprehend.

Then, abruptly, something lashed out at them—a tongue of pure white energy. She felt motion, acceleration, penetration, reorientation—

Time passed in an unmarked blur. It seemed to Lucia as though her internal clock had slowed right down to zero, freezing her in place while the universe moved around her.

Then all was quiet, and the fovea was gone. Lucia looked about her, confused as to what had just happened to them.

"Are we—?" Alander stopped, his question unasked. The view outside the spindle rendered all inquiries meaningless.

They weren't in HD92719 anymore; they'd moved again. Thor's home system was gone, and in place of its central star hung a maelstrom of unleashed energy. The system they were in had changed dramatically in the previous two days, but Lucia recognized it immediately.

"Pi-1 Ursa Major," she said.

"How the hell did we get here?"

"Maybe this was where the wormhole led."

"So where are the Starfish? What happened to the battle?"

Lucia examined the system in every frequency, but it was completely empty.

"They've gone," she said.

"I can see that, Lucia. The question is *where?*"

"How the hell should I know, Peter?" she snapped. Her confusion was making her less tolerant than she normally might have been.

Peter ran a hand through his hair, sighing. He looked haggard, much older than his rejuvenated body had before. "I'm sorry. It's just—"

He stopped.

"It's just what, Peter?"

"It's just that it seems so empty," he said after a moment. "So quiet. And I don't want to hope that—" He stopped again and shook his head. "I just don't want to hope, that's all."

She did know what he meant. As they searched the system,

looking for any sign of alien activity, the same thought occurred to her, too. Just because they found nothing—no Source, no Tridents, no cutters—did that mean that the aliens had really gone? Was it too much to hope that Thor's strange dance had somehow saved them?

But like Peter, she didn't want to jump to any hasty conclusions. The system *was* empty, though. There wasn't any wreckage that didn't come from ruined planets and shattered asteroids.

They waited for the fovea to reappear, but nothing disturbed the violent beauty of the expanding clouds of gas that had once been the system's primary. They waited for Thor, but she didn't come, either.

"Maybe they kept going," Alander said. "Maybe the fovea pushed us out of the way while they danced on, system by system." A slight pause before: "And maybe we've just been wasting our time here all along."

Lucia's stomach sank at that notion. Time was so precious right now, and the idea of having wasted any was depressing. "So where do you want to go, then?"

He didn't even hesitate.

"To Sol," he said. "I want to go home, to see if there's anything left."

3.0.0

UEH/ELLIL

Ueh/Ellil *stepped out of the hole ship and onto the surface of* the unnamed planet. Dense air whipped around him, catching his body off balance. He slipped to one knee and put a hand into the dirt to steady himself.

Yu-qiang was beside him in an instant, helping him up.

"This is so *not* a good idea, Ueh." Weak sunlight painted her skin a deeper green than normal. She looked decidedly unwell. It matched the unease she had expressed throughout the short journey down to the planet.

"I shall be fine," he assured her.

"Well—just so you know—if you die I'm not carrying you back."

He shifted his faceplates in acknowledgement of what she'd said but realized immediately that she wouldn't have understood the facial gesture. He was too preoccupied with the sense of joy that was thrilling through his body to say anything. Something wonderful was about to happen.

The soil was rough and stony beneath his feet—but it *was* soil. He rubbed his fingers together, enjoying the graininess of it. He was standing on a real planet for the first time in many, many long cycles. The higher gravity dragged him down; the weather was completely unnerving; the light lacked the controlled qualities of *Mantissa A*'s artificial sources. And yet here he felt complete—or nearly so, anyway.

Atonement stirred within him. He could feel its tendrils writhing under his skin, yearning for something he could no longer give. It had outgrown him and longed for its next phase of growth.

It would be a difficult birth, he knew. But he didn't mind. Strangely, he held no fear whatsoever.

"Well?" said Yu-qiang. "Now what?"

"Now I think I understand," he said. The yearning of Atonement filled him like light, granting him insight into things he never thought to question. "I understand what *Goel* means."

"Don't go all mystical on me, Ueh. This isn't the time for epiphanies."

He laughed. For the first time in cycles, he felt truly alive. "My name is no longer Ueh," he said. "I am changing again. I am *escaping.*"

"You're making me nervous is what you're doing," she said.

He could sense her fear and concern as clearly as he could feel the thing inside him straining for release.

"The Ambivalence is gone," he said.

Yu-qiang stared at him for the longest time, mystified and intrigued simultaneously. He could see the flicker of hope behind her expression. "You can't possibly know that."

"The Praxis knows it. He knows things we cannot. He sensed its passing from this universe."

"So we're *saved?*" She hesitated again, clearly wanting to embrace this news with delight but reluctant to do so until she understood everything. A brief scan of the turbulent sky seemed to galvanize the doubts she still held. "We won't have to keep running?"

"You can go home now, *Caryl/Hatzis.* Just as you wished."

"As can you."

"That is something the *Yuhl/Goel* cannot do."

"I know it's a long way, but you have navigation records. I'm sure you could find it again."

"You misunderstand," he said. "We never *had* a home."

She stared at him. "What are you talking about?"

"*Goel* means *made,*" he said. The simple truth, the realization, warmed his insides, lit up areas of his mind that had until then been dark.

"I don't understand what you're trying to tell me," Yu-qiang said.

"The Praxis made us," he explained. "We served him, attended him, kept him company. We gave him a reason to keep running. Perhaps we were modeled on a species he encountered in the past—maybe even more than one. Whatever the origins of our forms, we were given false memories, myths that gave us a sense of who we are but did not hold us back or undermine our true purpose. We were the perfect companions." His understanding grew the more he thought about it, but it came only with feelings of compassion, not anger. "The Praxis lied to us for all these years."

"You don't seem too upset about it," she said. "He *used* you—and he would have used us, too!"

"How long would you engrams have lasted without his help? He may have used you, but it would have been for your own benefit. Only by being remade by the Praxis, as were we, would you have been able to survive in a universe containing the Ambivalence."

Yu-qiang didn't look convinced. "That still doesn't give him the right to—"

But he wasn't interested in her objections. Something more important was about to happen—something that would justify the Praxis's lies.

"I understand now," he interrupted her. "I know what has to be done."

He opened his arms to embrace the wind and ordered his I-suit to open.

Ueh gasped as bitter cold struck his chest and shoulders. Primordial winds tore at his skin, making every nerve scream. The widening seams of the suit slid slowly down to his waist and around his back, then spread along his limbs and up his back.

"What the hell are you doing!"

He ignored her protests. The exposure to alien air sent a completely new sensation thrilling through him. He felt as though every cell in his body had woken. He halted the I-suit's progress at his neck, wanting to savor every last sensation he was experiencing. He opened his wings sheaths to their full extent, as though he was gliding in the wind.

Yu-qiang tried to grab him, presumably to drag him back into the hole ship cockpit, but she stopped short when a flurry of mist rose up between them, accompanied by a strange and alien hissing sound. It took him a moment to realize that it was coming from himself. His skin was decrepitating; every exposed cell was popping open, releasing genetic material to the wind.

"I am Atonement!" he shouted over the rising noise.

"Don't do this, Ueh!" she shouted back. "You're going to die!"

But the thought didn't bother him. He embraced it, knowing that his death would bring life to a barren world—life based on *his* life, on his genetic material. Atonement had made him a catalyst, the seed crystal for an entirely new biosphere. A *home*.

What was death in the face of such transformation? Who wouldn't give up their life to give his people what they had lacked, without knowing it, all their existence?

With a feeling of the most profound accomplishment, he ordered his I-suit completely open and gave himself up to his fate.

"Ueh!" was the last thing he heard as Yu-qiang made one last, desperate plea to him.

But the word was meaningless to him now. The name no longer belonged to him. And as the winds carried his substance across the face of the planet, part of him wondered if it ever had.

3.0

EPILOGUE

It had been three whole days since the Starfish had last been
seen by anyone—three days of almost unnatural calm and unspoken apprehensions. Sol understood those apprehensions
well, and as she faced her third sunset on the ancient regolith
of Luna, she couldn't help but wonder if humanity would ever
stop holding its breath in anticipation of death striking once
again from the skies.

"You okay, Sol?"

She glanced over to where the barely visible shimmer that
was Lucia Benck's new body stood. If she looked above the
north horizon she would have seen the golden gleam of the
orphaned spindle from which Lucia was conducting her part of
the conversation.

Sol nodded, smiling. "I was thinking of that carbon disk
Peter found in 53 Aquarius," she half-lied. "The one that you—
that one of your engrams—left behind. Do you know what it
said?"

"I had a list of quotes," said the former scout pilot. "Was it
Noel Coward? 'Why, oh why do the wrong people travel, when
the right ones stay at home?' "

Sol laughed at this, and realized as it lasted just how *good*
it felt. "Actually, I think it was Wordsworth."

"Ah, yes," said Lucia, taking another step forward, glancing in the direction of the sun. " 'Bliss was it, in that dawn to be alive.' "

"That's the one."

"Why were you thinking of that?"

Sol shrugged, sobering. "I guess because this doesn't feel much like bliss to me."

"But we *are* alive, Sol, and that's what matters. As long as we stay that way, there's a chance things could get better; then we can find the bliss."

"He still wears the disk around his neck, you know."

Lucia didn't respond immediately, and when she did, her tone was defensive. "We'll figure out how to change. We have to."

"Not all people want to change."

"Then maybe we should just figure out how to be people again."

"You make it sound like that's a good thing."

Her bitterness surprised even herself. After all, she *was* still alive, like Lucia said. Surely she should be grateful for that? She should be grateful for every day she got to see a new dawn.

Sol shook her head, smiling wryly to herself. That was crap, and well she knew it. She tilted her head to look up at the sky, where the stars would have been had not the glare of the sun swamped them—and where Earth might have been had it not been destroyed ninety-eight years ago. Human nature being what it was, survival alone wasn't enough. There were precious few people left with which to rebuild, and none of them were more than passably human; Lucia, Alander, and herself were extreme examples.

Since the destruction of Sagarsee and the last of the gifts three days earlier, she had remained on Luna, here in Sol System, waiting for humanity's end—waiting for the Starfish to come and trample the remaining survivors underfoot. But they had never come, and this had left her feeling profoundly exhausted. She was tired of the apparently endless ebb and flow of change. She wanted to settle down and grow old as humans were supposed to, to quietly die on some porch while sitting in a rocking chair and watching her grandchildren playing around her feet.

She almost laughed again. The image was a ludicrous one.

She'd never been interested in children, let alone grandchildren! And with Peter, the closest thing to a lover she had had for over a century? The thought was absurd. The circumstances that had brought them together were passing; both the whim and the need were gone. And the sports they might produce didn't bear contemplation.

No, her engrams had been the closest she'd come to off-spring, and they had been imperfect and resentful, just like her.

The truth was, she didn't know *what* she wanted. But she knew what she *didn't* want, and what she didn't want was to be sitting around waiting for death to come and take her.

"I called you here to ask you a favor, Lucia," she said.

Lucia's I-body moved closer, kicking up moondust that slid unimpeded off her invisible legs and fell with unnatural rapidity back to the regolith.

"I've already agreed to act as a shuttle for people between Ellil and here, if that's what you want," said Lucia. "The Unfit asked me to do that yesterday."

"And I'll put you onto that as soon as Yu-qiang arrives. Once I see through her eyes what happened there, we'll know better what to do."

Sol still didn't quite believe the testimony of those that had followed the Praxis in the wake of the Starfish. A new world flowering from the nanotech dust of Ueh's body; the Praxis gone, vanishing with a significant chunk of *Mantissa A* to destinations unknown; no sign of the Starfish anywhere, for hundreds of light-years ahead or to either side . . . ? It seemed almost incomprehensible.

"But that wasn't what I was going to ask," said Sol. "This is more of a personal favor."

Lucia's ghostly image inclined her head slightly, as if curious. "What kind of favor?"

"It's going to take a while to work out exactly who's going to live where, and how. I'm intending to stay right here, but that doesn't mean everyone else has to." Sol imagined a similar transformation of the lunar surface as was occurring on Ellil, the new Yuhl home world. Set free from Earth and nudged by the AIs of the Spike, Earth's old moon rotated once every ten hours and followed a stable, life-supporting orbit around Sol. Enough raw material—in the form of shattered molecule chains and radioactive ions—had fallen from the destruction of the Shell to make nanofacturing a habitable biosphere a relatively easy task. It wouldn't be Earth when she finished, but it would be somewhere to call home. With the exception of Venus, another victim of the Spike, the starscape was reassuringly familiar. Her ancient genes responded to its call.

Sol told Lucia, "I want you and Peter to find the others."

"What others?"

"The missions that didn't arrive at their target systems. The ones who drifted off course, whose acceleration or deceleration phases were mistimed, or who ran into any one of a dozen different types of trouble. Some will have been destroyed, and some won't be what they're supposed to be—if Axford is to be believed—but not all of them will be out of commission. Some might be waiting for rescue. They're needles in a very large haystack, I know, but I'm sure the spindle will make it easier for you to search that haystack. And it's worth it. We need everyone we can get, Lucia."

Lucia didn't respond immediately, but Sol could tell that she was taken by the idea.

"You can get started as soon as things settle down," Sol said into the silence.

"There are more of me out there," Lucia said finally. "As well as more Peters."

Sol nodded. "And you'll get to explore, too."

"What if I come across Axford?"

"Ignore him," she said. "Don't listen to anything he has to say and get the hell away from him as quickly as possible."

"Okay. Why not? It might be fun. And who knows: we might even find Thor in the process."

Sol didn't feel the same enthusiasm with which Lucia clearly viewed the possibility. She'd heard all about her hybridized engram's dance with the fovea and its climax in HD92719. Thor hadn't been seen since, and neither had the Starfish or any of their attendant species. She hoped her attempted, futile, final stand in Sol System hadn't driven Thor to do something equally self-destructive. As if diving into the Source of All hadn't been enough.

If it *was* true that Thor had tried to sacrifice herself again, the fact that it appeared to have worked made Sol's vague feelings of guilt even worse. Had the memories she'd given the engram contributed to her demise? Was she in some way responsible?

"If you do find her," said Sol, "then tell her she's welcome back here any time. Tell her—" She paused for a moment, thinking of the last time she had seen Thor back in the cutter. "Tell her I'm tired of being in charge."

"Do you really mean that?"

"Yes," she said, smiling faintly at her own routines, and the traps from which even she couldn't quite escape. "Sometimes I do."

"Bliss was it . . ."

Even as she smiled, the quote haunted her. Lucia's disks, like the Yuhl death markers, were totems that were never truly intended to be seen. They were gestures flung defiantly out to the stars, as if daring the universe to ignore them. That they would be ignored was indisputable. The universe as a whole didn't care if the disks or totems—or engrams or humans— faded to dust and were forgotten forever.

Still, she was determined to fight the natural progression. She would write her will large across the stars by any means possible. And if she failed in the attempt, then so be it. But having come so close to pointless immolation, she vowed to do her best to avoid it happening again. Whatever life brought her, it had to be better than the alternative.

"So we still don't know, then?" Alander looked away from Rob Singh's virtual representation. His ability to participate in conSense events was improving, but it still unnerved him. "That's what you're saying, isn't it?"

Singh cleared his throat. A slim, tall man with dark hair graying at the temples, he looked more like a high school teacher than an astronaut pilot.

"That's it in a nutshell," he said. "At least I can tell you the difference between what we don't know for certain, and what we only *think* we don't know."

"I can do that for myself." Alander raised a hand and began ticking off points on his fingers. "We don't know where the Starfish and the Spinners came from."

"No," said Singh. "But—"

"We don't know where they *went.*"

"Again, no; however—"

"We don't know if they'll come back."

"If you'll just let me—"

"And we don't even know why they came here in the first place, right?"

"Ah, now that I think we *do* know." The enthusiasm in Singh's tone was short-lived, however. "Well, actually, we don't think they *had* a reason at all. I think we just happened to be in their path."

"So they're not time-reversed humans from the distant future covering their own tracks?" Alander had heard that rumor within a day of returning to Sol System. It had the merit and pull of a satisfactory narrative, but he wasn't convinced.

Neither was Singh. "Wishful thinking, I'm afraid. The chances of humanity surviving the near-heat death state at the other end of the universe are very slim. And even if we did make it, we'd be so unrecognizable as to be effectively alien anyway. The time scales we're talking here are fantastic."

"How long?"

"The current estimate puts the entropy switch to occur at five to ten times the current age of the universe."

Such a length of time was too much to grasp, especially given that humanity had barely managed to survive just the last few weeks. That it could last not just to the end of the universe, but back again, seemed utterly impossible.

"Not that I'm dismissing the reverse time arrow scenario," Singh went on. "In fact, I don't think we should be ruling anything out just yet. Personally, I think there's a real chance that one of the migrations came from another universe—perhaps even both of them. As well as the—what did the *A/kak/a/ riil* call it? The Exclusion?"

Alander nodded. "That was their word for the Spinner ecosystem."

"If all of the races came from different universes, you know what that means, don't you?"

Alander frowned. "No, what?"

Singh smiled broadly. "That your theory of quantum evolution could still be right, of course. Humanity might still be the only intelligent life to have evolved in this universe."

Alander acknowledged the gesture, even though he was no longer as convinced of the idea as his original had been.

"It would also explain the gaps in the Map Room and the Library," said Inari, one of the many who had gathered to hear Singh's analysis of the situation. The simulated lecture hall was a fair approximation of one from the late twentieth century, with scuffed walls and graffitied desks that strongly echoed the ones from Alander's artificial memories. In reality, humanity's surviving minds were huddled in a complex assembled from seventy hole ships presently in a lunasynchronous orbit above the ruins of the Moon's Yi Base.

"If the Spinners came from another universe," Inari went on, "albeit one slightly different from ours, then the gaps aren't deliberate at all. They're just evidence of those differences."

Singh nodded. "It makes sense, doesn't it?"

"As much as anything does around here," said Cleo Samson, glowering from her end of the table. She was still smarting over the loss of Sagarsee, her own colony, in the last of the Starfish attacks. "If they're not from around here and we don't really matter to them, then why the gifts? Why bother with us at all?"

"Well, we mattered to somebody. If not the Starfish or the Spinners themselves, then perhaps a subspecies traveling with them. We know of at least six attendant species in the Exclusion."

"Which might have been seven, had things gone badly for us."

"You think they *didn't* go badly?" said Ali Genovese of Demeter.

"We're still alive, aren't we?" Singh was grim-faced but determined in his opinion. "Without the gifts, there's no way we could have survived the Starfish."

"Without the gifts," said Jayme Sivio of Zemyna, "maybe we wouldn't have had to face the Starfish in the first place."

"That's the trillion-dollar question, isn't it?" said Alander. "Were the Spinners trying to give us a fighting chance against the Starfish with the gifts, or were we just being used as a diversion for the Starfish while the Spinners hid out in pi-1 Ursa Major?"

"Maybe both," said Singh. "I know that sounds crazy, but we need to remember what we've been dealing with here. We have a large number of species interacting around a core of hyperintelligent beings. Whether the core is comprised of organic life-forms or AIs, or something else entirely, we'll probably never know—and neither is it terribly important. It's the peripherals we're interacting with that matter—the lesser species. They might have their own priorities, within or alongside those of the Spinners. Two different groups with quite different agendas could have arrived at the same simple tactic with equally mixed results: one gave us the gifts; another instructed them to talk only to Peter; a third selected Lucia, the first human they encountered, to be the one who could inhabit the Dark Room. I see lots of possibilities but little consensus."

"And let's not overlook the time arrow possibility here, either," said Inari.

"That raises a number of complex possibilities," cautioned Singh. "If the Spinners are going forward in time and the Starfish back, then that makes *both* of them benefactors—in their eyes, at least. But if it's the other way around, then they're both destroyers."

"Or maybe the Starfish *are* the Spinners," said Sivio, "going backward to the big crunch."

Inari let out a long, low whistle. "Now *that* would be seriously fucked up."

"I agree." Singh affected an eloquently weary expression via his conSense image. "Once we start talking about the possibility of time working in both directions, we end up with a terribly confused mess: a crack in the normal flow of things, as Lucia described it to us earlier—a kind of casual singularity. How do these things work? Shit, I have no idea, and if you'd asked me a month ago, I would've said it wasn't possible on this scale. Elementary particles, yes; atoms and small molecules, possibly; but *entire civilizations?* No way."

"I guess we're limited by what we can understand," said Alander. "I like the idea of a causal singularity, but maybe that's just me clutching at the basest explanation. It could be something we haven't thought of yet."

"Or something we don't have the *capacity* to think of yet," added Samson.

"If it was a singularity," said Sivio, "then what ended it?"

"Or indeed what started it?" said Singh. "It all depends on how you look at it."

"Perhaps it was the mission to the Starfish itself," said Inari. "That must've had some effect."

"Delayed, though," said Sivio. "Because the killing continued after you got back."

"Maybe Thor finally got through," said Genovese.

Singh shrugged heavily, tiredly. "Maybe both theories are true," he said. "And maybe we'll never know. But it has to be *something*. I can't believe the whole thing came out of existence from nowhere."

"From nowhere in *this* universe, perhaps," said Inari.

"If it was a singularity, or if they have gone to another universe," Alander said, "then at least we can breathe easily now. We made it out the other side."

"Only by the skin of our teeth," said Genovese. "Not what I'd call a conclusive victory."

"But we made it," he said. "That's the main thing."

Singh shrugged again, more wearily this time. Alander was beginning to feel a little sorry for him. The ex-pilot was in the awkward position of having to explain the inexplicable. But how *could* he give a satisfactory explanation for something that couldn't be explained?

A moment of silence claimed the gathering. Alander was reminded of something Ueh once said to him when asked if what he was saying was the truth.

"*I/we* do not believe in truth," the alien had said. *"Since we cannot see the truth cannot be spoken."*

That was very much how Alander felt at that moment. Of all the intriguing possibilities raised by the Ambivalence, none of them seemed quite right. He doubted they would ever know for certain, and arguing about which theory was better seemed a little pointless. As the horrors of the rout of humanity slid ever so slowly into the past the question, perhaps became less important.

"There is no *wrong/right*," Ueh had said. "There are only degrees of aptness."

The thought of his lost alien friend put him in an even more melancholy mood than he'd already been in.

"So, now what?" asked Singh. There was a challenging tone to his voice, as though he was glad for the spotlight to be shifting off him. "If we *have* come out the other side, then what do we do now?"

"Ah, well, there's the rub," said Genovese.

"I see us and the Yuhl going our separate ways for the time being," said Sivio. "They've got their new home to monitor, and we've got ours."

"That's if we decide to stay here," said Samson.

Sivio nodded. "Neither of us have huge resources, but there's enough to keep us flexible for a while. Sol has committed to making the engrams more robust, this time with full disclosure." He added the last with a glance at Inari, who was still annoyed at Sol's surreptitious manipulations. "If she can do that, then I think we might have a chance. And when we're stable, or at least know what our limits are, then we can talk about treaties and the like."

"There's no point thinking too far ahead," said Inari. "With Axford out there, and the Praxis, the only thing we can be certain of is that *nothing* is certain."

"Not to mention what might come along next," said Singh. He looked at those around the virtual hall, meeting their challenging stares. The thought wasn't one they particularly wanted to dwell upon. "There was a wake behind the Spinners. We don't know *what* could be following the Starfish, out of range of the fovea."

"So we batten down the hatches for a while," said Cleo Samson. "Is that it? Ride out whatever comes our way next, and hope for the best?"

"What else *can* we do?" asked Sivio.

Alander bowed out of the discussion, already tired of it, and sick of fighting the disorientation of conSense, too. Whatever they planned, he was sure the universe would surprise them. He would leave them to it, happy to let them shoulder the responsibility, along with the guilt.

Shrugging from the illusion, he took a brief, centering walk through Lucia's pristine corridors. The motives of the many aliens that had passed so disruptively through Surveyed Space might always remain a mystery, but he took hope from one thought. Lucia had encountered them before anyone, in pi-1 Ursa Major, and that encounter had shaped much that followed. If the Spinners had picked Peter based on her impressions of him, it wasn't because he was flawed. She couldn't have known that in advance, and he found that comforting.

Barely had he gone one lap around the spindle when he heard light footsteps from behind him—which was odd because, as far as he knew, he was the only embodied person aboard.

He turned and saw Frank Axford approaching him from along the corridor.

"How the—?"

"Relax, Peter," said the ex-general, raising his hands innocently as he came to a halt several meters away. "This is only an illusion."

Alander didn't let himself relax. "You've hacked into me?"

"Do you think I'd risk coming any closer after what you did to 1313 and 1041?" He smiled. "I'm 1699."

Alander wasn't interested in pleasantries. "What do you want, Frank? To say good-bye?"

"Maybe just au revoir," said Axford, smiling. "I'm not here to play games with you, Peter. I just wanted you to know that I'm only leaving now because I feel you have nothing I can use. But know that I'll be back, should that ever change."

"Don't think we won't be waiting for you."

"I'm sure you think you'll be ready for me," said Axford. "But you won't be, and deep down you know it. Face facts, Peter: you lot are completely unequipped to handle someone like me."

Axford's image was so realistic that Alander had to fight the urge to throw a punch at him. "Selling us short would be a mistake."

Axford's snort was loud and amused. "Don't kid yourself, Peter. You used to have brains, but now you're just brawn through and through. The Praxis made you that way. Otherwise, you'd be doing the same thing as me."

"Running, you mean?"

"Expanding," corrected Axford in a silky voice. "Exploring my options."

"I'd rather consolidate what we've got, thanks all the same."

"And that's why you'll always be a sitting target."

Alander shook his head. "You're beginning to sound like a broken record, Frank. Your mind is stuck in a rut, just like mine was."

"If it *is* a rut, then it's a superior one."

"If that's so, then why do you keep coming back? Why did you welcome us when we found you in Vega? I'll tell you why: because you need us around to make you feel superior." Alander took a step closer to the conSense illusion, the certainty of his diagnosis of Axford's mental state giving him confidence to stare down the man he had killed twice already. "And I'll wager everything we have left that you'll burn out on your own. Ten years, maybe less, and you'll be dead, or stagnant, and we'll still be going strong. All we have to do is ignore you, and you'll go away without any effort on our part."

Axford's lips tightened in a furious line. "You have no idea what you're talking about."

Alander barked out a laugh. "If that's so, then why are you so angry?"

Axford glared at him, and for the briefest of moments Alander thought he might be about to argue the point. But in the end, he simply vanished without another word.

"Who were you talking to?" asked Lucia, her voice filling the empty corridors.

He looked around to find a reference point and ignored the question. Lucia was nowhere to be seen. "Where have you been?"

"Down on Luna, with Sol. She wanted to talk to me about an idea she had."

"About you and I going off to look for the others?" He nodded. "Yeah, she bounced that one off me earlier, too. She also said that she'd look at your hardwiring when we get back. Reward or bribe, I'm not sure which."

"As long as we all get what we want, it doesn't really matter, does it? She'll get more of her engrams, the colony gets more hands to help out, and I get—" Lucia hesitated. "And I get *me* back."

He half-smiled at the memories her comment awoke. His feelings for the original Lucia were irrelevant now, as was her betrayal of him in Sagarsee. She had done the right thing. He was learning to enjoy her company in new ways, new times.

"Except it won't *be* you, will it, Lucia?"

Her laugh echoed along the corridor. "Let's not go there again, Peter."

With a chuckle, he turned and headed back to the Dark Room, wondering what his original would have thought if he could see where he and Lucia had ended up. His original, no doubt, would have argued that it wasn't him at all, that the hybrid Alander was another person entirely, and that any continuity he shared with that person was purely an illusion.

But the old Alander had been wrong on plenty of points so far, and he was quite happy to let him go, at last.

"Who *were* you talking to back there, anyway?" Lucia asked again as he walked along.

He shook his head but didn't stop. "Just ghosts," he said.

Somewhere, deep in the construct called "Thor" by the pinprick intelligences who had accompanied her to the discontinuity point, part of her stared out at the universe in awed wonder. She saw particles like stars streaming by; she saw space in all its foaming, multidimensional splendor; she saw time curled up in a plait that flexed and snapped like a whip. She felt a strange sensation rush through her, a sensation for which she had no word.

IT

The light of the fovea seared into her, stripping away all illusions, all hope that she could possibly comprehend the minds who had made it and who directed it according to their will. There would be no merging with that intelligence, if indeed intelligence it was. It was beyond anything she had encountered, before the Nexus and since. She was a grain of sand riding out its breakers, knowing that somewhere nearby was the promise of an incredible sea.

WHERE

An endless rush of photons bombarded her. Seeing was like trying to find a straw in a stack of needles. Blinking, bewildered, besieged by new sensations, she thought she might still be in HD92719. The sun shone brilliantly in an infinite array of colors. Its planets appeared to her down to their molecular level: every detail of their cores, atmospheres, magnetic fields, and other structures was revealed to her staggered senses. She felt gravitational interactions sweep through her body as the dance of the planets continued, not in the slightest bit disturbed by her presence.

IS

She wondered if she was hallucinating. Part of her couldn't believe that she was still alive, in any form. She had dived into the fovea. What was she thinking? Where did she imagine *that* was going to get her?

HERE

But somehow, through the sensory bombardment, came the certainty that her actions *had* mattered. Her presence was noted, just as a single particle's trail in a cloud chamber could make the difference between abandonment and proof of a theory. She felt giant forces turning around her, as though she was floating in the center of HD92719's primary, staring at the planets sweeping chaotically across the starscape.

The pressure of those forces was daunting. She felt squeezed, probed, mapped, examined, and pondered. She dissolved under the combined gaze of creatures she might have called gods, had she ever believed in such things. She lost all sense of herself as the thing she had become was unraveled and stripped back to its essences.

HOME

When she returned to herself, the stars were streaming again—but this time they *were* stars. They were moving across her field of vision like water down a window. She wasn't an astrophysicist, but she knew enough about the relative motions of the stars near Sol to know how they were supposed to shift. The odd thing was that they seemed to be moving *backward*.

AM

Verbs took on a whole new meaning. She followed the fovea as it jumped from place to place in the wake of lesser emissaries. Or were the emissaries—the cutters and the Tridents—following the fovea? It depended on where she stood, she guessed. Now that she saw it from the other side, swept up in the momentum of the fovea's mission, she began to wonder if her memories were correct. Had the Starfish come last, or had they arrived first? Had the fovea been following her, or had she been following it? Was she leading it now, or was she trailing along for the ride? Had she finally convinced the Starfish to leave, or had she brought them and the entire causal singularity down on humanity? In the cloud chamber of her mind, there was only one certainty—only one thought streaked white and clear. *I'm still here.* It didn't matter who she was or where she was going; nor did it matter that she had already been there and that "she" no longer existed in her former future. She still *was,* and *that* was all that mattered.

I

For the moment . . .

THE ADJUSTED PLANCK STANDARD INTERNATIONAL UNIT

After several notable mission failures in the late twentieth and early twenty-first centuries, the United Near-Earth Stellar Survey Program (UNESSPRO) developed a single system of measurement to prevent conflict between data or software from nations contributing to joint space projects. The following charts summarize the results, as adopted by UNESSPRO in 2050, using Planck units and other physical constants as starting points.

1 new second		= 0.54 old second
1 new minute	= 100 new seconds	= 0.90 old minute (54 old seconds)
1 new hour	= 100 new minutes	= 1.5 old hours (90 old minutes)
1 new day	= 20 new hours	= 1.2 old days (30 old hours)
1 new week	= 5 new days	= 0.89 old week (6.2 old days)
1 new month	= 6 new weeks	= 1.2 old months (5.3 old weeks)

1 new year	= 10 new months	= 1.025 old years (12 old months)

1 new centimeter		= 1.6 old cm/0.64 inches
1 new decimeter (dm)	= 10 new cm	= 6.5 inches
1 new meter	= 10 new dm	= 1.6 old m/3.3 feet
3 new meters		= 10 feet
1 new kilometer	= 1,000 new meters	= 0.97 mile

1 new hectare	= 2.6 old hectares	= 6.4 acres
1 new liter (dm³)	= 4.2 old liters	= 1.1 gallons

1 new g		= 2.2 old g
1 new kg	= 1,000 new g	= 4.8 old pounds
1 new tonne	= 1,000 new kg	= 2.1 old tons

1 new ampere		= 2.972 old amperes

New	Centigrade	Fahrenheit	Kelvin
1°	= 1.415°	= 2.563°	= 1.415°
0°	= –273.15°	= –459.67°	= 0° (absolute zero)
193°	= 0°	= 32°	= 273.15° (freezing point of H_2O)
264°	= 100°	= 212°	= 373.15° (boiling point of H_2O)

c (the speed of light)	$= 1.00 \times 10^8$ ms^{-1}
1 light-year	$= 6.00 \times 10^{15}$ m
1 light-hour	$= 1.00 \times 10^{11}$ m
1 parsec	$= 2.0 \times 10^{16}$ m
1 g	$= 1.0$ light-year/year^2
1 solar radius	$= 430,000$ km
1 Earth radius	$= 4,000$ km (equatorial)
geostationary orbit	$= 22,220$ km (Earth)

DRAMATIS PERSONAE

Human

Peter Alander (*Geoffrey Marcy*)
Peter Alander (*Michel Mayor*)
Peter Alander (*Fred Rasio*)
Peter Alander (*Frank Tipler*)
Francis Axford (996)
Francis Axford (1041)
Francis Axford (1313)
Francis Axford (1699)
Lucia Benck (*Andre Linde*)
Ali Genovese (*Freeman Dyson*)
Caryl Hatzis (Sol)
Caryl Hatzis (*Roger Angel*)
Caryl Hatzis (*Debra Fischer*)
Caryl Hatzis (*Martin Heath*)
Caryl Hatzis (*Michio Kaku*)
Caryl Hatzis (*S. V. Krasnikov*)
Caryl Hatzis (*Tess Nelson*)
Vince Mohler (*James J. Funaro*)
Owen Norsworthy (*Freeman Dyson*)
Kingsley Oborn (*Marcus Chown*)
Kingsley Oborn (*Alice Quillen*)
Cleo Samson (*Marcus Chown*)
Cleo Samson (*Frank Drake*)

Donald Schievenin (*Frank Drake*)
Rob Singh (*Marcus Chown*)
Rob Singh (*Frank Drake*)
Jayme Sivio (*Freeman Dyson*)

Yuhl/Goel

Ueh/Ellil (Conjugator)
Vrrel/Epan

Alien Races

A|kak|a/riil
The Asteroid
The "governors"
The "black ladybugs"
The Nexus
The Praxis
Pllix
The Spinners
The Starfish

APPENDIX 3

MISSION REGISTER

#	Target System	Core Survey Vessel	Primary Survey World
13	23 Boötis	*Maroj Joshi*	(unknown)
17	chi Hercules	*Geoffrey Marcy*	Vahagn
31	Beta Hydrus	*Carl Sagan*	Bright
44	BSC5581	*Seth Shostak*	Geb
95	94 Aquarius	*Larry Lemke*	(unknown)
154	HD92719	*S. V. Krasnikov*	Thor
163	Tau Ceti	*Brian Chaboyer*	New France
180	Dsiban	*Geoffrey Landis*	(unknown)
182	Altair	*Didier Queloz*	(failed)
183	Van Maanen 2	*Steven Weinberg*	Aretia
205	Theta Perseus	*Debra Fischer*	Mahatala
219	BD+14 2621	*Douglas Lin*	Medeine
253	Gamma Serpens	*Stephen Hawking*	Juno
267	mu Ara	*V. S. Safronov*	Pan

278	HD113283	*Lee Smolin*	Fu-xi
306	beta Cane Venatici	*Siegfried Franck*	Amun
321	HD132142	*Freeman Dyson*	Demeter
340	HD165401	*Michio Kaku*	Marduk
344	BSC8477	*Anna Jackson*	(unknown)
373	iota Boötis	*Heather Hauser*	Candamius
387	BSC8061	*Jill Tarter*	Heimdall
391	pi-1 Ursa Major	*Andre Linde*	Jian Lao
400	BSC7914	*Fred Rasio*	Eos
402	HD203244	*Ronald Bracewell*	Fujin
416	Delta Pavonis	*Martyn Fogg*	Egeria
477	Hipp1599	*Roger Angel*	Yu-quiang
512	Head of Hydrus	*Michel Mayor*	Athena
538	61 Ursa Major	*Fred Adams*	Hera
543	zeta Dorado	*Steven Vogt*	Hammon
564	gamma Pavonis	*Jack Lissauer*	Diana
567	zeta Triangulum Australe	*Stephen Udry*	Walaganda
636	BSC5148	*Frank Drake*	Sagarsee
639	psi Capricornus	*Tess Nelson*	Inari
647	Procyon	*Philip Armitage*	(failed)
648	Luyten's Star	*Alan Boss*	Jumis
666	Vega	*Matthew Thornton*	(none)
707	AC +48 1595-89	*Frank Shu*	Ea
709	Sirius	*David Deutsche*	Sothis
711	lambda Auriga	*Donald Brownlee*	Gayomard
713	BSC5423	*James J. Funaro*	Zemyna

726	BD+14 2889	*Norman Murray*	(failed)
754	Hipp61053	*Amy Reines*	61053/3
755	zeta Serpens	*Henry Throop*	Rama
784	Hipp64583	*Robert Haberle*	Adammas
794	Asellus Primus	*Shelley Wright*	(failed)
805	Zeta-½ Reticuli	*Paul Davies*	Tatenen
833	Mufrid	*David Soderblom*	(failed)
835	HD194640	*Carol Stoker*	Varuna
842	Upsilon Aquarius	*Frank Tipler*	Adrasteia
861	Alpha Mensa	*Subrahmanyan Chandrasekhar*	Pugu
906	58 Eridani	*Martin Heath*	Gou Mang
919	64 Pisces	*Miguel Alcubierre*	Ilmarinen
934	10 Taurus	*Alice Quillen*	Shang-Di
950	Groombridge 1830	*Sarah Manly*	Perendi
992	BSC5070	*Marcus Chown*	Rasmussen

TIMETABLE

Universal Time		Mission Time
1988, 17 Dec.	Peter Stanmore Alander born	
2049, 26 Nov.	UNESSPRO engrams activated	2049.9.29
2050, 1 Jan.	UNESSPRO launches commence	2050.1.1
2062, 8 Jul.	Spike	2062.3.3
	Lucia Benck's flyby of pi-1 Ursa Major	2117.3.18
	Breakdown of Peter Alander engram in Upsilon Aquarius	2151.1
	Spinners enter surveyed space	2160.8
2163, 10 Jul.	Gifts arrive in Upsilon Aquarius	2160.8.17
	Adrasteia (Upsilon Aquarius) attacked	2160.8.26
2163, 24 Jul.	Sol System attacked	2160.8.28
	First contact with the Praxis	2160.9.15
	Lucia Benck (Jian Lao) recovered by Caryl Hatzis (Thor)	2160.9.18

	Starfish attack Beid	2160.9.19
	Sothis (Sirius), Rama (zeta Serpens), Hammon (zeta Dorado), Hera (61 Ursa Major), Inari (psi Capricornus) destroyed	
	Lucia Benck arrives at Sothis	2160.9.20
2163, 28 Aug.	Sagarsee (BSC5148) contacted by Spinners	2160.9.26
	Departure of *Mantissa A*	2160.9.27
	Thor's mission departs	2160.9.29
	Rasmussen (BSC5070) attacked	2160.9.30
	War erupts in pi-1 Ursa Major	2160.10.1
	Zemyna (BSC5423) and Demeter (HD 132142) attacked	2160.10.2
	Geb (BSC5581) attacked	2160.10.3
	Thor's mission returns	2160.10.3
	Sagarsee (BSC5148) attacked	2160.10.4
	Ellil "colonized"	2160.10.4

AFTERWORD

Our thanks go to many of the usual names. We hope they're not getting blasé about this, because our indebtedness to them only increases, and this is the only way to repay them. (Sorry, guys.)

Hála vminek the wonderful Ginjer Buchanan for giving us space when we needed it. *Tank* to Richard Curtis, Stephanie Smith, and Shelly Shapiro for possessing between them all of the holy virtues. *Grazie,* Ralph Buttigieg at Infinitas and Justin Ackroyd of Slow Glass for rock-solid support on the front line. *Asante* to Erik Max Francis, Winchell Chung, and Claus Bornich for reasons spelled out in previous Afterwords. *Oatlho,* Marcus Chown (the real one, author of *The Universe Next Door*) for compiling so many wonderful ideas in such a slim volume. And a rousing cheer of *"Obrigado!"* for Nydia Dix, Vanessa Hobbs, Rob Hood, Kim Selling, and numerous other family members and friends who have inspired and put up with us for the last year.

It seems unlikely to an extreme that, given such support, we could possibly make *any* mistakes. But we do, and we ask that those named above not be held guilty by association. *Merci.*

The ultimate invasion begins here,
in the national bestseller

DEATH DAY

BY WILLIAM C. DIETZ

"A classic alien-invasion tale of survival."
—*New York Times* bestselling author
Kevin J. Anderson

"Intriguing...an exciting, action-packed thriller"
—*Midwest Book review*

"Well-drawn, fast intelligent action"
—*Booklist*

**Available wherever books are sold or
to order, please call 1-800-788-6262**